THE LAST LETTER

KIRSTEN MCKENZIE

SSP

First Published 2016 by Accent Press

This edition published 2019
by Squabbling Sparrows Press

ISBN 9780995117075

ALSO BY KIRSTEN MCKENZIE

The Old Curiosity Shop Series

FIFTEEN POSTCARDS

THE LAST LETTER

TELEGRAM HOME

Standalone Novels

PAINTED

DOCTOR PERRY

Anthologies

LANDMARKS

This book is not dedicated to my former publisher.
It is dedicated to the
Alliance of Independent Authors.
Thank you for your invaluable assistance.

THE LAST LETTER

PART ONE

THE PACKAGE

*A*nnabel Lester sat at the scrubbed table, hands in her lap, a leather-bound bible open.

'Impossible' she whispered, tracing the spidery words with trembling fingers.

"To Sarah,
With the greatest love I gift this to you.
May God fill your soul with the light of this country.
May He bless your footsteps through His land, from this day on, and for
all your days, wherever those steps take you.
With Love, Christine Young,
March 1864"

She passed a hand across her brow. There was no possibility that this Sarah was her Sarah, absolutely none that it was her daughter - the clever, tousle-haired daughter she'd left behind in London. Annabel's heart constricted as she remembered a distant lifetime, a different century, a home and a family lost forever.

Annabel slammed the book shut, folding the brown paper wrapping into smaller and smaller squares - saved for a future use.

She wound the twine from the package onto a tatty ball of string on the mantle, but the bible she left on the table. A misdirected piece of mail sent based only on her surname, and nothing to do with her daughter. Annabel left the room, casting no glance backwards towards the unwanted bible.

Barely two steps out of the kitchen, and Annabel returned. Reopening the bible, its inscription leapt out at her, sweeping across the page in bold strokes. She reached out towards the ink. Her finger hesitantly brushing the swirl of the 'S' of the word 'Sarah'.

Of all the possibilities, this was the one she'd never expected. She recalled her first days in New Zealand; how she would have traded her soul to the devil to see her daughter once more. The nights spent shivering in squalid shacks, hiding from men who considered her fair game without a husband to protect her, were never far from her mind. Her unimaginable life path stunned her. But for the grace of God, she could have become a lady of the night, a harlot, plying her wares to every drunken sailor, soldier and sinner who had coin to pay her, had the Reverend Howard Cummings not rescued her from the streets.

At the thought of Howard, Annabel scooped up the book and thrust it deep into her pocket. She wiped the tears which had dared gather at the corners of her eyes. *What rubbish was I thinking? A mere coincidence.* In this small backwater of a country, everyone assumed that if you had the same surname birth or marriage related you. But not her. She had no relations here. And there was no way on God's great earth that her daughter could be in New Zealand. Sarah was at home in England, teasing her father about his messy hair, or his inability to use email or navigate the Internet.

Annabel had made the best of her situation. As a live-in housekeeper — without electricity, she'd blundered her way through bread baking, laundry, gardening, and cleaning, with no modern-day conveniences. No supermarkets, or washing machines, just hard graft. She missed the freedom of summer shorts and singlets. The high-necked dresses of the day felt like ivy wrapping its vines around her throat and her legs got tangled in her skirts constantly. But it was at least a life. And if her employer thought it odd she spoke so little of her family, he kept his own counsel.

Annabel left the kitchen, making her way to a small room at the back of the wooden house. There she placed the bible on her cluttered nightstand. Her bedroom was overflowing with treasures she'd collected during her time in Dunedin. Nothing of any great value; mundane day-to-day objects, the sort you see for sale at car boot fairs. Earthenware jugs from England, a piece of etched ruby glass, green leather-bound books of common prayer and hymns. All gathered to remind her of home.

'Home' is such a powerful word. When life rips you from your home against your will, and forces you to assimilate into a new life, does that become home? Or is home where the heart is? Or where you live and breathe? Until she returned to her husband and daughter, she had no home. She was a refugee of time.

THE HOUSEKEEPER

*A*nnabel Lester leapt from her chair at the kitchen table – it felt like she'd only just sat down! As housekeeper at the parsonage of the newly appointed Bishop of Dunedin, hers was a job which had no down time. No tea breaks, nor leave. Her master, her lord, was as much a slave driver as the overseer on a southern cotton plantation. And there was nothing she could do about it.

When she'd first come to the parsonage, she was employed by Howard Cummings. A kind, jovial minister, his personality was eminently suited to the rigours of a new country. But he'd been displaced by the new bishop, under some duress from the local congregation. The Bishop had wasted no time in sending Reverend Cummings to an outpost far away from the rising city.

Annabel shook her head. Waimate was as foreign to her as North Korean cafés. And the Bishop was making her life unbearable, constantly questioning her about Dunedin's decision-makers, influencers and troublemakers. He'd asked about her, and her family. *The worst of questions.* She wasn't overly religious, but lying to a man of God still didn't sit comfortably. Cummings never questioned her history, he'd merely taken her in, his Christian duty above all else. The *Bishop's* duty, above all else, was to himself, and that went doubly for his weasel-like assistant, Norman Bailey, who scurried silently about the house.

When the Bishop first arrived, Bailey appeared as if out of thin air, and had barely left the prelate's side since. He had the innate ability to sense when the Bishop was on the move, and within moments would be loitering at hand. When he wasn't shadowing the rotund cleric, he was under her feet – watching her, judging her, questioning her.

The brief moment at the table felt like it'd been the only time she'd had to herself in weeks, and now the Bishop wanted her, *again*. Hurrying to his office, she practically tripped over Bailey, lurking as he was in the dark hallway.

'What the hell!' she exclaimed, rubbing her shoulder as she eyed the shorter man in the gloom.

He'd recoiled at her use of the expletive, his pock-marked skin flushed with the indignation he had no chance to express, as she turned away from him and hurried into the Bishop's office. *She is definitely possessed*, he decided, for the umpteenth time. He crossed himself for protection, and stepped out of the shadows, hurrying towards her room at the back of the house. A parcel had arrived for her today and he needed to know what was in it, to protect the Bishop from the evil she had within her – and to satisfy his own curiosity.

THE RESPONSE

'Ou'd think these provincial ministers would have more than enough time to secure the only thing of worth entrusted to their care!' raged the man clothed in the decadent robes of a bishop.

His assistant waited, nib poised to record the portly Bishop's words of reply to the letter received from the wayward minister stationed at Bruce Bay.

'Spreading God's word seems to be nigh on impossible when the lesser servants of God are imbeciles. How could he allow someone to steal such magnificent candelabra from his own home? Defies belief. No news of this must reach England. The embarrassment would ruin any chance of us leaving this cesspit.' Slamming his hammy fist on the desk, he continued, 'No, we must bury this disaster. Reply to the idiot, but keep no copy of his letter, nor of our response.'

'Should I perhaps suggest that he ask the local community for funds for a replacement? A project for the settlers?' the diminutive assistant suggested, his nasal voice symptomatic of hay fever, caused by an abundance of lily filled vases in the study.

'Yes, yes, whatever seems appropriate.'

The Bishop waved his assistant away, his mind on something of far more import than missing silver candelabra. Still incensed the Church had sent such exquisite silverware to a muddy heathen-filled settlement, instead of keeping it for the new diocese of Dunedin — his diocese — and now those pieces were lost. *Thieved, no doubt by a digger, and bartered for Heaven knows what.* And this diocese needed more than a candelabra to pull it out of the cesspit it seemed to be.

Bishop Thomas Dasent gazed out the parsonage's window, faced with the glorious colours of gladioli, carnations and calendulas. His eyes did not appreciate their beauty, his mind fogged with fury and frustration at this backward nation. He could half hear the choir rehearsing next door — indifferent but improvable, if he'd felt so inclined to help, which he did not. His energies were best spent preaching the glories of God, not singing them.

He was to travel the provinces later, a whole host of baptisms and betrothals to bless. The faster God-fearing folk populated this country, the better which was why baptisms were almost the favourite part of his job. *That and preaching.*

After kissing the heavy gold crucifix slung around his neck, he bellowed for the housekeeper.

'Mrs Lester!'

THE BAY

Christine Young worried at the cuff of her shirt, the once-white cotton grubby for want of soap.

Wife of the only minister in Bruce Bay, on New Zealand's west coast, sat waiting in the parlour for hours, refusing even the cups of tea offered. Samuel Sinclair leant against her feet, his pale, freckled face gazing up at this woman who'd taken him in, after his father Bryce had disappeared with the peculiar Mrs Bell so many months ago.

Together they waited for the Reverend to return from meeting with the local Māori tribe. Troubled times in the region meant Christine couldn't be sure he would return.

Footsteps on the wooden porch steps startled them both — so much so that Samuel uttered one of the choice swear words he'd learnt from his abusive father. Uncharacteristically silent, Christine didn't rush to admonish him like normal. Although he *had* been improving, he'd limited his swearing to twice a day now, at least within her hearing, and almost never in the Reverend's presence.

The front door opened, allowing a swirl of damp air into the house. Samuel hugged his knees closer to his body. Half a year ago he'd been all angles and bones, starved by his father, and beaten into submission like a dog. The Reverend and Mrs Young had given him the first home he'd ever known. They'd shown him more love in six months than he'd had in the rest of his short life.

Christine half stood, not knowing whether it was her husband returned or someone bearing bad news. The brass door handle turned, and Reverend Gregory Young slipped inside. Samuel launched himself at the minister, wrapping his arms around the man's muddied legs. Christine collapsed onto the couch, biting back any cry she might have let slip if they'd been alone. Protecting Samuel from the terrors of her thoughts an overwhelming priority.

'There, there, steady yourself, there's no reason to worry. Look at Mrs Young, as calm as a summer's day. Now, Christine, how about a nice cup of tea and I can tell you all that's happened. I hope never to have another like it.' He collapsed on the opposite chair, closing his eyes to the swirls and whorls of the ivy patterned carpet.

Christine brightened — a pot of tea was something she could manage — and vanishing into the kitchen, she returned moments later with a tray filled with steaming tea and buns still warm from the range. Samuel sniffed appreciatively as he hurried to help Christine.

'Ah, much better my dear, that will hit the spot. Nothing like a good pot of tea. We built the Empire on this stuff, Samuel. Blessed be the men who made it so. After God, and my good wife — and you — it's the thing I love more than anything else.'

He lapsed into silence, sipping his tea, eyes glassy with thought. Samuel returned to the floor, devouring a warm bun lathered with freshly churned butter.

Christine was not as patient as her ward, 'Gregory, tea may well have made the Empire but, unless you tell me straight away what happened this afternoon, the Empire will have to do without its minister.'

'Such an eloquent way of asking me to hurry. Yes, well, the natives were most generous towards us. They've heard about the troubles up north, and they're most uncomfortable. We've been very fortunate with our relationship with the local *iwi* and I tried to reassure them that as far as I knew, no British troops were being sent here. Which took a while. The new Premier seems more sensible than the last, but time will tell.' Draining his cup, he continued, 'There's been no reason for a military presence here. The militia has kept the miners in check, and since Seth and Isaac died, and Sinclair disappeared, there has been no further trouble. I'd say most of the troublemakers have found their way to the northern goldfields now, although that won't be helping the situation up there. All those men.'

Christine had crossed herself at the mention of Seth and Isaac. She'd had no time for Seth, but Sarah Bell had talked fondly of Isaac, believing him led astray by the older man. She shuddered at the memory of the blood at the front steps.

Although the Reverend appeared happy with the situation in Bruce Bay, Christine was far from reassured. His natural acceptance of the word of others was a constant source of frustration. *How can someone be so trusting?*

'Samuel, help Cook in the kitchen whilst I talk further with the Reverend,' she suggested, mindful that his ears were too immature for the words she wanted to say.

Samuel scurried from the room, pulling the door shut.

'So they're not about to murder us in our beds then?' she asked, tugging the curtains closed, as if armed warriors were peeping into their Victorian parlour waiting for an opportune time to strike.

'They've enough of their own troubles to contend with. We're not doing them any harm. I've told the Church that our lot aren't keen to have their souls saved. And other than acknowledging that we lost the silverware for the altar, they haven't even bothered making further contact...'

Christine interrupted, 'We didn't *lose* it, Sinclair stole it, right from under our noses. And Sarah, I shudder to think what's become of her. How do we know that that "our lot" haven't eaten both Sarah and Sinclair and sold the silver candelabra?'

'You've read too many novels. The Māori don't eat people. They may shoot us with the guns we've traded with them, but they won't eat us. You're confusing them with natives in New Guinea-they eat their captives-dreadful practice. No, my dear, our home is safe. I can't say the same for all those in our flock, given some stories I heard today about the goings on all over country. We're in the safest place in New Zealand.'

THE WARDEN

*F*or a man content with a solitary existence — who devoted his working time breaking up fights, mediating between natives and settlers, and answering to the Crown — losing Sarah Bell was the most bewildering experiences of Warden William Price's life. After she disappeared with Bryce Sinclair, he'd spent days searching for information about their whereabouts: combing the bush; haunting the wharf questioning the miners flooding out of Bruce Bay for the goldfields in New Zealand's North Island; and manhandling every reprobate he knew. Despite years of experience, he couldn't find any trace. Exasperated and exhausted he'd retreated to his cabin, descending into a dark depression.

With Price's temper turning volatile, in a town struggling under a cloud of alcoholic dependency and mistrust, Christine had suggested he travel to Dunedin, to call on the woman to whom she'd sent the bible — the bible Sarah had left behind. She'd proposed it more to save his life than to find the girl. But Price believed it would be futile, and his place was here in the Bay.

Price sat alone at a table in Sweeney's Bar. Miners came and went; the hardcore losers of the mining world. Too poor to leave, they worked the remnants of the West Coast goldfields. Anything they earned, they poured down their throats, either here or at one of the other half dozen establishments in town. Most would become 'Hatters' — men too old or sick to continue panning for gold. And if they weren't drinking in the bars, they were buying it out the back of someone's shack, although that supply had shrunk when Bryce Sinclair vanished.

The stench of strong alcohol and unwashed bodies churned through the room every time the door opened. Incessant rain and insidious conditions fuelled gloomy emotions, giving rise to the vilest behaviour. The pervading air of despair manifested itself in front of Price, with a scuffle between a scrawny Scots redhead and a belligerent Irish boy. Sweeney had his rifle cocked behind the counter as the brawl ranged across the floor, and their fellow drinkers placing wagers on the potential outcome.

'Come on, Mac, kill him.'

'Don't let a feckin' Scotsman thrash ya, Paddy.'

The jeers were coming thick and fast, as fast as the fists were being thrown. Price let them go. As long as Fred Sweeney wasn't too concerned about the mess, he was loath to intervene. He'd learnt early on that it was better to let the frustration play out, than to intercede, unless it looked like someone would die.

Sweeney nodded at Price, who stood up, and tipped his ale over the two fighters. Gasping and spluttering, they stopped brawling long enough for Price to haul the scrawny Scot off Paddy, who, despite his bulk, had been on the losing end of the fight.

Margaret Sweeney peeped round the corner from the stairs, a wrapped infant sleeping in her arms, unfazed by the ruckus in the bar. Friends lifted Paddy up into a chair, one of his eyes already swelling closed. Sweeney poured another handle of ale for Price, and, with barely a ripple, peace returned, money changed hands, and Margaret slipped into the room. Fred kissed the forehead of the tiny bundle, 'Where are you off to, love?'

'Mrs Young invited me round this morning, to discuss the Easter celebrations and, I reckon, to see wee Jillian again, although she only saw us two days ago.'

'Do you need me to walk with you?' he asked, trying to sound casual.

Margaret Sweeney looked into the eyes of her husband, struggling to gauge the level of his concern, 'Not unless you don't think it's safe...' she stammered.

'No, I'm sure it's fine. I was... well, I was just offering in case you wanted my company,' he shrugged.

She peered around the bar: spilt ale seeping into the *kauri* floorboards; broken chairs, tangled together like the roots of the trees they'd been born from.

'Best you clean up here, Fred. I won't be long. I'll be back in time for lunch.' Kissing his cheek, she tugged baby Jillian's knitted hat over her ears, and ventured outside. Using her free hand to lift her skirts over the worst of the churned mud, she shivered at the deep cold carried into town by the West Coast winds.

'You think it's still safe here, Price?' Sweeney asked, watching his wife make her way up the road, her hems forgotten in her efforts to keep the wind off their child.

After draining his ale, the Warden handed the glass to Fred, 'She'll be fine, no harm will come to her at the Reverend's. Not now, anyhow.' The unspoken message was that, since Sinclair had gone, everyone was safer — everyone except Sarah Bell. Price pulled on his oilskin coat and stepped out to the chill air, 'It's as safe as anywhere, Fred. As long as you've a good shotgun and someone to watch your back.'

Hands deep in his pockets, Price trudged towards the wharf in the vain hope that today there'd be word of Sarah Bell's whereabouts.

THE BAR

*W*arden William Price ran his hands through his long hair. It was as if Sarah Bell had just disappeared; vanished, along with Bryce Sinclair. He'd found no sign. None of Sinclair's associates would admit to having seen him with, or without, a woman.

With a jaw hidden by a week's worth of stubble and hair loosed from its regular tie, his wild look was enough to keep the other drinkers away. He sat nursing a whisky, his large hands grasping the barely clean glass, trying to think where else to search. Dunedin was his destination, but he had his suspicions that Sinclair had somehow got another boat, abducting Sarah Bell via water. That was the only logical answer. They couldn't just disappear like a winter's breath.

It was killing him not being able to find her. It made no sense at all. He'd never married, preferring the company of soldiers and his horse. He was a man comfortable with his being alone. So why was he pining for a woman he hardly knew? There'd been something there. Was it love? As intangible and untouchable as a ghostly vision, deep down, he suspected it was.

Knocking back a drink in a tavern near the bottom of New Zealand's South Island wasn't ideal, but he had good reason for dallying in this undesirable environment. He'd heard Sinclair had at least one friend, Saul Hunt, another ferryman. An ex-convict from Australia who'd made his way to New Zealand to bury his criminal past, to start afresh here. And the *Waimate Hotel* was his favourite haunt. The barman had assured him Hunt would be along soon, but only after Price had passed over enough small change to satisfy the alcoholic habits of his host.

If Saul Hunt was a dead end, the only possibility left was Dunedin, and beyond that... he didn't have the means or time to continue the search. He'd have to return to Bruce Bay, to carry out the duties the government was paying him for. This trip was under the pretext of finding Sinclair and the stolen silverware from the Bruce Bay church. That was always at the back of his mind, but enquiries he'd made during his journey down the coast, and across the island, had proved fruitless.

The door opened, bringing in the nor'wester and a smoky odour; a daily occurrence in these parts, as settlers cleared vast tracts of land for new houses. Blowing in with the wind was the man the hotelier had described as Hunt. Tall and mangy like a malnourished dog, a droopy left eye completed the picture. He wasn't alone, following behind was Shrives, the local bullock driver — a hulk of a man, with as much sense as his teams. Laughing, they sauntered up to the bar, leaned against it like regulars, and waited for their drinks.

'Here you are, lads. These drinks are on him over there,' the barman tilted his head towards Price.

Price lifted his glass to acknowledge the suspicious look Hunt and Shrives gave him. The men conferred. Evidently Price's looks were enough to assure them he posed no threat.

By and large, Shrives was a law-abiding man; Hunt, not so much. Together though, that was another story. Price bore no man ill will; judgement wasn't his to give. Time, however, was of the essence, and becoming embroiled in policing these two was not high on his list of priorities.

The men moved as one towards Price's table. Hunt then took the lead. 'I'd say thanks, but I'd rather know who I was thanking, and why, when I don't know you from shit.'

'William Price. Figured it was the right thing to do when you're the new guy in town, trying to figure his way round. Just got here. The barman suggested I catch up with you — you know, find out how things are around here.'

Price stoked Hunt's ego like a fire. It worked.

'Always happy to help a new arrival. What brings you to town?'

'Just came from the West Coast. Had to get out of that rain. Bloody rain every day. Heard it was warmer here, and they needed men for the forestry. Thought I'd try my hand. Given up on the gold. That's all gone. Is there good paying work here?'

'Only if you want to break your back. Nah, you're better off going to Timaru or Oamaru, get into the building industry up there. You know how many men've died chopping down those bloody big trees? What do you reckon, Shrives, at least twelve this month?'

Shrives took a long sip of his grog as he mulled over the question. Draining his glass, he replied, 'Nah, fifteen maybe? It's been a bad month. Last one was better; only three or so then.' He looked expectantly at his empty glass.

Price motioned to the barman, who'd been listening to the exchange while cleaning what few glasses he had left. The room was filling and, with that, the noise increased. Price needed to find out about Sinclair before any friends of Hunt and Shrives turned up, making conversation more difficult. With replenished drinks, Price took a punt, 'It wasn't just the barman who recommended we talk. A guy I met by the Moeraki river suggested I get hold of his mate over here, said he might get some info on a girl I used to know. She thieved some stuff of mine I'd like back.' Price swallowed the hard liquor, staring at Hunt the whole time.

'A mate, you say? Can't say that I've many of those!' Both men laughed, before Hunt continued, 'You must mean Sinclair? Yeah, we go way back. Haven't seen 'im for two years now. Last I heard he was still in Otago. He's always had a nose for following the money. If he's saying there's more money in this shit hole of a town, then hell knows where he heard that. Got his ideas wrong, that boy. Yeah there's money in the trees, but better money in staying alive, and well away from those things. Haven't heard of no girl round here, not unless she's the sort that makes you pay for it.' Another chorus of bawdy laughter followed.

'I'm not after what's between her legs, just what's in her bags,' Price interjected.

'That's what they all say,' Shrives quipped, looking to Hunt for validation of his pithy comment.

'Never knew a man who wasn't after what's between a woman's legs, apart from those queer bastards who we haven't strung up yet. Leave it with me. How long you in town for then?'

'Taking it day by day till my money runs out, or till I find the girl. Goes by the name of Sarah Bell. She left me high and dry. So you haven't seen Sinclair for two years then?'

'Yeah, gotta be at least two years. Hope he's not telling everyone that I owe 'im anything. We had a thing going in Dunedin, but it went a bit south, so we split up. It'd probably be okay to go back there now, but those army boys 'ave got long memories. Thought it best to stay away a bit longer, steer clear of Sinclair, so's they can't accuse us of anything. Some people pin everything on an ex-con, regardless. A man can turn over a new leaf, you know.'

Price nodded in agreement, noting Hunt's insistence that he hadn't seen Sinclair. Seemed that this avenue of enquiry was at an end.

THE MORNING

$\mathcal{P}$rice rolled onto his side, his head felt as if someone had split it with a ball-pein hammer. He hadn't drunk so much since he'd first left home. After a couple of incapacitating sessions in his early days, he'd vowed never to do it again. That vow had lasted till last night. To ingratiate himself with Hunt and Shrives, he'd consumed what seemed like a barrel-full of gin and whisky, with nothing solid in his stomach to absorb the toxic mixture. He'd no recollection of putting himself to bed. The bedpan on the floor beside him held a mass of regurgitated alcohol and bile. *Better in the pan than the bed.* He tried sitting up, but his head hurt more than he'd ever known. Groaning, he fell back onto the lumpy mattress, his pillow only the folded oilskin that travelled with him.

The tilt of the sun coming in through the window proved it was well into the day, dawn a distant memory he'd never have.

His tongue curled around a dry cave of a mouth. It was this that forced him up. He'd kill for a drink, and not the alcoholic kind.

He didn't need to put his hobnail boots on, he'd never taken them off. Somehow he'd stripped off his shirt before getting into bed, showing off a torso banded with muscles that years of outdoor work had formed. Confused, he looked around for his top. *There, balled up in the corner, with a silk garment. Wait… a what?* He hooked the silky fabric with his finger — the creamy folds shook out revealing a chemise of foreign origin.

Price scanned the room. There was nothing else obviously feminine. He dropped the chemise, grabbing his shirt instead and pulling it over his head, grimacing as the sudden movement jolted his hung-over skull. Thrusting his arms into the sleeves of his oilskin, he tarried long enough to splash cold water on his face. He put the lingerie out of his mind. Perhaps the rooms last inhabitants had left it there?

He slipped down the stairs into the tavern, already busy with no-hopers filling their stomachs with ale, or something stronger depending on the coin in their pockets.

The room fell silent as Price appeared. He felt the mood shift from congenial to feral in the space of a heartbeat. Unarmed, his rifle left for safe keeping with the publican when he'd first arrived, he shifted his weight, unsure whether he was in any fit state to defend himself.

'Morning,' he said to the barman, who maintained the same look of disdain as he had the night before. Warden William Price had seen much in his life — little surprised him and, with a remarkable tolerance for animosity, provided violence didn't accompany it, he chose not to react. There was no point making a mountain out of molehill over bad manners.

'I'll just grab my rifle and be on my way,' Price said quietly.

The barman slipped through a door marked "Private", returning moments later with Price's well-cared-for rifle, its cherry wood stock gleaming in the antipodean light that seeped in from the windows.

Price muttered his thanks and, avoiding the looks of the other patrons, made his way outside, only to walk straight into Hunt.

'Hang on there, friend, we got some unfinished business from last night. Figure you owe me and Shrives here some money for the bit of fun we passed your way yesterday.'

Shrives peeled himself off the white-painted wall, and matched pace with Price, as he tried to sidestep Hunt. The trio made an odd picture, with the healthy-looking Price towering a good head above the other two. In contrast, Hunt and Shrives both had the sallow sheen of the malnourished, and bandy legs, signs of childhood rickets. Their clothes, the same sets they'd worn on the journey out to New Zealand, had more repairs than a patchwork quilt. Both peered at Price through bloodshot eyes.

Price rubbed his hand across the lengthening stubble on his chin, 'I've no idea what you're talking about, gentlemen. My head is killing me, and I really must find Mrs Bell, which means I've to follow her trail down country as there's no sign of her here.'

'Surely the taste of Waimate you had last night is enough to make you want to stay — you know, to try it again?' Both men laughing at their private joke.

'I thank you for your company. It was eye-opening, but I must move on.'

'You need to reimburse us for your woman. She wasn't free, you know,' Hunt drew out the words, as if he were talking to a simpleton.

'There was no girl, gentlemen, I believe you are mistaken. Again, thanks for the company, and for your efforts in trying to locate Mrs Bell. Sinclair was correct when he said you were the men to help.'

'Stop pissing around, Price. You had a right royal romp with our Sue last night, but you didn't pay.'

Price stopped. 'Look, I'm sorry but I don't recall meeting any Sue yesterday evening. You're mistaken. Now I must be on the road.'

Hunt slapped a hand on Price's shoulder, his strength a surprise to the taller man.

'Pay up. Sue doesn't spread her legs for free. Your Mrs Bell is doing the same wherever she is, and you wouldn't want to think that some fuckwit has just stiffed her out of enough money to feed her brood of bastard kids, do you?'

Price fixed Hunt with a steely glare, 'Take your hand off me. I've been more than pleasant, but that's at an end.' Price shrugged off the other's grip.

A pointed dagger, reminiscent of a Scottish dirk, appeared in

Shrives' hand. Short and skinny, just like him, it was the only well-kept article Shrives owned.

'We gave you Sue, whether or not you remember her — she serviced you, and needs paying. Her unique skills usually leave men with a hankering for more. Perhaps your tastes run towards something a little different?'

The men laughed. But it was no joking matter to Price. There were very few women he'd found himself attracted to. As with most men, there was always the first love, someone from his adolescence, a girl who made you so tongue-tied, that it went no further than 'hello'. Then there was that first real love, one which arrived and fled faster than a summer storm, but one you remembered for her freshness and vitality. And, if you were lucky, there was a girl like Sarah. A woman whose presence gave warmth to the sun. A simmering love, its ignition hard to pinpoint but undeniable, and when you found that love, you'd do everything in your power to hold on to it.

Despite losing Sarah, Price would do nothing to jeopardise his relationship with her, which is why he was adamant there'd been no 'interlude' with Sue — nor with anyone else. These men were lying. Shrives' blade was evidence of that.

One last effort at peace, 'Thanks for the help, and company.'

As Price made towards the stables, Shrives lunged for him, aiming for the stomach. Hunt went to grab Price's arms, only to find an empty oilskin in his hands as his target squirmed out of reach, using his bulk as a weapon against the smaller man. Hunt stumbled forward, thrown off balance, clumsy with the heavy oilskin.

Shrives yelled in frustration. Price hadn't trained in any of the ancient Asian defensive arts, but he'd had enough experience of men gripped by rage to know their fury diminished their decision making. He deflected Shrives' thrust with his forearm, bone on bone. Still holding his rifle, he swung it like a hockey stick against Shrives' shins — the man's thick corduroy pants absorbed the impact. He slashed at Price again, the dirk tracing an arc through the air towards his face.

The sharpness of the honed blade took the top off Price's cheek effortlessly. Blood flowed. Clenching his teeth, he swung the rifle towards his assailant again, aiming for his less padded torso, a thin cotton shirt no protection for his ribs. The crisp sound of them snapping punctuated the air. Price took in a breath and, as he wiped away the blood pouring from his wound, Hunt tackled him. They toppled to the ground, where — grappling like Graeco-Roman wrestlers — they grabbed and tore at each other. Hunt ground his palm into Price's lip. Price flipped Hunt onto his back, pinning him down with his superior weight. His strong hands squeezed Hunt's windpipe and the slighter man struggled, his face turning puce, his lips parted, trying to pull in even the smallest amount of air. Gradually the struggling stopped, followed by a random jerking of his oxygen-starved limbs, then nothing.

Hunt lay there, a soulless cadaver cooling in the morning breeze. Death's distinctive odour mingling with fresh sawdust carried on the colonial wind. The same breeze bore away Shrives' moans. Price pressed his hand to his cheek, adrenaline failing him now. Pain came in crested waves, and he stumbled from the men.

He scooped up his rifle, pain screaming his name with every footfall. Someone would clean up this mess, but it wouldn't be him. He doubted anyone would take umbrage with a Warden ridding the country of types like these.

He turned his back on the township of Waimate, and continued his journey to Dunedin, to Sarah Bell.

THE ARTIST

*A*nnabel Lester hovered in the study of the Bishop, ostensibly to dust, but was reading the spines of the hundreds of leather-bound volumes decorating the shelves in front of her.

Other than hot showers, electric ovens, central heating and the local Waitrose, the one thing she missed more than anything else was the comfort of curling up on the couch with a good book. To dive into a make-believe world, to lose yourself for hours in someone else's life, from the safety of your paperback, was a joy.

Reverend Cummings had kept a decent library, with a wide variety of material. The Bishop's taste, however, was as bland as butter. Running her fingers along the titles, she'd only encountered various bibles, psalters, religious texts, and illustrated history books.

Where were the bodice-ripping yarns she'd heard the Victorians loved? Or even something by Dickens? *Anything*. She needed means to shrink from this life, wrapped in the familiar arms of a book.

A set of matching volumes caught her eye. Clad in burgundy leather, the gold-embossed lettering too joyful for the dour Bishop. Intrigued, Annabel knelt down, running her worn fingertips along the letters. Angling her head, she read the spines, "Ruskin. Modern Painters. Vol. I-V".

Ruskin, that name's familiar. From her crouched position on the floor, she pondered the link. *Ah yes, Ruskin was a watercolour artist* - a favourite of the Bishop's because there were at least three signed John Ruskin works hanging around the house — vapid, hinting towards being unfinished, as if you were looking at them through grimy windows. Not her style at all. Curious, she pulled out the middle volume, leafing through the gilt-edged pages. Pages and pages of in-depth analysis of the work of another artist, Turner. Discussing, at length, symbolism in art and in nature. *Dry material, but better than the Bible.* The Reverend had been partial to reading 'sensation novels'. Although he tried to maintain that someone had left them in the church accidentally — one of his parishioners, she doubted the veracity of that story. *No, even the good Reverend needed a dash of escapism in his role. As do I.* All the Wilkie Collins books sat on his shelves, and volumes written by James Payn and Edmund Yates. One of the last works she'd read before he'd left was by a woman; *Danesbury House* by Mrs Henry Wood. Written by a female, but convention dictated that she had to use her husband's name.

With the undue haste they had moved Reverend Cummings on, he hadn't had time to pack his books. They made promises to send them on, but no sooner had the Reverend left the parish, than the Bishop ordered the 'filth' disposed of, by fire. That had broken her heart. No one should ever burn books, not just because of their monetary value, but because they were treasures in their own right. Just as valuable as a diamond brooch or a marble statue. Their covers held between them ideas and knowledge, hopes and dreams.

So, for now, she had only the words of art critics and long-dead disciples of Jesus.

'I don't think you have the time for reading.'

Annabel dropped the volume in fright. Looking up, she saw the Bishop's assistant — his narrow teeth bared in a macabre rendition of a smile, one which never reached his hooded eyes.

She stood up, the book abandoned, 'I wasn't reading,' she protested, 'I was dusting the cobwebs...' she trailed off, uneasy under his suspicious gaze. If she didn't find a way out of this house soon, she'd scream. Or stab someone. Someone like Norman Bailey.

Bailey scurried over, fitting the book back into its allotted slot. 'How upset would the Bishop be if he knew you'd been reading his volumes of Ruskin's Modern Painters. He likes his books to remain in perfect condition, you see.' Taking Annabel's fingers in his tiny hand he carried on, 'Dirty fingers may damage the gilt edging, hmm?'

Annabel jerked her hand out of his grasp, wiping it against her skirts, removing all traces of his clammy sweat.

'Best you don't touch them then. Sweat damages books more than dust,' she muttered, turning her back on the smaller man.

Bailey grabbed her a second time, 'There's something not right about you. Can't put my finger on it, but you watch yourself. I'll not have you ruining the plans Bishop Dasent has. He is a great man, and his reputation should not come under scrutiny for engaging a woman of dubious morals. I think your service here will soon be at an end.'

With his ominous words ringing in her ears, she fled from the Bishop's study, tears threatening to spill down her cheeks. Never had she wanted to go home as much as she did this very minute.

From the moment Reverend Cummings rescued her, and for a long time after, she'd been secretly happy with her predicament. Her duties were light, the lifestyle suited her. No husband, no child. None of that all-absorbing guilt over whether she was a good mother and an adequate wife, or functioning as an employee. Certainly no frustration over whether she could be all three at once. Here, in this time, she was just Annabel Lester.

THE TOWN

*W*arden Price stood at the entrance to the Dunedin gaol. He should let the constabulary know he was in town, but was in no real hurry to lose anonymity. After the debacle in Waimate, the rest of the journey had been uneventful, and he'd merged seamlessly with the other travellers — disillusioned prospectors, families trailing behind their patriarchs, farmers riding in to visit with the bank.

Young men surrounded him on the road, all still cocky enough to believe life owed them and would deliver, the concept of being rewarded for hard work as far from their mind as abstinence for the alcoholic, and he admired them for their resilience.

Running filthy hands through his wild hair, he attempted to make himself presentable. Sarah's whereabouts weighing heavily on him, he'd barely given any thought to what he'd do now that he'd arrived. All he had was the family name 'Lester', and the suggestion that there was a connection to his Sarah. To find them would be like searching for a needle in a haystack, or an honest man in a gaol. He was also looking for Sinclair, and he knew it wouldn't be as much of a stretch to start his search with *that* name. It was peculiar how criminals achieved a level of fame, of notoriety. They never told stories of how kind an elderly neighbour was. History never remembered how his generosity was legendary throughout the district; that his preserves were award winning. But the gangs; the robbers and the rustlers, had songs sung about them, legends forged where the mere mention of their names had widows quaking in fear, their infamy transcending the centuries and the classes.

Price tugged at his shirt, and straightened his wool waistcoat, brushing off the evidence of his journey. Tendrils of curled fern still clung to his collar; thorns from the invasive yellow gorse had woven themselves into the fibre of his coat. Mounting the wooden steps, he went into the gaol.

Prisons had the same aroma regardless of their location; a foul stench of desolation. Cramped spaces filled with a sector of society not known for their hygiene habits before they entered the penal system, culminated in rank bodies filling the limited accommodation, and their scent permeated through every corridor and doorway of the *ad hoc* gaol. The man on the formidable front desk was the sort you'd expect to be fronting any modern-day prison; huge, with hands like sledgehammers. The kind that could well be on the other side of the bars but for the grace of God.

'Morning, sir, what can I help you with?'

'Good morning. My name's Warden William Price, down from Bruce Bay. I'm in town and thought it best I check in with the authorities. I need some assistance to find a man who's wanted for murder on the coast.'

The desk sergeant stood up, extending his gargantuan arm across the counter, shaking Price's hand with a firmness a wrestling champion would be proud of.

'Great to have you here, Warden. Damn sure we'll be able to help you out. You got a place to stay?'

'No, not as yet. Thought I'd stop here first, then find the nearest hotel.'

'There's *The Queen's Arms*, but it's rough, with prospectors taking most of the rooms there. Probably better to try *Wains Hotel* on Manse Street. The Press Club meets there, so, as long as you don't say who you are, you might pick up something from them. Once they get a whiff of who you are, they'll clam up tighter than a nun's arse.' He laughed at his own bawdy humour and carried on chuckling as he sketched out directions to the hotel. 'There you are. I'll send someone over tomorrow to get you, once the boys return from Clyde.'

'Clyde?'

'Ah, they're escorting the gold. It's pretty much just me, and a few others holding the fort here. Not sure we'd be able to hold back a mass breakout, but me,' patting his sidearm, 'and my trusty revolver would reduce the overcrowding by a good amount if they tried.'

Price nodded and, taking the crudely drawn map, left the premises, the stink of the gaol clinging to his skin. Outside, the emerging freshness of the city struck him. Everywhere new buildings were crawling upwards. Sawdust danced on the wind, its woody scent on a par with English roses, after the stench of the gaol. It wasn't a far walk to the *Wains Hotel*, twenty minutes maybe. Supper and a wash had never been more welcome. He raised his eyes to the heavens and prayed for an available room.

With his horse stabled behind the gaol, Price strode down the bustling road, taking in the prosperous shop fronts. Each had a generous window displaying their wares. Stopping for some time outside *Hislop's Watchmakers*, he admired the range of gentlemen's pocket watches on display. Sterling silver half-hunters lay gleaming in the sunlight, and in the centre was a James McCabe pocket watch — an 18-carat gold, full-hunter minute-repeating pocket watch made by England's best known family of watchmakers. A trinket which epitomised success, waiting for its new owner — probably a boy from the provinces, flushed with the thrill of finding his first gold nugget, before time taught him that that nugget was a collision of fate, a one-off; and before the year was out, that same watch would find its way to the pawnbroker's counter.

Shaking his head at the frivolity of man, he carried on towards Manse Street, passing the Shamrock Auction Rooms just as a sale had ended. Be-suited men flowed out the doors, their black suits and hats making them as indistinguishable from each other as grains of sand.

Amiable chat swirled around him as he negotiated the human tide on the semi-formed footpath. Snippets of conversation reached him, nonsensical without context, like so many overheard conversations, which morph through Chinese whispers into damaging gossip, and character assassinations.

'He'll not last this one, too inflexible.'

'Did you hear him a fortnight ago? All fire and brimstone. Surprised lightning hasn't hit us all!'

'If I wasn't already going to hell, he'd send me running there just to get away!'

The group laughed, slapping each other on the back, none of them paying attention to the stranger among them.

Price shook his head; *peculiar conversations, to be sure.* City conversations.

The *Wains Hotel* appeared before him. Simple, solid, and with a "Vacancy" sign in the window's bottom. The structure swallowed him as he walked through the door.

THE SERMON

arden Price sat on the wooden pew, hat clasped in his lap, well aware of the admiring glances the young women seated around him were casting his way. But his thoughts were elsewhere. Was there anyone here he recognised? Anyone there with a hint of Sarah about them?

The priest droned on about sloth, extolling the poor parishioners to work harder, to look upon laziness as a sin. It astonished him that priests lectured their congregations like this. The church heaved with hard-working folk with patched clothes, faded trousers, chafed hands and wind-damaged faces. Few parishioners lived an indolent life. In Price's mind, the most slothful persons there were the priest and his lackeys.

Price was all for religious worship, but he preferred his messengers of God to be more of *this* world — more like Reverend Young and his wife Christine in Bruce Bay. A married priest was far better placed to understand his parishioners and their sins than this man pontificating at the front of the church.

The building was so full of extended families in large clusters of several generations, that it was impossible for Price to recognise who went with whom. He didn't know if Sarah Bell's family was big or small, whether she was an only child, or one of many. Self-doubt seeped in. It could be a fruitless journey, this quest to locate Sarah, and Bryce Sinclair. And then there was the possibility that she may not be interested in seeing him. There'd been no agreement, just a feeling; a once in a lifetime feeling.

The service over, the crowd rose as if released from purgatory with the flick of a wand. The tidal wave of churchgoers made for the door, making way for the elderly and the women, the children showing a level of respect unheard of in modern times. Price held back, nodding at the strangers who met his eyes, some curious, some outright flirting. *There.* A whisk of a skirt and the glimpse of a brow. *Sarah?*

There were too many people, and he lost sight of her. The hotelier from the *Wains Hotel* laid a hand on his arm, 'Mister Price, let me introduce you to Bishop Dasent. He is also new to Dunedin.'

The blackness around the Bishop wasn't because of his cassock. An unpleasant aura emanated from the man, who was even more distasteful up close than when he was castigating the congregation.

'How lovely to meet you,' Bishop Dasent greeted Price, his words not reaching his eyes. For a man ordained to save souls, it didn't appear to Price that he himself had one.

'Bishop Dasent,' Price was curt, looking beyond the Bishop for any sign of the woman who had that wisp of familiarity to her.

'Mister Price has travelled from Bruce Bay. He was telling us over supper that there was a theft from the church before he left. How anyone could desecrate a church? It's an affront to Christ.' As a godly man, the hotelier crossed himself, his eyes shining with the fervour of the righteous. 'Did you hear about the theft, Bishop Dasent?'

The Bishop steepled his fingers, his eyes travelling over the sorry-looking congregation. He knew of the theft of the candelabra — he'd anticipated this very thing after hearing of the gift of such valuable items to a church in the middle of nowhere, instead of to *his* diocese, but he wasn't about to tell these peasants of his knowledge.

'No, that is a shock.' Looking behind him, he summoned forward his assistant, who'd been hovering around like a seagull hankering after food scraps. 'Norman, please remind me this afternoon to write to the minister at... where?'

'Bruce Bay, it's on the West Coast, several days travel away from here,' the hotelier offered.

'Yes, thank you. At Bruce Bay, to enquire about their theft.'

Norman's mouth gaped like a carp, well aware the Bishop had already destroyed the correspondence relating to the candelabra. He nodded, so used to ingratiating himself with the Bishop, that his ability to discern right from wrong, truth from lies, had long since disappeared.

His instructions dispensed, the Bishop moved away to find someone more worthy of his time. A hotelier and a drifter from the country weren't worth his precious breath.

Puffed up with pride that he'd conversed with the Bishop, the hotelier attempted to introduce Price to those still milling around the aisles, eager for local gossip, but Price was past pleasantries. He knew the woman he'd glimpsed must be Sarah Bell's relation. His heart knew it. Shaking off the other man's hand, he pushed through the knot of parishioners into the daylight, the fresh air a balm to a man who felt constrained inside the hypocritical walls of this church.

Casting his eyes down the slope, all he saw were the erect backs of women held up by whalebone stays, and strict upbringings. Children were delighting in their own freedom. Fire-and-brimstone preaching were mere gibberish to the ears of the young who'd wiggled and squirmed on the uncomfortable pews, release a few steps away.

There. At the bottom of the hill. Turning right. The turn of the hips, the angle of her shoulders. The auburn highlights in her hair.

His long stride an asset, he raced down the hill, holding onto his hat, barely refraining from calling out to the woman, to Sarah. Ignoring the startled glances of the families returning home for their weekly roast in their Sunday best, he hurtled towards her. Breath ragged in his throat, he reached her, grabbed her shoulder, spun her around.

The woman screamed, wrenching her shoulder out of Warden Price's grasp, and backed away from him, eyes wild.

Price crumpled. This woman wasn't Sarah, nor was she any relation, maternal or otherwise.

'I'm so sorry, madam,' he mumbled, 'I mistook you for someone else. My deepest apologies.'

With a swish of heavy skirts, she hurried away, looking back at him until she rounded the corner, and disappeared from view. *What now*, he wondered. Other members of the congregation were making their way down the road, each holding their own conversations, not seeing his pain. Dunedin was full of men who came then disappeared; one more stranger meant nothing to them.

For Annabel Lester, a newcomer was an opportunity to escape her reality, and so it was when she came across him standing on the road, looking disoriented.

'Excuse me, can I help? Are you lost?'

Price turned towards the voice and fell into her eyes. *Sarah's eyes*. The green of ivy, narrowed against the morning's sunlight. His breath caught, and she repeated her question, 'Are you lost? Do you need directions, perhaps?'

Clearing his throat, Price found that he'd lost the inability to articulate, and stood gazing at the apparition in front of him.

'Right, well, I'll leave you to it,' she said before edging past him on the street, the same way one might avoid a filthy beggar ranting about the end of the world.

'No! Please... I mean yes, I need help,' Price finally managed, coming to like a man surfacing from a coma.

The woman paused, stepping back a pace, ready to flee should he turn out to be in the grip of opium delirium, which was prevalent among the gold miners, especially since 'The Doctor' had arrived — a Chinese miner supplying the drug to all and sundry, causing mayhem in the town, and at the various claims around Otago. This man could be under the influence of 'the smoky dragon', although he did not have that manner about him. She waited for him to speak again.

'I'm sorry, you took me by surprise. You... you look so much like a woman I have been searching for, and you surprised me. Please do not think me rude, it's just that you have her look about you. I'm probably mistaken, but I'd been told she had people in Dunedin...'

Annabel Lester listened to his words, her stomach churning with every sentence, until she could stand no more, and blurted out 'I have no family here, sir', and hurried down the street towards her home. To the only life she had left.

Price stood befuddled. The woman's manner of speech was like Sarah's, strange intonations, like no other he knew. It was as if they were the same person. This woman was older than Sarah, but not by much. Shaking his head, he continued on his way, puzzling over this development. There was no other path now — he must turn to the police for help. Walking the streets of Dunedin, or the goldfields of Otago, would gain him nothing but a need for new boots.

THE SEARCH

The Dunedin constabulary welcomed Warden Price, where they quizzed him on the goings-on up country, and filled him in on the flood of humanity at Westport. Together they commiserated with the lot of the police stationed there. Sergeant Nash was getting a good round of praise for his leadership there, before they moved onto the reason Price was in town.

Sinclair's reputation ranged far and wide across the country, and only the newest recruits were not familiar with the man.

'What's he done this time, then?' Sergeant Jock Crave asked, the pipe clamped between his lips.

'Abduction and murder,' said the young Graeme Greene.

'Gone up in the world then, hasn't he,' Jock observed in his deep Scottish accent. He'd been in New Zealand almost as long as the Māori, yet there wasn't a hint of the colonial to him. Scottish, through and through, a tiny piece of thistle under the long white cloud.

'He abducted his lady friend!' Greene recounted, as excitable as a puppy with a ball.

Price corrected him, 'Not a "lady friend", lad, an acquaintance, and a *proper* lady. Best you not get your words mixed up when describing a lady, or it'll not end well for you one day. Ladies prefer being described decorously.'

Graeme Greene blushed, his own ladylike features flushed with embarrassment at being corrected in front of his colleagues. He knew he was inexperienced with women, although that wasn't the only thing against him. His high voice a constant source of amusement for the other men. He neither drank nor engaged in the typical male banter that occurred. His private life was as circumspect as it needed to be.

'Oh don't worry about our Nancy here,' guffawed another officer. 'He's new, been dying to get his hands dirty. It's no fun just locking up the drunks has it, young Nancy?'

Greene's blush had made it all the way to his ears, bright beacons in a room filled with testosterone. The worst part of the job was that his colleagues had nicknamed him 'Nancy'. A name that would stick like glue for the rest of his days.

'It's fine — but, with a lady, it's not just treating them well, it's important that we think well of them too. Now what's your name, it's not "Nancy" is it, unless your father was one of those drunks you've incarcerated?'

'No, sir, it's Greene, sir, Graeme Greene. Not sure my father had much to do with my naming. My mother made the decisions in our house. Pa spent most of his time away.'

'That'd be right,' muttered a constable under his breath, falling silent when Price shot him an unwavering glare.

'Graeme, how'd you like to make the rounds with me. The lads here have given me some ideas so having a local to guide me would be more than helpful, and I can fill you in on the smaller details?'

Greene looked towards his sergeant; Jock agreed, 'It's good for Nancy to understand how others work. Gets a ribbing round here, being the new boy.'

'Hmm,' replied Price. 'Let's head off then, Graeme. I've no idea if Sinclair is even *in* this town, but it's the only lead I've got. We'll start with the port.' Price strode out, with the lithe Greene following behind, thinking all his wishes had come true.

They arrived at Port Chalmers just as a coastal steamer arrived. Burly Scottish dockworkers, and a smattering of Chinese workers, swarmed over the busy port, preparing to load the spring clip from the sheep being farmed in Otago. Like the Red Sea being parted by Moses, the workers avoided the two policemen. A landing waiter intercepted them and escorted the men to the Customhouse.

Along the foreshore, banded dotterels squeaked their way about, high-pitched and urgent; the Collector of Customs they encountered was anything *but* urgent. He wasn't bald from moving too fast. Sloth-like he emerged from behind his desk, crumbs from morning tea clinging to his black beard and his woollen uniform. Once-proud epaulettes sat grubby on his shoulders; he belched before greeting them, setting a farcical tone amidst the stunning scenery.

'Gentlemen, an unusual time for you to be passing by? What could bring you this far out of Dunedin on a day when we aren't expecting any vessels carrying delinquent treasure hunters? Today is just wool and provisions, not worth your attention.' Merv Kendall wiped his perspiring brow with a napkin sorely in need of a hard scrubbing with laundry soap.

'Sir, we are making enquiries about two persons may have departed this port in the past week. I request your leave to make your passenger lists available for us to examine.'

'My passenger lists? Hmm, I can't say for certain.' Again he wiped his brow, the musty smell of unwashed man wafted towards Price and Greene, the younger man bringing his own handkerchief up to his nose. 'Come into my office, while I enquire after these lists. The past week, you say? That may be hard... hmm, yes tricky. Come sit, and I'll see what I can muster up. Busy place this... yes... hmm, very busy. Our paperwork, while accurate — yes it's always accurate — but not always filed on time... too many arrivals, too few staff... you understand, yes?'

Price would have preferred taking the passenger lists away to examine them in a more congenial environment; a sideways glance at his colleague confirmed those were his thoughts. The lad had stationed himself in the chair closest to the door, the furthest away from the lopsided chair the customs officer favoured, spread as it was with a sheepskin rug of dubious colouring and cleanliness.

The spring heat seeped through the wooden walls of the new Customhouse; Price could only imagine the stifling temperature inside the building come the summer months, and what that heat would do to a man like Mervyn Kendall, Collector of Customs.

An interminable length of time passed. The two men watched bulbous flies gorging themselves on the remains of a hare pie left half-eaten on the desk — the morning tea they had interrupted — the gelatinous chunks of meat unappetising in the warming room.

A great hoicking sound from the corridor startled them. Their stomachs turned even more when Kendall entered, wiping a glistening glob of phlegm from his mouth. His only redeeming feature was the buff folder clenched under one arm. 'I had to harry the clerks to find this... overworked here, you might mention that when you report back the help you received here, hmm, yes? Takes time to gather this information, yes?'

Greene jumped up to respond, 'We are most appreciative of your help, sir, I'll write it in my report. Anyone just has to look outside to see how busy this port is. It's a travesty you are so understaffed.' By now Kendall was nodding so hard and sweating so profusely in agreement that Price feared his head would snap off. 'It's best if we take these off site, to stay out of your way. We'll have them returned to you by teatime tomorrow. I should imagine that suits?' Without giving the public servant any time to agree or otherwise, Greene grabbed his hat, and that of Price, and led the way out of the Customhouse.

'Fine work there, lad. Who taught you to be such a statesman?' Price slapped his young companion on the back. Greene beamed from ear to ear, his face flushing with delight — his standard reaction to both embarrassment and joy.

'Well, sir, when your voice sounds like mine, and God didn't see fit to bestow muscles of any note, you learn darn quick how to talk yourself out of situations which might have resulted in a beating. I've always been a talker. Just haven't had much of an opportunity to show anyone.'

Price lapsed into his customary silence as he pondered Greene's words. Whilst not all men were equal, a true man learned to use what he had to make himself equal to those around him. 'Can you recommend a hotel where we can go over these lists? Somewhere not serving hare pie!'

Greene looked at Price, before recognising the older man had made a joke and was chuckling. Greene joined in, both still smiling as they entered the *Surveyor's Arms*, Port Chalmers' first public house.

Taking a table under a window, and taking a gamble, Greene ordered two Phoenix ales, an amber beer from the brewery established in Reefton which was proving to be a hit with the miners flocking to find their fortunes. Ale was a welcome change from the fortified sherry his parents had consumed in vast quantities.

'Can you read, Greene?' Price asked, bowing his head over the first passenger list.

'Yes, sir, did my schooling through the Church. My brothers are farmers, but they decided that I needed something more office-based. I expect my parents assumed I'd join the Church, but that wasn't for me. This suits me.'

'Good,' Price handed half the papers to him, 'Run your eyes over these.'

'What am I looking for?'

Price hadn't given Sarah's name to the men in the station, only Sinclair's. His emotions were causing foolish mistakes. 'Bryce Sinclair, and Sarah Bell. That's her married name, so also check for Sarah Lester, I think that's her maiden name. Sinclair had a son, Samuel, so look for that too. He's still in Bruce Bay, but Sinclair may use his son's name.'

Turning of pages and the sipping of ale were the only communication at their table. Around them, the busy bar filled and emptied several times over as the day progressed. One or other would start to say they'd found something, then shake their heads, and lapse back into silence. The handwritten records proved as hard to read as they'd been for Merv Kendall to find; the penmanship of the clerks varied widely. Until Price closed his last folder, 'Nothing.' Greene scanned his last page and shook his head in response.

'There's the Cobb & Co. coaches they could have taken? We could try there next.'

'No, I questioned several drivers on my way here. None of them had seen anyone matching their descriptions. They use the same men all the time, and I trust their answers. No, we should look elsewhere. He had his own boat, but left it in Bruce Bay, so perhaps he had a collaborator somewhere on the waterfront, someone who would have let him and Mrs Bell board with no paperwork changing hands. We'll take these papers back tomorrow and question the other workers at the port. We may as well try Dunedin — they could have transferred to a larger vessel from one of the small ones operating out of there. This could be a devil of a job. Anyway, let's go, I need to freshen up for supper. Mrs Stewart expects a certain level of decorum in her establishment. Never cross a Scots woman, Greene — let that be a piece of advice to you.'

The ride to Dunedin was quiet, the roads emptying as people hurried home in time for supper. The coach delivered Greene to the police station. As he was disembarking, Greene's next words stopped Price's heart.

'We could always go speak to Mrs Lester at the Manse tomorrow, after we've been to the port. She could be a relation of your Mrs Bell, and may have had word from her.'

THE INTERVIEW

'*D*o you not think that you could have told me before about Mrs Lester?' Price asked Graeme Greene, forcing the words through clenched teeth.

Greene turned around, one foot on the wooden step, 'Only just thought about it. Mrs Lester has been here for years, lives at the Manse, does the cleaning and things, the flowers for the church too on Sundays. I've never spoken to her, just know who she is, but like most people here, we recognise everyone, except the new miners who float into town every day now, it seems, but then you can identify them because they aren't anyone you already know.'

The boy's logic made sense. You knew who you knew, and if you didn't know them, they were strangers. The permanent population, while large compared to the rest of the country, was still small enough for everyone to know you and your business, often before you learned yourself.

'Where's the Manse then?'

Greene looked amused, before answering, 'On Manse Street. I wouldn't go calling there today, though. Wednesday is the day he receives his visitors. Bishop Dasent isn't as open as the last minister; keeps strict "business hours" and gets upset if he's bothered outside of Sundays and Wednesdays. A funny one, that one.' Flushing at his baseless observations, he added, '... someone told me. I've not met him myself cause I go to a different church, but Wednesdays, that's the best time to call. He'll be busy, and won't worry if you speak with Mrs Lester because she has to speak to all the callers, doesn't she?'

'Thank you for your help today, Graeme, and for the information. We'll call by on Wednesday and you can introduce me.'

Nodding to the carriage driver, he carried on to his lodgings where supper was waiting for him. *Damn supper, damn the bishop, and damn courtesy.* He wanted to speak to Mrs Lester now, this minute. Head in his hands, he never saw the Manse as they drove past, its glorious gardens shrouded in shadows, dragging the night behind them.

No matter how much you wish time to pass, it carries on its progression regardless of your desire. Morning follows night, night follows day, the sun rises, the moon chases the day away. Babies are born, the elderly die. And so it was that Price spent Tuesday walking through the new streets of Dunedin, peering into shop fronts; passing time. He stopped to admire the skill of the workmen installing stained-glass windows festooned with English ivy in the empty sockets of a building precariously placed across the road from a cricket ground. Cries went up as a batsman thwacked his ball over the roof of the Albion Hotel. Price took one last look at the master craftsman and his windows, and chuckled to himself, recognising the grim determination of a man paid to do a job, regardless of the perils. Those windows wouldn't remain intact long.

People carried on with their lives, the high and mighty as invisible to him as the Chinese hurrying through the streets, long black braids swaying with their strangely quick gait. Travelling in pairs was the safest option in these times of mistrust. Men throughout Otago were succumbing to madness brought on by greed. Nothing changed a man's nature as much as money. Fascinated by the twin backs of the Chinamen, Price turned to watch them a moment longer, and promptly walked straight into a woman coming the other way. The woman tumbled to the ground, her woven basket disgorging its contents over the hard pressed dirt, her hat stolen by the wind.

'Jesus!' cried the startled girl.

'Sorry?'

It was then she realised she'd spoken aloud, 'Oh my God, I'm so sorry... oh my goodness. You must think I'm dreadful. I never meant to say...'

Taking Price's proffered hand, she pulled herself up. Meeting his eyes, her cheeks blushed red with embarrassment at her swearing. As he examined her, Price realised it was the same woman from Sunday, the one who'd offered him directions.

'I seem to making terrible habit of causing you harm, madam. It is I who must apologise.' Price removed his hat and gave a little bow, drawing a self-conscious laugh from Annabel Lester. Regardless of how long she lived in this time, these small decorous moments caught her off guard. She never remembered whether she should nod or curtsy in response.

Recovering her composure, she ventured forward, 'Perhaps we should introduce ourselves?'

'I am William Price, and it has been a great pleasure running into you again. Please forgive the physicality, and my behaviour on Sunday.'

It had been quite some time since anyone had spoken to Annabel in such a flirtatious way. She never imagined feeling the fluttering of temptation again, but that explained the sudden joy coursing through her body.

'Annabel Lester, of the Manse,' she said, shaking Price's hand.

Instead of releasing her hand, as common decency dictated, Price clung harder. 'Mrs Lester? You are the lady I have been seeking.'

Confused, Annabel tried to extract her hand. Why would this man be searching for her? Something to do with the Bishop? Uncertainty gripped her, and she searched for an escape.

Price wouldn't let her get away. 'I was coming to speak with you tomorrow, but here you are, like a gift from God.'

'I doubt He had anything to do with it, more the case of you not keeping your eye on the road,' she parried, trying to lessen the intensity of the moment. He was the best looking man she'd stumbled across in Dunedin — the tallest *and* the most intriguing — but he scared her. There was something in his eyes she couldn't interpret. The last thing she needed was another religious zealot in her life. She lived with a pair of them and, although she'd become resigned to her living arrangements, there was no space in life for those who believed in the divine right of their god above all else. Pulling her hand free, she continued, 'I'll be seeing you at the Manse tomorrow then. Good day, sir.'

Annabel tried smothering the short-lived feelings of attraction. She didn't need a man in her life, they only complicated things. Besides, she was a married woman, albeit to a man she hadn't seen for over a decade, but that didn't diminish the vows she'd made, *did it*?

Price called out to her, 'Mrs Lester, perhaps we could take a cup of tea together, there are things I must discuss with you that cannot wait until tomorrow.'

'Oh I'm sure they can. Good day, Mister Price.' The curious glances of other women on the street pierced her back. Busybodies too uncouth to keep their noses to themselves. Another downside of living in a small town. At least in London, a city teeming with every form of humanity, you never need see the same person again. But on the streets of Dunedin, they'd be talking about this interlude from now till Sunday. Fuel for the fire that she was a 'fallen woman', kept by Reverend Cummings for his personal entertainment until Bishop Dasent deposed him.

Annabel hurried off, leaving her spoiled goods on the ground, never once looking back at the pained face of Warden William Price.

THE LETTER

"Darling Elizabeth,

Thinking of you keeps me going. Were it not for the mere thought of your welcoming arms upon my return, I swear I would have laid down in some foreign meadow and let the others run me through. To plough me into this land that we are defending.

We are little more than fertiliser for the fields here. These virgin fields, fields we have yet to rake with our boots, swathed in a carpet of pristine white snow, ice crystals cling to every naked branch, like jewels in a crown; until we get there, and then it turns dun. A dull muddy brown, stained with the red blood of men. If the enemy reaches it before we do, it becomes the blackened carcass of a vulture. An ugly, stinking carcass.

There's no word of when we'll return. It's laughable to imagine celebrating Christmas with you this year. I'm truly sorry, my love. Remember our first Christmas together? Our tree? Almost every tree here reminds me of our first tree. You'd hung so many decorations on it that it barely had the strength to stand up straight. That's how we feel out here. I'd do almost anything to be up in the skies looking down on all of this. They're asking around to see if any of the lads have flying experience. I've put my hand up. How hard can it be?"

THE SHOP

*a*fter their first meeting, Richard Grey had kept his word, and once Sinclair found the address on Grey's card, he introduced himself to the man waiting there. He'd frisked Sinclair, furnished him with a weapon of some sort, and issued orders to stay close by and await further instructions.

Sinclair didn't know what the small black object was, but assumed it was an obscure modern day weapon, so pocketed it without question to avoid looking stupid in front of the other man. He'd endured enough of that at home.

It hadn't taken long to wheedle out the name of Grey, the man he'd followed from *The Old Curiosity Shop* to the *George and Vulture Inn*. And despite orders not to leave, Sinclair promptly left to find a bar where the clientele didn't look askance at his rough clothes and pugilist face. A mock-Tudor travesty called the *Jolly Farmer*-fit the bill. It came complete with condom vending machines, stained carpets, and a bartender whose blindness to the goings on around him was legendary. Sinclair found more of his ilk in the bar's dark corners, and, like a lord, held court.

Sinclair's minder was a goon called Stokes — a short weasel-faced man with close-cropped hair who held a much higher opinion of himself than anyone else. Kindred spirits — both enjoyed inflicting pain on those who crossed them, and the men spent an enjoyable evening preying on tourists, before Sinclair scored a pistol from a thug who'd mistaken them for naïve tourists. Forensic dental work would be the only tool left to identify the thug's bloodied corpse.

Sinclair had jumped at Grey's order to attack Sarah at the shop. He had his own reasons for agreeing to the job and Grey's reasons were of no concern. It was what happened afterwards that shattered any illusions he held about the position he was now in.

After the disastrous attempt to retrieve the Indian knife for Grey and his silver candlesticks from Sarah at *The Old Curiosity Shop*, he and Stokes had run like the devil himself was chasing them. Sarah's disappearance as he pulled the trigger had scared him more than he'd ever admit, and they'd leapt into the waiting Peugeot, both as white as sheets, with Stokes screaming 'Drive!' at the young Nigerian boy behind the wheel.

They'd returned to the apartment, empty-handed after heaving the pistol into the Thames, where it sank to the silty bottom, joining countless others under the murky waters of history. Stokes poured two large tumblers of whisky and they collapsed onto the couch with their drinks.

'What the fuck was that?'

Sinclair shook his head, 'The work of the devil, that's what it is.' He'd expected to see the remains of Sarah Bell's head after he'd pulled the trigger. He'd expected blood and carnage. But now *his* head was screwed.

'Fuck off. How the fuck am I meant to tell Grey what happened? Jesus, he'll kill us.' Stokes drained his glass, refilled it, and knocked it back a second time, before wiping the nervous sweat from his brow and stubbled head. 'She did just disappear didn't she? Fuck, if you hadn't of fired that bloody gun we could've searched the place for the stuff. Now we are fucked. You really are from another planet, aren't you?'

Sinclair sat sipping the malty amber liquid, taking the time, even now, to enjoy the best grog he'd ever had. A thousand times better than the stuff back in Bruce Bay. He wondered if Sweeney kept any of the good stuff for himself, only selling the swill to the miners. The abuse from Stokes rolled off his back and his anger simmered unseen.

From the depths of Stokes' jacket pocket came a shrill ring. Sinclair couldn't help but stare in fascination at the magic box making the sound which Stokes now held in his hand, a name displayed in a lit rectangle.

'Shit, it's Grey.'

He stood up, his face alternating between shades of fear and subjugation. He stabbed at the phone.

'Yes?... no, we didn't get... no, she said she'd already handed it over to Christie's... there was trouble.' He winced, before carrying on, glancing at Sinclair, 'Yeah, the new guy shot her... no, no one saw us.' Stokes listened for an uncomfortably long time. Sinclair drained his whisky, confident he knew what the magic box was saying, and he wanted to be ready. Stokes swallowed, before speaking again into the phone, 'Yep, I understand, no problem. I'll handle it.' The phone disappeared back into his jacket.

Sinclair rearranged his solid bulk on the couch, every sinew ready for whatever was coming, his inbuilt survival mechanism ready to kick in at the slightest provocation.

'Another drink?' Stokes asked, moving towards the cabinet, his hand back inside his coat.

'Nah, mate, I'm right,' Sinclair replied, his empty tumbler in his left hand, as if he were about to pass it to Stokes to put away. Sinclair stood up at the same moment Stokes withdrew a knife from his cavernous pocket and slashed at thin air.

THE ANTIPODEAN

Sinclair smashed his empty glass into Stokes' head, stunning him with the heavy crystal. Unexpectedly agile for a man of his size, Sinclair wrenched the knife from Stokes' grasp and plunged it into the smaller man's lean stomach. The knife sliding deeper into Stoke's bowel as Sinclair twisted it malevolently before releasing it, allowing Stokes to slip to the floor. Blood painted the polished floors a red Monet-like pattern.

Sinclair frisked his victim, liberating a clunky gold sovereign ring and cash. He stared at the remaining wallet contents: credit cards and loyalty discount coupons. Snorting in disgust, he tossed these new-fangled objects aside. Then, satisfied there was nothing else of value, Sinclair eased himself out of the apartment, engaging the lock behind him and never looked back.

Safely ensconced in fresh premises, courtesy of the bartender at the *Jolly Farmer*, Bryce Sinclair watched the saturation coverage on the magic box, he now knew as a 'television'. He'd seen so much he felt he could picture the whole scene. The various broadcasters relished replaying the live Internet footage of the murder, the facial features of the dying clerk blurred out in mock respect to his grieving family.

The arrest of Richard Grey fascinated him. He'd rightly assumed

Grey would want him dealt with after his failure to get the *katar* before Sarah consigned it to Christie's. But a man doesn't survive the goldfields of the colonies by being easy to kill. And London was no different.

In fact, Grey had received the call from Hannah Gardner at Christie's, saying that someone had picked the *katar* up from Sarah at *The Old Curiosity Shop*. He'd then phoned Stokes, instructing him to dispose of the 'luggage' from New Zealand. What Grey hadn't counted on was Sinclair's innate sense of self-preservation. Which Sinclair was now toasting with a pint of London Pride, wondering where to from here.

THE INVESTIGATION

"*The Metropolitan Police have concluded that there were no other persons involved in the alleged murder of Leo Hayward, the clerk at Christie's, other than the one man arrested at the scene. Mr Richard Grey of London City has been charged with murder, and released on bail under strict conditions, including the surrendering of his passport, pending trial to be heard next month. The Health and Safety Executive are continuing their investigation.*"

$\mathcal{T}$he article was short and to the point, omitting the gory details of the slaying. It ignored the splatters of blood on the frocks of the woman in the front row of Christie's auction room, and the unfurling of a man's intestines on an international stage.

Sinclair carefully folded the newspaper and slipped out of the café. In this century, he may be a bit backward, but he'd quickly understood that Grey out on bail might pose some difficulties. This time wasn't one he was born to, but revenge was surely as common now as it was in the colonies in the 1800s.

He hurried down the street, his back prickling in anticipation —

for what, he didn't know, but he'd learned to trust his instincts. His tattered fighter's ears attuned to any change in his environment, he sidled towards his squalid flat, checking first that all looked as he'd left it. The tenement filled with the dregs of society, and Sinclair slotted right in. His peculiar ways didn't interest the drug addicts, dealers, and mentally impaired residents who shared the building. This was a 'cash up front, ask no questions' place. As long as you had cash, you were in.

Sinclair unlocked his door, his nose curling at the decaying scent pervading the room. He'd rather be in New Zealand without running water and electricity than living in this hovel. Mind you, the ripe odour of mouldy carpets and filth-encrusted toilets — almost as bad as the long-drops in Bruce Bay — were a small price to pay for hot showers and food he never believed could have existed. Until he found Sarah Lester or Bell, or whatever the hell her name was — and, figured out how to get home, or decided if he wanted to, he was stuck.

Closing the stained curtains, he flicked a magical switch which illuminated the room. This always cheered him, and he took a moment to admire the glow from the globe dangling from the discoloured ceiling, before he focused on the task. Unzipping a sports bag, he pulled out his latest acquisition; a small black handgun, well used and comfortable in his hand. There was no doubt he'd need it soon. It galled him no end that Stokes had made him ditch the last one in the Thames; a bloody stupid waste. The bag held several other things every modern 'gentleman' needed: boxes of ammunition; a light flick knife; a larger all-purpose butcher's blade; duct tape; and clothing.

He'd replaced his filthy antipodean rags once he'd met Grey, although his new ensemble was not that different from the outfit he'd discarded, just cleaner and more contemporary, enabling him to merge with the general population.

It amazed him how easy it was to walk out of shops with anything he desired, without paying. Most assistants seemed to be vacuous young girls with other things on their minds, and who never gave his ugly countenance a second glance. So he'd gone on a shoplifting spree around London.

Unloading his five-finger discount 'purchases' into wire baskets left by a former tenant, he changed into a more upmarket outfit — moleskin jeans, a lightweight sweater and a fancy wristwatch. Wearing it on his wrist was a novel feeling, and he kept glancing at the Casio as he pondered his next move. Today he'd go back to the antique shop. It might be fun living this modern time rather than going back to a life of bloody hard work in Bruce Bay, but he couldn't appreciate it until he'd dealt with that bitch Sarah. Only then would he be able to prove to Grey that he'd repaid his debt. And then he'd begin enjoying his new life here.

Of his son Samuel, he gave no thought.

THE EXPERTS

*W*hen Richard Grey eviscerated the clerk, the armed security guard present had fired wildly, the shot incapacitating the crazed man. It would have been a better if the bullet had taken Grey's life.

The Metropolitan Police spent five hours at Christie's, interviewing every witness - where they were; what they heard; and what they saw.

Don Claire and Jay Khosla had retreated to Don's office to run damage control with the PR team. The adage that all publicity was good publicity debatable in this case. It was not profitable business to have one of your best customers gut an employee, on stage, in the middle of an auction, streamed live across the Internet.

Detained with the rest of the attendees, the police funnelled Ryan Francis and Gemma into the boardroom with the other key Christie's employees, because of their connection with Richard Grey and the *katar*. There, they spent several of those hours talking with Andrew Harvard and Patricia Bolton, supervised by a lone constable who'd given up trying to follow the convoluted conversation.

'So they're a pair,' Ryan muttered, not for the first time. They'd all repeated themselves, incredulous at what they'd witnessed earlier.

'Sarah knew that the *katar* was part of a pair that a lord owned...'

'Lord Grey?' interrupted Ryan. Patricia shot him an annoyed look.

'Yes, Lord Grey — but it belonged to the Raja of Nahan, in India. That was what the seller told her-'

'But we've no evidence,' Andrew interjected, also earning him an exasperated look from Patricia.

Unfailingly loyal to her friend, Patricia replied, 'If Sarah were here, she'd be able to say more, but she's not, so this is what we have to work with for now.'

'The police will have to look into the likelihood of Grey's involvement with Sarah's disappearance?' Andrew offered.

Patricia fiddled with her coffee mug, and mumbled, memories of the bizarre conversation with Sarah fresh in her mind. She was certain Sarah must have travelled back in time, the same as her parents, but there was still the nagging fear that Grey had hurt her. 'I'm sure after today they'll go through his dealings with a fine-tooth comb,' she muttered.

Andrew, misunderstanding Patricia's reluctance to discuss Sarah's disappearance, put his arm around her shoulders, comforting the woman who'd agreed to be his girlfriend. His once-despairing, and now jubilant, mother had all but taken out a full-page ad in *The Times*, telling the world. He suspected she'd already knitted several pairs of booties.

'If only the police would let us see both knives, to compare. Looks like Grey was right; that Sarah's *katar* is the mate to the one his grandfather bought from Christie's in the forties.' Ryan shuffled the papers until finding the copy of the auction receipt.

'The receipt says Mrs Elizabeth Williams was the seller, earning just over two hundred pounds for the Red Cross and St. John Fundraiser. The file only had the sale and purchase receipts, but not a photo. I'd need to see the original auction catalogue, and hope that has a picture. It's a shame no one checked the archives before this...'

Their conversation ended when a constable came to collect Patricia for her witness statement.

'How much longer are we going to be kept here?' Gemma demanded from the uniformed man.

'Sorry, but we have to talk to every witness tonight; time warps the memory.'

The constable escorted Patricia out of the room, and handed her over to a plain-clothes detective, one younger than she expected. He walked her through the process until they reached Sarah's disappearance, 'What do you know about Sarah Lester's whereabouts?'

'Nothing. I've told the police everything I know.'

'You haven't told me. So humour me, and fill in the gaps,' Detective Sergeant Owen Gibson said.

'Are you joking? It's ten o'clock, I'm tired and hungry, and, to be honest, I need to go home and have a bath. You weren't here when it happened. I will never get the sight of that man's stomach splitting open like an overripe grapefruit. And you want to ask me about Sarah? It's all on file somewhere.' Turning away, she stared at the opaque glass of the office door.

Detective Sergeant Gibson read through his notes, eyes gritty, his cheap suit crumpled from the late hour. Being surrounded by such ostentatious opulence confirmed that the world wasn't fair, and the last thing he needed was a rich tosser making the job any harder. 'Miss Bolton, I appreciate that you are tired but I'm not sitting in front of a computer to check the veracity of your story. This will go faster if you fill in the blanks. So I'll ask again, and if you choose not to answer this time, we'll move to the station, where it will take much longer. I'm well acquainted with long nights, and it'd be no trouble to resume this conversation there. So, what can you tell me about Miss Lester's disappearance?' He waited, his point driven home by a heavily chewed pen poised above a hard-sided notebook.

Biting the inside her cheek, Patricia looked at her options. Answering honestly may be considered backchat; but feigning no knowledge unbelievable; which left using a version of the truth the easiest answer. Taking a deep breath she replied, 'Well, you know both her parents disappeared? One of the last things she told me was the rumour that her father was in India...'

Gibson tried interrupting.

'No, you wanted me to answer, so let me finish. She heard a rumour — where from I don't know — but I haven't seen her since just before the shooting in the shop. She must have run off when they came in, So maybe she went to India to find her father? If someone was shooting at you, and the police hadn't caught them yet, would you go back to work?'

Gibson massaged his temple, a full-blown headache forming. He scribbled a few words before looking at Patricia. 'Thank you Miss Bolton, we'll be in touch. You're free to leave.'

Patricia stood and left the room without a backward glance. Harvard was lingering outside the office, his interview over too. Others were gathering up belongings and streaming towards the lifts. 'Come on, we'll take the stairs,' Andrew offered, motioning to the door, away from the herd of tired interviewees waiting to leave.

Ryan and Gemma were now the only ones left in the opulent boardroom. They'd each had a cursory interview with a constable, with the police satisfied they were of no interest, being ostensibly 'on the same team'.

'What do you think, Gem?'

'That I need a bath,' she answered, her black pencil skirt crinkled beyond what she considered acceptable.

'I meant, what do you think about Grey? And the *katar*? I'm trying to block out what he did but now we're alone should we ask the police to let us have a look at the knives?'

Gemma looked aghast, 'I can't believe your one-track mind. You and your antiquities! The last thing I want to see is a knife covered with someone's stomach contents. At least we won't be dealing with Mr Grey for quite some time, and god knows if we'll ever see a penny of what he owes the firm. That'll give the Accounts Receivable team something to do.'

THE CANDELABRA

'*G*em, what have you got? Anything yet?' Ryan Francis quizzed his colleague from his side of the token partition as he peered over at her computer screen.

Gemma Dance sighed, her fingers poised over the keyboard, before answering, 'For the tenth time today, no. I'll let you know when I've something to say. I'm not keeping secrets, Ryan, I haven't found what I'm looking for yet. It's here and I *promise* to tell you as soon as I find the needle in this electronic haystack. So please leave me alone.' She stabbed at the keys, driving her point home.

Ryan huffed in his cubical, leaning back in his ergonomic chair and studied the ornate ceiling rose above him. While London was buzzing over the tragedy at Christie's, he and Gemma, and several other Art Loss Register staff were puzzling over the origins of the two *katar* and, more, the Paul de Lamerie candelabra, also auctioned through Christie's. The antiques trade knew De Lamerie as the greatest silversmith in eighteenth century England. A silversmith who'd supplied Tsarinas, Earls, Counts and Kings, de Lamerie's body of work was huge, but pieces as spectacular as the matched pair of candelabra should be recorded somewhere. *Someone* had owned them, had them commissioned. Records *must* exist. At some point last week, Gemma had declared she'd found the hint of a lead, but hadn't shared it with her colleagues. She had drive, he'd give her that, but she also had an annoying habit of trying to score points by being the one to deliver the goods, regardless of who'd helped her along the way. A glory hound, who was magnificent at her job.

Meanwhile, he sat here, at her beck and call, waiting to cater to whatever crazy research mission she assigned him next. So far she'd sent him to the London Silver Vaults, and back to Christie's to search their archives, but his most interesting visit had been to the library at the Goldsmiths' Company. Over eight thousand books, and countless magazines, journals and papers from private collections. He could have spent days there delving into their material, surrounded by the life stories of the world's treasures. He'd returned with a mountain of papers Gem had already ordered online through the librarians at the Company, leaving him no time to wallow in the incredible depth of history within the library. What the papers had in them — well, she hadn't involved him in that particular treasure hunt. So in the meantime, he tried working on cases for his other clients, but everything else he looked at was as dull as watching paint dry.

'I've got it!' Gemma yelled.

The office erupted. Half a dozen corporate lackeys crowded around Gemma in her cubicle, high fiving as if she'd won the lottery.

'It's here. Can't believe I didn't think to look here first. It was the church all along,' Gemma announced, gesturing towards an enlarged image on her computer screen.

Ryan tried to peer between his colleagues. There was nothing he could see providing evidence of the original source of the candelabra. It perplexed him why they were bothering with this folly. No one had registered the items with the Art Loss Register. The police didn't seem worried, and Christie's didn't care, since they'd received their massive commission from the sale. But Gemma had insisted there was something fishy about the whole thing and, given her position with the Register, they'd given her free rein to pursue her hunch. It's how they operated, and a reason for their past successes.

The Register had an impressive track record of reuniting stolen art and artefacts with their original owners — rare tapestries, Matisse artworks, the Duchess of Argyll's jewellery. All done with decorum and subtlety using the world's largest private database of lost and stolen art, antiques and collectables.

As the hubbub cooled down, Ryan pulled up a chair next to her, so he could see exactly what she had found, 'What is it, Gem?'

Gemma pointed a manicured nail at the grainy picture on her screen, 'There's de Lamerie's name in the header, with his Gerrard Street address. The date is clear, "May 29, 1739". In the body you can just make out the words "Pair of altar candelabra". And underneath that, you can see they also ordered a large oval platter. I guess it was to match the candelabra. The hardest part has been trying to decipher *who* the invoice is for — up here, in the top left-hand corner? I've got as far as deciphering the first word, "Bishop". But I can't read what comes after that.'

'Don't you have the original to look at? Wouldn't that be easier?'

'Trust me, this enlarged version is much clearer than the original. Water damaged it, which is why it's so hard to read. The IT people played with the image, and this is as good as they can get it.'

'But you still don't know who ordered them?' Ryan offered.

Gemma rolled her eyes.

'But we know *when* the Bishop of *Somewhere* ordered them, and a matching platter which may still exist unless someone melted it down. I can use some word recognition software I've downloaded to match up the letters we *can* make out, to known bishops in 1739. It can't be that hard. Just a few more hours. And from there, we can track it through church records. The church are worse than Inland Revenue with record keeping. Somewhere they have everything. Thank God.'

Ryan rolled his chair back to his cubical, resigned to waiting till Gemma's program had done its thing. Clicking on the *katar* file, he reread the notes on the knives, hoping that the raised energy levels in the office might offer some clarity. But without the actual dealer who'd consigned the *katar* to Christie's — Sarah Lester — the investigation had ground to a standstill.

He noted the address for *The Old Curiosity Shop* on a piece of memo cube, underlining it several times. He didn't need the owner of the store at all, just access to their records.

THE PLAYER

*T*he soft plunk of balls against racquets echoed around the tennis courts. Abrupt yells of players commingled with the low conversations of spectators, the barks of coaches, and the sounds of diners knocking back healthy concoctions made from the current trendy 'super food'.

Grey sipped on a tea. The green sludge in his companion's glass looked as appealing as Thames river water. He'd foregone his normal structured black suit for a pastel polo shirt and cream-coloured slacks, finished with leather boat shoes. His suit would have been an anomaly among the sea of white-uniformed players around him. Hannah Gardner squirmed in her seat. If she could have hidden behind her blunt blonde fringe, she would have. Being seen talking to Richard Grey in public would be career suicide. Meeting with a man charged with murdering one of her coworkers was the stupidest thing she'd ever done. She'd never regretted her involvement with Grey as much as she did now.

Their relationship had begun when she'd been at a low point in her life. Her elderly parents both required full-time nursing, depleting their savings, and requiring the sale of their comfortable semi-detached home, the one she'd expected to inherit. Her salary at

Christie's, and the occasional split of a sales commission, was barely enough for her to live on, let alone to assist with the care of her parents. When Grey had approached her, with what seemed like a minor query, she was all too happy to help one of Christie's most moneyed clients.

Cultivating customers was a major part of her work — the more distinguished they were, the more money spent, and you received a greater portion of the commission, especially if you sourced the object they purchased, or helped broker the sale, either by private treaty or by bringing the winning bidder to the auction.

Grey had called her to ask one minor question; who had consigned a piece of art, a late 1800s painting, by Russian war artist Vasily Vereshchagin. Not a piece that would break any records under the gavel. She'd been so flattered that he'd contacted her, since they'd only met the once, that, without thinking, she'd looked up the details, sharing the confidential information.

A few days later, Grey had a small bouquet delivered to her home, as thanks. In all these years, she'd never thought to ask him how he knew her address.

When Grey rang with a second question, about the reserve price of an urn — a piece of Doulton Lambeth pottery — she hadn't hesitated, the lilies still fresh in her mind. The piece only warranted a reserve of three hundred pounds, and he wanted to buy it because his great-grandfather had talked of owning a similar item. She was more than happy to oblige. She'd seen him at the auction, and it felt natural leaning towards him to whisper the confidential reserve price of a lacklustre piece of pottery, for sentimental reasons. The smile he'd given her was reward enough. She'd fantasised that, before long, he'd be whisking her away on trips to Aspen, and winters in Bermuda. He was the only man ever to send her flowers, or shower her with compliments.

Was she breaking the rules? *Absolutely*. But it had seemed like such a minor infraction that it hadn't bothered her. He'd always seemed so grateful. Half a dozen bottles of good French wine had arrived on her door step after he'd won the urn. After that, tickets to the Royal

Ballet, seats at Wimbledon. She'd only ever answered innocuous questions about items consigned to Christie's. Over time, the requests had increased, and became more complicated, involving more subterfuge. By then, she was in too deep. At some point, the gifts evolved into payments, the money a welcome boost to her haemorrhaging finances. By then it was too late to back out, and she was sending Grey the contact details of people looking to consign goods in which Grey had expressed an interest. He had a very specific list of things he desired and didn't want to pay market price for them. Grey wanted them before they even made it to the auction floor.

'Couldn't we have just talked over the phone?' Gardner whined, peering at the people surrounding them.

'The police will be listening to my conversations, hoping I'll incriminate myself. Any fool can see on the CCTV footage that I slipped and, in my haste to claim my stolen property, it was physics, the sharpness of the antique blade, and the reactions of the idiot on the stage that led to his death. And this sham of a trial will prove that.'

Gardner choked on her smoothie, coughing into her serviette, eyes darting around to check if anyone was looking. After wiping her mouth, she tugged her cap down tucking her blonde hair out of sight.

'Surely you can't want anything further from me now?'

'On the contrary, Hannah, I require you even more than before. Now I am *persona non grata* at your place of work now, I need your help more than ever. I cannot stop my quest to reunite my family's belongings. Our task here has only just begun.'

'You can't expect me to continue giving you confidential information? The whole office is going through a massive security crackdown...' Gardner's voice cracked under the strain.

'Hannah, you don't understand the position you've put yourself in. But I'm sure your employers will, once I instruct my solicitor to release the evidence of your efforts to curry favour with me to supplement your income. Rather daring of you. You were also hoping for a smidgeon of romance, no? And to think I kept rebuffing your naïve advances. Do you imagine I *like* the ballet? Dire rubbish, tiresome and devoid of imagination. Did you *really* believe I would have gone with you? How many nights have you sat in a theatre with an empty seat next to you? Oh yes, it is all well documented, your pathetic attempts to seduce me...'

Hannah interrupted, her heart hammering, she pressed her hands to her chest.

'No, no, let me finish. You need me. Your parents need my money. Yes, I know all about them. I knew all that and a lot more about you before we began this dance. But your dance card is full now, and my name is the only name on there, so we shall continue dancing. We needed to get that clear. I expect the same level of service that I have received from you up to this point.' Grey took a final sip of his tea, before wiping his lips.

'Thank you for your time. Good luck with your game.' With that, he left the table, and wound his way past the other tables filled with oblivious diners, his height casting shadows in his wake.

Gardner fiddled with her phone, struggling with her decision. Deep down, wasn't her relationship with Grey the bright spark in a monotonous life? She only had her job, her failing parents, and a crummy flat. And because of Grey, a tidy sum in her bank. An amount that facilitated membership to a club like this one.

THE ASSOCIATION

$\mathcal{T}$he room hummed with the genteel murmuring of suppressed excitement. A hundred women wearing pearls and cardigans — and a smattering of men in sensible shoes — sat their stout behinds on unforgiving conference chairs. The fabric of the stackable chairs and the well-worn carpet showing the age of venue.

Mired in the nineties, with salmon pink and beige the predominant colours, the room stood in stark contrast to the ecclesiastical robes displayed on the stage under spotlights highlighting the gold thread embellishments.

'May I have your attention?' A robust woman at the lectern waved at the assembled crowd, tapping on her microphone with short blunt-cut nails. There were no pretensions of beauty bound up in her dated woollen suit.

Tracey Humphrey, Chairwoman of the Royal School of Needlework, was more at home with bobbins and Buckingham lace than she was in front of self-proclaimed needlework experts. But here she was. Today's lecture series on 'Samplers, Genoa Point Lace and Ecclesiastical Robes' was a sell-out. That so many people paid twenty pounds to listen to lace experts always amazed her.

'Thank you, and welcome to the first lecture of this series of the

School of Needlework's "Stitch In Time" programme. We have a marvellous line-up of speakers — comprising conservation professionals, collectors and museum curators.'

There was a rousing round of applause before Tracey could continue, 'After our first speaker today, we will run our popular "Open The Trunk" service in the foyer where you can present your treasures to our panel of experts for valuation, advice on restoration, or information gathering.' A wave of shuffling rippled through the hall as the attendees patted their treasures concealed in a motley assortment of carrier bags and tapestry totes.

'I'd like to introduce our first speaker, Eliza Broadhead, curator of the Department of Furniture, Textiles and Fashion at the Victoria and Albert Museum, with her presentation on their collection of samplers and their conservation.'

Enthusiastic applause greeted the formidably buxom Eliza Broadhead as she ascended the stage, jet beads jockeying for space between her enormous breasts. Panting into the microphone, she acknowledged the crowd with a smile, and a tilt of her head.

Famous for her precise eye and extensive knowledge of all things textile, Eliza was renowned in the world of needlework. She was also believed that any tapestry or textile of historical import should be in the safe hands of the V & A, not those of unscrupulous collectors. Which was why her broad grin faded was when she noticed Andrew Harvard from Christie's in the third row, his black suit incongruous in the sea of tweed and cashmere.

Unsmiling, she recognised the vulture among them. Then, catching her breath, she launched into her presentation about the quirks and intricacies of samplers and their conservation.

'And now we reach the V & A's latest acquisition', she paused, as the next slide illuminated the stage.

There, in all its glory, was Sarah Lester's sampler, the one she'd brought back from Lord Grey's house.

'Signed by 'R. J. Williams' and dated '19 June 1726'. Whilst we have older pieces in our collection, we consider one in such immaculate condition to be our finest example. Unfortunately the V &

A had to purchase this piece when, normally, families are more than happy to bequeath items such as this to us, so everyone can enjoy them. As a consequence, we have almost exhausted our acquisitions budget for the year.' Eliza glared at Andrew as she delivered the verbal jab.

Harvard busied himself with his notes. Eliza may not have realised it, but he agreed with her. There was no greater enjoyment than to wander the halls of a museum, soaking up the reflected grandeur of the past. Collectors who paid obscene amounts for objects which then disappeared into their personal collections, locked away from sight, were cultural vermin.

As she came to a close, those seated around Harvard chatted among themselves about Eliza's presentation, oblivious to any friction. Each harbouring the tiny hope that *their* family heirlooms would be worth thousands of pounds. Although they might nod in apparent agreement, for most, money exerted a stronger pull than charity.

The lecture broke for lunch; a sorry-looking smorgasbord of chicken curry and dry roast beef, followed by an insipid trifle with *faux* cream. The attendees scoffed the lacklustre food in a trice - 'Open The Trunk' was a highlight no one wanted to miss. Everyone needed to be at the front of the line with their family treasures.

For the event, Christie's had negotiated a booth with the Royal School of Needlework, and Harvard was there to enable the easy consignment of any special articles which might come to light — a bone of contention with the V & A, who had their own appraisers there. Eliza Broadbent's goal was to have those same pieces gifted to her establishment instead.

For a group of well-heeled and educated grown-ups, there was an unseemly amount of jostling for space around the tables scattered throughout the foyer. Hairspray and perfume, fused with decades of dust, created a near-toxic cloud in the confined area.

Other auction houses and dealers had representatives there; some specialists, some sharks. Harvard's booth was far enough away from Eliza's that he couldn't hear her words, nor discern whether this crowd was more likely to donate or sell their treasures. The more altruistic attendees would *never* consider coming to his table, so he wanted to see what else was out there.

Leaving the gathering hordes to an assistant, he wandered the foyer, just in time to overhear a slender young woman comment to Eliza that she, too, had a sampler signed by 'R. J. Williams', but dated 1728.

THE ARGUMENT

'What do you mean I can't have a look at it? I'm not about to run off with it.' Harvard argued with Eliza Broadhead outside the conference hall.

'They donated it to us, and we need to undertake serious conservation work on it. Letting non-museum staff near it is against our policies. I shudder to think what you would have done with it if it had come to you. I've seen the *repairs* your so-called conservators do. Sacrilege. Your lot have no regard for history. Rapists of history, and thieves. All of you.' Eliza turned away from Andrew, gathering up her bags, waving imperiously at her assistant to collect the rest. Now resembling a real-life caricature of a bag lady, Eliza squeezed her immense bulk between the table and Harvard. He put out a hand to plead his case further, but, in his haste, and as she was navigating the tiny gap, he pushed her. Eliza Broadhead toppled over, and fell to the ground — voluminous skirts, bosoms and beads tangling with overstuffed carry bags, handbag and laptop. Eliza's assistant squealed in fright, dropping her things in a rush to help.

Harvard bent to offer his hand, apologies tumbling from his mouth.

'Get away from me. How dare you?' Eliza panted, trying

unsuccessfully to disentangle the jet beads from her bag, 'You assaulted me. I shall lodge a complaint with your employer and with the Association — and the police. You're a menace.' Sweat blossomed on her forehead.

'It was an accident, I only wanted to examine the sampler; if you'll just listen? I'm sorry, it *was* an accident.' Harvard tried stuffing bits of fabric back into bags, the floor awash with skeins of thread and lace trims chopped from long-discarded wedding gowns.

Like a *Benny Hill* farce, Eliza's tiny assistant tried heaving the larger woman off the ground, instead slipping on silky remnants and landing on the floor herself.

'Christ, girl, what are you doing? Get me up. And you go away. Leave my things alone,' Eliza squealed at Harvard. Panting with exhaustion, she made it to her feet.

Harvard's concern for Eliza and what she might say to Don Claire, his boss, was all but forgotten as he froze. He'd grabbed a handful of fabric, and was about to shove it into a bag, when he caught sight of the very distinctive embroidery of the mysterious 'R. J. Williams'.

Eliza ripped the textile from his hands, but not before he'd read the embroidered passage:

"Time is an illusion. The minutes that have gone may still be ahead of you. Embrace every second."

THE INKWELL

'No, I only want inkwells which are Victorian or earlier, and I'd prefer sterling silver, but I'll look at anything unusual.' His black top barely holding in his enormous girth, the man was creating an effective blockade of the aisle. The young girls wanting to sift through the old vinyl records had already asked to get past twice, before the tallest pushed by, her handbag bouncing off the man's bulging side.

He grunted, whether from annoyance or escaping gas as his belly slapped against the counter, Patricia Bolton couldn't tell.

She looked around the shop, trying to identify where on earth inkwells might be.

'Um... best if you have a look in those,' gesturing towards a series of cabinets filled with every type of Victorian and Edwardian sterling silver objects, including a few pricier pieces of Georgian silverware.

Again he grunted. 'Where's Sarah then? She usually sorts me out,' he asked, tapping his grubby fingernails on the countertop.

Sarah Lester's closest friend grimaced, so tired of explaining that she was filling in at *The Old Curiosity Shop*, while Sarah was having some time out. At least, that was the answer Patricia gave the customers. For the police it was a particular version but, the reality *was* very different.

She painfully recalled when she'd last seen her friend; handing over the *katar*, an Indian knife, to a representative from Christie's, before vanishing. Sarah hadn't been at the auction house to witness the horrific murder of the young clerk, gutted in front of Patricia and a roomful of onlookers and Internet viewers worldwide. The weapon used had been a second *katar*, the twin of the one Sarah had consigned to Christie's to sell on her behalf. A veritable nightmare for the audience, not to mention the Christie's public relations team.

Which left Patricia Bolton trying to run her own semi-successful clothing design business and keep Sarah's antique shop solvent in her downtime. Although she was making a fortune on that front. *A hundred and thirty-two pounds today, and on a weekend too.* She was far better suited to selling clothes than other people's stuff.

Patricia wrinkled her nose at the back of the obese man now shuffling towards the silver cabinets, jersey threatening to give way with every lumbering step. She whipped out the well-thumbed copy of the *Miller's Collectables Price Guide*, scanning the index for inkwells: Staffordshire inkwells in the shape of greyhounds on cushions; travelling inkwells; a grotesque stoneware inkwell in the shape of a mask; and a heart-shaped Wemyss inkwell.

'Bloody hell,' she muttered, aghast at the prices quoted. 'Two hundred and sixty pounds for that! Looks like something I painted at school.'

'What did you say, love?', the walking heart attack asked her, followed by yet another grunt as his girth toppled over a tower of ephemera, only tidied that morning to be less an obstacle.

She shook her head, and continued flipping pages, furthering her antique education within the disorganised confines of *The Old Curiosity Shop*.

'There's nothing here for me today. Just tell Sarah I was in. Needs some tidying up in here, getting a bit hard to move round,' he suggested as he eased his way past the centre tables, although his bulk was more the problem than the state of the aisles. Patricia would be the first to admit that the insurmountable clutter had defeated her, but being obese was as hazardous as the precarious piles of stock.

For what the hundredth time that hour, she checked the clock, waiting for her boyfriend to come rescue her from the purgatory to which she'd submitted herself.

Andrew Harvard was due any minute to take her away from this repository of dead people's treasures. Senior Specialist, Costumes and Textiles at Christie's, he had stood by her through it all: the auction fiasco; Sarah's disappearance; the unrelenting attention of the police; and various antiquities organisations curious about the origins of the articles Sarah had consigned to Christie's.

Patricia had become so fed up with the number of collectors coming into her clothing shop to ask when *The Old Curiosity Shop* would reopen, that she and Andrew had organised limited opening hours, now displayed on the cluttered window. No new stock was coming in; that was where Patricia drew the line. She'd sell, but she wouldn't buy.

The media attention generated by the murder had done nothing but bolster Christie's reputation, and that of *The Old Curiosity Shop*, now inundated by macabre sightseers and serious collectors alike, looking for hidden treasures within the muddled aisles.

With a sigh, Patricia slipped the price guide back into its slot on the shelf behind her, and left the counter to pick up the mess of papers scattered on the floor by the man. She shoved them on top of a nail box full of napkin rings.

Patricia picked up the last of the postcards and letters held together by a corroded bulldog clip, rust marks staining the edges of the papers, and threw them on the pile, without noticing who they were addressed to.

THE CUSTOMER

*B*ryce Sinclair pushed open the door of *The Old Curiosity Shop*, revealing an eclectic mishmash of antiques and second-hand junk.

A disembodied voice called out from behind a tall cabinet, 'Hi there, I'll be with you in half a minute. Just call out if you need anything!'

Sinclair wandered around the dusty shop. Relics from his past brought back memories he'd rather forget: a wooden washboard, its ridges scored by a century of laundry; an iron boot scraper, the ornamental lily design on its edges incongruous with its muck-wiping function.

Most things in *this* life seemed magical to him, such as the traffic lights and hot running water. Sliding his hand over a grey box on the edge of the counter, he marvelled at the feel of the materials they made it from. *What is this machine?* The acronyms CD and DVD were as foreign to him as Arabic to a farmer in the highlands of Scotland.

Sinclair had discovered this time was much more to his liking, and after mulling over the possibilities for an even *better* life, he'd made a decision. He'd spent a fair amount of time checking out antique stores near his flat and the value of articles from his past amazed him. It perplexed him that punters were clamouring for cut-throat razors, pocket watches and sovereign cases, old coins and fireside tiles. Ivory trinkets and ladies' hatpins. Menial items. All obtained by sleight of hand — or by force.

If he *could* find his way back to his former life to do some 'shopping', all he'd need to do then would be to return to this present and he would be a very wealthy man.

A dishevelled Patricia Bolton made her way over to the counter, a stack of German beer steins in her arms. 'Old stock,' she announced, carefully lowering them onto the glass. The china mugs clinked in protest.

'Old stock?'

'Yep, from what I can see by the stock numbers, these beauties have been here for at least twenty years, if not longer! Most of these aren't German, they're Japanese. You can tell the difference, based on how heavy they are — you don't even need to check the base stamps. Listen to me, talking like I'm an expert!' She laughed.

'Uh huh,' Sinclair said, not interested. German beer vessels weren't something he was familiar with and, compared to the antiques he'd been studying, they appeared worthless. 'Where's the woman who owns this place?'

'Who? Sarah?' Patricia stopped fiddling with the steins, looking instead towards Sinclair, uncomfortable under his direct gaze and butchered ears. 'She's not here.'

'Where is she? See, she has something of mine that she owes me for, and I need that money now. You could tell me where she is, and then I'll leave you to your... your party for one,' Sinclair gestured towards the empty shop.

'She's away on holiday. I won't be able to help you, anyway. I can't make heads or tails of her record keeping, so, unless you have proof that Sarah owes you any money, I can't help, sorry.'

'She back in New Zealand then?' Sinclair chanced.

Patricia froze. She considered Sarah her closest friend and based on that she was sure Sarah wouldn't have told anyone else about her time travel. Besides, Sarah had no one else to tell. So how did this man know about New Zealand?

Sinclair looked at Patricia, surprised that his question about Sarah being in New Zealand had thrown her so much.

'Yeah, New Zealand. Last time I saw her she was saying how much she wanted to go back there. Good source of antiques, she told me,' Sinclair continued.

Patricia nodded, rearranging the beer steins in rows as she pondered his query.

As a child, Patricia was renowned for being unable to keep a secret. She'd forever be telling her cousins what was inside their birthday wrapping paper. Her school friends knew never to tell her anything confidential. She never meant to divulge things, it was just her way. Despite her unease in Sinclair's presence, she couldn't help elaborate. She could still keep Sarah's time travelling secret whilst answering the customer's question. 'To be honest, I'm not sure if she's there. She also mentioned India, so she could be in either place — I'm just looking after the shop while she's away.'

Sinclair's piggy eyes watched Patricia for any signs of fabrication, interrupted when the door opened and the postman appeared with the day's mail. With the finesse of a champion darts player, the post sailed through the air, landing on the counter. The uppermost letter emblazoned with the logo of a London Port storage company.

'More bills. It's never-ending,' Patricia complained, gathering the white envelopes into a tidy pile.

Sinclair picked up a beer stein, trying out its weight in his rough hand.

'That one's German. See, on the inside, it's all smooth. The Japanese ones don't have the nice finish like the German ones,' Patricia prattled away. 'Sorry about the dust, though. Thought I'd give them all a wipe before I tried restocking the shelf.'

'I'll take this one,' Sinclair announced, to Patricia's astonishment. 'I haven't got one of these. But it needs a clean...'

'Sure,' Patricia agreed. A sale was a sale. And besides, it would be one less stein for her to have to fit back on the shelf. 'I'll pop out back and wash it.'

As she made her way out to the sink, Sinclair whipped the storage envelope off the stack of mail. His next course of action was clear.

THE BISHOP

'here's no record of this piece. We've been through everything. Every scrap of documentation, all the vaults, the libraries. There's nothing about a matching pair of altar candelabra, which means these markings could be counterfeit.'

The diminutive woman in the room sighed in frustration, 'It's genuine. Why you persist in questioning our results defies belief.' Gemma Dance thumped the papers in front of her.

The portfolio assessors on the other side of the table shook their twin heads. Their matching bald pates shone under the harsh fluorescent lights, their client sitting beside them, his black robes an anomaly in the soulless corporate space.

'It's not that we're disputing your expertise — it's just that our client wants to be sure that the article they purchased is genuine.'

'Really, this is an issue you should have taken up with Christie's. Querying the authenticity of a piece after buying it is the same as questioning the spiciness of a meal after you've eaten it.'

The accountants sniffed, affronted.

'They're just doing their job, Miss Dance. Let's refrain from personal attacks and concentrate on whether Paul de Lamerie made these candelabra?'

Gemma Dance drew herself up, fixing her glare on the cleric filling her boardroom. 'You hired us. We have told you again and again that there is no evidence that these candelabra are *not* genuine. Unless you have evidence that you've yet to share? Our investigations show that *your* Church commissioned them. And it's lovely to see them returned to their rightful owners...'

Bishop Shalfoon averted his gaze, inspecting instead his manicured nails, a rather effeminate affectation, given his role. 'The Church is not withholding any evidence — we're not Catholics.'

Gemma winced, but turned her winning smile towards the Art Loss Register's newest clients. 'As it says in our report, it's well documented that de Lamerie was a prolific silversmith, but he also ran a large workshop, and allowed his apprentices to apply his silver mark. Despite being known for his personal commissions, time has lost those records. Documentation sometimes surfaces giving the provenance of an item — but only occasionally. Sadly, most laymen view ephemera such as bills of sale as rubbish. It's our opinion that these candelabra are by the silversmith de Lamerie.' Gemma closed the file with finality as her words made their way across the laminated boardroom table.

The Bishop nodded to his advisors, and they scurried away in tandem, practical shoes carrying them to their sensible offices.

Tapping the folder on the table, Bishop Shalfoon smiled at Gemma, 'Thank you for your efforts, Miss Dance. The Church appreciates all the work which has gone into this report. Insurance is one of our largest costs these days. We have to be so careful to ensure that what investments we make are for the best. So many natural disasters, earthquakes in New Zealand, erosion in the Islands, wars in Europe... our land holdings are not proving to be as robust as we once thought.' Gathering up his belongings, he rose, a faint stench of body odour lingering in his seat. Gemma's professionalism preventing her from screwing up her tiny nose.

'It's been a pleasure, Bishop Shalfoon. Please let me know if the Register can provide any additional help?'

The Bishop nodded, like a bobble-head dog in the rear window of a car, before leaving.

Gemma moved to the back of the now empty room, away from the smell of unwashed sweat permeating the area. She wiped her own sweaty hands against her skirt. *Jesus, he was a difficult customer. Who on earth buys at auction and then queries the provenance?* Not for the first time she wished they could open the windows, if only to remove his stench. But the Church was a good client, and he *was* working on their behalf.

If she'd been a party to the conversation Bishop Shalfoon was now having via cellphone in his car, she'd have been less conciliatory towards the man.

'She's confirmed it, these are the ones stolen in New Zealand... yes, I am sure... no! That's the last thing that needs to happen to them. We'd be mad if we sent them to that backwater. Do we have a representative there?... I doubt there's even a congregation let alone a functioning church... no, these should go to one of our higher profile congregations. Let's discuss it further when I return to Salisbury... no, I'll be there tomorrow, I have other business in London.'

Ending the call, Bishop Daniel Shalfoon ran a finger around his collar, his other hand holding Gemma's meticulously prepared file on the authenticity of the de Lamerie candelabra Sarah Lester had consigned to auction. It would be a damning indictment if anyone were to find out how much they'd paid out for the pair of candlesticks, but then the lay-person rarely had any idea what the Church did to ensure its survival in these times of disbelief.

Tapping his driver on the shoulder, they drove off into London's spaghetti-like traffic. On the leather seat next to Shalfoon was a second folder. Older and slimmer than the one from the Art Loss Register. Within it were two pieces of paper, foxed with age. Sloping lines of faded ink marched sideways across the page. *Here* was evidence that the Church had once commissioned a piece from the silversmith Paul de Lamerie; a pair of candelabra, destined for the newest church in New Zealand, one in Bruce Bay. What a personal coup it would be when he recovered the funds he'd spent acquiring property which he'd just proven was stolen from the church. The potential media opportunities had him salivating.

THE TAPESTRY

*H*arvard returned to Christie's, tail between his legs. The jungle drums would have been banging during his long journey back to work. Why anyone drove a car in London was beyond him, and he felt the sharp pinpricks of a migraine starting its slow onslaught behind his eyes.

Slipping into his windowless office, the airflow hampered by the biblical tapestries covering the walls. Hung by one of his predecessors, unclaimed auction articles, 'saved' from festering in storage. Such pieces decorated most of the offices in the building, rightly or wrongly. Processes were tighter now — electronic banking and credit cards made it almost impossible to avoid paying for something you'd bid on. But these *perks* were a leftover from a more paper-based record system prone to errors.

He gazed at an embroidered scene of Ruth gathering threshed wheat in her arms. *Simpler times, woven into wool, one of the most dynamic and tactile materials used by man.* It was odd, he'd never paid too much attention to his office decor — downtime wasn't a luxury Christie's employees enjoyed — but in this rare moment of solace, he examined Ruth with a critical eye. Age-worn and fraying at the edges — fortunately the absence of the sun's ultraviolet light in his office was more beneficial to the art than the employee, and probably the only reason this piece kept from disintegrating. Ruth's dress featured a myriad of reds, giving her skirt folds and complex shadows. Dark hair peeped out from her headscarf, her eyes downcast, demure. The flowers in the foreground were foreign to him... *old fashioned poppies?* The boffins would know.

In reality, he was filling in time before someone received a complaint from the V & A. This might be the end of the line for him.

The quotation on the sampler he'd failed to secure swam before his eyes, "Time is an illusion. The minutes that have gone may still be ahead of you. Embrace every second". *A family motto?* Just as he was reaching up to lift the tapestry of Ruth from the wall to better examine her, a knock sounded.

'Redecorating, Andrew, or packing up your office already?' Hannah Gardner stood in his doorway, one hand planted on her waist, the other gripping the handle, as if holding it gave her enough moral support to behave like an obnoxious cow.

Andrew returned to his seat. For whatever reason, Hannah Gardner continued to haunt the halls of Christie's, despite being distrusted by most of the staff. No one knew exactly what she did. Historically she had negotiated valuable commissions for the auction house, and had a variety of clients she entertained on behalf of Christie's but, apart from that, she was more a lackey for Don Claire. Some even alluded to a secret relationship between her and Claire.

'Yes, Hannah?'

She edged into his office, surveying his space, but taking care not to touch anything, before replying.

'How was the School of Needlework thing? Full of buxom ladies in pearls and twinsets? Or the stern studious kind, with glasses and frigid nether parts — *museum* types?'

Andrew sighed, 'What have you heard, Hannah?'

Recognising she was getting under his skin, she perked up. 'Oh, nothing much. Just Mr Claire got a call from one of those institution women you hang out with. I could almost hear her from my office. You seem to attract more than your share of controversy. That's why I wondered whether you were packing up, preparing to be... how do they put it, *let go?*'

'Seriously, Hannah? I've got work to do. I'm sure if Mr Claire wants to talk about what happened at the needlework lectures, he'll call me — unless you're here to tell me that he's asking to see me?'

Gardner flushed at Andrew's abruptness. 'No, I was just passing. I'll leave you to it then.' Tossing her blonde hair over her shoulder she scurried away like a threatened rat.

Sinking back into his chair, Andrew rubbed his eyes. His headache was a constant companion now. He checked his watch. If only it were home time — but that was about an hour later than other City types. Going home to Patricia would be nice, but they weren't at that stage yet. All he had waiting for him was half a bottle of mediocre wine, and a frozen chicken Kiev.

He looked up at Ruth. 'What are you having for dinner tonight?' he asked the wall hanging. With no answer forthcoming he attacked the contents of his carry case, the fruits of his time at the School of Needlework lectures.

THE STAFFROOM

*E*liza Broadhead slowed her breathing. No piece of tapestry was worth another heart attack. For the hundredth time that morning, she wished she'd chosen a different career; a simpler career, teaching young girls the basics of sewing. Darning, gathering, pleating. Simpler things, easier things. But the die had been cast, and her role in life was as the head curator of Textiles and Fashion at the Victoria and Albert Museum – the V & A. Working there had been a dream come true. But, as is the way with dreams, they can turn into nightmares.

She wiped the perspiration from her face and adjusted the long strands of jet beads around her neck. As her heart rate slowed, she mentally composed the scathing email she was going to send those thieves at Christie's. She wished she could tell the world how many of their treasures had been sold through the outwardly illustrious rooms of both Christie's and Sotheby's. It made her sick to her stomach to think of the pieces the public would never get to enjoy, probably stored in damp cupboards or attics, rotting away.

She tried to calm herself, as her heart rate escalated again, fingers poised over her keyboard. How *does* one address the head of an organisation complicit in stealing the treasures of a nation? It was only through sheer luck that she'd rescued that sampler from the slimy hands of Andrew Harvard, and he'd assaulted her.

Logically, she knew it had been an accident, which was why she hadn't insisted on calling the police yesterday, but she wasn't above milking the situation for all it was worth. And if that resulted in never having a representative from the auction house at any needlework event again, then she'd be happy with that outcome.

Turning away from her laptop, she unpacked the boxes from the lecture series. Placing the other articles to one side, she reverently laid the sampler out in the middle of oak drafting table. Deep drawers, reminiscent of old fashioned map drawers filled one side; a huge flat expanse on the top existed for cutting out fabric and patterns – not that she did that any more. Now it was used for laying out new acquisitions while she and her team decided on a course of action for each piece – restoration, storage or display, or a mixture of all three. As with any museum, her role at the V & A was a fine line between presenting the exhibits as antiques or presenting them as part of an 'experience'. The world wanted to be entertained. They weren't satisfied just viewing a piece of fabric behind glass with a card proclaiming its origins and composition. The viewing public, the great unwashed, *demanded* to be entertained. She suspected many of them couldn't actually read the information cards presented with the exhibits. The uneducated hoi polloi were the bane of her life, second only to the auction houses.

The sampler spread out on the well-used table was irresistible. The stitching was beautifully rendered and vaguely familiar – she waddled around the table, her critical eye taking in every detail.

There was the date, picked out in faded green thread, 1728. The sampler was filled with flora and fauna, stunningly lifelike, their colours sadly faded over time – undoubtedly the sampler had been hung up in direct light. Although England's sun was weak compared with the harshness of the Southern Hemisphere, it still had the capability to fade fabrics. She was lucky – it didn't appear to be suffering from dry rot. Fingering the sampler, she could tell the base fabric was pure linen, with the threads a mixture of silk and cotton.

The silk threads were close to disintegrating, as was the wont with silk suffering from sun damage. The cotton threads, used for the larger sections looked to be in good repair, apart from the fading. But all of that was by-the-by – it was the name embroidered on the sampler which had given her more of a shock than Andrew Harvard's push. "R. J. Williams" – the exact same name as the one she'd purchased through Christie's for an indecent sum of money. Merely thinking about the chances of owning two pieces by the same woman, but from two different sources, was enough to send her heart rate stratospheric again.

'Breathe,' she said aloud, sitting heavily on her work stool, panting. It was all too fantastical, and undoubtedly the museum director would be more enthusiastic than he was when she'd spent half a year's budget on the purchase of the last sampler. This one had been free. Ah, the joys of the altruistic. There was a place in heaven for them, that was certain.

Her ample stomach rumbling, she left her office in search of a soothing cup of tea, and some shortbread from the staffroom. There was a firm rule at the V & A, at least in the Textile and Fashion Department – no liquids or foods were allowed in offices or workrooms. The risk they posed to the collections was too high.

The staffroom was lightly populated this early in the day, and was filled with the overpowering scent of brewing coffee. Eliza took her mug of fragrant Earl Grey tea, plunged her hand into the biscuit barrel, withdrew three sugary treats, and sat down next to a colleague.

'Good morning, Brenda.'

The slightly older Brenda Smith looked up from her toast and paper, 'Morning, Eliza. How was the lecture yesterday?'

'Brilliant this time. We had a full house – they'd really marketed it well.'

'Makes it easier doesn't it, having a full room.'

'Only thing that marred it was they'd let one of the auction houses have a table there, so he was touting for business like a pimp at a plumber's convention. I'm going to make it clear to the School of

Needlework that I won't be available for any more of their lectures if they insist on allowing those bloodsuckers to attend.'

Brenda raised her painted eyebrows, the victims of over-zealous plucking when she was a teenager, consigning her to a lifetime of artistic pencilling.

'Never, Eliza?'

Eliza harrumphed, vigorously stirring sugar into her tea.

'Did anyone donate anything good, then?'

Eliza brightened considerably, 'Oh, absolutely. But if I never see another embroidered handkerchief, it will be too soon.'

Both women laughed, knowing full well that the basement of the V & A held the *largest* collection of embroidered handkerchiefs in the world. The Cooper Hewitt Museum in New York had a comparable collection, but the ones held by the V & A were eons older, and dwarfed the American set.

Eliza's laugh turned into a breathless wheeze, her beads rattling dangerously as the wheezing escalated into a hacking cough.

With the best of English manners, Brenda ignored her colleague's coughing fit, choosing to sip her coffee until Eliza had it under control, before questioning her, 'So tell me, other than handkerchiefs, what did you get?'

'You'll never believe it, and I still have to work through its provenance with the family, but I truly believe it's the sister sampler to the one I bought the other month.'

'No! Really?' Her curiosity piqued, she went as far as lowering her mug, a sure sign she was interested.

'Same initials, the date ties in with the first one, so yes, I think it's from the same hand – sadly not in the same condition.'

Wickedly, Brenda asked, 'Refresh my memory about the one you bought at auction.' Every V & A employee knew the ruckus Eliza had caused by spending half her department's acquisition budget on one sampler.

Reminding herself to stay calm, Eliza recounted how she'd had to spend an obscene amount of money to secure the sampler signed by

R. J. Williams – the very one Sarah Lester had taken from Lord Grey's house and had given to Andrew Harvard to auction on her behalf.

Brenda, with her own budget to manage, tutted at the necessity of spending such a huge proportion of one's annual budget on one item. She would love to believe that national treasures could be gifted to the nation, and not sold for profit. 'Profit' was a dirty word amongst the curators at the V & A. But she was also disillusioned at the sheer number of articles gifted to the museum which never saw the light of day, left wallowing in storage.

Eliza was a card-carrying unionist, more suited to communist Russia than democratic England, hence her compatibility with the museum and academia, a world where you were more likely to be rewarded for perseverance than excellence. Brenda, however, saw the value in selling off excess objects to fund the acquisition of more notable pieces. This continual squabbling over budgets would vanish overnight, should the V & A ever slough off their excess and focus on truly exceptional exhibits.

The two women commiserated over their drinks – one more honestly than the other – each sharing stories about the ill-informed public, the vapid young things in charge of marketing whom they blamed completely for the public's insatiable appetite for entertainment instead of education, and the shameful way the auction houses conducted themselves.

Other staff ebbed and flowed through the staffroom, feet scuffing the old linoleum, the coffee machine whirring off and on in the background. Most ignored the two older women gossiping in the corner. Both V & A 'institutions', they kept their own hours and seemed to be above reproach, modern-day employment conditions completely unknown to them.

Finally, a much younger woman stopped at their table, a look of superiority on her face – the sort only the young can pull off – as she interrupted the older women.

'Excuse me, Eliza, but we had a meeting scheduled for nine o'clock with the Learning Team, and the team are waiting for you now ...'

'Goodness, yes, I'd forgotten.' Eliza heaved herself out of her seat, beads jangling loudly. 'Brenda, you must come by my office later this morning to see the sampler. I'd love to have your opinion. Sorry, Jasmine, I'm coming. Completely slipped my mind. You'll never imagine the textiles we had donated to the V & A yesterday.'

The two women walked off, Eliza oblivious to the sighs the younger woman was holding back as she listened to verbal diarrhoea about tapestries and linen from a woman most considered a dinosaur.

THE KNOCKER

The shop bell tinkled, interrupting Nicole's private musings as she sat behind the cluttered counter, waiting for Sarah to return from Patricia's. *Will I still have a job* uppermost in her mind. She'd found her niche in running the shop. Yes, it had its moments of frustration, but she'd done her best given the circumstances.

A man entered. His legs encased in grimy track pants; his bulky stomach constrained by a taut sweatshirt, the logo in the upper right corner faded, looking as if swirls of toothpaste had migrated onto his chest from his distasteful mouth. A riotous head of stringy grey hair, as unacquainted with a hairbrush as his body was to deodorant, topped off the filthy human who sidled up to the counter, a battered banana box balanced on his hip, threatening to take out half the items on the edge of the long table as he edged past.

The carton safely deposited onto the counter, he stood in front of her.

'What have you got for me today, Wick?' Nicole asked, trying to inch unnoticed away from the smell emanating from the other side of the counter.

'Not much for you this week, Nicky.'

She cringed at his unwelcome use of the diminutive of her name, 'Unpack it all then. I can't offer you a price if I can't see it.'

Wick Farris, a 'knocker' for *The Old Curiosity Shop*, ferreted through his box, the slow extraction of treasures part of his show. *How do you ever persuade people to let you into their homes, let alone sell their valuables to you*, she thought for the umpteenth time. Yet, according to the stock book, he'd been 'knocking' for the shop for years. She'd looked through the old stock books stacked up on shelves behind the counter and, almost without fail, every week there'd be at least one entry for goods purchased from Wick Farris.

'Knocking' was a distasteful profession. Tapping on the front doors of strangers, and persuading them to sell their treasures, usually for the lowest price possible — a practice frowned upon by every auction house, antique dealer and constable in the country — but an integral part of the chain. Not *all* of them were as dodgy as sin but, in Nicole's opinion, Farris was top of her list of the most untrustworthy of suppliers.

He unpacked a blue Bristol glass scent bottle, complete with its stopper. *Good.* Cameo glass goblets. *A pair, also good.* Two sets of sherry snifters. *Glass, not crystal.* Two *millefiori* paper weights, different sizes, although one had tiny nibbles in its base, not visible on display. *Potentially saleable.* Nicole checked to see if it was marked "*Baccarat*" — alas no, just a run-of-the-mill paperweight, its coloured glass rods nevertheless forming a pleasing image inside the bun shaped glass. The *Baccarat* name would have been better, adding another hundred to the price.

Next came a small brass carriage clock, its leather case battered and held together with yellowing tape. A plastic bag bulging with coins, its heft not at all indicative of its value. Just last week she'd paid forty pounds for a box lot of china, medicine bottles, biscuit tins and a handful of costume jewellery. In amongst the jewellery was a tiny bag containing what she thought were four coins, so she hadn't factored those into her offer. It was only when she was pricing them up that she realised one was a worn gold sovereign. She'd made back her money several times over with that one coin.

The pile grew larger — a cigar box filled with military buttons, badges and medals, including a rare Indian Mutiny Medal from 1858. Nicole crossed her fingers that Wick wouldn't know the true value of that. A wooden barometer, missing its hands, and glass — *worthless*. Two silver-plated chafing dishes. *Quite desirable*. And an ornate *betel box*. That one she'd need to research.

Farris looked up from the empty banana box, the greed in his eyes as filthy as his nails. 'How much do you reckon for this lot then? There are some lovely things here this time. Some old duck up in Salisbury let me have a right ferret through her stuff. There's jewellery too, but I'm saving that for a rainy day.' He winked.

Nicole eyed the *betel box*, admiring its fine floral openwork. Decades of dust obscured its true beauty, but a quick dunk in some warm water with Sunlight soap ought to clean it up.

'I don't know, Wick, none of this is that moveable. Where's more of that Lladro you bought me last week? Or some silver? You know I'm running low on good sterling silver. Don't you ask people about their silver?'

'Come on, Nicky love, you know this stuff's good. It'll sell. I guarantee if Sarah were here she'd buy it in a heartbeat. Let's say two hundred quid and we're sorted.'

'Jesus Christ, Wick, if I paid you two hundred quid, Patricia would fire me. There's no way this stuff is worth that.'

'What about that military stuff? You've got a guy that buys all that straight away. I've met him in here before. Come on now. How about a hundred and eighty? I'll discount it some for you, cause you're still learning the ropes and all.'

'A hundred and fifty, and not a penny more.'

Nicole opened the till, the bells inside adding a merry tune to their conversation. She counted out the money, knowing Wick would accept her offer because no one else dealt with him. *She'd* rather not trade with him, but it seemed Sarah trusted him, as had her father.

'Here, a hundred and fifty quid.' She handed over the money, before thrusting the purchase register at Wick for his signature. He scrawled his details, which hadn't appeared to have changed in the ten years of record keeping that she'd had access to.

'A pleasure, Nicky, as always. You got time for a coffee? You couldn't nip out the back and make me one? I've got a drive today, heading up north. There's more up where I got this lot from. Might sniff around a while up there.'

Nicole had no intention of 'nipping out back' and leaving Wick alone in the shop was the *last* thing she planned on doing.

'Sorry, Wick, ran out of coffee yesterday — meant to buy some more, but I forgot. The bakery across the road does good coffee, most days.'

Wick looked at her from under his hooded eyes, before turning to look out the window at the place she'd mentioned.

'Right, till next time then,' and he sidled out the same way he came in, crablike and suspiciously.

Nicole reached for glass cleaner and sprayed the spot where Wick had leant on the counter. She knew it wouldn't dispel the sick feeling in her stomach that he'd swindled some old lady out of her treasures. If what she'd offered made him happy, it meant he wouldn't have paid even half that for them.

After wiping away all evidence of his being there, she transcribed her new inventory into the purchases book, wondering what Sarah would say when she returned.

THE AMERICAN

*W*ith no summons from Don Claire's office, Harvard felt secure enough to sign out for the day. Leaving through the staff entrance, he'd avoided the preparations downstairs for that evening's auction. Had he made his way through the crowded foyer, he might have seen Bryce Sinclair lurking to the side of the proceedings, himself looking for some glimpse of Sarah, who was the key to untold wealth and fortune, after he persuaded her to share her secret with him.

The security personnel to guest ratio was high, unsurprising given the tragic incident between Richard Grey and the Christie's clerk Leo Hayward. The firm had toyed with installing a small plaque commemorating Hayward, but had decided against it, arguing that *no* publicity was now better than some publicity, and therefore there was no visible reminder of that fateful auction, apart from the increased number of security staff, most of whom were too elderly to be really effective.

Sinclair had bluffed his credentials. Given the economic climate, the institute's focus was more on the amount of money being spent than *who* was spending it, or where it came from — a vast difference from the pre-financial crisis times, when you had to be someone to receive an invitation into the esteemed enclave.

Sinclair was not the only dubious character attending tonight. The room trilled with foreign accents — bidders from former Soviet states, and the unfathomable languages and dialects of more than two dozen Chinese gentlemen, wives draped over their arms like porcelain dolls — perfect skin, their jet hair styled by the best hairdressers in London. Jewels which would feed entire villages graced their slender fingers and necks.

With neither the language, nor societal skills, to converse with these oligarchs, he loitered at the back, drinking rather than sipping the Taittinger a supercilious waiter had served him.

Sinclair took in the jewellery, the foreigners, the overt and subtle wealth displayed in the room. It was the subtle riches which interested him more. Those who flaunted their wealth were usually teetering on the precipice of insolvency, or they tied their prosperity to the coat-tails of someone more influential, who had the power to take it away with the stroke of the pen — or the knife. No, the faint touches, indefinable but obvious, showed class, longevity and serious money. With Sarah still missing, someone else would do to assist in his quest for a comfortable life, a life denied to him by the circumstances of his birth. A life owed to him.

Centre stage was a bloodwood and kingwood ormolu cabinet by Beurdeley, dated 1894. Women clustered around it, like flies to a honey pot. It was unlike any piece of furniture he'd ever seen. He was used to utilitarian pieces hewn from ancient *kauri* trees, knocked together, not by a master craftsman, but by a journeyman. Such examples would never have entered these doors; more than likely they'd have become firewood, or sold as 'shabby chic' at a High Street design store; code for falling apart.

He approached the cabinet. He could admire its lines, even if it didn't move him as much as it did the crowd of women cooing over its serpentine shape, and the Chinese *chinoiserie* figure playing a mandolin on the centre door.

Picking his moment, Sinclair bumped into a woman with a dead animal reclining on her shoulders. From behind she'd looked alluring — her buttocks shown off to their full advantage in a pink sheath, her calves extended by the highest of heels. Almost every woman there looked like some version of this one, but she was the only one on her own. Everyone else was with a partner, or travelling in a pack.

She turned to admonish him on his clumsiness and he almost gagged as he inhaled her perfume, for it smelt like she'd bathed in the stuff — or perhaps been preserved in it, for her face told a very different story from her backside.

Sinclair appraised her features — eyebrows pulled almost into her hairline giving her eyes a feline quality, but did little to disguise all the wrinkles. But she *was* alone, so, swallowing, he apologised, his accent enough to pique her interest.

'Oh, isn't your accent adorable. Are you English?' Her elongated vowels marking her as an American.

'No, but I live here.'

'That's a mysterious answer, I like it. So, Mr *I live here*, what do you think of this piece? I fell in love with it, and I could have bid online, but I need to see something in person to imagine how it will fit the aesthetic of my home. So I flew fly out to have a look.'

Sinclair smiled, the concepts of 'online' and 'flew out' as foreign to him as her accent. He listened as she recounted the salient facts about the cabinet, the trellis and its gallery. Words like 'encadrements' and 'acanthus swags' tumbled from her pouty mouth. He watched in amazement as she wrapped her plump lips around the descriptive words; words as comfortable to her as violence was to him. Despite her animated speech, her face didn't register the same enthusiasm as her voice. *A miracle or a curse?* Regardless, here was someone who didn't know him, nor what he'd done. It was as if someone had given him a clean slate, albeit one he was about to blot.

A waitress sailed past, a tray of canapés in her hands, offering them to a distinguished couple nearby; the greying gentleman took a sliver of Canadian salmon laid over a cracker and consumed it in one movement. The waitress judging too-tight pink dress, and Sinclair's more casual attire, and by-passed them, offering her tray to another group conversing in Russian — or she would have, had Sinclair not stopped her with a sudden grip on her arm.

'Seems you didn't offer your fish to my friend. Do only old people get to eat here?' he asked, his mouth twisting.

Her training took over. 'My apologies.' Sinclair noted her staring at his companion's immobile face. Even when she placed a cracker in her mouth, the only thing which moved were her oversized pink lips.

The waitress carefully arranged her own facial features until there was nothing but professionalism showing as she waited for these two 'new money' guests to stuff themselves. There was a world of difference between old and new money — the staff knew it and the customers knew it. *Everyone* knew it, except these two.

When they had finished, she moved off, rolling her eyes as she left.

'Did you see that? She wasn't even going to serve us. This country! When are they ever going to get in the twenty-first century? Service is a concept they seem to have forgotten.'

Sinclair stared at her. This world still shocked him and the smallest things tripped him up: coins; banknotes; her *ankles*. The only ankles he'd been on familiar terms with were those belonging to prostitutes at home. But here, he could look out his window, day or night, and see ankles, and more: calves; knees; thighs; breasts barely restrained by singlets. Most of these modern women might as well forego clothes altogether, given how they presented themselves. His companion was no different.

'But you showed her. Silly girl, head so high in the air you could see up her nose. Half the time, these wait staff think they're better than us, and *we're* the ones with the money, paying their wages.' Tossing her hair, she cast a grin at him — or what would have passed for a grin had her face had any natural movement.

Sinclair made appropriate murmuring noises, his mind struggling to understand why her face wasn't moving. *Apoplexy perhaps?* He didn't know much about medical stuff, but recognised she wasn't well. No one could survive long with that level of paralysis. The perfect partner for him then, and he ran through the possibilities.

'Were you planning on buying this, then?' he asked, gesturing at the grand cabinet.

'Could be. Were you?'

'No, I'm here more for the foreign stuff. Also to see if a dealer who robbed me was here.'

'Ooh, that sounds fascinating, another story for later, like your accent,' she enthused, checking her watch. 'It's time, let's go in.' With her arm linked through his, she marched forward, passing through the elegant crowd like a bulldozer, before plonking herself down in the middle of the front row. Not as circumspect as he'd imagined. However, being with her lent him a certain level of respectability. She seemed well known, and many of the attendees greeted her by name.

'Good evening, Melissa,' said a sallow-looking.

Melissa Crester swung round in her seat. If her face could have fallen, it would have. 'Hello, Johnson. Can't say it's a pleasure to see you.' Turning back towards the rostrum, she prickled at the proximity of the man seated behind him. Sinclair turned to face him.

'Mister, I think it'd be better if you moved to another seat.' Sinclair's tone as menacing as a junkie on the streets of Detroit, and Johnson Perry feigned spotting a friend, hurrying from his seat to greet an astonished acquaintance like a long-lost friend on the opposite side.

Melissa put her bejewelled hand on Sinclair's thigh and whispered her thanks. 'Every time I'm here, he bloody well bids against me. I'm sure it's because I turned him down once when he asked me out. As if anyone would want to go out with a stiff like him. He must have cost me at least sixty or seventy grand in the last few months, bidding the price up just because he knows of my interest in something.'

Sinclair followed her gaze, taking in the blue suit, leather loafers and an ostentatious watch taking up his entire left wrist. 'What does he do?'

'He fancies himself an interior decorator.'

'Interior decorator? Someone who paints inside a house? Sounds like a real nancy boy if you ask me.'

Melissa threw back her head and laughed, earning her a chorus of frowns and tutting from those seated around them. 'You have a way of hitting the nail on the head! You're not far off the money.'

'He does building too?' Sinclair asked, puzzled over her terminology.

That question left Melissa in gales of laughter, until the auctioneer stepped up to the microphone to begin the night's auction.

THE AUCTION

*A*s the auction progressed, Sinclair watched the room, the bidders, the money flowing unfettered from their pockets. Never had he heard such sums as the ones pouring forth from the auctioneer's mouth. Hundreds of thousands of pounds were being bid for fanciful pieces of furniture, trinkets to adorn the mantelpiece, and silverware he'd have given his eyeteeth to sell. And no one seemed to care about the cost, least of all his companion. Melissa's paddle went up with gay abandon, for anything decorated with the slightest bit of gilt, or with a hint of *belle epoch* glamour. She was nothing but consistent in her bidding. At one point, she turned to Sinclair, 'Are you not bidding tonight?'

'There's nothing here I want, save the candlesticks that dealer stole from me.'

She smiled, as if his reply was completely understandable, and turned her attention back to the auctioneer, eyes gleaming, clenching her numbered paddle.

'Lot 193, a pair of French ormolu and painted metal five-light candelabra. Louis VXI style, by Emmanuel-Alfred Beurdeley. Bidding set to start at twenty thousand pounds. Do I hear twenty? Yes, madam, twenty from you... twenty-five, sir... thirty, madam? I have a phone bid for thirty-five. Forty, do I have any bids for forty thousand pounds?... Yes, sir, thank you. Madam?'

The auctioneer looked to Melissa and paused. She wasn't looking at him. She was, instead, scowling at Johnson Perry, whose paddle was dangling over his crossed knee, a sly smile on his face as he absorbed Melissa's gaze.

Turning to the auctioneer, Melissa called out 'Forty-five thousand.'

'Thank you, madam. Do I have any further bids? Sir? No? Thank you. Final call. We are at forty-five thousand pounds for this exquisite pair of Beurdeley candelabra. Going once. Twice. Sold.'

His gavel hit the hardwood sound block, and the room erupted into bemused applause. Many of the attendees had seen these two battle it out before, and tonight hadn't disappointed.

After the auction wound up, the place emptied of unsuccessful bidders, and Melissa stood, stretching like a cat.

'Come with me while I settle my account, then we can go find something to eat, and you can tell me about the dealer who robbed you. I am *starving*. They never feed you well here. They'll drown you in champagne, but they give you almost nothing to line your stomach. If you're tipsy, you're likely to bid more.' She laughed at herself, 'I guess it works.' Tugging on Sinclair's arm, they made their way to the business end of the auction process, the exchange of money for goods.

Sinclair hung back as Melissa arranged to ship the larger pieces to America. He was so busy watching for any sign of Sarah, that she caught him unaware when she thrust a large cardboard box into his arms.

'For you,' she beamed, as far as her fat pouty lips allowed.

'What is it?'

'Those Beurdeley candelabra. You shouldn't live life hankering after something. Think of it as a gift to celebrate our new friendship. Come on, we'll catch a cab and go for dinner. I've finished here now.'

'You bought them for me?' Sinclair stood in the middle of the foyer, shocked. No one had *ever* given him a present. Not his parents, nor his friends, who had been few. He couldn't recall being given anything other than a clip round the head. He'd had to fight for everything. Food, clothing, shelter. Nothing in his life had been easy. This woman had just spent forty-five thousand pounds on the ugliest pair of candelabra he'd ever seen, and he'd never been happier.

'I did. Let's go, my car is waiting for us.'

THE SAVOY

*B*ryce Sinclair stretched out in the luxurious king-sized bed, the crisp white sheets crackling under him. The steady splash of the shower was the only sound invading the peace of the hotel suite. From the bed he watched the London Eye turning against the frame of the watery Thames. Crystals dripped from a lit chandelier, the ornate ceiling rose painted white in contrast to the dusky pink of the walls, and the upholstery of the couches tastefully positioned around the suite. A bunch of purple lilacs was the single jarring note in the bland room.

This was a much lower standard than the absolute luxury Sarah had experienced lunching here at the Savoy in the 1890s, served by Escoffier himself. But, as far as it concerned Sinclair, anywhere with a bed was sufficient, and this room far surpassed any luxury he'd ever dreamt of.

Silence fell as the shower switched off. With the bathroom door ajar, he could see Melissa Crester, the American, vigorously towelling herself off. Her body was no mystery to him after a night spent together. It was that of a considerably older woman than her face had led him to expect. Parts of her were alien, and he'd spent much of the night pondering those peculiarities. *Her breasts* sat high, like those of a young woman, but were solid, more akin to over-baked bread rolls. There had been no joy in fondling them, not that that had stopped him from enjoying her other offerings.

'What shall we do?' Crester trilled from behind the towel.

'Buy more wardrobes?' Sinclair offered, causing Crester to howl with laughter.

'Oh, you funny man. Truly, I've reached my limit for wardrobes this trip. A girl only has so many clothes. No, today we will go hunting off-piste.'

'Hunting? With guns?'

Crester laughed again, although the laugh never made it to her frozen face, 'No, they wouldn't let me bring my guns here. Crazy right? How's a girl meant to protect herself? What I meant was, we'll head off round the local antique shops, have a look see what they've got. Often they have stuff just as good as the stuff at the auction houses, but without the price tag. Pays to keep your fingers in as many pies as you can, that's what I've always thought. Will you come with me, be my protector?' She giggled like a schoolgirl flirting with the young caretaker by the bike sheds.

Sinclair considered her proposal, 'I will. Case is I know a place we can visit.' He slipped out of bed, London's sights no longer of interest. The cash cow, his American golden goose, was far more exciting than anything else he'd ever had on his horizon.

Pulling an envelope from the pocket of his discarded trousers, he read out the address of the storage unit company to Melissa. 'You know that place?'

She mumbled in the negative while towelling her hair dry, and Sinclair smiled, his mind already on the potential riches held by the elusive Sarah Lester.

He gave Melissa's buttocks a quick squeeze on his way to the bathroom. He'd never known a woman to have muscles in the places Melissa had hers. Even his favourite whores were soft and pliant, comparable to sinking into a feather bed. This American was as hard as wood, petrified wood.

Despite Sinclair's plans to visit Sarah's storage locker, he and Melissa spent the morning perusing the dozens of cabinets in the Silver Vaults of London in Chancery Lane. Melissa collected sterling silver place card holders. Sinclair had absolutely no idea what they were, but had been on a crash course for the last two hours as she spent an average worker's annual salary on several sets.

'You're crazy, you know?' Sinclair said as she showed him yet another set and asked him for his opinion.

'Crazy yes, but I'm rich too. What else am I going to spend my money on?' she joked back, nodding to the woman behind the counter who rang up a sale for three hundred pounds, before wrapping the four fox-head place card holders in a mountain of tissue paper.

Sinclair had no answer for her. He'd never had cash to spare; using any cash he had just to survive. Spending it on trinkets seemed a waste, but then he couldn't think what he'd spend it on if he had as much money as his companion.

'Shall we have lunch now? I'm famished. Let's find a nice wine bar and plan our attack for this afternoon. I've some old favourites I must visit; they'll be expecting me—'

'Expecting your *coin*,' Sinclair interrupted. His annoyance at the delay in searching Sarah's storage locker had vanished. The contents of the locker could wait. He didn't want to do anything to jeopardise this *wealthy* relationship.

Raucous laughter erupted from Melissa's immobile face. 'Silly man. I'm not that gullible that they're pleasant because they want to be friends. So far you're the only person in this dreary country who's seemed the slightest bit more interested in me than my money.'

Sinclair rubbed his bald head in confusion, and taking the silver-laden shopping bags, he took her hand in his free one. It seemed like the right thing to do and felt peculiarly nice. 'Lunch it is,' he announced. 'There's one place I need to go to, and that warehouse at the docks, so we can add them to your list while we eat, if you like.'

Melissa's idea of 'a nice bar' for lunch, and Sinclair's were vastly different, so, when they entered the Lobby Bar at the *One Aldwych* hotel, Sinclair was more than impressed. Described as the most beautiful hotel lobby bar in London by the *Evening Standard*, the Savoy had nothing on this place. Recognising Melissa as a regular, the waiter took them straight to a table where Melissa wasted no time ordering for them both, an assortment of sushi, sashimi and duck spring rolls, accompanied by a Malt Jockey cocktail, a twist on the classic Manhattan.

When the fancy cocktails arrived, Sinclair's mouth dropped, 'What's this then?'

'You'll love it. It's got scotch in it. Just taste it.'

Pushing it away from him, he summoned the waiter back over and ordered a proper whisky, 'None of that nancy boy rubbish for me.'

Melissa smiled into her cocktail. *A real man.* How hard had she looked for one of those? *A bit on the rough side, but don't all girls enjoy getting a little dirty sometimes?* Worked for Elizabeth Taylor.

The food arrived, and Melissa watched Sinclair pick through the dishes, pulling the seaweed casings from the sushi, and spitting out the slivers of salmon and tuna. She only just stopped him from sending it back for being raw.

'It's *supposed* to be raw,' she laughed.

'Like hell it is. That's the last time you order for me. Next time I'll order for myself. I've eaten raw fish in the past, but as a last resort. Never thought they'd be serving it in a place like this.' Sinclair pushed his platter away, instead throwing back the nuts served with the cocktails. They'd hold him until he could find a good piece of lamb or beef. As Melissa ate her portion, they chatted about life, the state of the weather — always a safe subject — and the antiques they both liked. An odd topic for Sinclair, in that the things Melissa waxed lyrical about, were everyday articles, albeit ones he'd never owned, but he had seen them in the shops and on the persons he carried in his boat back and forth. How something so mundane became collectible was unbelievable.

The bill arrived and, to his surprise, Sinclair threw some cash down to cover it. The cash wasn't his — he'd taken it from Stokes, who was now rotting away in the apartment — but the bulk in his pocket had provided a measure of comfort, and here he was using it to impress a lady. *A miracle.*

Melissa smiled, and this time the smile made it all the way to her frozen eyes. 'Come on then, the waiter said *The Old Curiosity Shop* is only four minutes walk from here. We'll go there first, so we're not weighed down by too many other packages before I continue my shopping spree.'

THE LETTER

"*Flying training has been keeping me busy. Have you ever wished you could fly? I swear I feel like an angel when I'm up there. Free of all my earthly shackles. Free of worry, or fear. Oh, I know the fear will come when we're finally let loose on the Germans, but while I'm still training, I feel nothing but freedom. I wish I could have you sitting beside me. So hard to describe, it's like boating on a summer's day; like eating plump berries straight from the vine; like the sun warming your face when winter has finally passed. If you were able to package them all up, to bottle those moments, that still wouldn't be as euphoric as the moment your wheels first lift off the ground.*

They say we'll be ready to fly solo soon. Another week or so. I shan't be able to tell you any more than that. I can't even tell you what sort of aircraft I am going to fly – sometimes I think the air force doesn't know themselves. I'll write as often as I can. I look forward to your postcards. They bring such happiness to my days.

There are some Indian chaps joining us next week. Do you still have that snuffbox your father had from India? The small gold one? It would be interesting to see if the Punjabs know anything about it. Can you send me a little sketch when you get a moment?"

THE ADVISOR

'What have you done with her then?' he asked, sinking into a leather chair, amber liquid sloshing near the rim of his glass.

'She's with Mrs Abbott, upstairs. Did you want to speak with her?' Captain Doulton's hands were barely steady as he poured himself a generous measure of scotch.

'No, she's being well cared for. Tell me about the body. I suppose I should have a look myself, but hearing it from you may suffice.'

Doulton closed his eyes, and the scene replayed itself in his mind. *The Indian girl screaming, as if hell had taken up residence in the house. Looking past Sarah's shoulder. A solitary fly circling around the body, waiting his turn at the still warm flesh of Simeon Williams.* He shook his head, trying to dispel the image. 'It was a mess. Still in his uniform, sword within reach. They must have surprised him, to overpower him. Much as I disliked Williams, there's not a chance he just sat there — not without a fight anyway, if you know what I mean.'

Albert Lester remained seated, sipping the fine single malt he had shipped in from Scotland. Ostensibly, he ordered it for the Governor General, but consumed far more himself. Whisky numbed his feelings and memories. He never drank himself into a stupor — that was how you ended up dead. No, he drank just enough to forget that this was not the life into which he'd been born. He drank to forget a wife and a daughter. A daughter he'd given up hope of ever seeing again. Until... until he'd heard about the peculiar Sarah Williams. The Sarah Williams who'd fired a shot from a rifle, killing a rogue tiger intent on mauling one of the local members of Indian royalty. Nice English ladies didn't do that. Nice English ladies fainted. 'What's happening with his body?'

'They've moved it to the doctor's rooms. I've asked him to give us more information on his death... although it's bloody obvious that if someone cuts you from navel to neck, you will die. Sorry for being so blunt.'

'No need to apologise, it was hard to like him, and after the chaotic events of last night, anybody could've taken a knife to him. But being surprised, that concerns me more. I'll talk with Miss Williams when she has recovered in a day or two — no point distressing her further now. Thank you, Captain.'

Captain James Doulton returned his glass to the tray, and took his leave, pulling the heavy door shut. Leaning against it for a moment, the image of Simeon Williams flickered behind his eyelids. Death's sickly scent lingered in his nostrils. He'd hoped the peat of the whisky would chase it away. *An odd fellow that Albert Lester*, he thought, as he gathered himself to return to his men. For some of them, it would have been the first time they'd seen such a brutal murder. *He* was used to death; his posting to India these past four years had seen to that, which well equipped him to counsel his men. *But dealing with Lester?* There was something off about him. Doulton struggled to understand the man, and his role in the Empire. The Governor General and Lester were inseparable. There was no doubt he had an uncanny way of predicting trouble in the colony but, apart from that, he didn't seem to fit in. Doulton shrugged it off; it was above his pay grade to worry about the man.

He set off to debrief his men, wiping warm perspiration from his face. Long years in India and still its cloying heat invaded every part of his being. The warmth was intoxicating, but had the devious ability to send you mad should you succumb to its wily ways.

THE VISITOR

*A*lbert Lester, the grey-haired missing proprietor of *The Old Curiosity Shop*, father of Sarah, and husband of Annabel, sat in his rosewood chair, gazing at the surrounding room, its overt grandeur now as familiar as his own face. There had been a time once where every item here would have caused his heart to race. The value, rarity and provenance of the furniture alone would be worth a staggering sum on the open market — a market one hundred and fifty years away, give or take a decade. The workmanship was like nothing he'd ever come across in his day, unless you took into account pieces on display at Hampton Court or Windsor Castle. And it killed him that there was no possibility of him ever being able to deal in these things. All his life he'd been a wheeler and dealer. His life revolved around buying and selling antiques and bric-à-brac. "Buy low, sell high, always leave some in it for the next guy", that was his motto. He'd never imagined his daughter following in his footsteps. All that money spent on her education at the best schools and university, and she'd turned out to be a damn second-hand dealer.

A single tear trickled down his face. There'd been a point early on, where, for one more moment with his family, he would have given up this lifetime full of antiquities. But he'd so fallen in love with this life,

119

a daily *Boy's Own* adventure, that he hadn't had the time, or perhaps the inclination, to find a way back. Five years of pondering his predicament provided some theoretical answers, which he shamefully refused to investigate further. And now his daughter just proved one of them — that you could come and go — he assumed. He wouldn't know for sure until he spoke with the distraught Sarah Williams — if it was her, and not his daughter, Sarah Lester. He couldn't go rushing into her room to ask.

Lester knocked back his whisky and left, other errands barging in on his jumbled thoughts. The moisture ring from the cold glass the only trace he'd been there. If anyone had sought evidence of Albert Lester's existence before his appearance in India in the early 1860s, they would have found nothing. He was a visitor to this time. One who'd been unable, and unwilling, to leave.

THE RETURN

*S*arah Williams shrugged away the tray of tea things the sari-clad serving girl offered her and turned aside. This room was as foreign as the people in it; her last memory was of boarding the steamship in England, then being struck with crippling seasickness. Now strangers surrounded her.

The bedroom emptied. Sarah remained in bed, covers held tight under her chin, though not from cold, as the humid warmth of northern India forced its way inside. She huddled there, frozen with fear.

The bedroom door opened again and stale lavender wafted over her, reminiscent of her childhood. She turned, half hoping to see the snowy white hair of her English grandmother. Instead, she faced the whirlwind personage of Naomi Abbott; her dimpled cheeks rosy with purpose.

'Enough of this turning away food; you need your strength. You've had a nasty shock, but you must eat. No one is expecting you to decide right now, but in the next few days, the Viceroy will no doubt arrange for your return to England.'

Sarah's eyes widened. Almost everything from this woman's mouth made no sense. *A nasty shock? Return to England.* She tried to interrupt but Naomi held up a bejewelled hand. Gold rings jarred with her lily-white fingers.

'Not one word, young lady. I know you'll want your things, but we'll wait till they clean the house up before we take you back there. In the meantime, your girls are trying to salvage your clothes. I'll pop round to the other ladies' and between us we'll rustle up whatever you need, so for now you're not to worry. The regiment always looks after their own, regardless of the fact that Simeon was an absolute cad.' Another commanding finger thrust this point home.

Sarah had some vague memory of being on the ship to India to join her recently widowed brother, Simeon Williams, an older brother she barely knew. *A cad?* Nothing made sense. She smiled weakly at the nonsense surrounding her.

Naomi took the smile for compliance. 'Good, I have your word you'll eat? Then you're to get some sleep. No one can harm you here. The army will have Simeon's murderer apprehended in no time. Captain Doulton is leading the hunt right now.' Naomi bowed out of the room after dropping her verbal bombshell.

Sleep slipped over Sarah, bringing flashbacks of Simeon's body slumped in a chair, his skin pasty with the colour of death. Although what came before that eluded her.

For the Sarah Williams lying in bed was not the same Sarah who'd hunted tigers with the Raj, nor fought with Simeon. That Sarah was long gone, sent back to a future this Sarah Williams couldn't possibly comprehend.

THE RAJA

The Raja of Nahan adjusted his black turban, the one which matched his mood. Not even the gleaming strands of pearls — some the size of quail eggs — slung around his neck, could ease the darkness that had settled over his household.

Never had he encountered such hostility from the British. It was as if he were being held responsible for both the uprising, and the death of that pompous English officer Simeon Williams.

They all knew in Simla, and beyond its verdant hills, that Williams was a brute of the first order. His avarice was legendary and, more than once, other members of India's aristocracy had come to him with complaints at Williams' 'procurement' of treasures which belonged to India.

The turban wasn't causing the band of pain around his head, it was his obligations. Never had he put his own needs ahead of those of his family, or those under his patronage. Just once he wanted to run off without worrying about the consequences. But, if he abdicated his responsibilities, the Empire would absorb his lands and property, and he'd have nothing.

Briefly he thought of the last moments with Miss Williams, before the conflagration had caused him to send her home. *Home to safety,* he'd assumed. He'd had Saptanshu punished for abandoning Sarah Williams on the side of the road, for protecting his own skin, and not that of the English lady. His orders carried out with no questions from the other staff. This was the way it had always been — orders given and obeyed. He had given Saptanshu no further thought. Servants were plentiful in India.

He'd sent gift after gift to her, but had heard nothing. The servants reported that Miss Williams had fallen into a stupor, where she remembered nothing other than the trip out from England and then finding her brother's eviscerated body in his room. He understood shock could incapacitate, but it had been days now, and the latest information seeping out of the Viceregal Lodge was that Miss Williams was being sent to Delhi to convalesce, before returning to England.

Probably for the best, he told himself for the tenth time that morning. Jasmine clung to his skin as he splashed toilet water over his face, patting the back of his neck with the cool liquid. Winter would be welcome, with its crisp air and dustings of snow, a respite from the disease-laden summer heat.

Nodding to his image in a silver-framed mirror, he left his dressing room, ready to prove to the British they'd never be able to subjugate his people, not while he stood.

Today he would call on the Viceroy in person. It would be a simple act to ask after the welfare of Miss Williams — she had saved his life when she'd shot the tiger which had attacked him.

Climbing into his decorated palanquin, he gazed out towards the majestic Himalayas. He could never grow tired of this sight. Their presence filled his soul with enough energy to live, and to understand that the problems of man were never bigger than the mountains overlooking them, and that, like mountains, obstacles were not insurmountable. Difficult to climb, but not impassable. He *would* see Miss Williams.

Soldiers surrounded the Viceregal Lodge. After the superior fire power of the British Army quelled the uprising, the executions of the ringleaders had dampened down the remaining pockets of dissent. But tension was palpable in the air and the soldiers looked at him with distrust. Ignoring them, he tilted his chin higher. Their opinions were of no consequence.

An aide escorted the Raja through the glorious entrance hall of the Lodge, and taken straight through to the Viceroy's study, where Albert Lester met him.

'Your Highness,' bowed Lester.

The Raja nodded in acknowledgement — his disdain for the British didn't extend to Lester, who'd been one of the few true English gentlemen he'd encountered in recent years. Different from the others; more relaxed, less judgmental — an unusual man.

'The Viceroy will join us shortly. I've sent his aide-de-camp to locate him. He's out on the tennis court; please forgive his tardiness — we weren't expecting you.'

'I understand, do not apologise for the man. Exercise is as good for the country as is efficient management.'

Albert Lester laughed. Only an Indian could give a compliment with one hand and take it away with the other in the same sentence.

'And the girl, Mr Lester, how does she fare?'

Albert contemplated his answer. He'd heard the rumours about the Raja and Sarah. No father wanted to contemplate their daughter's love life in any depth, even if *his* daughter was now back in her own time. But he felt responsible for the *real* Sarah Williams, who was close to a complete nervous breakdown.

'Gone. Left just before dawn, so she wasn't travelling in the day's heat. Did you not know?'

'This morning? I didn't know. But the gifts I sent? I had hoped to express my condolences to her myself for her brother's death.'

'You'd be the only one concerned about the death of Simeon Williams. I wouldn't concern yourself with that miscreant, and I — '

Interrupted by Viceroy's arrival, his tennis whites stained by the reddish dust which residents of Simla were all too familiar, Albert Lester lapsed into silence.

'So sorry to greet you like this. You should have sent word that you were visiting today. Would you take tea, perhaps?' The

Viceroy's training concealed from all but the most observant that he was a man who considered himself above the native Indian. They had trained him to play a part on behalf of Her Majesty Queen Victoria, and if that meant taking tea with a minor upstart who thought himself royalty, then needs must.

Both men knew the part society expected them to perform. The wild card was Lester. Raised by a father who worked for the postal service, and a mother who supplemented her housekeeping money with selling knick-knacks at community hall collectible fairs and car boot sales, no one in their right mind would have classed him as anywhere near upper-class, let alone royalty. Yet it was through the strangest quirks of fate that he was here in this room, advising the man second only in importance to the longest serving queen of all time, and he would do all he could to avoid further bloodshed in his country.

'Tea would be most agreeable, thank you. From Mr Lester, I understand that Miss Williams has left for Delhi. This saddens me, as I had wished to speak with her before she left. She saved my life. There is a debt of gratitude there that I can't repay.'

'Yes, we struggled with that decision, but she has distant family in England, and for her to remain in Simla seemed to be hindering her recovery. Too many reminders of her brother. Best thing for her. But enough of Miss Williams. Shall we speak of the troubles, or do you believe that they have passed us?'

'The "troubles", as you so describe them, have not gone away, they are but hidden underneath the carpets littered about your houses.'

The tea arrived, interrupting the Raja, and providing the breathing space for the Viceroy to recover from the gentle insult loosed among them.

'That is not reassuring. I understood that they had rounded up the ringleaders—'

'And shot,' the Raja interrupted.

'Yes, well that was unfortunate. But, like a snake, once you remove the head, the danger has passed?'

'You have forgotten about Medusa. The threat is in the shadows now and you must act or your empire will tumble.'

The veneer gone from the conversation and the Viceroy flushed. 'You speak in riddles, man. The Empire will never falter when our power spans the entire globe. Not just some shabby band of disgruntled *sepoys*.' Struggling to manage his anger, the Viceroy took a deep breath. 'Come, let's drink our tea, and talk no more of uprisings. Peace will reign. Can I interest you in scones, perhaps?'

The Raja declined. He noted that Lester had been shaking his head during the Viceroy's diatribe, as if he alone understood the Raja's position and agreed with it. 'Mr Lester, your opinion?' he probed.

Lester drew down on his pipe, its acrid smoke filling the wood-panelled room. History had been his favourite subject at school, despite leaving as soon as he'd completed the minimum requirements of secondary level, he had a fairly clear memory of how the Indian rebellion would play out, how the British Empire would disintegrate, falling like ivory dominoes.

Exhaling, he chose his words delicately, 'I feel we have not seen the end of unrest in India over the sepoy's treatment. It would be my advice that we tread carefully, and take measures to assure the Indian commanders, and soldiers, that they are an integral part of the Empire.'

'A wise position to take — a prudent man would listen.' He'd watched the Viceroy spend the entire conversation spreading English jam on fresh English scones, reinforcing his opinion of the British ruling class, and so he rose. Brushing down his immaculate *churidars* — his trousers — he bowed stiffly to the Viceroy, 'Thank you for your time but I have business to attend to in Delhi, so I must prepare for the journey.'

Shocked, Albert almost choked on the bit of his pipe. He was about to question the Raja, but thought better. His daughter was home. Sarah Williams was no longer his concern. Interfering would complicate matters needlessly.

'Before you go, Raja... this Simeon Williams business, I don't suppose you know anything about it?' the Viceroy asked, slathering another piece of scone with sticky jam before looking up at his guest.

'I understand you were rather close to his sister — perhaps she shared some information with you? It's just we're having no luck in tracking down his murderer, and... well, it's bad for morale. Rumour is that it was a local, and so, on the off chance, I thought I'd check.'

'When one listens to gossip, the winds of mistrust seep in. Listen to your advisors instead of whispers from the staff. I bid you good day.' The Raja strode from the room, the Viceroy's aide-de-camp hastening to hold the door open for him.

Lester stamped out his pipe, 'That could have gone better.'

'The Indians are all the same, Albert. They think they rule the place. Swanning around with pearls round his neck, like a peacock. Wouldn't have put it past him to have had old Williams knocked off himself, to get his hands on the sister. Yes, it's for the best we sent her away.' He addressed his aide-de-camp, 'Call Doulton here — I want to talk to him about the possibility that the high and mighty Raja may have had something to do with Williams' death; it's an interesting angle. One I hadn't considered.'

The ADC hurried off.

'You don't think the Raja had anything to do with it? It will have been a gambling debt — we've talked about this. You've just insinuated that a member of Indian royalty murdered an English officer. By now every coolie south of Simla will have heard the rumour.'

'Poppycock, Albert, there was no one in the room apart from us.'

'Sir, you know as I do that India has eyes and ears everywhere. They know what you think before you do. God knows what will happen now.'

'Albert, you need to trust me on this. My information is that we've settled the uprisings. If you'll excuse me, I must change out of these clothes.'

The Viceroy left Albert in the study shaking his head at the arrogance of the Victorian ruling class. Mind you, nothing much had changed in the one hundred and fifty years after. Eyeing the decanter, he decided it was never too early for the stuff when surrounded by idiots. Pouring two fingers into a crystal tumbler, he relit his *meerschaum* pipe, gripping the natural amber stem with his work-worn hands, and moved to the wingback chair. Sipping his scotch, he surveyed the great expanse of lawn. The sheer numbers of staff required to maintain the Empire in India was staggering, and the British treated them like dirt. It was no wonder the people of India were about to rise and shrug off the imperial yoke. Not in his lifetime, but it was coming.

THE JOURNEY

he Raja rearranged his aching legs on the divan. The road to Delhi had never seemed so long or rough. Monsoons had wreaked their usual havoc on the roads, reducing them to a morass of churned-up mud and broken wheels abandoned by travellers who'd gone before. But there were pros and cons with every season; at least the rains had lowered the temperature to a bearable level — more so for his staff. The muddied roads were unlikely to affect him; that was what servants were for.

Losing time to the weather frustrated him. For each day it delayed his journey, Sarah Williams drew further away from him. Once again he rapped on the roof of his *gharry* — his carriage — urging his *gharry-wallah* to move the bullocks faster, which was as hard as swatting away the mosquitoes lingering in the humid air. For good measure, he rapped on the roof a second time, the carved ivory lion head and ebony walking stick creating a satisfying thud against the silk-covered ceiling. He sank back into the cushions, their soft caress reminiscent of Sarah's hands upon his chest, her words in his ear.

He was certain that once he arrived in Delhi and found her, she'd snap out of the grief consuming her. In his mind, he visualised her ensconced in one of his homes. Closing his eyes, he allowed his imagination to drift, luxuriating in the release only available in daydreams. Freedom where, released from cultural expectations, following your heart's desire is easier than breathing.

He had other work in Delhi to attend to while Sarah was being tracked down. His land holdings were extensive, but he feared that his portfolio was not diverse enough. He'd inherited a successful export business, sending Indian textiles to the buoyant British market. The civil unrest unnerved him. His family had done well working with the British, dabbling in both indigo and opium, and although their foreign overlords considered themselves the masters of India, he felt this was a passing phase, as history had shown throughout time. Everything passes, and history repeats. He maintained publicly that he was coming to Delhi to investigate the increasing demand for cotton; whether expanding his investment in this quick cash crop would be beneficial to his people.

With dreams of wealth, health and happiness filling his thoughts, he slipped into the sleep of the pampered, dozing away the days on the journey from Simla to Delhi.

He could smell Delhi before he saw it. A myriad of pungent odours surrounded the *gharry*. Squalor mixed with an infinite number of residents and no discernible sanitation system mingled with aromatic spices, fragrant oils and a carpet of flowers.

Only the kaleidoscope of colour on every corner overpowered the scent; reds, yellows and greens. Copper browns and shimmering golds oozed from the pores of the buildings, as if someone had emptied a paint factory over the city, smearing colour from every tin and, even then, that couldn't truly describe the colourful symphony on display in the streets of Delhi.

The Raja of Nahan was all but blind to the riot of colour and poverty beyond his carriage. It had taken so long to travel to Delhi, his heart bled with the certainty that he'd lost Sarah. There was no chance of finding Sarah in this teeming city now. If they'd dispatched her back to England, he decided he'd go too — although, deep down, he suspected he'd never follow through with that rash decision. 'Foolhardy' was not a term coined for him. There was no room for recklessness. He had obligations, which allowed no time for chasing English maidens across the oceans. Valid sensible arguments, but when has the heart ever known sensibility?

Banging the roof of the *gharry* with his lion-headed walking stick, he called to his driver to take him to the missionary school instead of his Delhi home. His heart was taking over his decision-making, the vice him chest squeezing tighter and tighter.

'School' was too grand a name for the structure in front of him. Before today, he would have climbed back into his carriage without a second thought, and driven off; educating the lower castes none of his concern. Now he'd arrived, he cast an appraising eye over the establishment — the Anglican Mission School for the Society of the Propagation of the Gospel. A uniformed student popped out from the gate, astonishment all over his face at the mirage of the opulent Raja, resplendent in gleaming golds, pearl strands encircling his elegant neck, his turban the same tint as his brocade coat. Whilst the Raja considered himself dishevelled, to the young lad he looked like a god.

The boy disappeared, leaving the Raja standing puzzled on the street. A mere tilt of his head, and one of his servants scurried into the school yard, a haven of quiet in the teeming streets.

Within moments, Alice Montgomery appeared with efficient haste. Widowed on the road from Kanpur to Delhi in the company of Sarah Williams so many moons ago, she showed no sign of grief, save tiny extra lines at the edges of her kind eyes.

'Good afternoon, sir, how may the Anglican Mission School assist you?' Dressed in stark white, she was the angel to the Raja's godlike appearance.

'Good day. Would you be Mrs Montgomery?'

'Yes I am. Can I help?'

'Forgive me, Mrs Montgomery, for appearing unannounced, but I'm hoping for your aid with a personal issue?'

Alice smiled, and invited the Raja inside out of the sun, 'Would your companions like to take refreshments while they wait?'

The comfort of his staff had never crossed his mind, and he turned to look at his *gharry-wallah*, and the rest of his retinue, the heat casting a sheen on their dark faces.

'Yes, that's very thoughtful of you.' Nodding at his staff, they scurried into action, moving the Raja's belongings through the driveway into the courtyard of the school, now adorned by little faces wide-eyed at the windows of the classrooms; their immaculate outfits and haircuts making them peculiar clones of each other in ascending sizes.

It perturbed him to have so many people witness his affairs of the heart, but he squared his shoulders and entered the lion's den.

Alice showed the Raja into the administrative office, cooled by the ministrations of a *punkah wallah*, whom Alice dismissed, waiting until he'd left, before offering the Raja a glass of *aam ka panna* (green mango juice).

'Thank you.'

'You have had my name, but I fear I am at a loss why you're visiting our small school?'

'My apologies, madam, I am the Raja of Nahan, just arrived from Simla, on a matter of much urgency.'

At the mention of his point of origin, Alice's face paled, as she anticipated the Raja's next words.

'I am calling upon this fine establishment to enquire after a dear friend of mine, who left Simla before I had time to speak further with her. Time was of such importance, I came straight here, without any attention to my appearance, or the required letters of introduction. I am truly sorry.'

Alice looked past the Raja's bowed head towards the door where the dark head of her friend Elaine Barker lurked. Her age and experience should have emboldened her to enter the room, to be part of what would be a difficult conversation for Alice.

'I'm not positive we'll be able to help. The only women here are myself, and my colleague Miss Barker. I've never quite made it to Simla, I'm not sure about Miss Barker.' Summoning her eavesdropping friend she called out, 'Have you ever been to Simla, Miss Barker?'

Elaine entered the room, her sensible shoes silent on the tiled floor.

'Let me introduce the Raja of Nahan. Your Highness, this is Miss Elaine Barker of Salisbury in England. We have been running this school now for some months. It was to be my husband and I, but unfortunately he lost his life in a carriage accident, and Miss Barker agreed to stay on as my companion.'

If the Raja knew any more of what had happened to the Reverend Montgomery between Calcutta to Delhi, he kept his own counsel, rising instead to greet Miss Barker.

'A pleasure to meet you, Miss Barker.' Like honey dripping from a hive, his voice flowed around the two women, his presence reassuring, his intentions shining through.

Elaine wasn't as taken with the Raja as Alice, having met minor Indian nobility on her previous journeys to and from India. She dropped an infinitesimal curtsey before joining Alice on one of the chairs scattered around the room. For a small office, there was an abundant supply of seating in various states of dishevelment.

'Have you ever been to Simla, dear Elaine?' Alice asked, trying to delay the inevitable.

'Only once, but years ago. I suspect very few of my acquaintances are still there.'

'Ladies, I have to interrupt you. I wasn't clear; there is a particular lady I am seeking, and I'm told they sent her here to recuperate from the shock of her brother's murder; Miss Sarah Williams.'

Alice and Elaine exchanged what they thought were subtle glances.

His heart racing, he forgot his station and pleaded with the English women, 'I was not wrong. Is she here? May I see her?'

The two women both spoke at once.

'No,' said Alice.

'Yes,' said Elaine.

In something akin to a farce, they clamped their hands in unison over their mouths, before Alice took the lead.

'She was very ill when she came to us and recuperated here, but she has since left.'

Which was technically true, but Alice didn't want him to see Sarah's growing pregnancy. That perhaps the father of Sarah's baby was *this* man, and not Sarah's brother Simeon, filled her with relief, but did nothing to dampen the potential social damage to Sarah's family name should word get out that she had slept with a native, regardless of his status. It was a basic truth that in England, the mere hint of an assignation with a man of colour would ruin a girl. No, the course they'd agreed for Sarah Williams was the best one. A quiet birth, then returned to England, the baby named as Simeon's child, with the story that the mother had died in childbirth, and was being returned to England by his aunt. It was the only option given the circumstances. The best for Sarah, and for the baby. Alice frowned, appraising the Raja's coffee-coloured skin. If this man was the father, would the child take on the father's hue? Or the mother's porcelain white tones? It was in God's hands now.

'It is urgent I speak with her. I owe her an enormous debt. She saved my life, yet I had entrusted her care into one of my servants, and he abandoned her to great peril, and I must apologise. Sadly Miss Williams took ill before I could address this properly. And you can see... how badly I am affected by this terrible state of affairs. Therefore it is a necessity you tell me her whereabouts.'

Elaine cleared her throat, before replying with her sensible voice, 'It has been very tragic. She refuses to speak of Simla — it's as if the trauma of finding her brother has caused her to lose all memory of her time there. Perhaps if you come back tomorrow morning, after you have recovered from the arduous journey here, we can talk more?'

Recognising that uniquely British way of dismissing guests, the Raja stood, defeated by their English manners. These women had cared for Sarah, and now they were protecting her. He could understand that.

His travelling retinue were waiting for him, and after settling into his carriage he spoke to the women again, 'Tomorrow then. Thank you, ladies. It is thus that the heart shall have to wait a few beats more.' Thumping his walking stick on the roof, the carriage moved off.

'What do you think, Elaine?'

'There'll be trouble if we let them meet. She's not right. I don't think she will ever be, but this will set her back after everything we've done.'

'So we'll say she's gone, then?'

Elaine agreed, her greying curls bouncing unhindered under the Indian sky.

THE SICKNESS

*T*he Raja coughed into his white silk handkerchief; the lace edging rasping at his face like sandpaper. He'd been in this interminable city for less than twenty-four hours, yet a fever had struck him down in the night, developing into a hacking cough. And he daren't leave the confines of his room, lest he became any sicker.

He'd had word sent to the ladies at the Anglican Mission School that he couldn't attend them today because of a sudden illness, and that he'd be in touch in due course, but to please pass on his regret to Miss Williams. He'd added that last bit to his message, his staff having told him that Miss Williams was still in Delhi, and that the two women were trying to protect her from his advances. Their position was understandable, but he wanted it known that they could not sustain their ruse. Once he was well, he would call upon Miss Williams. She would be his.

The Raja called for a cool compress for, as the headache he'd woken with worsened. He shivered under his covers, yet knew he was too hot. This cursed fever. A tiny boy laid a cold cloth against his brow, and as he waved him away, his arm was as heavy as lead, weighed down by an invisible force. Still, he forced himself to reach for a drink — he had kept nothing down all morning, and he knew he needed to drink. Dehydration in this climate would kill you. He fumbled with the glass, which slipped from his fingers and crashed to the ground. A thousand shards of Irish crystal decorated the floor of the Raja's sick room. He turned his head away, towards the open verandah doors where a breeze gathered, teasing him with the scents of the garden. In the ornamental pond outside he imagined the golden carp sunning themselves in the shallow water. Another coughing fit interrupted his musings, and he held a lace kerchief against his mouth, waiting for it to pass; each cough sapping his strength.

The Raja slipped into a fretful sleep; the fever ravaging his body. Staff came and went, replacing cold compresses on his forehead, tugging the mosquito netting around him as night fell. Closing doors and wetting his lips with water. Taking away the uneaten meals.

By the next morning the bell by the Raja's bed broke the silence. With his headache gone, and the fever broken, he ordered a simple flatbread, devoid of any spices or accompaniments. Washed down with chilled lemon tea, he felt he was almost back to normal. He'd take things slow and then send word to the school that'd he'd attend them late afternoon. For now he would wash and change out of his fever-laden clothes — leaving them for the staff to get rid of.

THE LETTER

"You'll never believe who have joined us now – some jolly chaps from New Zealand. Had to look the place up on a map. Had no idea where it was. Right next to Australia, at the very bottom of the world. You'd hardly know that they'd travelled 12,000 miles to get here, to help us out. Most of them have already had air time before they got here. A godsend, if you ask me. A quick classroom lesson, if they're lucky, a quick one-two round the old bird, and then they're being sent off. This could be it, you know. A few more of these fly boys, and we'll defeat those Germans quick smart.

There's a couple of native boys from New Zealand here too – the rest have all joined the army it seems, not so much into the flying thing. Not everyone's cup of tea.

Darling, the one thing I want to do, still, is take you up into the air. Not in the middle of the war, of course, but when it's over. Maybe we'll do it down in New Zealand. By all accounts, it's everything England is, only with better weather, and actual real beaches, the sort where you can build entire cities out of sand.

Anyway, I digress. I asked the New Zealand lads about those stones your father had – you know, that old box rattling round in the attic. God knows why you've kept it all these years. We should have donated it to the British Museum last time we were in London – better than collecting dust up there. Anyway there

I go again, off on a tangent! Anyway, the boys said that they'd be more than happy to have a look at them for us. Seems they would be able to tell us which tribe made them based on what they'd been made from. Sounds slightly far-fetched to me, but I've given them our address. So don't be alarmed if a couple of Air Force lads turn up out of the blue asking about stone adzes in our attic – they haven't just escaped from the lunatic asylum!

THE CELLAR

If saints perform miracles, which one just performed the miracle of saving my life?

Sarah Lester huddled in a corner of the dark room. Her faith that everything would be okay this time round was being tested by the intense cold gnawing at her bones. She drew her legs tighter into her body, willing the rustling noises around her to go away.

Clenched in her hand was the greenstone adze she'd grabbed at *The Old Curiosity Shop*, its unnatural smoothness a comfort. That a Māori warrior had honed this weapon, with no metal tools, gave her an other-worldly feeling of strength.

Her stomach cried out for food, but still she didn't move, staying wedged in the corner of the... of the what? *A cellar?* With no light, and only her sense of smell and touch to guide her, that was what she'd discerned. An earthen floor, rodents scampering away from her bulk, and wooden crates stacked against a wall. Running her hand over the cartons, she'd recognised heavy glass bottles. Sarah removed the stopper from one, trusting her senses to warn her before she drank something potentially toxic. Her eyes watered as the harsh liquor hit the back of her throat. Coughing at its intensity, she cast the bottle aside, the remaining contents seeping into the hard packed earth.

Anything more than a moderate slug of that and she'd have been comatose in minutes.

Sarah slunk back to her corner to wait, sure that someone would be down for more grog, and then she'd judge what next. There was nothing else she could do — her blind fumbling hadn't located a door or an access hatch, or any means of escape. She was in a super-sized, gin-filled grave.

THE PRISONER

*S*hivering and clumsy, her limbs felt as heavy as lead, and her eyes kept closing against her will — typical symptoms of the onset of hypothermia. First-aid classes at school had described in detail the symptoms and if she'd been in a better state, she would have been able to recognise them herself. Not that she could do anything about it.

Heralded by the rasping of a metal bolt, someone flung a trapdoor open. Faint light filtered through the freezing void but did not reach into the corner where Sarah lay huddled, semi-conscious.

The sweaty fug of unwashed man followed as boots, legs, then man, climbed down a short ladder lowered into the cavity. In one of his huge fists, a bear of a man carried a lantern. The hair on his hands trailed all the way up his exposed arms to the back of his thick neck. Seemingly impervious to the cold, he set the light down as he hefted wooden crates of liquor through the hatch as if they weighed nothing more than a sack of feathers.

About to pick up his third crate, he paused. One slot was empty. The eight remaining pig-snout bottle tops stared back up at him. Grunting in surprise, he swung the lantern backwards and forwards to

KIRSTEN MCKENZIE

locate the wayward bottle. And there it was — next to the recumbent body of Sarah Lester.

Joe Jowl's eyes widened in amazement. This was his cellar, and he was damn certain he'd put no one down here, at least not this month, and not with this current stock of grog. Surprise gave way to anger as he considered the loss of profit from the missing bottle.

'Oi, you!' He nudged Sarah's form with the scuffed toe of his boot. No response. Frowning, he shook the thief. 'Oi!' He tried again. *Nothing.* Exasperated, he clumped off to the ladder calling to an unseen associate, 'Oi, Jimmy, give us a hand here,' before returning to the unconscious girl.

A mirror image joined him, complete with hirsute hands and neck, matching rough pants and filthy cotton shirts. The two men were identical in every respect.

'You put her there?' Joe asked.

Jimmy shook his head.

'Who put her down here then? You letting your friends use our place? Giving them free grog too?'

'Nah, not me, Joe. Got no idea where she came from.' Jimmy lumbered over to look at Sarah, as you would a tiger in a zoo.

'Stop your gawking, Jimmy. Give me a hand to move her upstairs. Don't want her dying down here and stinking up the place,' Joe growled.

The men bundled Sarah out of the cellar and none too gently. Barely conscious, she didn't even register being dumped onto a lumpy bed in a room not much warmer than the cellar. Gentleness, like cleanliness, was not a concept with which the Jowls were familiar.

Profit was their abiding life mantra, and Joe was already calculating how he might turn this unexpected gift into cash. *As long as I can keep her alive, that is.* Just how a young woman had ended up under their house was irrelevant; perhaps his twin had forgotten he'd put her there. Regardless, she was theirs now.

'Fetch the lantern and then light the fire, Jimmy. Let's have a better look at what we've got here,' Joe directed.

The elder twin by only fifteen minutes, Joe was the undisputed leader. Jimmy had always done what his brother told him. It never crossed his mind to question this. If Joe decided that the girl belonged to them, then that was the truth of the matter.

Joe sat on a spindly rocking chair, which creaked under his weight, and rocked waiting for his dim-witted brother to return with the lantern. Neither man had a wife, or any romantic interest. Women cost and, despite a normal sexual appetite, Joe wasted none of his money on whores, nor did he allow his brother to partake. There were enough women around willing to give it away for free, in the hope they might marry into the Jowl wealth. He wasn't stupid enough to believe they loved him for his looks. No, women were only after their cash. This one probably was, too.

The fire coughed into life, lending a smoky haze to the proceedings. Two candles supplemented the lantern's light. Jimmy slouched against the far wall, eyeing the woman on the bed. Normally he gave no thought to the opposite sex. His twin had drummed it into him that women were gold diggers, and if he ever gave into temptation, that would be the first step to ruin: the poorhouse; hunger; living off scraps to survive. The only thing scarier than losing his brother was the fear of being hungry. Now, Jimmy's simple mind couldn't fathom the unease bubbling inside him. He didn't understand why Joe didn't dispose of her, like the others.

Sarah stirred. Her heavy eyelids stretched open in response to the warmth penetrating her chilled form. Her eyes focused on the dancing reflections in the glazed tiles surrounding the hearth, the red poppy in the centre of each tile alive with the flames.

A man's voice drifted in from somewhere past the fireplace. 'So, you're awake then?' Sarah struggled to find its origin, her eyes and mind not functioning as one yet.

'I... I can't quite...' she trailed off, the effort of trying to talk sapping what little strength the fire's heat had given her.

'Get her a cup of tea, Jimmy — not in the good china, mind; just a mug'll do,' ordered the disembodied voice. The floor heaved a sigh of relief as Jimmy slinked off and disappeared out the door, allowing enough light to reveal Joe in the rocking chair. Sarah tried to focus on this mountain of a man.

'Thank you,' Sarah managed.

'No point thanking me till you've explained who you are and why you're in our cellar, drinking our grog. There's a bill owing you know, for the bottle you stole.' The rhythmic rocking continued as he delivered the words, a plan forming in his entrepreneurial mind.

'But I didn't drink it, I only sipped it, once. It was ghastly,' Sarah countered.

'Be that as it may, I can't sell that bottle now, so you owe me a debt. To cover your board too. Not sure how you will repay us for our hospitality, though I've had some thoughts on it while you've been sleeping.'

Jimmy returned, a steaming mug of tea in his huge hands. He handed it to Sarah before scuttling away to the far corner.

Sarah did a double take as she registered the similarities between the men, making Jimmy squirm under her scrutiny, till he could handle it no longer. 'I'll see to the chickens then, Joe,' he said, edging out of the room, refusing to meet Sarah's gaze.

Joe nodded at Jimmy's departing back. 'He's not so good with women. You take care not to bother him while you're under our roof. Do what you're told, leave Jimmy alone, and work off what you owe us, and we'll be fine. Cross me and... well, then I'm within my rights to punish you for the theft of my liquor.' Enjoying the sound of his own voice, he expanded on his lecture.

'Jimmy and me will have to rearrange things to make room for you here. It's a bother, but we'll add that to what you owe. You must earn your keep, so finish that tea, and I'll show you the kitchen where the two of you can get acquainted in time for breakfast. Idleness is a sin, and I cannot abide idleness.'

The floor groaned as he stood up, moving closer to the bed. He leaned over Sarah, his odour mixing with the smoke from the fire, 'Just know that there's no point you trying to leave till you've paid your debt, one way or another. It's never been said I forgive a debt.'

He left the room, taking the lantern with him, closing the door hard enough behind him to cause the candles to sputter and die, like the hope in Sarah's eyes.

THE TOWN

*T*he Jowls sang to the glory of God with lusty fervour, their piety as legendary as their illicit gin.

Singing His praise was the highlight of the younger brother's week. Under God's watchful eye, Jimmy knew his place in life, and where his worldly body would go when no longer required. Believing in Him was like hoarding money. With God and cash, your soul was safe from torment and your earthly hunger assuaged. Jimmy needed nothing more in his life other than God, Joe and cash. And his brother made sure they had plenty.

After the service, Joe lingered to exchange banter and business jovially with the town 'nobs'. Jimmy hung back. Talking to others made him uncomfortable, and he was nervous about the girl in their cellar. He wanted nothing to do with her, afraid he might let slip about her if he dared speak, even to the Minister's wife; the only woman he felt at ease with. Married to God's servant, she was the one woman who would not try to lead him astray. *No, best I wait here for Joe to finish.* Later, away from their devil-filled women, these men — pillars of the community, would drink the Jowls' gin, then fornicate with whores. Jimmy shook his head to dispel the evil crowding him. *Dear God, make it stop; it hurts*, he thought, holding his head in his hands.

'Come on, Jimmy, let's get home. We've things to do; there's trouble down south. That fool of a governor just declared martial law down Taranaki way. Armed men up and down the country will need the refreshments we provide. Bloody hope that girl has sorted out some tea. I'm parched. He's a good man that minister, but he goes on. Stop dawdling — you're to make some deliveries straight after.'

The brothers, mirror images when asleep, looked poles apart as they walked home: one brother, shoulders back, head held high with the world in the palms of his meaty hands; the other, hunched, boots scuffing the dirt, trailing at least half a pace behind, eyes downcast.

Joe halted; Jimmy nearly bowling him over.

'For the love of God, Jimmy, pick up those bloody feet of yours and walk like a man. Anyone would think you were walking to the gallows at that speed. D'ye want to get home for tea, or is it breakfast you're after?' Joe gave his twin a clip round the ear before he turned and carried on.

Jimmy picked up the pace, although his shoulders remained hunched, under the weight of his brooding thoughts. Gaining on his brother, he asked, 'Is keeping the girl a good idea, Joe?'

'Shh, don't you talk about family business on the streets. What've I told you a hundred times before? *Family business is for behind family doors.*'

Jimmy fell into step with his brother up the rutted path to the house they'd built with their father. Soon, other settlers would realise that land on the hill, above the filth of the lower streets, was premium real estate, but, for now, the seclusion was their friend.

The turning key broke the silence, followed by the thumping of the tumbler falling open in the lock. They looked askance at one other, expecting to hear hammering or yelling, but heard only breathing — their breathing.

'You lock the door, I'll check on our guest,' Joe directed.

Jimmy did as instructed, the outside world's tension sloughing off him. His shoulders straightened, his mood lifting. This was his safe place. He pocketed the sturdy key, its heft a reminder that, through the grace of God, he had a solid roof above him, and was about to have food in his belly. *As long as the girl doesn't ruin everything.* He muttered a short prayer; that temptation wouldn't visit him — again.

THE KITCHEN

Sarah had touched everything in the room trying to find a way home. It hadn't taken long. The bedroom was Spartan - a bed, a functional chest-on-chest, a transfer ware basin and jug, and two candlestick holders with old beeswax clinging to the sides like a climber on Everest.

Left with no lantern, or matches to light the candles or fire, she operated in the dark, trying to prise the wooden boards from the window frame. She could feel curls of wind seeping through the window sashes. Freedom so close. So unattainable.

She'd screamed herself hoarse trying to summon anyone's attention, until wrapping herself up in a quilt made from red, black and cream squares, sewn together in intricate geometric patterns — and curled up on the bed, too cold, hungry and despondent to do anything else.

The key turning in the old iron lock was a welcome noise compared to the silence she'd endured since they'd locked her up following a harrowing breakfast.

That had started with her being hauled out of bed. Half asleep, she'd stumbled along the corridor to the kitchen where Jimmy was feeding the fire in the black range, refusing to meet her eyes, as Joe pointed out oats, sugar, bowls, and cutlery. Sarah never cooked porridge herself in London — and that had been with access to a microwave and instant sachets from the supermarket. Her lack of culinary knowledge had been a family joke, to the point where she'd had to ring her father when she was away at university, to ask him how long it took to boil an egg. Cooking porridge from scratch, for two strangers, in what she considered a medieval kitchen would be beyond her.

For two men on their own, the kitchen was a shrine to cleanliness. A delicate tea service sat on a hutch dresser, its golden rim winking in the sunlight that flooded into the room through the thin glass windows. The fabulous view of the emerging settlement down the hill wasn't enough to distract her from her predicament. Standing there, she made no further move. Joe stepped forward and slapped her.

'We're waiting for our breakfast. It won't get cooked by you stopping there. God gave you hands to use and to serve. And while I allow you to live under our roof, you'll cook, or there's room back in the cellar. You liked it enough to sneak in there before.'

Sarah held her hand to her cheek. The power behind the slap had thrown her into the table. Glaring at Joe she replied, 'I don't know how to make porridge. So you can bloody well cook it yourself.'

Joe jerked his head at his brother. The twin pushed back his chair, stood up and, like a well-mannered child, returned his chair under the table. Seeing his huge hands resting on the chair, Sarah felt the hairs rise on her neck. Her heart rate quickened.

Jimmy walked towards her. Joe moved to block the doorway, cutting off any potential escape route.

'You sure, Joe?' Jimmy asked as Sarah backed away.

Joe nodded.

Jimmy lunged at Sarah, his bulk belying his speed and strength. Grabbing her in a bear hug, he dragged her to the range. Bending down, he opened the cast iron door, the fire-hot metal barely registering on his labour-toughened skin.

Sarah struggled futility against him pushing her closer to the fire. She screamed as the heat singed first her hair, and then her eyebrows.

Her bruised cheek brushed against the edge of the range, and her screams of fear turned to those of absolute pain.

'Enough,' Joe commanded from the doorway.

Jimmy released Sarah, who scuttled away from him like a crab, till she hit the furthermost wall.

'We'll have our breakfast now. Best you put some butter on that burn. Can't have that pretty face scarred can we?' Joe decreed, taking his customary seat at the table. Jimmy joined him, and together they sat in silence as Sarah picked herself up off the floor, her cheek in agony, and made her way towards the pantry.

THE NATIVE

*S*ilent like the surrounding air, Wiremu Kepa slipped down
the slope of the grassy hill with only the sunlight watching
him. He'd seen enough to get the gist of what was going on but was a
little nonplussed by the sight. It was all very well agreeing to bury old
ancestral hatreds and jealousies, but whether the chiefs would abide
by that was another story.

Wiremu wanted to worry about just one thing — his family. And
that meant keeping them safe, especially from the white man's
influenza. He'd scoffed in silence as the Governor handed the Māori
chief a staff. No fancy pole trimmed with silver and carved with the
Royal Coat of Arms would protect the chief or the members of his
tribe from the *pākehā* disease. Too many had died during its relentless
march.

Gangs of men were clearing the land, forming the long ribbon of
road to make it easier for soldiers and settlers to travel. *Easier for them
to massacre my people.* Steering clear, Wiremu ran down the scrubby
slopes, only pausing as he heard the faint screams of a woman. As he
tried to locate the sound's direction, it faded. There was a smattering
of houses on the hills, their owners oblivious to the sacred nature of

the ground where they'd built. It was beyond him to judge them, but their complete disregard for his culture rankled.

The sound had gone. Striking it from his mind, he carried on, not noticing the covered-over windows of a substantial weatherboard house less than two hundred yards away.

With ragged breath, he made it home after a marathon run to the settlement of Onehunga. The town clung to the harbour side, the smell of the mangroves crowding its shores, salt hanging in the breeze. Here tiny two-roomed fencible cottages huddled next to each other like women gathering water at a well. Given to Wiremu's father after being wounded defending Auckland in 1849, like the other Fencibles — retired soldiers — he'd set about building his own cottage. Wiremu had been born there and knew no different.

Ducking his head as he entered the doorway, a veil of peace descended on him. Time slowed, as did his heartbeat. A beautiful man, skin the colour of fine coffee tempered with cream, his muscular frame was evidence of a life lived on the move, exercising every muscle, all day. His dark eyes had a haunting look to them, as if they saw more about you than you knew about yourself.

Wiremu's father had built the cottage using native timbers. The knots still visible in the planks of wood were like eyes accusing him of destroying the forests which had graced the harbour's edge. He shuddered and averted his gaze. To cover them, he'd have to get some of those paintings the white men hung on their walls — depictions of the lands they'd left behind. He'd want paintings on his walls of the land he felt in his heart too. *This land.* The land of the long white cloud.

Moving from the all-purpose space that served as kitchen and dining room and lounge into the only other room in the house, the bedroom, he found his wife asleep, a tiny bundle curled up next to her. He admired how they slept, knowing that he protected them. Wiremu started toward to the bed, and his boot caught on a rogue nail jutting up from the floorboards. The noise caused both his partner and baby to stir.

'Wiremu?' she murmured, fumbling to feed the mewling infant in her arms.

He sat on the bed's edge, smoothing her sleep-mussed hair.

'How was it? Did it go well?' she asked, as she remembered the reason for her husband's absence. It was a long trek to Kohimarama from Onehunga and, although Auckland was at peace, there was never any certainty that a native could pass through the township without being assaulted. Through fear, or more likely alcohol, the unexplained deaths of natives had risen in recent months.

'I kept away from the work gangs. I'm as fleet on foot as the *weka*,' he laughed. The *weka*, an ungainly bird, more at home in the forest's undergrowth, but a poor master of disguise despite its unassuming brown plumage. Curious and fearless, it was easy prey, and often ended up on their dinner table.

'The talking was just wind, but peace will hold, for now. We've got bigger problems coming. All that alcohol those gangs are drinking. Tau said it's getting worse, and it's them that I worry about, especially with you here alone with the baby.'

Wiremu prayed that this child would survive. Their first, a boy, born in winter, and influenza had spirited him away a few weeks after his birth. They were better prepared this time. Baby slept wrapped in a feather-filled quilt, or warm against her mother. The fire never went out, and they did not mix with anyone else.

Wiremu earned the white man's dollar at one of the native mills. Today there was no work. The grindstone had slipped off its shaft, cracking the metal, and he had no expertise to fix it. One of the English millers had agreed to help repair it, but not today, for today had been the spectacular conference in Kohimarama.

Would his family have a better life down country with his wife's extended family, her tribe, her *iwi*? He hadn't grown up on the *marae*, but an *iwi* gave you protection. The only problem was that there were more troubles the further down New Zealand you went. Lawlessness increased, soldiers who'd gone rogue haunted the Waikato.

He threw a couple of rough split logs on the fire, the fresh sap spitting as the flames hit the new fuel. He allowed himself a few moments to reflect on the *tangi*, the funeral they'd held for his son — the last time he'd seen any of their family.

Wiremu shook his head to dispel the black thoughts, he grabbed the sweet potatoes from their garden, and put them to the boil. He chopped up a handful of bright green *puha*, before preparing a simple dough to make fried bread to serve with their meal.

THE ESCAPE

*S*arah bent over the sack of potatoes, counting them in her
head, checking each knobby blob for blight — the weeping
burn on her cheek a reminder of what her captors would think of her
serving up anything less than perfect. She'd resisted lathering butter
on the burn — *silly old wives' tale* — but it had helped somewhat. She'd
have preferred a tube of Silvadene, but there was nothing else, so
butter it was.

Jimmy sat stock still in the kitchen, eyes on his empty plate. He
hated Joe being away when the girl was cooking for them. He could
sense her feminine wiles from his side of the sparse room and he
knew if he looked at her, she would ensnare him with her evil magic.
Joe had told him women were all like that — only after the brothers'
money — and that they had to protect each other from scented
vultures. What Joe really meant was that *he* needed to save Jimmy
from gold-diggers. Jimmy was slower than his older brother; Joe knew
that he was easy to snare, and there was no way he would let his baby
brother fall into the clutches of some low-born scullery maid, fresh off
the boat from the penal colony in Australia.

Jimmy sniffed the air and tasted daisies. There hadn't been flowers in this house since their mother died, so it must be the girl. He shifted in the wooden chair; his boots scraping against the floor.

Sarah jerked back from the potato sack. Used to the silent treatment from Jimmy, any sound from him took her by surprise. There were times she almost forgot about his presence. Joe was the only person she ever conversed with. Her life was a lonely one, though not for want of trying. She'd lost count of the number of times she'd tried to slip away, but Joe Jowl anticipated every move, regardless how surreptitious she tried to be.

This was the first time he'd left her alone with Jimmy, and she knew enough to understand that Jimmy was as uncomfortable with her in the house as she was herself.

Sarah tried engaging the young man. 'Jimmy, could you help me move this sack of potatoes back to the pantry?' He responded by moving his chair further away — its wooden legs protesting once more — turning from her as if her mere proximity was causing him physical pain.

Deciding a different tack might be more effective, she tried again, 'Excuse me, Jimmy, I need your help to move the sack. It's too heavy for me. Joe normally carries it for me, but, well... since he isn't here to help, could you please?'

Jimmy sniffed, clamping his huge hands over his ears to block out her words. *Women are the devil. Women are the devil,* he whispered to himself, wishing his brother hadn't left him alone with her. The last time he'd been alone with a woman... well that didn't bear thinking about.

Sarah stood, hands on hips, trying to decide whether to risk one more request when she realised Jimmy had closed his eyes. Without a second's delay, she took her chance. Backing out of the kitchen, she pivoted and raced down the darkened hallway. Weeks of cleaning the house made it easy to navigate. The front door was the only obstacle in her way now.

Jimmy rocked himself in the chair. The voice in his head almost loud enough to drown out the temptresses words, whose echoes sent ripples through his mind. He pressed his fists harder against his ears, the vibrations of his chanting adding to crowded noises in his skull.

Sarah fumbled at the door. The old iron handle refused to turn. Grasping it with both hands, she tried again, hoping Joe wouldn't have locked it when he'd left his own brother as a guard.

Silence. Jimmy took his hands away from his ears and opened his eyes. He expected to see the witch still waiting for help. *Gone.*

Jimmy swung his head towards the pantry. *Empty.*

Then he heard the striking, rasping sound from the hall — realisation hit him with the force of a jackhammer. Enraged, he leapt back from the table, sending his chair careering backwards, to bounce and smash against the wall.

She wiped her sweaty palms on her filthy skirt and tried a third time.

Jimmy launched himself towards the hallway, unhindered by the murkiness. The faint outline of the woman at the door provided the only target he needed.

Sarah finally found purchase, and twisted the handle, pulling the banded door towards her. Slipping through the narrow gap, she tumbled down the stairs of the stoop. Like a rabbit, she hopped up and sped down the path.

She could hear Jimmy puffing behind her. He was not as fit as his brother, despite being no less bulky. It was unsurprising — Joe rarely let him out of the house, apart from church on Sundays or to make their regular deliveries.

She zigzagged her way down the hill, hoping there'd be a high street of sorts at the bottom. Her lungs devoid of air, the stitch in her side threatened to immobilise her. A fork in the road ahead, a split second decision; she chose left — and ran headlong into Joe Jowl.

THE MILLER

*W*iremu left his wife and baby reluctantly. Around the shores of the Manukau harbour, soldiers were mustering, ships docking and scavengers loitering. Throughout history, someone has always profited from war, and it was the profiteers that most concerned him.

There was one thing you could say about the British; their officers held their men on tight reins. Once the army had dealt with the troubles down country, he was sure things would change but, for now, they kept the soldiers billeted around town busy training. The staccato sounds of rifle shots rang through the settlement, reverberating off the water and the surrounding hillsides, birdsong replaced with gunfire and the shouts of forestry crews sawing and swearing in equal parts.

Wiremu had to go to the mill to repair the shaft for the grindstone, so he could get back to milling the flour destined to feed an army. He laughed at the irony of feeding men who, in all likelihood, would kill the native warriors of New Zealand, his blood relatives, many generations past.

There was no fancy carriage for him, or even a horse to ride. His transport was on foot — and he needed to hurry — to meet Vaughan

Hughes, the English miller who'd been the only white man to treat him as an equal. Perhaps their profession fostered solidarity, or maybe Hughes was one of those rare fellows who believed God created all men equal.

Hurrying to the mill, he pulled up sharp at the sound of bottles smashing on the metalled road. In front of him, at the intersection, was the source of the noise. The innkeeper, Joe Jowl, with a wooden crate at his feet, was bellowing at his halfwit brother and holding a writhing girl under his arm, one hand clamped across her mouth. She was struggling against his bulk.

The breaking bottles brought half the neighbourhood out to watch the fracas. The sight of Jimmy Jowl lumbering down the hill enough to get tongues wagging. And Joe Jowl taking the Lord's name in vain as he restrained a young woman, was so disturbing that several men looked tempted to intervene.

One unbroken bottle, an escapee from the crate, rolled to a stop at Wiremu's feet, its branding visible on the thick opaque glass, "Jowl Bros. Auckland".

Wiremu debated the wisdom of his next action. *Walk away?* It was nothing to do with him. Leave it to others. 'Don't get involved,' his wife always told him — but fate decreed that he ignore her advice. Scooping up the bottle, he carried on toward the brothers.

Aware of their audience, Joe had fallen silent. Being a public laughingstock was shameful, and he glared at the onlookers, daring them to interfere. Anger at his brother simmered under the surface. He'd deal with him later. *Family business was for behind family doors*, he berated himself. He'd tamed the now-docile Sarah, and would punish her in due course. Then, out of the corner of his eye, he spotted Wiremu. His rage-clouded mind mistook the bottle for a weapon and, flinging the girl to the ground, he swung around, his arms free to defend himself against the *savage* approaching him.

Joe threw himself at the would-be attacker, his clenched hands forming a pair of massive weapons. Wiremu staggered under the onslaught, and the clunky glass bottle fell from his grasp, bouncing on the road and rolling to a stop next to Sarah.

Sarah lay there, winded, watching in terror as Jimmy stomped towards her, an unnatural light shining in his eyes.

Jimmy knew from the start the girl was trouble. Never in his life had his brother sworn at him, blaspheming the Lord's name. God would mark their souls as blasphemers. Jimmy shuddered. There was only one thing for it. Sarah was a pox on their family and had to go. He was oblivious to the stares of the womenfolk from behind their fences, and unworried by the surrounding men. His size, and his brother, had made him untouchable growing up. No one challenged them, because together they were too strong. *Until this witch magicked herself into our cellar.* He'd prayed for answers. He hadn't put her there — not this time, anyway. God knew there were other women buried under their house. Joe occasionally brought home entertainment for himself. Jimmy had watched his older brother play with his living toys, but he had never partaken. He enjoyed helping dispose of them, though. Which was why keeping Sarah to cook and clean was against the natural form of things. But now it was time for Sarah to join the other *scented vultures* in the cellar.

Wiremu ducked the first punch that flew past his head. Enraged, Joe lined up for another shot, fists up by his square jaw, a stance more like a professional fighter in the ring than a street brawler. He went into survival mode. This unexpected turn of events was what his wife had warned him about. There wasn't time to think 'what if?'. He couldn't rely on the watching crowd for any help. Most of them thought the Māori no better than dogs, and now that the fight had gone from between a man and a woman, to one between a man and a dog, it was much more entertaining to watch. Had Wiremu looked, he might have noticed the men placing wagers on Jowl to thrash the native.

A vicious upper cut from Joe's left hand caught Wiremu by surprise, and he reeled backwards. The crowd circled round the men, and the cheering intensified, the onlookers happy to see a native get a thrashing. They'd lost interest in the woman on the ground — all except Jimmy.

He'd slipped past the crowd. He knew his brother didn't need his help. Their father had taught them both how to box by belting the living daylights out of them — his way of showing them love — their mother had explained. Until the night he'd beaten her to death in a drunken haze while showing her his *love*. That's what love did for you. After her death, the boys stood side by side, and showed him their brotherly love, with their four fists and boots.

Jimmy moved towards Sarah. Bloodied hands, elbows and face made it difficult to pull herself together. Pushing herself up, she winced in pain, tiny grains of gravel embedded in her hands like needles. Her foot nudged the glass bottle, which tinkled on the ground — a merry sound amidst the jeers of the crowd witnessing a fight between two men who'd never met, and who were nothing to each other. The hand of fate, and a fork in the road, responsible for their meeting — and Sarah herself.

Jimmy crept closer, his bulk oddly agile in his wary approach. You couldn't be too careful; she'd already proven herself to be unpredictable, like a cornered beast. How else could she have escaped his watch at the house? He primed himself to grab her. He knew he had to be quick; had to get her back to the house before Joe could punish him for his mistake. No, not his mistake, hers.

With her back to Jimmy, Sarah bent down to pick up the glass bottle. Jimmy's subconscious queried why she was bending down but he was too intent on his course of action to give it any rational thought.

The raised lettering was slippery in Sarah's bloodied hand, but why was her head so sore?

Sarah disappeared.

THE MEN

*W*iremu struggled to his feet, the ragged sounds of the crowd ringing in his ears. Joe reared up, ready for a second go, when the onlookers fell silent.

Sensing an opportunity, Wiremu shot through a gap between two roughshod settlers, legging it for home before Jowl could refocus his attention, distracted as he was by the sudden hush.

The injured native struggled through the scrubby brush clinging to the hillside, vicious fingers of cutty grass slicing into his limbs. Stumbling onto pitted lava rocks, smashing his knees on the unforgiving surface. Wiremu stifled his screams with his fist, panting with the pain. From this vantage point, the tableau below was an arresting sight.

Joe Jowl was standing over Jimmy, who appeared to be supplicating to his brother. As if with a single thought, the surrounding crowd was backing away, in an ever-widening circle, almost balletic in its formation. Spectators peeled off in twos and threes, checking back at the Jowl brothers — whether in fear or amusement, Wiremu couldn't tell. He looked in vain for the girl, but couldn't see her. She must have escaped.

Wiremu stumbled onwards; they needed him at for the repairs to the grindstone's shaft, although in this condition it would take him much longer to get there. He only hoped Vaughan Hughes would linger at the mill; his injuries could wait, but the wheat couldn't.

Reaching the mill, the sun high overhead, he leaned against the wooden doorway. Most days he paused to admire this marvel of engineering. He recognised he'd already strayed far from his tribal roots, and that sat uneasily within him, but needs must. And he had to do what he could to provide for his family. After that, he would do his best to feed his soul.

THE BROTHERS

Joe Jowl stood over his brother, who quivered beneath him. Joe's face as dark as the sky had become. Without respite, the elder twin hammered the younger with question after question, 'What happened here, Jimmy? What was the girl doing out? Why are *you* out? Where has she gone? Did you want the neighbours to gossip? What would Mother say?' Pausing for breath, he homed in with the last words, 'You have shamed the family.'

Leaving his brother cowering, Joe spun around, scanning the retreating audience for the native and the girl. He planned very short lives for both of them. There was no sign.

Joe spat in disgust at the backs of his sanctimonious neighbours, then kicked Jimmy in the side, encouraging him up off the ground — the closest form of affection he could bother with. Without a word of complaint, or instruction, Jimmy hurried to pick up the bottles strewn over the road. Two were beyond redemption, fragments thrusting their jagged edges skywards. Six bottles had survived the altercation, leaving one unaccounted for.

'There's one missing Joe.'

'That filthy bitch. She's stolen from us again. No one steals from the Jowls. Come on, we're going home. Family business is for behind family doors. We'll talk about it there.'

Together they trudged up the hill, Jimmy's eyes on the ground, avoiding the curious curtain-twitchers in the houses along their path. Joe held his head high, looking neither left nor right. Neighbourly relations were not the Jowl brothers' strong suit and not having their neighbours know their business was a basic rule.

The front door stood ajar, causing Joe to freeze at the gate.

'You left it open?'

'She was getting away. I said she was trouble. Didn't I tell you? I was trying to get her back for you.'

'Did you not consider that someone could have gone into our house?' Joe's face was incredulous, challenging his brother to answer.

Jimmy's head hung low, his shoulders already pulled forward by the weight of the crate in his muscular arms. It was a miracle Sarah had escaped his wrath. His strength was such he could have throttled her with just one of his huge fists. He twitched thinking about the fear in her eyes when he closed his hands around her skinny white neck. The way he'd make her eyes bulge out, like bubbles in boiling water. He longed to hear those tiny noises only true strangulation could bring. Not the rasping sound a choking victim made, but an almost silent panicky flailing, followed by the most delightful blue tinge, as if he'd applied an artist's palette to her lips. The fantasy would carry him through whatever punishments Joe was about to inflict.

'Inside,' Joe directed, letting Jimmy mount the steps before him, the clanking bottles reminiscent of the bells used in to herald the weekly church service.

With the door closed behind him, Joe shed the mask of restraint he'd held in place since Wiremu and Sarah's disappearance escape. The first punch landed in Jimmy's soft solar plexus. Stumbling in shock, the crate careened corner-first into the *kauri* floorboards. The remaining bottles protested their latest treatment by shattering within the crate. Wafts of pungent alcoholic fumes enveloped both men. Hunched over, Jimmy struggled for breath, his back an open invitation. Another blow, this time to Jimmy's exposed kidney. Jimmy gasped in pain, crumpling to the ground, but still he didn't retaliate. Like any long-term victim of domestic abuse, he took his punishment, knowing the less he fought, the sooner it would be over.

'It gives me no joy, brother, but you have dishonoured the family.' A well-aimed kick to his silent brother's stomach concluded his attack, leaving Jimmy wallowing in the bitter alcohol saturating the golden floor boards.

'Clean up that mess. I'll be working on the books. These breakages need to paying for.'

Jimmy curled into a ball, detached from reality, watching the broken bottles around him swim in and out of focus. He imagined each glassy peak plunging into Sarah's stomach. In and out. Over and over. As dreams of Sarah's violent death mingled in his damaged mind, he disappeared into himself, and his subservient side emerged, ready to bow to his brother's demands.

THE BOTTLE

A loud thump from upstairs echoed in the empty shop, leaving dust motes dancing down the stairwell on the disturbed air.

Sarah stirred on the floor of her lounge. The thin layer of grime over the furniture showed that this time she'd been gone longer than any of her previous experiences. Her heart constricted. *How long have I been away?*

Letting go of the old glass bottle, she watched it roll away until hitting the leg of the coffee table. A glass bottle, not the most valuable of items and the last thing she would have expected to bring her home. She made a mental note to look up the bottle online, later. *Much later.*

It seemed her gravel burns had made their way back to England with her, given the pain she was in. Gritting her teeth, she stood up, limping to the bathroom. Turning on the shower, she stripped off and waited for the water to warm up. Her colonial clothes lay in a bloodied heap on the lino floor.

This she loved — it'd been one of the few things she'd done to the flat above *The Old Curiosity Shop* before moving in after her father vanished. She wasn't up for paying to varnish the floors, but a small piece of black and white lino gave the bathroom a retro modern feel, if such a thing existed.

She put her hand under the water. *Stone cold.* Sarah fiddled with the ancient taps, turning the cold off, and the hot tap all the way round, stinging her hands. She needed to get the gravel out.

'Damn it,' she exclaimed, realising someone had turned the hot water cylinder off. Standing bloodied and naked in the bathroom, that there was only one thing she could do. Steeling herself, she climbed under the freezing water. Teeth chattering, she sat in the bathtub, and sluiced the blood from her body. She wasn't sure what was worse, the chilly water or the pain of picking the gravel from her wounds, with the shower head clamped between her knees.

Sarah could bear the cold no longer, so, struggling to her feet, she rinsed off. There was no chance of using any form of soap or shampoo when her wounds were this fresh. Her hair would be fine in a ponytail and she was mostly clean. There was nothing more she could do for the burn on her cheek but hope like hell that it wouldn't scar.

Drying herself off, she dressed in the loosest clothing she could find. An old pair of Singapore Airlines business class pyjama pants a boyfriend had left behind, and a sweatshirt of her father's that she'd kept, made even more poignant now she knew he was alive. Slipping her feet into oversized bed socks, she made herself a black tea in the kitchen, with copious spoonfuls of sugar to make it palatable without milk.

Carrying her favourite 'Antiques Roadshow' mug into the lounge, she slumped on the couch. The light outside told the time better than the railway clock on the wall — frozen at five thirty-eight. Like most of the objects, a thin sheen of dust covered the oak frame. The piece had been one of her early purchases after she'd taken over the shop, and she'd paid way too much for it, a trap for the uneducated, so she'd kept for herself.

Old railway clocks were wildly popular, and a week didn't go by without someone asking her for one. And, as was the way of things, she'd never seen another. This one had come from a defunct railway station in Harlington, salvaged by the retiring station master. She'd also scored branded china cups, monogrammed silver-plated teapots and the most *spectacular* wooden filing cabinet. That had flown out the door, off to some industrial-turned-residential warehouse on Canary Wharf.

She fought off sleep, her stomach competing for attention. *When did I last eat?* Sleep won. Curled up in the lounge she drifted off, the couch a welcome change from the lumpy horsehair-filled mattress in colonial Auckland.

THE ASSISTANT

*P*atricia unlocked the door of *The Old Curiosity Shop*, resentment filling every fibre of her body. Each minute she spent here was one less in her own shop. One less minute designing the clothes she loved. One less serving *her* loyal customers. To remove such negative feelings at this imposition brought about by her missing friend, she'd hired a girl to run the antique shop, but hadn't yet felt comfortable handing over full access. That would change today. She couldn't carry on doing this. *Hardly a girl though* — Nicole Pilcher had moved to London for love, and had come highly recommended from her previous job at the historic Tamworth Castle, where she'd been the curator of the museum. *It's time to trust her with a set of keys*, she thought through gritted teeth, as she struggled with the padlock on the door.

As usual, she scouted around the shop, hoping against hope that her friend might have reappeared. But, like every other day, nothing. She and Andrew Harvard had agonised over what to tell Nicole but had decided on the simplest explanation; that Sarah had gone travelling, and they didn't know when she'd return.

Patricia sat behind the counter, counting down the minutes till

Nicole started. She was normally on time, as one is prone to be when starting a new job. She flipped through the sales book. Things had improved since Nicole had taken over, that was for sure, although there were her wages to take into consideration. She groaned and let her head bang against the counter as she considered how much energy she'd spent on her friend's business instead of her own.

The door flew open, and in bounced Nicole, with the passion and excitement peculiar to the young.

'Good morning, Patricia, thanks for opening for me again. How was your weekend?' Nicole bubbled over with joy.

Patricia plastered a smile on her face, 'All good, thanks. Just checking... do you have any calls planned for this week?'

Now there was a licensed dealer in the shop, Patricia only needed to be there when Nicole went out to buy new stock. In asking, she deep down hoped that the answer would be 'no'.

'There's only the one on Wednesday, but I made it for first thing, so I thought, if you didn't open till eleven, that would work better for both of us?'

'What have they got?'

'They said they had some Lladro, a pile of crystal... and a sterling silver pin cushion collection. It's those I'm excited about. At the last auction I went to, a pin cushion, shaped like a camel, of all things, sold for nearly *seven hundred pounds*. So, fingers crossed, these are sterling and not silver plate.' Nicole threw her jacket over a stool and flicked on the cabinet lights Patricia had forgotten.

'Right, well, I'll be next door if you need me...' Patricia paused, weighing her words. 'Look, it seems silly you not having your own set of keys, and mucking around with me opening and closing for you.' Handing over the keys, she couldn't help but smile at Nicole's face — like a child with a new puppy. 'This way, you won't need to worry about arranging calls around me. Anyway, see you later.' Patricia slipped next door, to open her own shop.

Something feels different this morning. She couldn't put her finger on it, but there was a feel to the air. She wished it were Sarah, but knew better than to wish for the impossible.

Nicole Pilcher busied herself behind the counter, she still couldn't remember where everything was. The shop was nothing like she'd expected. To start with, it was a complete *disaster*. Stuff *everywhere*. There was no rhyme nor reason to the shelving. It was dim, and hard to get around. Stock flowed onto the floors, shelves heaving so badly they threatened to break every time she placed anything new on them. There wasn't a day where she didn't expect one of the glass shelves in the window to crack and waterfall stock down onto the ones below. She was so fearful of this she'd emptied them, leaving artfully displayed pieces on the cleaned glass. The window looked fantastic but now she couldn't see the counter under the leftover stock. *What to do with it?* Her training told her to send everything off to auction and hope for the best. She wasn't sure if Patricia would go for that, but then again, she wouldn't realise.

Locking the front door, she ventured downstairs, where she'd seen a mountain of cardboard cartons. This was a treasure trove of unpriced stock. In her second week, she'd concluded that everything here needed to go upstairs, priced up, and put out for sale. She was no fool. She'd Googled the shop before accepting the position and knew the police considered Sarah missing and there was a genuine concern of foul play. Nicole suspected Sarah was never coming back, so if she did a good job here, her secret dream was that she'd be able to buy the shop.

With the front door locked, she spent a happy hour ferreting through the boxes stored by Sarah's father, stock he'd kept aside for selling on a rainy day — his 'retirement fund'.

Opening a crate, her breath caught in her throat. There was Ruth — Ruth from the bible who'd married Boaz, the great-grandmother of David. An exquisite hand-painted porcelain tile depicting Ruth with a sheaf of wheat under one arm, presented in an ornate gilt frame. *Got to be worth about five thousand pounds, give or take.* She ran a finger along the brushstrokes. The oil paint ghosted under her fingers; ridges and valleys she could feel, but which were only visible under a magnifying glass.

She lifted it from its bed of bubble wrap. Unseen, the auction receipt fluttered to the floor, slipping under a shelving unit.

Nicole carried it upstairs. Something like this needed to be on display, not hidden in a tea chest. She looked for an empty hook. That was another thing this place had plenty of; hooks. Scattered everywhere, but also inconveniently in weird places.

A faded Delft plate caught her eye. Delft normally held its vivid blue regardless of age. A copy? She removed it from its hook, replacing it with Ruth, who looked angelic in the half light of the shop. Satisfied, Nicole put the 1967 commemorative Christmas Delft plate on top of a pile she'd started for the nearest auction house, and didn't give it another thought.

Nicole decided her focus today would be the cabinet full of French *Limoges*. She wasn't an expert but, despite its garish images and dated colour schemes, *Limoges* was popular with the Chinese customers who ventured into the shop. As a start, she emptied the cabinet, cleaning the shelves, and examining each piece with a critical eye. No one, other than the *Limoges* factory itself, needed three hundred examples of chinaware on a shelf. She'd halve the stock and no one would be any the wiser. Anything that was a double up, missing its gold trim, or marred by knife marks, went into the box. She shook her head as she put two large knife-blemished wall plates into the carton. *Who on earth uses gold gilt display plates for eating off?*

Singing to herself, she contemplated how much she loved her work. She missed the hustle of the tourist season at Tamworth Castle, but here she had more autonomy and handled objects that didn't have five hundred years of history behind them. And that suited her perfectly.

Her humming drowned the creak as Sarah Lester made her way down the narrow staircase into the shop. Shielding her eyes from the brightness of the fluorescent lights, she tripped over one of Nicole's cartons left at the bottom of the stairs.

Nicole dropped a *Limoges* pepper grinder in fright, smashing it to smithereens as it hit a threadbare patch of carpet.

The women eyeballed each other. Nicole had the advantage of suspecting who the dishevelled woman on the floor was. Sarah was at a complete loss. The fall had knocked the fresh scabs off her grazes and she sat cradling her sore hands.

'Ah, hi. Sarah? I'm Nicole. Looks odd me being here, but I've been working here while you were away. Here, let me help you up.'

Nicole helped Sarah onto on a rickety wooden stool, scrawled with "Not For Sale" in permanent marker.

Sarah looked up at her, and around the shop. Everywhere she looked, there were glimpses of shelves and clear space. Patches of carpet which had spent the previous twenty years covered with nail boxes, now tufted up like new lawn. It was her shop, but it had transformed into a place she didn't recognise.

'How long did you say you'd been working here?'

'A few months. I'm... well, I've tidied up,' Nicole gestured around the shop.

Sarah sniffed, her hands in her lap. She'd have clenched her fists in frustration if they hadn't hurt so much. Her gaze took in the shelves behind the counter. Her voice trembled, 'Where's the pen and ink sketch of the sailing ship from up there?'

'Oh that? I sold it. An ex-Navy guy offered me ninety pounds for it, which I thought was a good price for an unsigned piece. It's all in the sales book. I've tried to follow your systems. I can take you through everything, but that only covers the time I've been here. Patricia and Andrew were running it before I got here, so I couldn't say how they were doing things...'

Sarah held up her damaged hands, stopping Nicole's ramblings.

Nicole's eyes widened in shock. 'Oh my goodness, your hands! Wait right here, I'll find the first-aid kit.'

'It's behind the counter, on the shelf above the reference books,' Sarah volunteered.

Nicole looked chagrined, 'I think that's the shelf I tidied up. A lot of those books were out of date. I mean, the 2003 *Miller's Antiques Price Guide* isn't relevant any more...'

Sarah stared at Nicole, her bleeding hands quite forgotten, 'You got rid of my reference books?'

Nicole squirmed under Sarah's glare and nodded.

'Well then, I guess you'll know where you put the medical kit then,' Sarah said.

Nicole rushed off and Sarah gazed around the shop. *This is a disaster.* Every time she'd 'disappeared' before, it'd only been for a fraction of time and there'd been no change in her circumstances. This was a whole different kettle of fish. Her father's favourite piece of art sold; her reference books hocked off. She shuddered as she considered the infinite possibilities of what this girl might also have done.

Nicole returned with the sparse first-aid kit, the one which Sarah always meant to replenish, but had never quite got round to doing.

'The antiseptic cream expired two years ago, but there are plasters and cotton buds' Nicole offered.

'The antiseptic will be fine. Pass it here and I'll put it on. If you could put the plasters on for me that'd be great. Then I must see Patricia. She'll be wondering where I've been, I expect.'

'I think there's a few people who have been wondering that... I can ring her for you?'

'No, I'll pop next door, surprise her. Best you stay here, but perhaps you could tell me how the shop is doing?' She steeled herself for the worst-case scenario, which, in reality, couldn't be any worse than when she was last here. So many thoughts reeled through her brain. *What happened about the katar and the candelabra? And the sampler?* Sarah groaned.

Nicole froze mid-plaster application, 'Sorry, did I hurt you?'

'No, no, I remembered I never found out how the auction of some things went. I should check with Trish, see if she heard anything from the guy at Christie's.'

Nicole looked sceptical. *How* couldn't *she know about what had happened at Christie's? Is she for real?* Nicole thought back to her second week in the shop, when she'd received a visit from some investigators from the Art Loss Register. They'd wanted to know all about the systems in the shop. 'What systems?' had been her response.

Although Patricia had done her best to show her the ropes, nothing in *The Old Curiosity Shop* made sense. Not the sales register, nor the stock register. Crates of stock from who knows where cluttered every corner. Then there was all the stuff stored downstairs. The place was a mess. Not that it was her business, but the shop was an advertisement for 'How *Not* To Run A Business'.

Nicole was used to worldwide museum-standard catalogue systems. Her dreams of one day purchasing the shop were going down the drain, but maybe she'd keep her job.

'I've met *one* man from Christie's, Andrew Harvard — he and Patricia both interviewed me for the job here. He's been helping look after things while you've been away.'

None of it made any sense, but at least her friend hadn't had to do it on her own. There seemed to be enough money coming in to employ a retail assistant — the one thing she'd planned to do herself after the auction of the *katar*, if it'd been a success. *Maybe things aren't as bad as I thought.* As for her father's sailing boat picture, sometimes you needed to let go of the past to let the future in. She knew her father was alive, albeit not in *this* time. He'd forgive the sale of the sketch if it meant the survival of his business; the only thing he loved more than his family — with golf a close third.

With her hands covered in plasters, held in place with old strapping tape, Sarah stood up, her body aching like she'd gone ten rounds with Mike Tyson. She made her way out of the shop, choosing to ignore the artful displays dotted about, and the now visible areas of floor. Perhaps this was the way of the future, although what her regular customers thought of it was something she refused to consider.

Sarah opened Patricia's door, the bell heralding her entrance. Two women were by the mirror admiring the Victorian era-inspired skirt being tried on by the taller one and paid no attention to Sarah as she limped towards the workroom. Pushing open the door, she greeted her old friend hunched over her sewing machine and a swath of snowy white fabric. 'Hello...'

'Sorry, this area is private. I'll be with you in just a moment. Just got to finish this seam.' Patricia never looked up from her sewing machine.

'Trish, it's me,' Sarah replied, walking in.

Patricia froze. Her hands clenched the snowy fabric. She looked up.

'You'd better have a bloody good explanation for what you've been doing and why you've been away for so long.'

THE RUG

Sarah surged forward, gathering her friend up in a clumsy embrace, trying to protect her hands and comfort the woman sobbing in her arms.

'Hey now, I'm back, it's OK. I'm here and, apart from some grazes, I'm fine.'

'Well, I'm *not*,' Patricia retorted, wiping her eyes on a scrap of fabric. 'Gone for months. *Months*. What do you think I thought? Huh? I'll tell you. That you were dead. Either dead or never coming back. Do you know the *pressure* I've been under? *And* Andrew? The police constantly "drop in" to ask about you. That's not good for business, I can tell you that for nothing.'

Sarah held up her hands, 'I'm sorry. I don't know how to explain, it's...'

Hesitating, Sarah tried to think how best to convey in words what had happened. Her time locked up by the Jowl brothers was too raw, too painful for her to even comprehend, let alone share. 'I can't describe it, it was different this time. I *can't* explain it, and to be honest, I don't know if I want to. Not now, anyway.'

Patricia shrugged, her pain at being abandoned by her friend still slicing into her gut. 'Whatever, Sarah, but you just have some explaining to do, and to people other than me. The police wanted to hear from you as soon as you showed up. The auction house has your money, so I'll ring Andrew, and tell him you're here. It will get messy.'

'Messy?! Do you imagine I've been sunning myself in the Caribbean? Jesus, Trish, two lunatics locked me up, assaulted me. I can't remember my last coffee, let alone a wine or a hot shower. That's another thing, someone turned off my water heater! Anyway, you could give me a break at least. I told you before what's been happening, you *said* you believed me. What more can I say?'

'"Sorry" would be a good start.'

'Fine. I'm sorry. I had no way of coming home, and I didn't know how long I was away for. It didn't feel that long. But did you *have* to employ someone for the shop? How do you know she's trustworthy?'

Patricia stood up, her bottom lip wobbling, fresh tears in her eyes. Pointing to the door, and without meeting the eyes of her friend, she said 'Out.'

'What? Come on, Trish, we need to talk about this, you've got to fill me in on all that's happened. Last time I was here, someone was shooting at me.'

'I can't have this conversation with you now. I've been trying to get on with my life, so can you leave? Just go.' Patricia wouldn't meet Sarah's eyes; instead, she stared at the floor, her arm stretched towards the workroom door.

Sarah stepped away, shoulders drooping. Trish was her closest friend, and Sarah never dreamed it would've been possible for her to be like this. It wasn't in her nature; she was a constant source of sunshine in *everyone's* life. Turning, she made her way out, oblivious to the stares of the customers whose ears had pricked up at the mention of the police, a shooting, and the other delicious tidbits of gossip they'd overheard.

Looking in through the window of *The Old Curiosity Shop*, Sarah could see the interloper bustling around inside. Her life was a mess, that was for certain, and now she needed to straighten it up. *But where do I start?*

First things first, reconnecting her hot water. That seemed to be the easiest to deal with. She'd just call the...

She shook her head. *Who am I kidding?* It was completely unlikely that her cellphone was still active. With a deep breath, she walked back into the shop.

'Um, Nicole? By any chance would my mobile be around here somewhere?' Sarah ventured.

Nicole paused, a small bronze bust in her hands, furrowing her brow, 'Um, not that I can recall.'

'What about when you tidied up?' Sarah gestured towards the now-immaculate shelving behind the counter where chaos had previously reigned.

Nicole looked over at the wooden shelves, 'No, I don't remember seeing one. Maybe Patricia put it away before I got here?' she added, 'But I've got one Trish gave me for shop stuff.' Plonking the bust onto the countertop she rummaged behind the counter, unaware of the thunderous looks Sarah was giving her, this stranger in her shop.

She held up an iPhone, clad in a gaudy bubblegum pink cover. 'This is the one; it's my cover, but is the phone yours? You can use it?'

'Too kind,' Sarah replied, her sarcasm lost on Nicola who was busy unlocking the phone, and checking her email before she handed it over.

Relief flooded Sarah that her best friend hadn't given this enthusiastic puppy-like employee *her* phone, but a newer one; one without the telltale crack on the bottom corner where she'd once dropped it on a marble-topped washstand she was trying to move.

'No it's not mine. I'll have a look upstairs, and sort out some stuff. I'll pop down if I need to borrow yours.' Inhaling, Sarah broached the other question which had been niggling away ever since she'd come downstairs, 'So, Nicole, where do you live?'

'Oh, not that far from here. A friend has a place in St. George's Square, in Pimlico, and the timing was perfect, because she'd just been told she was being transferred to the Paris office of her company at the same time as I got this job. So I'm flat-sitting for however long she stays there. That way she doesn't have to let it out to strangers. Perfect.'

With relief, Sarah smiled. The notion that this girl, regardless of how nice she seemed, could have been living upstairs in her flat filled her with a sense of invasion.

'Right, well, I'll just pop upstairs, till Trish isn't so busy in the shop, then we'll have a proper catch up with her, so she can fill me in on everything that's happened.'

'You don't want me to talk you through the books for the past few months?'

'No, not now. Tomorrow?'

'Good idea. Anyway I've got to finish getting all the props ready for Trish's show this weekend. With all this stock, you'd have more Indian antiques, but there aren't any. Don't suppose you remember if you've got any downstairs in storage? I've been through lots of the boxes. Found the tiger-skin rug and the...'

'The what? What tiger-skin rug?' Sarah paused on the bottom step and grabbed Nicole's skinny arm, her eyes bright.

Squirming of out Sarah's rough hold, Nicole rubbed her arm, eyeing Sarah warily.

'We... ell,' she hesitated, drawing out the word '... there were some crates stacked up by the stairs. Trish asked me to move them down just after I started, and the rug was in one, along with some other bits and bobs. All Indian stuff, I thought.'

'Where is it now?' Sarah demanded.

Nicole squirmed under Sarah's intensity, 'It's in the back of my van, um, I mean *your* van. I'm delivering it for the show tomorrow.'

'For Trish's show?' she said frowning.

'Yes, for Patricia's new line. The one she's been working on since I've been here.'

'Let's go.'

Confused, Nicole just stood there. 'Go where?'

'To the van. Come on, grab the keys, I need to see what's in there.'

Sarah veered off, leaving Nicole frozen at the bottom of the stairs.

'But it's all packed up ready to go. There are loads of boxes in there, all heaped on top of everything.'

Now moving towards the back door, she stood by while Sarah

struggled with the old latch. It had taken Nicole weeks to figure out the complicated system of locks and bolts. There was even a random panel of trapezoid shaped tin screwed to the bottom, as if covering up a giant cat flap or similar, which had another floor bolt screwed to it.

Going out the back door to the van was a constant annoyance, so she'd negotiated with Patricia that on Monday's she wouldn't be at work, instead using the van for pickups and deliveries, giving her a vehicle to use over the weekend, and meaning she only had to struggle with the old door a few times a week.

'Maybe you could come and help set up at the show? I'm sure Trish would be more than happy with an extra pair of hands — and it'll give your hands another day to heal,' Nicole offered.

Sarah whirled around and, through gritted teeth, replied, 'I'm sure *Trish* would appreciate my help, since we are friends, but to do that, I need to sort out a few things first, and checking which of *my* stock is being used for *my* friend's show is something I want to do. So please, spare me your helpful suggestions, and fetch the keys to *my* van. We'll make this quick, then you can go back to work.'

The sniping from Sarah was undeserved, but she had set the tone, and she couldn't bring herself to turn on the charm now. This stranger wouldn't bloody well understand that the skin could be from the animal which had attacked the Raja of Nahan. *It could be a link back to my father, dammit!*

Nicole squared her shoulders. Sarah may be the owner, but *no one* spoke to her as if she were a servant. Her mother had raised her better than that. 'The keys are hanging on the same hook as they were when I first started here. You're right, I should get back to work, so look through the van, but do it without me, as I have to close early today. I'll lock up out front, and I'm busy at a fair tomorrow morning. Have fun helping *your* friend with her collection. Please pass on my apologies; I don't think I'll have finished at the fair in time to help.'

Feelings hurt, but pride intact, Nicole left the astonished Sarah by the door, the cool air complementing the frosty atmosphere inside the shop.

THE VAN

*S*arah stood by the open door, watching Nicole walk away, torn between her business and her past. Or was it her future? Standing in the chilly air, she wasn't sure whether the goose bumps on her arms were from the cold or the knowledge that the contents of her van might hold the key to her father. A sob escaped her throat. All these thoughts of her father, yet she'd barely given her mother a thought. Her wonderful mother. When she was younger, there were delicious moments when Mum would emerge from her bedroom, dressed for a night out, made up like a model, jewellery glittering in the evening light. The distinctive of scent of Chanel perfume wafting behind her and an Oroton bag slung over her shoulder, her silver high heels completing her outfit. Always the Oroton, and always the diamonds.

Sometimes Sarah's mother allowed her to try on all the rings in her Victorian jewellery box, each layer spread out on her parent's bed. With her fingers brimming with rubies, emeralds and pearls, she'd felt like a princess. Her mother reminded her of one.

Sarah rested her forehead on the peeling paint. She'd wait. With no one else to turn to other than Patricia, she'd wait. A headache crept around her head, until her whole skull pulsed with pain.

She fumbled her way upstairs, sinking into the couch. Her whole life was a complete muddle. Now she had nothing. The weight of depression settled on her shoulders. That, coupled with the headache, saw her stumble from the couch to her bedroom. Without undressing, she slipped under the musty covers. Expecting sleep to take her, she lay there, eyes open, replays of her life running on a loop: a bike accident when she was nine; alongside her father at work; her mother dressed up for an evening out; the police — so many police; her parents gone. Then Lord Grey; India; the strange Arab; Betsy. Warden Price; Major Brooke. Seth. And finally Isaac. The memory of him dying in her arms made her ache, and the tears flowed; giant, all-engulfing sobs. The sort that starts from your stomach, and cascades out of your body in relentless waves. It was her fault he was dead. She knew it. And she'd never felt worse than she did now, alone in the world.

Tugging the duvet tighter around her shoulders, she stared unseeing at the pile of unread books on her bedside table. It seemed so long ago that she'd had the time and the luxury to loll about reading. On the bottom of the stack was a novel by Stephen King, although she'd been too chicken to read it. Above him was a well-thumbed copy of *The Hobbit*, there as her go-to comfort read. Then the first two instalments in a fantasy fiction series she'd found among her mother's belongings. A series she kept meaning to start, but some other book always seemed to be more enjoyable than reading a series with a cast of a thousand characters with peculiar names.

And on the top of the pile was a slender volume on the archaeological investigations at the Vindolanda fort in Northumberland. It had long been a dream of hers to volunteer there, but the shop had made that impossible. Still, she indulged her daydreams by reading up on the excavations every time a new publication came out about the latest developments at the site.

Her eyes slipped past the stack of books, each one mocking her with their air of neglect, until they fell upon a dirty sheet of paper, covered with scratchings of smudged ink, held down by a lumpy rock masquerading as a paperweight.

As her be-fogged mind processed this, the clouds in it parted, her eyes widened. Not *just* a rock, a nugget. *A gold nugget.* She remembered at once that this was the nugget from Isaac's pocket, with a letter to his mum. Her heart plummeted further. She'd promised to deliver it, and she'd failed.

Sarah dredged up all the history she could recall about life in Wales around 1860. Receipt of this gold would have changed the life of Isaac's family, and she'd let him down. He'd died, just after she'd vowed to send his letter and his gold to his mother, and she had not followed through on her promise.

She knuckled her eyes, rubbing away the tears. So many lives ruined because of her. It just wasn't fair. She was alone in this world, with no responsibilities to anyone other than herself. Yet, through no fault of her own, she'd wrecked lives and lives had ended because of her.

She stared at the ceiling. *Something else that needs attention* — the cream paint tarnished with past cigarette smoke and stale air. *Perhaps I could trace the descendants of Isaac's family?*

Sarah rolled over and buried her face into the soft cotton of the spare pillow, long since void of its clean washing powder smell, yet there was still a vague hint of domestic bliss, of times when her greatest worry was which café to go to for breakfast at the weekend.

Later. She could trace Isaac's family later. For now she just needed to sleep, and then everything would be better. Even sorting through the stuff in her van wouldn't be so daunting, later.

THE FAIR

he cavernous hall echoed with the voices of traders from around Europe, with a smattering of antipodean twangs, and the harsh vowels of South Africa.

Furniture polish shone on Georgian side tables and Regency chests. Ornate ivory-topped walking sticks and battered old cricket bats leaned against shiny silver spittoons, everything mellowed with age and wear.

Everywhere you looked, men were on the prowl for a bargain, and ladies loitered with lust in their eyes around cabinets crammed with rubies and gold bangles and baubles, glittering under the lights at the annual Alexandra Palace Antiques Fair.

Nicole Pilcher ambled through the hall, each stand more impressive than the one before. Her mental list was growing with every step. How she'd ever be able to remember half the things she wished to buy was beyond her. On the journey here, she'd struggled to put the altercation with Sarah out of her mind. She'd been looking forward to this event since starting at *The Old Curiosity Shop* and it wasn't fair that Sarah had ruined it by coming back. Nicole tried hard to regain her sense of excitement being at London's largest antiques gathering.

She'd planned to do a first pass around the hall — noting things she was interested in — and then buy them on her second run through; *if they are still there*, she reminded herself. The trouble with Sarah Lester clouded her thoughts. She had to concentrate; she had to prove her value and buying well was one way of doing that.

So far, she'd spied a cute vintage perfume bottle shaped like a Scotty Dog. Some collectors paid handsomely for certain *Avon* bottles, so she decided that building up a collection for the shop could be worthwhile. She'd even considered contacting the company itself to see if they were interested in taking part in a special 'collectors only' night. It would take work, but she was keen to try anything to make *The Old Curiosity Shop* an iconic place to visit, as opposed to watching it die.

High on her list were small items of pre-1900 sterling silver to replace the contents of her sparse cabinet — emptied by opportunistic punters because of the high scrap price, and because gold was so prohibitively expensive now so they'd turned to silver. Her regular scrap merchant told horror stories of other dealers scrapping exquisite articles to take advantage of the silver price. Melting them down was criminal, done for the sake of profit. She understood businesses had to be profitable, but sometimes they needed to weigh up whether it was better to preserve those pieces for their historical value?

Nicole wandered around, trying to keep to a logical pattern, down the left-hand side of one long row, then up the other side. Pause, examine, make a note, move on. The same faces kept passing her, possibly just variations of the same people. This was her first fair as a professional buyer. Although she'd been to plenty where she was choosing for herself, buying for a shop was a whole different experience. As a start, she knew she couldn't buy what *she* liked, otherwise the shop would be full to the brim with *Maling* lustre plates and *Sylvac* bunnies — most definitely not to everyone's taste. Trying to identify what was desirable was nigh on impossible.

She'd spent the previous night looking at all the hot auctions on eBay, hoping it might shed more light on the current trends. But several hours online had given her a headache, and reaffirmed her own knowledge that sterling silver was in high demand, which almost guaranteed there wouldn't be any bargains here today.

A cup of tea ought to help clear her head, so, after completing a whole circuit of the fair, she made her way to the crowded tea kiosk, pushing through a queue of elderly ladies with blue rinses, and carrier bags filled with *Lladro* nudging their baggy stockings. The one empty chair in the corner beckoned, and Nicole slipped into the seat, balancing her saucer on a knee, to review her notes.

Silver (pre-1900)
Avon bottles (complete)
Rodd Cutlery
Limoges (unusual)
Pipes

Finding affordable silver was proving difficult, resulting in only one eggcup — dated 1898 and hallmarked Sheffield. priced low because there was only the one, instead of being part of a boxed christening set, but even without the rest of the set, it was a desirable piece. The stand with the Scotty Dog *Avon* bottle also had another of their bottles in the shape of a pipe. Not quite the smoking pipe she was after, but it tickled her fancy. An elderly French dealer had two *Limoges* pepper grinders, complete with their original sales tags. *Limoges*, and different, and in mint condition. If they were still there, she'd buy them too. She sighed. So many beautiful things and she wanted to buy everything. *How do other dealers buy well and sell successfully?* It was akin to playing the lottery — you took a punt and hoped for the best.

Activity at another table caught her attention, as an older woman laid out her purchases for her companion to admire. Nicole couldn't help but 'admire' them too, albeit with her lips shut tight to avoid commenting. The neighbouring table groaned under the collective weight of Jim Beam bottles, many unopened and still full of the American whiskey. The sad thing was that most of those types of bottles were worth less than half of what they'd cost new. Because Jim Beam had had such great success with their novelty decanters, they'd produced tens of thousands, flooding the market, rendering any collection almost worthless. But, to the buyer sitting next to her, they were as exciting as a puppy is to a five-year-old. She was ecstatic with her finds. *Each to their own.* That was the beauty of an antique fair — everybody has different tastes.

Nicole finished her tea after convincing herself that she'd enjoy herself, despite the shadow of Sarah Lester over her shoulder.

THE SHOW

*T*humping her fist against the workroom table was the closest Patricia came to violence. Just look where her friend had led her. Patricia wanted to grab Sarah's head and knock it against the nearest brick wall — *bugger its heritage listing*. Georgian bricks were as good as post-war mortar-bound bricks. She'd promised to see Sarah after the shop closed, and that had been an hour ago. The shadows stretched so long across the floor; they threatened to consume her.

Time ticked on, pushing her closer to the door, and to her friend. What on earth was she thinking? She should be preparing for her fashion show, not leaving her studio to discuss the finer intricacies of time travel.

Damn it. She had to go, she'd promised. Well, the least Sarah could do was to drive her to the show's venue. They could talk while she was prepping. *Decision made*. She heaved one last box into her arms, locked the shop, and went next door, using her keys to let herself in.

Patricia tugged on the fraying cord at the top and light flooded the apartment. The smell of abandonment clung to the rooms. This had been one area Patricia had left to the police to search, wanting nothing about her friend's disappearance to tarnish her reputation. Whilst she believed Sarah's claims of going back in time, she'd kept that information to herself. Let the police turn themselves inside out finding Sarah and her parents. Keeping Sarah's business afloat had been above and beyond anyone's call of duty, but she'd done it, and she was tired of running both Sarah's life and her own.

The newspapers had run several stories about the shop being haunted, what with all three family members disappearing in peculiar circumstances. One detective had scoffed at that, preferring his theory that Sarah's disappearance was to perpetuate the rumour of a haunting to increase visitors to the store, which everyone acknowledged was on the brink of insolvency. Or it had been, until they had hired Nicole to run it. 'A magic touch' was how Trish and Andrew had described Nicole after her first month managing the shop. Fresh stock, tidier shelves, a window display devoid of desiccated insect carcasses. Shoppers liked the concept of a cluttered antique store, but they preferred shopping somewhere more curated. And that was what Nicole had achieved.

'Sarah, Sarah, wake up.'

'No,' came the sulky reply.

Trish sat on the bed and waited. She looked around the bedroom with its grandma-style rose patterned wallpaper, and extra wide skirting boards. It was the mirror image of the upstairs to her shop, which she leased but hadn't used other than for storage. She really should develop it and utilise it better than she did; play up the faded forties glamour. She again tried rousing her friend, the one person she didn't want to be spending time with given she felt an overwhelming desire to throttle her.

'Sarah, you can't pretend the world doesn't exist. You actually have to face it. Come on, sleepy head, I'll help you think up a story for the police, but I need you to get out of bed, and help me set up for my show tomorrow night. You know more about the bloody props Nicole has packed for me than I do, and if you won't get up, I'll drag you down to the nearest police station and tell them that you're mentally unstable, and need committing. So there are your options. You either help, or I tell the police you're a nutcase and they lock you up. What's it going to be?'

Sarah rolled over to face her friend, eyes puffy from crying and lack of sleep. 'Fine, I'll help you, as long as you promise to feed me, and let me use the hot water at your place. If I have to have another cold shower, I'll march myself down to the police station, if only to use the showers at whichever mental institution they commit me to.'

'Hah, that's more like it! I've only got a short window at the museum tonight, and tomorrow will be frenetic. All the clothes are being delivered in the morning, so I need to get as much done this evening as we can. And then I promise we'll go back to mine, have showers and a curry. Yes?'

Sarah wiggled her legs out from the duvet her hair worthy of a nest for starlings, 'Yup, let's do it. It's the hot shower that swung it in your favour.'

The friends hugged, before Sarah threw on warmer clothes for the evening air.

Patricia loaded the last box into the back of the van, and slipped into the driver's seat, Sarah's hands not up to the job of steering it.

'Where are you having your show?' Sarah asked.

'At the Foundling Museum. It's perfect. Creepy, but ideal. Have you been there before?'

'No, where is it?'

'In Brunswick Square, in the city. Parking is a nightmare, but today and tomorrow we get to use their loading zone. I'm picking tonight will be completely spooky, like *Night at the Museum*, but surrounded by abandoned children.'

'Abandoned children? Orphans?' Sarah's eyes were wide in the dark, lit only by the street lamps they were hurtling past and the minimal dashboard lights in the decrepit vehicle.

'No, not orphans — abandoned children. The parents, usually mothers, would bring them to the hospital if they couldn't care for them any more. You'll see when we get there. It's not the original building, they pulled that down. This is a replacement one, but they reused loads of the interiors. Can you believe that? Anyway, it's like taking a step back in time.' Looking sideways at her friend, she added, 'So, right up your alley then!'

Sarah smiled, her eyes misting up, holding her own counsel.

They pulled up to the Foundling Museum's rear entrance, directed by the shortest Indian security guard Sarah had ever seen.

'Pull into that bay there — best to back it in, make it easier to unload. If you wait until I've locked up behind you, I can give you a hand to lift it all in,' he said.

'That would be fantastic, thank you,' Patricia enthused. 'We've got two hours to set up tonight, is that right, Ravi?'

'Yes, two hours, that's why I'll help get it inside, then I have to go back to the security office.'

The trio toiled together, Sarah to a much lesser degree, her hands still too sore to carry anything substantial, and in less than ten minutes they'd emptied the van of its contents, with the boxes stacked in a room decorated only with sideboards and towers of stacked corporate seating.

'Thanks for the help, Ravi, we'll call you when we're done. Same number?'

'Yes, same number. Can't ever change it, too many casting agents have it.' Ravi smiled at the women and gave a theatrical bow before returning to his office. It was a lonely job being the night security guard at a museum, especially one as odd as the Foundling Museum.

Although Ravi had told them to stay in the function room, Sarah wandered into the adjoining hall, leaving Patricia sorting through her labelled cartons, deciding which ones to unpack first, based on the comprehensive lists taped to the sides of each.

Sarah called out descriptions of the more interesting articles on display in the next room, 'This is heartbreaking — it's an engraved coin, a token the mother left with her baby daughter, so she could recognise her if she ever came back to claim her. It says here that the baby Charlotte Louise, renamed Ethel Maud — who on earth would choose Ethel over Charlotte for a start — died a year after being delivered to the Foundling Hospital for safe keeping. Oh, it's got the face and wings of an angel. And here's another one, but this story is even worse. This baby boy, James Allen, renamed Charles Henry, came with a thimble engraved with his parents' initials, but by the time his mother returned for him — four years later — he'd died. I don't know if I can read any more of these. My heart is dying here. Are you ready to unpack?'

'I'm laying out the boxes in order now. Just promise me you won't touch a thing! It's best if you come back in here and sit down. I don't want to get in trouble. Ravi is watching on the CCTV and probably getting a little antsy about you being in there. God knows what he'd do if he saw you disappear on screen.'

Sarah pulled up a chair and watched her friend skitter about like a nervous foal. 'Why don't you just start with the first box? Instead of figuring out whereabouts in the room they go?'

'Because I labelled everything to speed things up.'

'To be honest, it doesn't look speedy from here.'

Trish laughed her northern laugh, and carried on checking her lists, moving boxes like pawns on a chessboard.

'Can you imagine being abandoned by your parents in a place like this? Well, worse than this because this isn't even the original hospital. Did you know that two thirds of the babies left here died? Most of them would've been better off being dropped on the doorstep of the nearest church, than being left here.'

'You know, Sarah, *you're* a foundling.'

'What?'

With a deep breath, Patricia addressed the elephant in the room, Sarah's disappearance. 'Your parents abandoned you, here in England. They haven't come back, although *you* seemed to have figured it out. How many times have you been and gone now?'

Sarah examined her hands, the grazes scabbing over. She picked at the edge of a scab. Trish was right. *She'd* come back every time — but was that because it was all tied in with the Elizabeth Williams estate? Was that the key her parents didn't have? But that didn't explain how both her mother and then her father had disappeared originally. A spot of blood welled up at the corner of the scab. Fascinated, she watched the tiny ball quiver, as it decided whether to grow or coagulate. *To stay or to go.* Had her parents stayed in their new realities because their lives were that much better than their life with her? She pushed down hard on the scab; refusing to consider that possibility any further.

'Maybe it was because of Elizabeth Williams? For all I know, Dad bought stuff from her in the past. I could go through all his purchase books. That would take days, but I...' She was trying to persuade herself that her parents just hadn't found a way home. Changing the subject, she asked, 'How do you know Ravi then? You seem quite close?'

Sitting back on her heels, Trish answered, 'I met him at a martial arts course I started after that thing at Christie's. Oh shite, I completely forgot — you won't know anything about that!'

'The auction of the *katar*? Tell me everything. How much did it go for? And the candelabra? And the sampler? That all slipped my mind. I'm such an idiot. No wonder you could afford to hire an assistant. Wait, they sold, right? This girl you've got working in my shop... I have enough cash to pay her?'

Trish looked at Sarah, 'You're worried about how much you made, after everything that happened there?'

'I don't know how long I was away, only that it was long enough for you to employ someone to run *my* shop for me, but I'm also not a mind-reader, so you need to fill me in. I asked you to do that earlier today, and you threw me out. Now I'm here, helping *you* prep for *your* show, so the least you could do is tell me what happened while I was away, and then I can fill you in. How does that sound?'

'Fine. Help me lay out these glasses over here. It was a nightmare you disappearing like that, but that was nothing compared to when they auctioned that knife of yours. Do you remember that weirdo, Richard Grey? Well, during the auction it turns out he had an identical knife to yours. He was waving it around, and yelling all sorts of things about how it was his, and then...' Patricia choked up, '... and then he stabbed the poor guy who was holding yours.'

Sarah paled at the mention of the second *katar*. How had she not connected Grey with *Lord* Grey, and the pair of *katar* sin the study? Of course — the second still existed after she'd taken its mate. 'He stabbed him?'

'He didn't just stab him. I was sitting down the back with Andrew, but we could see the poor man's stomach all over the stage. I don't think I'll ever forget it for the rest of my life.'

'Oh Trish, I'm so sorry. Did he die? What happened to Grey after that?'

'They say the clerk was dead before he hit the ground. They arrested Grey, but he has some huge legal team, so he's out on bail waiting for his trial. Gives me the shivers knowing I could run into him. Anyway, they haven't sold your knife because it's part of the case against Grey. I think Christie's is washing their hands of the whole thing. Especially since you haven't been here to explain how you had it to sell in the first place. A complete debacle. The candelabra sold, and your sampler, so, yes, there *is* sufficient money to keep your business going. But Nicole's done wonders — even without that money, the shop is going great. Enough about your finances, we need to focus on mine now and get on with this lot. If you've finished with the glasses, give me a hand with unwrapping this, I want to put it right up the front here.'

Without thinking, Sarah grabbed an end of a long cylindrical parcel, helping Trish carry it to the front of the room. As they lowered it to the floor, the paper ripped, and a rolled-up skin tumbled to the ground, both girls grabbing for it at once. *Both* girls. As one, seizing hold of the tiger skin — a skin which had last seen the light of day in an old home in Salisbury, owned and loved by Elizabeth Williams.

And Ravi, who'd switched from watching them unpacking to playing an absorbing game of Candy Crush on his phone, couldn't see them on his monitor the next time he looked up. Patricia had vowed to him they'd stick to setting up in that one room; that there'd be no wandering around the museum. *Unbelievable.*

After making a note in the log that he couldn't see them, he pushed his chair back, grabbed his keys, and set off to find them. *She'd promised him.* This was exactly what happened when you did favours for friends.

THE LETTER

"We're pushing forward now. Got them on the run, you could say. What's in the papers is the truth of it. We can taste the end. It's in the air, and we're the boys who're bringing it to an end, and not too bloody soon.

We've almost every nationality flying with us now – apart from the Germans, of course. I've made so many promises to visit the families of the lads I've met – you and I will be travelling the rest of our lives. First, we'll go to India. God knows I need some warmth in my life – not to say that your arms aren't warm enough for me, far from it, but once you've slept in the barracks here on base, you'll know the meaning of cold. I'm imagining taking you on long walks through the grounds of the Taj Mahal, and through the Red Fort, and to Jaipur, the Pink City and the Amber Fort. India is a country full of colour – colour which we Brits seem to have lost, probably around the time the Romans left. Why is it that we have no colour in our psyche?

The Kiwi boys say their country is just one colour, green. Green under a long white cloud. Can you imagine that? A green, green country, unscarred by war or poverty? We could move there, my love. Start again. Sell everything, and begin with nothing tying us to home. Nothing to remind us of the past, of what this country has sacrificed.

The Australian chaps describe their country as red. Not blood red. Not the red I see marring so many here now. So many lost lives and limbs. Not the red of sorrow, but an ochre, as if the land has been slashed with a giant scythe, and the earth scuffed to give it a depth of colour, a seriousness, but mixed on the palette with adventure.

Our country was once so beautiful, but like a butterfly pinned to a board in a display case, we cannot keep that beauty from fading. Coral plucked from the reef dies before our eyes, and I fear that that is what this war has done to our country. England is fading in front of us. We could stay, and try and find that beauty again – but perhaps we should flee before we, too, fade away to nothing?

Your beauty would shine regardless of where we live but I'm scared I'll never see it again.

I'll write more tomorrow."

THE ARAB

he gavel fell down, and in the ensuing silence came a gruff 'Not Guilty'.

With those two words, his life recommenced. He clasped the hands of his colleague, and those of his solicitor. The courtroom emptied. The spectators had been few. It hadn't been a riveting case. Tax evasion wasn't the most exciting of trials, but for those involved, the verdict was as important as oxygen.

'It couldn't have been anything else, now could it?' Robert Williams uttered as the two men left the marbled halls of the Old Bailey, their heart rates back to normal.

Samer Kurdi nodded.

'My friend, I shall meet you at the theatre tonight.' Robert slapped Samer on his shoulder, before he strode off towards a waiting hackney coach. His mind was already on his next deal; the court case, an inconvenient distraction, dismissed.

Samer stood for a moment, watching his friend and business partner leave. Turning, he walked off in the other direction, ignoring calls from cab drivers touting for work.

He headed for a specific street corner where they sold a particular paper; one not found in the London City railway stations. Small change handed over, he tucked *The Crescent* under his arm and strolled towards the Temple Gardens to a solitary bench overlooking the sluggish river. Alone, he tugged at the rigid collar of his uncomfortable English suit. He'd worn it so as not to cross His Lordship; His parents had taught him not to judge only by appearances but appearances mattered here. *If every parent taught the same lesson, the world would be a happier place.* Now, he relished this moment away from the mass of humanity inhabiting the filthy streets of London. A man with a newspaper, and a minute to himself, was a fine thing.

The Crescent, A Weekly Record of Islam in England was the only newspaper he'd been able to find written for the Muslim community in England. Reading it each week made him feel that much closer to home, despite being written by a converted Englishman, 'Abdullah' Quilliam, in Liverpool.

It was all very fine; working hard, providing for a family — yet he *had* no household. No dependants, he may as well still be living under his father's opulent roof for all he had to show for his life to date.

Samer lowered the paper as his thoughts drifted like the current of the river in front of him. He considered Elizabeth, the daughter of his business partner Robert Williams. A beautiful young woman, with a mind of her own. Blessed with her father's good sense and strength of character. But could she be strong enough to marry a man from another culture and live in a country foreign to her? *Would her father give his blessing? It would never happen.*

To distract himself from these gloomy thoughts, he resumed his reading, skimming an article about the plight of illegitimate children born in Liverpool, and a brief request for ladies to join the local sewing circle, before he came upon an advertisement. A *Mussulman*, living in England, was desirous of opening correspondence to do business with *Mussulmans* in India or China, dealing in tea or spices. Intrigued, he marked the passage with the tiny silver pencil at the end of his watch chain.

He was just about to close the paper, his interest piqued by a potential new business venture, when his eye skimmed a short article about a marriage which had taken place in the mosque in Liverpool.

The author described the bride as a wealthy English lady, heir to a title, who had renounced Christianity. The column bore all the vestiges of unbridled gossip, which would one day become its own sordid industry, but it also contained a paragraph which caused him to raise his dark eyebrows. He underscored the words:

"At the close of the ceremony, the bride and her sister, both veiled, and accompanied by her husband and a second gentleman, were driven away in a waiting carriage."

THE OFFICIAL

Clifford Meredith swore under his breath and stormed out of the emptying courtroom. At the two accused, he glanced at not, his bitterness at the verdict palpable. The Crown's solicitor stumbled behind, weighed down by boxes of evidence Meredith had conjured up against Robert Williams and Samer Kurdi.

In Meredith's eyes, Williams and Kurdi were as guilty as sin and, as God was his witness, he would make it his life's mission to destroy them. *Smugglers, both of them.* Their fine clothes and posh houses couldn't disguise that they were little better than the pickpockets infesting London's streets.

Anger and exertion flushed his face. He wouldn't normally walk this far, preferring to slouch in the back of a hansom cab whenever he had to travel. Walking through the filthy roads of London was not his style. He stopped, leaning on an ornate pilaster of some building whose owner was far above Meredith's station.

Catching his breath, his eye fell upon a pair of men struggling with a heavy wooden cabinet, sunlight flashing on its panes of glass as they tried manoeuvring the piece up a flight of steps and through the generous front door. The cabinet had come from a home more suited to its size than this town house.

Amused, he watched them toiling — it never once crossed his mind to offer help. As he stood there, he saw a woman come to the door, berating the workmen in a voice that only came with money and titles. *The worst sort of sound,* he thought.

Her upper-class speech assaulted his ears.

'You men be careful with that piece, it came back from India with Lord Grey. Now get it inside before the weather turns. Incompetent sods.' With that, she vanished, leaving an equally pompous uniformed man to take control of the situation, but without lifting a finger himself.

Meredith sniffed, disgusted at the whole scene. He spied a cab coming his way and hailed it. After climbing in, he issued curt instructions to deliver him back to the Customs House. He turned his face away from the 'Big Stink', as they knew the Thames, choosing instead to cast his eye over the warehouses they were now passing. Almost all had endured his presence. For some, he'd checked their paperwork or examined their cargo; for others, he'd had their staff arrested for smuggling. Small fry compared to his most recent case. But never let it be said that he, Clifford Meredith, would allow *any* form of corruption go unpunished.

He paid the driver, omitting tip; *let him work for his money* was a mantra Meredith used every day. There'd be no handouts from him.

Meredith walked through the building as if he himself were the Comptroller of Customs, instead of being one tiny cog in the wheels of bureaucracy. As he reached his office, he passed a young woman filing shipping manifests. Barking at her, he ordered a pot of tea, before disappearing behind his desk, running his hands over the pile of folders awaiting his attention.

'Come on, girl, a man could die of thirst around here,' he called out officiously, unaware of the resemblance his tone bore to the woman he'd just seen berating her deliverymen.

Now shuffling papers around he mulled over the day's failure. *Surely it is only a matter of time before Williams and Kurdi miscalculated?* He drafted a memo for the typists, directing that all imports by Williams and Kurdi were to be stopped for full inspections. Satisfied, he leaned back in his chair, sipping the tea that the girl had delivered, his mind wandering through the various files on hand. Any of them could lead to recognition by his senior officers and promotion. They'd overlooked him too many times now. And this Williams-Kurdi file had the potential to be a nail in his career coffin. He would do anything to ensure that that didn't happen.

~

'What do you mean, they have stopped the shipment for inspection? This is the third time this month. This is ridiculous; we have customers waiting on that cargo! There are spices in the hold which will spoil in this interminable damp.'

Samer Kurdi pulled his scarf tighter around his neck, his frustration at the clerk palpable. Fussing with the scarf was the only way he could stop his hands from throttling the man. *Just doing his job, just doing his job* Kurdi repeated over and over. *It's Allah's wish* also fleetingly crossed his mind. Sometimes he feared this life away from his homeland was turning him more English than Arab. And, not for the first time, he wondered what he was doing living in this dull grey world when his home was full of faith and light. He turned his attention back to the insipid Customs clerk. 'Perhaps if I could speak to your superior, we could get this cleared up?'

'Sorry. Mister Meredith is on an audit today and not expected to return before teatime. I could schedule an appointment for him to see you tomorrow?'

Kurdi shook his head, 'No, it's clear now what the delay is. Thank you for your time.' Pivoting on his polished heel, he made his way through the throng of watersiders, officials, and traders like himself.

Hailing a carriage, he climbed in and sat dejected, frustration written all over his swarthy face, as the carriage bumped over London's cobbled streets, jarring every bone in his weary body. Fighting the establishment had left him spent. Perhaps it was time to travel home and settle down — but first he must advise Williams of this latest development, and the expected reaction filled Samer with dread.

THE SHIPMENT

*R*obert Williams sat alone at his usual table in the Savoy dining room, mulling over the news from his sister Jessica. The appalling behaviour of the younger brother to Lord Grey hadn't perturbed him, but it had rocked his sister's world, and that was the world he wanted for his daughter. So, if Jessica had deemed the match unacceptable, unacceptable it was, and he'd instructed that they call the arrangements off, leaving him with a headstrong, intelligent, unmarried daughter, who stood to inherit everything once he died. He only hoped Jessica would come through with another option before he travelled to India to secure a large government contract for the exportation of indigo dye from India to Britain. *Why on earth it can't they negotiate here, in England! Governments — no better than a local church fair committee; made up of argumentative, egotistical layabouts, with nothing more on their minds than their dinner and the date of the next hunt.*

His wealth provided access to sublime restaurants and high end hotels. He had a carriage at his disposal, full-time staff and a country manor which wasn't crumbling around his ears. One could say his life was perfect. Mostly it was, but this trouble with Customs was wearing him down, and he suspected nothing would change until they Meredith on, or moved him sideways. Put where all they allowed him to do was count lumps of coal in Newcastle, or anywhere as far from his business as possible. The man was a power-hungry nincompoop, incapable of progressing any further up the ranks because of a lack of interpersonal skills and his shambolic management style. But this lunch would put an end to problems with Clifford Meredith.

Samer strode up to the table set for three and slipped into his usual seat. An odd couple they made — Samer dark, his stubble barely kept at bay by his fine razor, eyes the colour of coffee. A total contrast to the blue eyes of his partner — Robert, who was as white as an Englishman could be, sitting on his left. But their minds were equal, making them a formidable trading partnership.

'We're expecting someone else?' Samer asked.

'Yes. At a recent dinner, I was fortunate to make the acquaintance of the Surveyor for London. Quite intriguing, our conversation. I invited him to join us for lunch today, to discuss proposed tariff changes. But... should our talk steer towards staffing issues, or the timeliness of clearances, it would be remiss not to raise the unacceptable delays at the port. What do you think?'

'Cunning, Robert, hardly transparent...'

Robert lit a cigarette, offering one to his companion. Samer shook his head, already swathed in tendrils of smoke from a dozen other tables, the bitterness of the American tobacco an astringent to his palate.

'So we've decided on the offer we'll make once I reach India, then?' Robert queried, summoning the waiter to order a second scotch while waiting for Samer's reply, and their tardy lunch guest.

'When do you leave? After Elizabeth's wedding?'

'There's been a development on that front. It's off. "Unsuitable", according to my sister. It's done now, we move on. Jessica will sort something out, so I've brought my trip forward. I leave next Tuesday on the steamer, the *Jelunga*.'

Samer pulled the crumpled newspaper advertisement from his pocket, smoothing it flat on the table between the two men.

'What's this then?' Robert asked, settling his spectacles on the bridge of his quintessential Roman nose.

'It's a business opportunity. I've been corresponding with him for some time now, and it sounds promising. If you're leaving Tuesday, I'll take a trip up north, and see if we can arrange things face-to-face instead of this tedious backwards and forwards via post. With you in India, we should be in the perfect position to act on this before anyone else...'

Alan Bullard's arrival interrupted their conversation; a man whose girth was almost as wide as the spacious corridors at the Savoy. As he took his seat, Samer and Robert stood to shake his sweaty hand.

'Mr Bullard, such a pleasure you could join us today. This is my business partner, Samer Kurdi. Samer, this is Customs Surveyor Alan Bullard, for London.'

Introductions made, the three men sat. Bullard wiped his hands, and then his face, with the linen napkin, sweating in the unfamiliar environment. His club was one of the better ones in London, but it didn't rival the opulence of the Savoy. He was under no illusion why they'd invited him to lunch. It amused him that people underestimated him because of his girth; as if being fat was synonymous with being stupid, but he was more than prepared to play their game.

'Marvellous place this,' he enthused. 'Not where a civil servant normally eats,' he joked, accepting a cigarette, allowing the hovering waiter to light it for him.

The waiter set a bowl of Tortue Claire, turtle soup, before each man. Garnished with thin slices of carrot and turnip, the consommé rich and salty. In direct contrast, the conversation was informal and jovial. The men compared childhoods, holiday spots, horse breeds and clubs. They discussed mutual acquaintances as their second course arrived; a *lobster timbale*. Bullard was more than happy with the bill of fare, making what he expected would become an oblique request for a favour that much more palatable.

By the time they reached dessert — a *pêches cardinal* with the peaches drenched in a sweet raspberry puree — Robert made his thrust. They'd moved on to discussing the problems of finding good employees who wouldn't steal from you, or who weren't as lazy as the beggars on the streets, when Robert dived in with a pointed remark about the personal vendetta of some officials; Clifford Meredith, for example.

Bullard swallowed a mouthful of of the pêches cardinal, juice trickling down his chin. He wiped his face before answering, 'Well, yes, some officers can't comprehend the workings of a business, they become blinkered by their role; which isn't a bad thing,' he replied.

'It's the nature of the job to apply the rules, but what of the impact on legitimate businesses? What of the cost of goods left rotting at wharves, prey to thieves and corrupt officials? Are we to let them run riot over our futures?' Robert countered.

The sweat had returned to Bullard's brow. He didn't mind looking the other way when importers and exporters needed a shipment expedited, or a tweak to the tariff, if the inducement was tempting enough. But the criticism of another officer, even an overzealous one, didn't sit well with him. There was a limit to his sangfroid. 'I am sure he's just doing his job. Shipments get delayed all the time. We're not responsible for *every* delay at the port. They have the same issues with lax staff everyone of us endures. The unions are developing a stranglehold down there, and it won't be long before their calls for a strike will find fertile ground. Then we'll all know about cargo rotting on the wharf. What is it you'd have me do, gentlemen? Please, be blunt, before misunderstandings ruin this fine meal.'

'I think maybe you don't understand the severity of our position. They have delayed every one of our shipments. *Every* single one. Done at the behest of Meredith, and it has financial implications for the future of our business. He has a vendetta; extracting retribution for the court case we won...'

Samer interrupted his friend, before they lost the goodwill they'd garnered over lunch, such was the power of poorly chosen words. He offered instead, 'A small word in his ear, advising that we are a legitimate business wouldn't be amiss. Perhaps he is due a rotation to a role more suitable to his *tenacity*?'

Bullard nodded at the Arab — unusually sensible, for a foreigner which made it easier for them to persuade him that he should frame any action against Meredith as a reward for Meredith's work ethic. Bullard wasn't one for causing a scene. He knew an empire was through lunches such as these.

Sensing his mistake, Robert smiled at the civil servant, 'Getting back to your club... you were saying they don't run a shoot any more? I could invite you to our next shoot at Hurlingham? You're welcome to bring your own rifles, but there will be plenty spare for you to use.'

Bullard tilted his meaty chin; this was more like it, 'I recall that they need a man in the Stationery Office to deal with the papers from the new Merchant Shipping Act. It's taking a while to settle things down, he may be just the man.'

THE TRADER

With Robert en route to India, in a first-class cabin on the uppermost deck, Samer travelled north. Apart from his business interests, the intermingling of faiths intrigued him. He envied his friend his travel and chastised himself for not travelling with him. Travel was the world's greatest broadener of the mind. There was still time. He could conclude his business here, then find a berth on the next vessel heading to India. From there... perhaps it was time to return home. His parents were elderly, and they wanted him married to continue the family line.

Liverpool's greeting was damp and lacking enthusiasm. If he'd had to have described the city in a letter, he would have described it as 'dark'. Dark streets, dark stone, dark faces. There was none of the pearlescent marble he associated with Italy, or the refined palate which was daily Parisian life; nor was it the mass of humanity which London served up, where everyone came cut from a different cloth.

After checking into the Midland Adelphi, Samer strode off to find Brougham Terrace, the site of the first mosque in England.

The curious thronged the path outside 8-10 Brougham Terrace — a writhing sea of black outside a building which glowed an ethereal white against the bleak backdrop of the rest of the street. Three dark doors contrasted with the pallor of the white stone building.

On the edge of the crowd, he asked an Englishman what the fuss was about.

'He's opening an orphanage here. For a Mussulman, he's doing extraordinary things for this city. Those poor sprites have no chance on their own, so it's good someone'll look after them,' he explained, before turning back to his own companion to carry on their discussion about Lancashire's monumental cricket score against Gloucestershire.

Samer tried peering through the crowd, impatient to see the mosque, to connect with home. To escape from his perpetual pursuit of profit.

England's watery sun split through the clouds, showering the mosque with a rare burst of light, which lit up the white building, as if the hand of Allah had blessed the building. And Samer felt in himself a peace; knowing something meant him to be here, in Liverpool, for this moment.

If only Robert could feel such tranquillity, for his time in India was the complete opposite of Samer's experience.

T he voyage from England was uneventful, the company on board as diverse as always, a smattering of officers, wives, beautiful young women like his daughter, being sent abroad for betrothal and procreation — a hotchpotch of minor titles and complex history. A handful of religious missionaries, and returning Indian royalty, aghast at the dreadful weather they'd experienced in Britain, eager to return to their sprawling homes where shadows danced behind screens scented with jasmine, and food came in a thousand different flavours.

The passage through the Suez Canal was uneventful. He much preferred this route instead of the cheaper one through the Arabian Gulf, which was still fraught with danger, regardless of what his business partner thought.

Landing ashore in Bombay, he stretched his rubbery sea legs. The caterwauling of the port assailed his ears. An abundance of different scents — sandalwood and saffron, cardamom and cloves bombarded him. Unwashed men and the world's detritus lapping at the docks, all combined into a pervasive odour, one peculiar to ports everywhere.

'Mr Williams?' asked a dark native man, dressed in a stark white *dhoti*. How the Indian people kept so clean in this teeming mess of humanity was a perpetual mystery to Robert. Dust from passing carriages covered his trousers, and sweat stained his starched collar.

'Yes.'

'I to take you to your accommodation,' the man replied, his idiomatic speech common to those educated under British rule, but raised by families who were not.

Robert settled into his carriage, his handkerchief held to his nose, vainly trying to obstruct the smell. It was a pointless exercise, and as they got under way he lowered it, his eyes drinking in the kaleidoscope of colour Bombay excelled in delivering. Such a contrast to the stark black and white of Samer's Liverpool.

'Where do you take me?' Robert asked, increasingly aware they were not travelling towards the Great Western Hotel, his preferred accommodation in the city.

The driver ignored him, intent on the road, or on purpose, Robert couldn't tell. He settled back into the leather seat, fiddling with his signet ring, the black onyx matching his mood. He called out to the driver a second time, but the driver did nothing more than spur the horse faster, causing innocent bystanders to leap from the carriage's path.

Around them, other carriages crowded the road, jostling for space with rickshaws pulled by men who looked too malnourished for such labour, yet they kept pace with his larger carriage pulled by a horse better cared for than these disposable servants of the Empire.

'We arrive,' the driver announced, swinging down from his perch, opening the door with one hand, simultaneously unbuckling the luggage from the rear of the carriage.

Warily, Robert alighted. Nothing here was familiar. He was the only European on a street laced with ribbons of red lanterns, so quintessentially oriental, one could only be in a Chinese enclave.

Robert grabbed the loose *dhoti* of his driver, he questioned him, 'Where have you brought me? This is not my hotel. You will take me to my hotel.'

The little man struggled out of Robert's grasp, leaping back onto the carriage.

'Madame Ye waits for you inside. You come to see her. She will explain,' he sang out, whipping the horse into speed, scattering the silent Chinese men loitering in the street outside the home of the oriental woman.

THE OFFICER

*W*hen Edward Grey was in the army, his world spun on a known axis. His days marked by routine, orders given, and followed. He was neither junior enough to be cannon fodder, nor senior enough to be accountable for some heinous decisions made in India during his deployment.

His father's influence had wormed its way into most aspects of his career, and he forever came across officers who'd served with his father. Most had nothing but praise for Lord Henry Grey, although they chose not to regale Edward with the legendary stories of his father's gambling. On some level, part of him knew the untold stories about his father — *probably about his womanising*, he'd thought. What man, stationed away from his family for years on end, *wasn't* above finding comfort in the arms of another? If only his father's compatriots had at least hinted to him that his father was on the slippery road to ruin, he could have done something about it. He could have taken steps to ensure he protected his family.

As it was, he sat at his father's desk ploughing through the mounting paperwork generated by his mother spending at her usual level, the horrendous arrears left by his father, and exacerbated by his brother's bad debts, which had followed him from India.

Brittle paper crackled under his angry hands, as he perused each sheet with increasing concern, every spidery figure another nail in their financial coffin.

Grey rubbed his eyes, the creases in his forehead deepening more than was right for any young man with his life ahead of him. The weight on his shoulders was not of his making, and resentment seeped from him, adding to the tense atmosphere. The door swung open as he was about to abandon all hope.

'Hello, my dear.'

A draught ruffled his paperwork and lavender scent wafted across the desk, as his mother entered, her powdered face emphasising her weariness. It seemed old age had crept up on her, adding several years all at once. Edward stood, as she walked around the panelled room, running her hand over a book, a statue, the back of a chair.

'Your father loved this room. Sometimes I think he loved it more than me...' she hesitated before correcting herself, 'No, that's not right. He *did love* this place more than me, and his things, his collections. *I* was one of the beautiful objects he collected but, unlike his other pieces, my beauty faded. I wouldn't sit on a pedestal like he desired. Especially not in India.' Bitterness tainted her words. 'I detested it there. The filth. Those women throwing themselves at any man with breath in his body, regardless of his marital status. A godless country. One season I lasted — the voyage home was the best part of my time there.' Her eyes flickering to the mountain of paperwork concealing the desktop. 'Perhaps, perhaps if I hadn't... if I hadn't returned to London, the gambling...'

Edward rushed to his mother's side, helping her to a chair by the shuttered window. Crouching at her side, he stroked her hand as empty tears made their way through the powder on her face. Twin tracks of tiredness on her papery skin.

Their family had never been one for displays of affection. He'd grown up with tutors, and rare interactions with his parents. His father rarely returned to London from his posting in India, and His mother filled her days with society lunches, charity dinners and royal balls. There'd been no time for her children. *Isn't that what nannies are for?*

'Shall I call for tea, Mother?' he asked, uncertain as to the protocol for situations such as this.

'Tea, yes, thank you.'

Edward made his way to the bell discreetly hidden on the wall behind his desk, a long strip of fabric embroidered with a repeating pattern of an artfully arranged bouquet of roses and peonies, a hundred different shades of pink, ending in an ornate brass handle, and tugged on the cord, and although no bell sounded in the study, a strident jangling rang in the kitchen.

As Edward returned to his mother, he stopped short, 'Mother, the knife?'

'No, I need nothing to eat, just a cup of tea. That should jolly me up. Sorry, you have all these troubles and here am I adding to them.'

'No, one of Father's knives is missing. Have you moved it?'

Edward rummaged around his desk for the key to the cabinet, running his hands through his hair in exasperation.

Lady Laura Grey stood up, silk skirts rustling as she leaned over the curiosity cabinet.

'You know I've never paid much attention to what was in this. I've no idea if there ever *was* another knife.'

'Mother! There's a void. There have always been two knives in it. Father had his cabinetmaker craft these cabinets for the pieces they displayed. I should know, we're still paying off his substantial bill.'

'In that case, best you ask Sutcliffe, he'll know.' Dismissing the issue from her mind, Lady Grey made another circuit of the room, appraising its contents. 'I feel this room is due for modernising. Since your father has gone, there's no need for it to stay so dreary. The fashion for Indian decor has passed, and the latest *Woman At Home* magazine says Japan is in vogue now. There was a marvellous picture of hand-painted wallpaper with stunning mountain vistas and wooden pagodas which would suit this space. Yes, I think I shall order some.'

'No, you will not, Mother.' Edward yanked at the bell cord again, venting his frustration on the embroidered fabric.

'This is my house, and if I choose to redecorate, that is my decision. I was not asking for permission.'

'It's not a case of asking for approval, Mother — I said "no" because we don't have sufficient funds to accommodate your whims. We barely have the wherewithal to fill our stomachs, let alone paper these walls. The only thing we'll be doing in here is selling off its contents. I'll arrange for that auction house to call, to appraise some of Father's things.' Edward wrenched open the door, 'For Christ's sake, we pay their bloody wages, yet they can't bother answering the damn bell.' In the empty hall, he bellowed for Sutcliffe but may as well have been yelling into St Cuthbert's Cave for all the response he got back. Looking at his mother, who'd paled at his outright admission of their poverty, he shook his head and strode off in search of one of their dwindling number of servants.

THE LORD

'Mother, if that's the woman you'll have me marry, then that is what I shall do.' Edward Grey, the young Lord Edward Grey, took his mother's feathery white hand in his, and gave it a gentle squeeze.

Lady Laura Grey smiled at her son, her lavender scent stronger here in her bedroom, where, over a lifetime, it had seeped into the furnishings, making each of them a little part of her. 'Thank you, Edward, it is such a good match. Marriage wasn't for happiness, it was for convenience and profit. And in this case, both sides profit. They gain our name, and you acquire her money.'

'When you put it like that, Mother, it sounds damn mercenary.'

'Edward, your language. You may be the head of this house now that your father has gone, but I won't have you speaking like someone from the workhouse. We have not sunk to that level. Yet.'

Although he could see his freedom was slipping away, completely out of his control, he asked, 'How soon until it's arranged?'

'I'll liaise with the aunt on the morrow. From there it will take a few weeks for things to organise, but this side of Christmas. Nothing better than to celebrate the birth of Christ with a bride by your side, and our obligations paid off.'

'So that's the agreement then? Her father pays off my father's debts?'

Lady Grey sniffed, discussing money was distasteful, and she felt tainted talking about it, but when Henry had died, he'd left behind a tangled web of debt, stemming from rampant gambling both here in London, and from his time with the East India Company.

'The arrangement works for all of us. *I would* have preferred a viscountess or a duchess, but beggars can't be choosers, and so many of such families are in similar straits to ourselves. Now, let me get ready for bed. Today has been trying — not least of all your brother's behaviour, which has left me with a headache. If he has put this marriage at risk, I will shoot him myself. Goodnight, Edward.'

Edward kissed his mother's soft forehead, closing her door behind him. He'd never imagined having this conversation with his mother. All his life he assumed he'd meet someone at a society party and, suitably chaperoned, he'd call on her several times. He'd propose, and they'd marry. He hadn't expected a great love story but hoped to at least be fond of his future wife. With only a brief glimpse, he knew Elizabeth Williams was pretty, but of her nature he knew nothing. Did money confer good character upon a person? He thought not.

Shaking himself free of his melancholy, he checked his wristlet. He was still an anomaly amongst his peers, choosing to wear his timepiece on his wrist instead of in his waistcoat, but the ease of having the time so accessible overrode whatever qualms he had about fashion. His good friend George Garstin, another officer in India, had introduced him to the leather strap Garstin's brother Arthur had designed for holding a standard pocket watch in place around the wrist. Almost all their fellow officers had ordered one, setting in motion a new trend. A quick glance at the time and he was hurrying out of the house, an appointment scheduled with one of his father's creditors. An appointment he'd put off for as long as he'd dared.

THE MARRIAGE

'What have you done? All that work, and you've thrown it away. Foolish boy, you've ruined this family.' Lady Grey raged at her youngest son.

Benjamin Grey lolled on the seat, one leg flung over the wooden arm, 'Mother, you're overreacting. How was I to know some old codger had already married the girl? He should have been taking better care of her, instead of leaving her ripe for the picking, like the last of the summer strawberries.'

'I'm told he was in the study with the other gentlemen. He'd hadn't abandoned her. You, however, plucked her from the safety of the party of the other ladies, and were attempting to defile her in the gardens before being thwarted. The shame, Benjamin, on our family. To have you hauled off the young girl like a common cad.'

'Is that the strongest word you could conjure up, Mother? *Cad?* Makes it sound deliciously evil when, in reality, she was asking for it. The tart spent the whole night making eyes at me, practically asked for it on a silver platter and I obliged her.'

'You've ruined us.' Lady Laura Grey couldn't have looked any paler if she'd applied white lead powder so popular for painting ladies' faces a century earlier.

'Hardly not, Mother. A few disgruntled peers and their chicken-skinned wives telling tales over their sherry won't ruin our name. Your illustrious eldest boy will rescue us, he always does. I'm such a disappointment to you aren't I, Mother? Isn't it a shame you're stuck with me? No matter what you do, I'll always be your son. Doesn't that just stick in your throat?' Ben Grey laughed, an ugly sound, one which made his mother's skin crawl. Lurching to his feet, he tried leaving, until Lady Grey shot out her hand, her nails digging into Benjamin's arm.

'This is the death knell for our family.' Thrusting a stark white letter into his hand, she swept from the room. She was teetering on the edge of collapse, and one more minute spent in the company of her younger son would be her undoing. She'd bemoaned her child's lack of manners; complained about his behaviour; but never had she wished him dead — until today.

The letter from Jessica Williams — spinster aunt of Elizabeth Williams, had turned Lady Grey's hands clammy, and tightened a vice around her heart. The letter stated that betrothal arrangements between her niece and Lord Grey were no longer acceptable, given the proclivities of Lord Grey's brother. Mr Robert Williams could not bring himself to agree to the marriage of his daughter into a family which condoned such conduct.

There was no elaboration of the 'proclivities' and 'unbecoming conduct' in the letter. What did Jessica Williams know that she herself was not privy to? Surely the 'Indian Issue' hadn't followed him back to England? They'd dealt with that quietly and quickly. So quietly that she herself had only just heard of it. Summoning one of the staff she had left, her housekeeper Mrs Phillips, she'd requested they make enquiries as to Benjamin Grey's activities the previous weekend. What came back chilled her to the bone.

By now, every family in the greater London area would have warned their daughters away from the Greys, their ancient title insufficient inducement to attract even the most impoverished family. It was enough to drive a woman to liquor, except for the fact she'd seen the demon drink bury her own husband, his face a tangled mess of broken veins, his extremities decaying before her eyes. She *wouldn't* go begging. There was no need to lower herself to that level. There must be a way. A Northern girl then, an only child, no brothers, and no close family in London. It would be hard, but they could achieve it. Till then they'd sell off some of their belongings. There was no shame in that, as long as no one found out...

Lady Grey rang the bell for tea to calm her nerves. She still had to tell Edward, who was off conducting some business or other. She shivered, imagining her eldest son's reaction to this latest blot by his rabid cur of a brother.

Adelaide set the tray down, arranging the milk and the sugar just so, before pouring the boiling water through a fine silver strainer, the delicate Ceylon leaves caught before they could sully the china cup. There would be no filthy reading of tea leaves in this house, as much as Adelaide wanted to know the fate of those under whose roof she lived. Lady Grey would not brook with any of that nonsense. She wouldn't even allow a children's magician at any of the galas she hosted — or *had* hosted, before money had grown tight. The good lady passed off her parsimonious behaviour as the result of her bereavement, when the household staff understood it to be much worse than that.

Lady Grey sipped her tea, watching Adelaide lay the evening's fire, tidying as she went. A sense of resolution enveloped her, burying its vengeful tentacles deep into her soul. 'Adelaide, leave that now. Send an urgent message to Gowlings, asking them to call upon me here, I need some personal legal advice. Suggest they make haste — I'd hate to change my mind, or to have someone change it for me. And bring me my writing box; I have urgent post I need to send.'

THE TICKET

'If it's good enough for our Queen and our Prime Minister, then it's good enough for me, so please just pour the tea,' Lady Laura Grey waved towards the polished silver teapot.

Her youngest son smirked, his suggestion of starting afternoon tea with a dash of gin meeting with the expected resistance of his all-too-posh mama.

Being in this house was a living hell. Forbidden to interact with any of the female staff since the nervous breakdown of one of the clueless maids, he'd initially spent his time at various *sub par* establishments, where gambling and whoring were interchangeable. He'd have frequented more salubrious premises, but no one would have him, regardless of his family name. His descent as a *persona non grata* was almost complete, he just didn't know it yet.

'Wait until your brother arrives before starting,' her Ladyship ordered, signalling the conversation was at an end by gazing out the window and sipping the fine Assam tea. Prime Minister Gladstone had once joked he loved it so much that he filled his hot water bottle with the stuff, making it the most popular of the various teas the English consumed by the boatload.

Ben Grey sat nursing a splitting headache from his debauchery the night before, with a lovely Irish lass, who was far cheaper than the other girls in the brothel. He couldn't understand why the country of birth of a girl rendered her any less desirable than another. He'd tried girls from a dozen different countries and continents. Under the sheets, and in the dark, they all performed pretty much the same way. Some were better actresses, but it bothered him not a whit whether they were black or white, fat or thin, freckled or dimpled. He fancied himself akin to a *sommelier*, or a horse breeder; you had to sample all the varieties of wine or mare to find the best match, and he had an entire world left to try.

The door opened, 'Sorry for my lateness.' Lord Edward Grey strode into the parlour, his freshly pressed trousers, and clean-shaven face the complete opposite to his younger brother's dishevelled appearance.

'The tea is fresh,' his mother offered, picking up the pot herself.

'I wasn't aware you knew enough about the mechanics of a teapot to pour, Mother,' Ben threw out.

Unfazed, Lady Grey continued pouring for her eldest son, knowing the conversation she was about to have with the younger would be far more contentious than if she knew how to pour refreshments.

'Get on with it, Mother, I've some sleep I need to catch up on, and my dearest brother is getting poorer by the minute sitting here without a wealthy bride on his arm to prop him up.'

Lady Grey handed Edward his tea and pulled herself straighter in her chosen chair — an uncomfortable ladder-backed occasional chair instead of the more gracious armchair she normally favoured. Edward had noticed at once, but kept his own counsel. Benjamin was oblivious, his eyes glassy, yawning without the common courtesy to cover his mouth.

Months of sleepless nights, mounting piles of debt, whispers behind fans, the drying up of social invitations, and Edward's broken engagement to Elizabeth Williams, had all coalesced into her pronouncement. She slid a piece of paper from the table and examined the writing in spidery black ink, before handing it to Ben. Her hands returned to stroke the pearls at her neck, lips pressed together as if one word would reverse her decision, the hardest decision she'd ever had to make.

'What's this, Mother, an invitation to a charity ball you're holding? I didn't think I'd be welcome at any of your little soirées any more?' He didn't even look at the words, using it as a fan.

'That is a cheque for a thousand pounds. In the study there's a prepaid ticket in your name, for a berth on a boat to New Zealand, and an agreement you'll sign accepting this money on the condition you *never* return to England. I've amended my will, denying you any place in this family from this day forth. Should you not accept this condition, the cheque will be void, there will be no money, and you'll leave the premises by nightfall tonight.' Lady Grey's gaze was unwavering. Her fear of Benjamin providing strength to her resolve.

Ben stared at the cheque which represented an escape from this stuffy life, constrained by a society he had no interest in being a part of. He imagined his immediate reaction would be *fuck you, I'm off.* What he didn't expect was the pain coursing through his heart. With the stroke of a fountain pen, his family were ridding themselves of him, leaving him with nothing. No legacy, no ties. Humiliated that his own mother had placed a paltry value on his life. Racehorses were worth more than he was. The ridiculously ornamental Spode tea set they were drinking out of cost as much as she'd determined him to be worth.

He shot to his feet, sweeping the tea service from the table with one arm. Chinaware flew across the room, shattering. Assam tea stained the pale rugs Lady Grey had favoured for this room. The lid of the silver teapot caught against the table's leg and twisted, impossible to repair and destined for scrap. Boiling water splashed Lady Grey's ankles. Her screams echoed through the house, sending servants scurrying, and raising eyebrows out on the street.

Edward Grey rose to restrain his brother, but Benjamin Grey stormed out, his eyes filled with a burning hate, disguising the hurt that was engulfing him. With the cheque in one hand, he slammed the door behind him.

Adelaide crept into the room, aghast at the mess which greeted her.

'Adelaide, we'll need some cool water. There's been an accident, scalding Lady Grey. Send for Doctor Thomson — she needs her burns checked. Also, call for Sutcliffe. I have further instructions for him.'

Adelaide dropped a quick curtsey to Edward, and hurried off, the delicious gossip bubbling up within her. As far as the rumour mill went, no one had a better grasp than the servants of the upper classes.

Sutcliffe appeared as if by magic, 'I'm required, sir?' he asked, ignoring the mess, as if it were a normal occurrence.

'I've booked Benjamin on the *New Zealand Government*, departing this Friday. He'll need the bags and trunks packed with his belongings. Book a room for him at the wharf. His ticket is on the desk in the study, don't forget that. Leave the rest of the paperwork there. I'll bring it with me when I come down to see him off. Thank you.'

Sutcliffe slipped out as unobtrusively as he'd entered. Adelaide had already been in with a basin of cool water, and has eased Lady Grey's slippers off, putting her bare feet into the bowl. Relief that they had dealt the Benjamin issue superseded any embarrassment she might have felt.

'It's a solution, Mother, not an easy one, but one nonetheless.'

'I'm feeling quite unwell now...'

'That's shock, Mother, you'll be fine,' Edward interrupted. He didn't have the strength for any histrionics, she had to deal with the repercussions of her decision, and he had more pressing concerns than her health. 'The thousand pounds — how did you raise that sum of money without going through me? As you're no doubt aware, given our current finances, we can't honour a cheque for a hundred pounds, let alone a thousand.'

Lady Grey shifted in her seat, water sloshing around in the basin. 'It's a loan from an acquaintance, one who is very familiar with my concerns about your brother and the damage he has done to this family.'

'And do I know this *acquaintance*?'

Colour graced the powdered cheeks of his mother, and he watched fascinated as she fiddled with her pearls — as big a tell as there could be to anyone familiar with a poor poker player about to bluff their way through a hand. 'No, you don't...'

'I hope you know what you're doing. The consequences of losing this game you're playing are huge. This house you live in? Sold. Those pearls? Sold. The life you lead? Gone.' He bent down and took her hands in his. Kissing her palms took the sting out of his words, but couldn't soothe his fears that she was leading them straight to the poorhouse.

THE WINDOW

*E*lizabeth Williams sat at her window seat. The outside world taunted her fragile state of mind. As empty as her heart and home, the garden didn't whisper of the promises of spring or the delight of summer, rather its language was that of despair. Of loneliness, and the death of joy.

Clutched in her hands was a telegram. *Is it my turn? A funny day to become a widow, a Tuesday in January.*

There were no children to tell, her greatest disappointment. No family to speak of. Just her.

Unsteadily she unfolded the paper, scanning the contents.

It fell, floating down to the plush carpet like a leaf on a summer breeze. A sob escaped, transforming into laughter as she caught her reflection in the windowpanes. *Phil is coming home on leave.* She was to expect him in a fortnight. Oh, how she must apologise to the postman for the arctic reception she'd given him when he'd delivered the telegram.

The news would be right around town now. There were no secrets here, even though the posters plastered over England reminded them not to spread rumours; *Loose Lips Sink Ships.* They could prosecute most of the women she knew for espionage, given their inability to keep a secret.

With new eyes, the beauty of the world outside became self-evident — the potential in the barren branches, the hope in the silent soil. She flung herself from the seat, dancing around the furniture renewed hope giving wings to her emotions.

Pausing at her writing desk, she ran her hands across the stain of the wood. It hummed with the vibrations of all those who'd gone before. This was her absolute favourite piece of furniture, and she'd owned some remarkable ones, many of far greater value than this old thing. But this one always connected her to the past. She could almost see her mother sitting penning notes to the vicar, replying to invitations to take tea.

As a child she'd spent hours looking for hidden treasure within the dozens of tiny drawers, the functions of which were beyond her. Many were too small to hold anything more useful than paperclips and buttons. Intrigued, she'd drive her mother crazy opening each drawer to reveal its contents.

But, for now, she pulled open the top right-hand drawer, and slipped the telegram into the void where it landed on top of a bundle of postcards with tatty edges, from places she'd never heard of before the war. Places she never wanted to hear of again. Some of which no longer existed in any substantial form, and wouldn't for years to come.

It was a pile of short missives from her husband. Short and poignant, lacking detail. *Because of Philip's haste to write them, or the rules of the War Office?* It was enough he wrote to her at every opportunity. Each postcard further proof he lived, and that he loved. That he was still hers.

She closed the drawer. The faint impression on the ornate brass handle from the warmth of her hand fading as she walked away.

THE WAR

Flying Officer Philip Williams lit a fresh cigarette from the dying embers of his previous one, carefully crushing the stubby remnant before slipping it into his pocket to salvage any precious tobacco when he next got a chance; if he got a chance. The moon illuminated the sky as if daylight had dawned — easy for flying and easy for dying.

He sat brooding in the mess, waiting for his orders, any view of the airfield hidden by heavy blackout curtains covering the flimsy glass. Although if the Germans didn't know by now where all the airfields along the English coast were, their espionage chaps weren't doing their job right.

All around him dozens of young men, cookie-cutter versions of each other, sat laughing, gambling, smoking and carrying on as if life was every bit as fun as it was before the war. Pretending that losing your friends was of no consequence, and that the possibility of dying never crossed your mind. Ignoring the prospect of ending up in a foreign land being tortured for what you didn't know. For each of them, their behaviour papered over a very real fear of passing.

Their commanding officer strode into the mess, followed by his adjutant. The men turned all business: cards disappearing;

conversations cut short. 'Gentlemen, let's begin.' For the next thirty minutes, some of England's finest young men listened to the instructions which might end their lives tonight. Philip, dashing husband of Elizabeth Williams, never stopped to consider his future; he lived for the moment — it was the only one he allowed himself.

Before the outbreak of the war, he'd been muddling along as an archaeologist, working under Walter Pengelly, studying the Palaeolithic era in Devon — not a glamorous life — but one which suited his love of everything ancient. And it had been in Devon he met the young Elizabeth Grey, who was to become his wife just as his country called him up to fight in this accursed war.

Those magical weeks — where they'd found excuses to bump into each other at every opportunity: at the shops; the races; on the walking paths along the coast — were the sunlight to tonight's darkness. Philip shook his head. He forbade any thoughts to Elizabeth into his mind - a strict personal rule. The only time he let himself dream of her, to think of her, was his weekly postcard. Like the mortar holding the bricks of their house, those postcards tied them together. With no real privacy or time alone, the five minutes he had to read her precious cards carried him through the week. Her latest, filled with the minutiae of her life, warmed him more than his fur-lined flying jacket, where the card sat deep inside his pocket.

Briefing over, the mood turned sombre as they scrambled from their chairs, making their way to their aircraft. A field full of duralumin carcasses, flying coffins for the men about to climb into them.

'Come on, Phil old man, hurry up. You're slower than my grandfather,' jibed one man.

'You're a fine one to talk — I wasn't even sure you you would make it up in the air yesterday, you were taking so long shaving. Wanted to look decent for the Jerries?' Phil joked back.

And, as easily as that, they threw a veneer of normality over the tension, each man laughing with the aircrew helping them clamber into their Spitfire's cockpit. They carried out last-minute adjustments to their seats and straps in good humour — each pilot conducting his own personal good luck routines: placing photographs; kissing of lucky charms; and moments of prayer, before the throaty roar of the Merlin engines assailed the airfield.

In the blink of an eye, a squadron of aircraft filled the sky, leaving a peculiar silence on the ground. All over the English coast, women looked up from their sewing, from reading bedtime stories to fatherless children, and uttered silent prayers for the men flying above them.

Phil sat in his throbbing aircraft, surrounded by the inkiness of night, concentrating on holding formation with his brothers. Thoughts strayed to Elizabeth as the green grass of home gave way to the choppy seas of The Channel. A memory of their last trip to Paris before the war. They'd walked for hours along cobbled streets looking for the perfect something for a corner of the house. Her pedantic nature infuriated him at times — something was not quite right, or the piece had a tiny flaw which didn't fit her vision. He'd rather they'd just sat in a café by the Seine sipping strong coffee, but she'd been adamant they needed an Empire style, burr walnut inlaid side table, with gilt ormolu mounts. *Specific requirements.* And, as the day progressed, *and* after they'd visited at least fifteen antique shops, he was ready to leave her to it. She'd been impervious to his impatience, intent on her mission — as he should be now, not reminiscing about days when he should have shown more patience. Taking his hand off the throttle, he pressed it against his breast, against her postcard. Then, dismissing Elizabeth from his mind, he turned his focus towards Germany.

THE LANDING

*T*he Spitfire landed on a vacant field and taxied. Phil thanked his lucky stars he'd been able to avoid the stand of old oaks bordering the field, despite the engine's loss of power.

Suddenly the nose of the plane dipped, and its forward momentum ceased like a garden hose being shut off.

The realisation he'd hit an 'anti invasion' hole came as his machine somersaulted and his canopy smashed into the loamy soil. The massive impact annihilated the Spitfire's elegant tail. One wing lay half attached, its leading edge ploughing the fallow field.

The once-proud tool of war, now resembled a baby bird thrust from its nest too early, lying broken on the ground.

Phil moaned, more in shock than pain. His harness holding him against the seat. Blood filled his head as he fought to release the metal clips. Burning to death in the cockpit was his greatest fear. The scent of aviation fuel mingled happily with the night breeze and the disturbed soil.

The high-pitched scream of a family of foxes punctuated the air around the plane, as if they were providing a soundtrack for his crash, mimicking his anguished cries for help as he struggled with his harness.

Barry Wentworth awoke with a jolt. His room was pitch-black — the blackout curtains were performing their role admirably.

The screaming of foxes punctuated the darkness, but their otherworldly sounds were not what had woken him. He was well-used to the sound of those vermin, killers of chickens. Thieves who stole into his coop at night, regardless of the protective measures he took. No, the noise was something foreign to the night. *Germans?*

Flannelette-clad legs emerged from under the eiderdown. Goosebumps rose on his bare arms — not from the cold, but from the real fear that they'd arrived. That Churchill was right, in all his pipe-smoking, bowtie wearing pudginess, he was right. The Germans had invaded.

Slipping feet into boots at the end of his bed, he grabbed his rifle, which stood ready propped against the wardrobe. Wentworth threw on a coat and eased open the bedroom door, stepping cautiously into the inky hallway.

He muttered his old army motto under his breath, 'Pro Patria', *For My Country*, before creeping down the stairs, remembering to duck at the bottom to avoid the low lintel. At the front door, he straightened his shoulders and disengaged the rifle's safety catch.

The foxes fell silent and Barry Wentworth paused on the front stoop, blood pounding in his ears drowning out the other sounds of the night. Straining to hear what he assumed were invading Germans, he willed himself to calm down.

A flickering light in one of his upper fields caught his eye.

'Right then, that's it, you bastards,' Wentworth whispered, striding across the gravelled drive, stones crunching under his feet, intent on doing his bit for Mother England by killing as many of the Nazi swine as God and his ammunition supply would allow.

The flickering turned out to be flames, licking the wing of a plane nestled into the barren field.

Wentworth smiled; *one downed plane is one less the Germans can use to bomb us.* His grin disappearing when the marching flames illuminated the unmistakable red, white and blue roundel, the distinctive emblem of the Royal Air Force.

Barry couldn't tell the difference between a Spitfire or a Harvard, a Bristol Freighter or a Hurricane, but the roundel was as British as his morning tea. Abandoning his rifle on the dewy field, he raced to the burning plane.

Coughing in the acrid smoke, Wentworth struggled with the external latch on the canopy, fingers useless in his panicked state. The flames threatened to ignite the remaining aviation fuel in the tanks — if that happened, neither of them would do any more fighting for King and Country. With the heavy-duty heel of his boot, he bashed at the latch several times, smoke stinging his eyes, his breath wheezy with the toxic fumes. Every kick becoming more frantic than the last.

At last! The canopy popped open. Expecting the pilot to obey the laws of gravity, it took Wentworth valuable seconds to understand that the aviator couldn't get out. The rush of adrenaline and the heat of the fire thwarting his ability to process the scene, and it took Phil's hoarse cries to jolt him back to reality.

'Bloody thing's stuck' Phil cried, tugging on the webbing.

With no knife to cut the jammed belt, Barry searched for something, anything, to cut the straps.

The firelight danced across the ground, catching on a tractor on the side of the field, an abandoned plough in the next field over, and on something embedded in the exposed earth in the anti-invasion hole he'd dug himself months earlier.

Not a knife, a buckle perhaps, Barry rationalised as he grabbed it, its jagged end the perfect tool for plunging into the webbing — anything to create a tear, a weak point in the fabric to wrench the strap apart; let the pilot to drop free of his harness.

The men scrambled from the would-be shallow grave, the conflagration singeing their hair. Only seconds later, the fire found the rest of the fuel, and celebrated with a violent explosion, sending both men headlong into the field.

The sickening snap of bone lost amidst the roar of the inferno behind them. The once proud Spitfire, all beautiful lines and powerful torque, was decaying before their eyes. There was nothing to do, other than let the fire run its destructive course. No fire brigade worked this far out, nor were there hundreds of villagers armed with wooden buckets. Only an overweight farmer and an injured pilot.

With the blaze well under way, and no means to extinguish it, Barry did what most Englishmen would do; declared it was time for a cup of tea. Helping Phil to his feet, the pilot cradling a newly broken arm, Barry introduced himself, with an awkward shake of the left hand. Common courtesy executed, they limped towards the stone farmhouse, both sure someone from the RAF would come along in due course to pick over the remains of the downed craft.

Maintaining blackout conditions seemed pointless given a plane was imitating a merry Guy Fawkes bonfire in his field, so Barry lit a lamp in his kitchen. He set the lifesaving buckle down on the table where it lay forgotten among jars of home-made jam and marmalade. As the kettle boiled on the stove, Barry pulled the light closer to have a look at both Phil and his broken arm.

'My young lad's in the Civil Defence, but in London. He's one of the night wardens there. Comes back here when he can like, but it's hard for him to get leave. He's the one who dug the hole you hit. He's lucky to get away as often as he can, given he's got such an important job. Yes, very important, my boy.' Barry sniffed. He peered at Phil's arm, poking at it with a nicotine-stained finger, 'It's a bad one, this break. I'm picking you'll be out of action at least six weeks, if not more.'

'Christ, it'd better not be that long, I'm training the Poles next week. Bloody hell, if they get old Barley to do that, we may as well surrender.'

Barry sniffed, 'Poles, eh? You letting them lot fly our planes?'

'They've lost their country, so if they want to help protect mine, they can fly every damn last one of our planes if they want.' It wasn't a polite reply to the man who'd just saved his life, but he wasn't about to let anyone insinuate that their allies were lesser men just because they weren't British.

Barry sniffed again, as he strapped a makeshift split to Phil's arm, and tightened the crudely fashioned tea towel sling he'd put round Phil's neck, their conversation at an abrupt end.

'You can kip on the settee in the front room tonight. I've only got the one bed since the Lloyds down the road needed my other one for the London kiddies they've taken in. Daft thing to do, if you ask me.'

Phil's hand tightened around his tea cup. He and Elizabeth didn't have children yet, but the War Office's decision to send children out of London into the countryside to keep them safe from the nightly bombing by the Germans, was one of its few *good* decisions. *This man was is a right piece of work.*

'I'll be back off to bed then. If you could put out the light when you're settled, I'd be much obliged. Don't want to be wasting my kerosene; rations and all.'

Phil said 'goodnight' and listened to the interminable sniffing as Barry ascended the narrow staircase.

His eyes closed, Phil savoured the strong tea and the solitude. The near-death experience replayed over and over in his mind. Quiet descended upon the house, and its natural groans and creaks surrounded him like old friends. Spying the buckle on the table, he put down his mug, and picked it up. In the flickering lamplight, the buckle looked old. Its age as curious as its corroded shape. Nothing at all like modern buckles, its pin was too long, its essence askew. The green pigmentation of its corrosion gave it an ethereal colour. *What's it made of? Bronze perhaps? Another alloy?* Regardless, it had saved his life, and he slipped it into the pocket of his drab flying overalls. He drained his now cool tea, turned down the lamp and found his way to the front room.

The settee wasn't long enough for his lanky frame, but he had neither the energy nor the strength to move an armchair closer to accommodate his legs, so he sprawled in an ungainly parody of a seductress draping herself along the edge of the couch. Despite the pain in his arm, sleep stole him away in minutes.

THE WRECK

*P*ots clanging woke him. Wincing in pain, Phil pulled himself up with his good arm, and made his way to the kitchen. The agony of his broken arm making itself well known now. Mingling with the odour of breakfast cooking, the vague scent of burning lingered, a reminder of how close he'd come to dying last night.

'You're awake then. There's bacon and eggs on the table, and tea. I've to get on with me jobs, so I'll leave you to it. Just you make sure the army gets that plane out of my field quick smart, and she'll be right.'

'The air force.'

'Sorry?'

'You said "army", but it'll be the air force who'll take the remains away.'

'Could be Adolf Hitler himself for all I care, as long as it's gone from my field.' Sniffing again, Barry left.

Phil recognised the intractability of someone whose approach to life was one of confrontation and affront. To his credit, Barry had saved his life, but sadly it was his type who made the world a very bitter place.

The divine scent of frying pork overtook the stench of burning, stirring hunger pangs in his stomach. Laid out was a farmer's size portion of fried eggs, bacon, and fire engine red tomatoes. Steam was still curling from the spout of the teapot shaped like a rooster. *A peculiar choice for a man as difficult as Mr Wentworth*, Phil thought, grasping the curly feathered tail handle to pour himself a cup.

Nothing had ever tasted so fine as that meal, although eating it one-handed proved somewhat awkward. Without an audience, Phil ate the bacon with his fingers, the use of a fork and knife beyond him this morning.

Unable to wash up, Phil left the crockery by the sink, and, with no belongings to gather up, save the unusual buckle already in his pocket, he went outside to survey his damaged plane.

A charred wreck surrounded by scorched field. Tendrils of smoke competed with tiny midges as he approached his once-proud aircraft. Upside down, its blackened belly resembled the carcass of a beached whale. Phil wondered whether it would be any use trying to recover the maps and charts from the cockpit, so climbed awkwardly into the anti-invasion hole dug by Wentworth's son. A quick glance at the now-unrecognisable wreck enough to see there was nothing left to retrieve.

He tried climbing out of the still-warm hole, only to crash down as his foot slipped on the crumbling earth. In a heap at the bottom, a vibrant green section of soil caught his attention.

Digging one-handed, the earth crumbled easily, revealing a misshapen object, similar in tone to the buckle in his pocket, but larger, sturdier. Plucking it free, he held in his palm: a small copper alloy bust of a bare-chested young man. No bigger than his hand, it was heavier than it looked. Antiquity etched on the face of the boy. Without thinking, Phil dropped it into his pocket, knowing at once that the farmer would see no value in such a trinket.

Like a bad penny, Wentworth suddenly appeared above him.

'Need some help, then? Saw you go in, and when you didn't come back up, thought I'd best check if you were okay.'

Phil wondered how long he'd been standing there — if he'd seen anything of the bust. But Wentworth's face was as clear as the skies. No suspicion lurked there, only annoyance that his field would be out of action.

'Yes, if that's OK? Seems I can't climb out with this bung arm.'

Barry hauled him out of the hole and the men stood next to the remains of the plane.

'Nothing worth saving then?'

'No. It's a lost cause down there. Not sure that the RAF would even bother with it, to be honest. Apart from making sure there's nothing the Germans can use. Mind you, there's been enough planes downed on their soil for them to scavenge if they wanted.'

Wentworth nodded.

'They wouldn't mind if I used the tractor to move it out of the way, then?'

Phil checked if Wentworth was joking. No, he was serious.

'I'd probably leave it for the RAF boys to clear it out, old chap. You never know, they could salvage something.'

Sniffing in disapproval, Wentworth ambled off muttering to himself, leaving Phil standing alone next to his plane, wondering what on earth he would do next. A rumbling met his ears. Phil looked towards the farmhouse where a military police vehicle was pulling to a stop by the front door. *The cavalry.*

THE PILOT

*P*hil Williams turned the little statue over in his hands. A beautiful example of Roman workmanship. By rights he should probably hand it over to the Museum of London, but there was something about a piece of treasure you'd found yourself. He tried to imagine the craftsman who had shaped it, and its journey to Britain. *Or was it crafted here?* If only Pitt Rivers was still around to ask. A leading light in professionalism's dawning of British archaeologists, who were now a cut above their philandering grave-robbing predecessors.

Convalescing in a military hospital was *not* quite the holiday he'd imagined. His injuries were so minor compared to those filling the surrounding beds. He shouldn't even be here, but an infection had set in. They would normally send a pilot with a compression fracture of his arm back to base on light duties, but it was amazing the damage one small microbe could inflict. So, here he was, surrounded by men who screamed in the night. Men without arms to worry about, or ears to cover when the screams got too loud, when demons came in the dark to haunt the men who feared they'd never be safe again.

As one who required minimal care, other than daily dressing changes and wound swabbing, they left him to his own devices. Philip read papers to the fellows who couldn't, all of them knowing that these barely covered the atrocities overseas, and only hinted at the losses on home shores. It seemed to the airmen and soldiers that the newspapers placated the populace, as if they were small children who needed the bosom of their mother to protect them from the truth that the bogey man was at the door.

The rest of his time he spent sitting outdoors. Never in his life had he imagined living in such surroundings. The sweeping lawns, views for miles, the peace. Cigarette butts littered the ground around the bench, from other soldiers seeking the same peace and solitude from the horrors they'd seen, but today he was alone, contemplating the statue he'd plucked from the earth. What else was there and would it still be there if he ever went back?

They had allowed him to send word to Elizabeth that he'd had a minor accident, and he was recuperating in hospital, and that she was welcome to visit at the weekend. It was now the weekend, and with every footfall on the gravel path his heart soared thinking it was her. But when he turned around, he'd see nurses, patients, harried visitors, and crying widows, until he gave up turning at every sound. It wasn't until her hand touched his shoulder, as light as a feather, that he realised she was there.

Philip pulled her to his body, breathing the happiness and freedom in her scent.

'Oh, my dear wife.'

Together they sat on the bench, Elizabeth careful to sit on the side without a sling.

'A "minor" accident then?'

'Broken arm, with an infection. The doctors are keeping me here to make sure it doesn't spread or get worse. Should be out by the end of the week, back into the classroom, but not the air.' He tucked a wayward bit of hair behind her ear, marvelling at how, despite not having seen each other in months, the same familiar ease was there, the comfort of a well suited couple.

'Thank goodness you're sitting here, on this bench with a dicky arm. I wish you had *two* broken arms, and that you didn't have to fly again in this stupid war.'

'Without our wings, we will lose this war, my love. I'm doing my part, although I'm guessing that from here it'll be in the classroom. When it's all over, I'll take you flying, and you'll feel as if you're a bird, soaring high above the land. There's nothing like it, Lizzie.'

Elizabeth harrumphed as only a wife can do. A sound imparting so much meaning, but without definition or defined form.

Clouds and sunlight made alternating shadows on their faces, shadows of things to come, when Philip's sudden cry broke the quiet, 'I almost forgot, Lizzie, look at this.' He pushed the Roman statue into Elizabeth's hands, the copper alloy cool against her skin.

'It's beautiful, Philip, just divine.' Elizabeth gazed at him, their togetherness enough for him to predict her question without it being asked.

'To be frank, my Spitfire found it, can't take any of the credit. Buried in a field. By rights I should have told the farmer what was there, but... well, I knew you'd see the beauty in it, and would appreciate it a darn sight more than he would.'

Elizabeth laughed, loud enough that the passing nurses giggled in response. 'Look at the glorious detail of his hair, those curls, just like a babe's. And this rough bit, he's off something, otherwise there would be clean lines here.'

Philip was nodding along with her monologue before interrupting, 'That's exactly what I thought. Someone took so much care in making this piece, why would one side be so coarse? It's definitely come off something. Shame I never checked for the rest. I'd love to go back and dig around — but without crash landing on it this time.'

'After we're done with this war, we will. Just promise me nothing more than a broken limb from now on.'

Elizabeth leaned into his shoulder, her felt hat crumpling under his chin, his good arm holding her to his chest. There they remained until the English sun pulled its vanishing act and the temperature dropped below comfortable.

'Time for you to go, my love. Matron will send out a search party if I'm not back by teatime; scarier than the Germans I tell you.'

Elizabeth giggled again, shivering in the country gloom.

'You think I'm joking. I've forgotten how to joke. They've sucked the life out of us here. Any banter, and they stick you in the arse with needles to dampen down moral. I kid you not.'

Philip kept a straight face while reeling off the woes of the ward, but lost control of his facial muscles at the end, his eyes crinkling in the corners. Elizabeth slapped him gently.

'You're freezing. Come on, off you go now. If I'm still here next weekend, I'll send you a card, but don't you waste any time worrying about me. I'll be as right as rain. So, when the rain hits your roof tonight, you think of me.' Pressing his hand to her heart he carried on, 'Remember, I'm always here. I always have been and I always will. Let your heart carry me, and I'll always have wings.' He finished his sentence by kissing her, throwing all of his passion into that one last moment.

THE LAST LETTER

PART TWO

THE DELIVERY

*T*he shop door opened, letting in a hint of warmth that the old double brick building seemed designed never to do. Nicole stood by her paltry fan heater, waiting to greet the day's first customer with a cheery 'hello'. The woman, however, revealed herself to be anything but.

'Is Sarah Lester in today?' asked the young woman, dressed all in black, like an undertaker's assistant.

'Sorry, no, I haven't seen her. She was in on Friday,' Nicole added.

The woman nudged a carton with the toe of her sensible pumps, 'I've another one of these outside, I'll just get it, then you can sign for them.' Not waiting for an answer, she stalked out, her black shift cinched in at the waist with an anorexic belt which, Nicole noted, had twisted at the back, to reveal a white backing, breaking up the impossibly well put-together young lady. Nicole looked down at her own tatty jeans and sneakers, and a cashmere jersey which had been machine-washed too many times for its fibres to cope with and they'd protested by pilling themselves into something akin to a crazy join-the-dot picture.

The door opened again, and the woman placed an identical carton on top of the first, and slapped a form onto the counter for Nicole's signature.

'Can you tell me what I'm signing for before I autograph this. I'm in the dark.'

The woman huffed, poking a finger at a line halfway down the page, 'It's all explained here; two cartons of goods from the Elizabeth Williams estate. Our firm was quite specific with Sarah that she was to remove all the contents from the house. However, the new owners found these in the attic. There were others left behind, too damaged to bother bringing here, so I gave them to the local charity shop. Please relay that to Miss Lester. I am parked on double yellow lines outside, so if you could sign this to say you have received them.'

Nicole did so, using a branded bank pen, of which there seemed to be a never-ending supply. They just appeared, she'd never bought a new one. Why would you, when banks spent an obscene amount of money on pointless marketing trinkets?

The woman left. *A solicitor*, Nicole decided — only a *solicitor* would be that succinct with her words and actions, and in a hurry to move on to another billable client.

She opened the hard-covered stock book, shaking her head at the antiquated system she had to work with. *Surely Sarah wouldn't mind if I implemented an electronic stock system.* Her father used one for his hotel business to track the consumables they used. *We needed it to track of all the stuff required to keep the guests happy.* She'd worked there every school holidays, in all the departments, so she knew their processes, and how transferable those systems would be to *The Old Curiosity Shop*.

Flipping through the pages of the register, she found the first entry for Elizabeth Williams, the alphanumeric numbering system marching down several pages. Again she told herself that there must be a better way. She started a new stock number, referencing it back to the original one, and opened the top carton.

A rusty blue Tilley lantern sat in a bed of old newspaper, next to a tarnished silver-toned box, probably an old cigar box, empty. Under the newspaper were an assortment of woodworking tools. Nicole piled them on the counter, counting them as she went: fourteen planes;

eight chisels; a small level; *a bow saw?* She wasn't sure about that last one, relying on hazy half-remembered details from her time at the Tamworth Castle museum, so, instead of giving it its own unique identifier, she entered it in the stock register as "Woodworking Tool", as for any other random tools she didn't recognise. *One box done. Why they'd even bothered contacting the law firm about it is bizarre.* They could have just dumped it in a rubbish bin. There was nothing of any great merit. The Stanley planes had some value. Sadly she didn't have the knowledge to recognise the darkest wooden plane in the group as an original William Madox plane from the late seventeen hundreds, so she priced it the same as the others, thirty-five pounds, instead of its true value of two hundred.

On to the second box. More layers of newsprint disintegrated in her hands, revealing ancient adverts for *Price's Regina Soap, Aspinall's Enamel* and the miraculous *Homocea* — a haemorrhoid cream, which doubled as a cure for the common head cold.

Putting the newspaper to one side, she focused on the next layer; lumpy packages, wrapped with the same crumbling paper. She unwrapped the first package; a glass — a large Victorian glass rummer — a glass for drinking fine Rhine wine. Decorated with an intricate engraved hunting scene — a man on his horse chasing the hapless fox across the countryside. Nicole twirled it round in her fingers, and then ran her fingertips along the rim and base, which was the only way to tell whether there were any chips, as the eye could easily deceive, whereas touch wouldn't. *Perfect.* Unwrapping the next package, she hoped it would be a mate to the first. She was right, *a matching pair.* Worth at least two hundred and fifty pounds on a good day, in the right auction, unless she sold them in the shop. No point sending *all* the great stuff off, otherwise you'd lose your regular customers wanting to see something special the next time they dropped in. It was a delicate balance trying to keep everyone, including the accountant, happy.

Next was a jumbled mess of porcelain thimbles — the sort you find in English Heritage shops the length and breadth of Britain. Quaint, pretty, and worthless. They fit into the same category as souvenir teaspoons, the popularity of which you'd have thought ended when the Queen Mother died but, no, they were one of the shop's most popular items. It defied belief. Thimbles and teaspoons were big sellers, probably because they cost peanuts. Searching through them, she found one marked with the Belleek black mark and set it aside for placement in a separate cabinet. She cringed as she recalled a moment of haste the previous week when she'd knocked over two Belleek trios, smashing both of the fine china cups. She hadn't told Trish, figuring that, in the scheme of things, broken cups were neither here nor there. No one would notice.

The next wrapped bundle had her frowning in confusion. *A bottle?* Hardly worth the effort of keeping, let alone wrapping up. The green glass was thick and clouded. Raised letters identified the bottle's maker as *Thomson & Co., Aerated Waters, Established 1865, Dunedin.* Shaped more like a modern bedpan than a bottle, with no flat base, it wouldn't stand up — its curved sides leaving it rocking on the counter, the clink of glass against glass echoing in the space.

Two matching meat platters depicting duck-hunting; a boxed horn-handled carvery set, with a hunting scene etched into the knife. Nicole decided that the original owner must have collected all things hunting related. And, lying flat on the bottom of the box, a framed watercolour of a church, no identifying features. Every lady of a certain ilk was prone to painting these sorts of scenes as an acceptable pastime. There was a crate of similar paintings under one table. No great call for them, but they *were* handy for prop buyers who needed something benign to fill a gap on set.

What a complete and utter waste of time. Dusting herself off, she broke down the cartons, leaving them by the back door. The only thing of any worth, the matched pair of glasses, already forgotten as she moved on to the next item on her list, polishing up some brassware she'd bought the week before. The law required her to hold all metalware for two weeks before putting it out for sale, but this stuff would be perfect to decorate Patricia's shop once the new collection arrived in store and, technically, she wasn't selling it, she was lending it out to the lady who paid her wages.

Thinking of Patricia made her pause. She hadn't spoken to her today. Since she had given her her own set of keys, she didn't expect to see Trish every morning, but it *was* weird she hadn't popped in to say how she got on with the launch. Nicole felt guilty about not helping, despite promising to. But Trish had Sarah to help her, so it had been easier to stay away. Nicole poked her head outside, the change in temperature a warm surprise. No, Patricia's shop *Blackpool Love* wasn't open yet — *not surprising* — she presumably had a million things to do today, like catching up on sleep. With the door propped open with an old iron, she reflected that she hadn't seen Sarah either, but assumed she was with Trish.

Polishing brass was not everyone's cup of tea, but she found it soothing, giving her the mental space for reflection. Her job, whilst arguably the best thing in her life, was in a state of flux, now that Sarah had returned. The love she'd followed to London was teetering on the edge of platonic friendship. And her flat wasn't quite as exciting as she'd imagined. Moving to London is meant to be one of life's great adventures. If you couldn't travel the world with only a backpack and a camera, then living in London was the next best thing. A cataclysmic crashing of humanity, hubris, culture and climate, London should have given her everything she desired. Sadly it was failing on many fronts.

She buffed harder with her polishing cloth, decades of dirt, and her own problems, vanishing under her efforts, the warm brass revealing itself like a courtesan in a Japanese bathhouse.

THE BOYFRIEND

*A*ndrew Harvard paced his small office. The halcyon days when he'd first started with Christie's, so long ago that the memory of them had faded. In the beginning he'd felt the office was the pinnacle of success for a new graduate. Now it seemed like a cell.

'Come on, Trish, pick up the phone,' he muttered.

She hadn't picked up the night before, and she wasn't answering again this morning. Today was the day of her show. He knew she was beyond busy, and planned to return his call later, but the sound of a friendly voice was what he needed. *Still no answer*.

Andrew threw himself onto his chair, which skidded across the floor, just as Jay Khosla peered in through the door.

Christie's well-regarded Senior Manager of the Indian Art Group's knowledge of Indian art was legendary. Employed by the Museum of London, Christie's had lured him, not by the offer of more money, but by the opportunity to handle the upper end of trade in Indian antiquities. Items the museum would never have had the funds to purchase. They could often find him in the bowels of the building staring at a piece the restorers were prepping for auction. It was as if he were trying to absorb by osmosis the glory of the item, its historical provenance.

'Having fun, Andrew?'

'Good morning, Jay. Sorry, chair skidded out from under me. How can I help?'

'The police have asked for the original paperwork relating to the *katar*, so I thought I'd come down, rather than email.'

A contrived excuse, Andrew thought. Jay obsessed over the latest Indian treasure to enter Christie's catalogues, or surfed auction sites around the world for a mis-catalogued treasure. He didn't wander the halls.

'I've given them everything I had.'

'No handwritten notes, or anything? Perhaps some information you noted about where the dealer got it from? Maybe in a notebook you forgot about, or something like that? Can you recall if she mentioned other pieces?'

Ah, that didn't take long. It surprised Andrew Jay hadn't quizzed him earlier about whether Sarah had any other Indian articles. The police thing was just a ruse. When it came down to it, the murder at Christie's *hadn't* been a public relations nightmare. They'd received days of free front page publicity. Even they didn't have the budget for the exposure they'd received after Grey had sliced open the clerk.

'To be honest with you, Jay, I know as much as you do. Even less, because I haven't spoken with the police since Leo died.'

Jay looked crestfallen, until Andrew brightened as he recalled something Trish had said to him a week ago, 'Wait, I've just remembered one thing — the girl working in the shop told Patricia...' and here he fumbled. Andrew wasn't sure whether telling his employers he was dating the friend of a missing person — a person linked Leo Hayward's death — was the best career move, especially with him already under the spotlight for the Textiles episode.

'The girl employed after Miss Lester went missing said that there are several cartons of goods in storage at the shop waiting for unpacking. I don't know if the police know that yet. The girl, Nicole, has been there a while now, but it's taken ages to sort through the mess Sarah left behind. Patricia and I weren't sure what to do when she disappeared, so anything which didn't have a price or stock number, we put downstairs out of the way. Seemed like the best thing to do at the time...' He trailed off, his own mind working through the implications of his actions, the potential of the stuff still in the cartons.

Jay's enthusiasm gushed like oil from a new well. 'Let's go! Let's go,' he sang.

Andrew shook his head. 'We can't just barge into the shop and ask Nicole if we can go through her basement. I should get hold of Patricia and talk it through because I'm not sure what the legal ramifications are. Should we tell the police?'

'No, not at all. Not unless there is anything worthy of their time.' Eyes shining, he rubbed his hands with glee as he pictured the treasures they might uncover. 'Imagine, uncovering Agra carpets or ivory chess sets or jade cups. We should go now.' He was hopping from one foot to the other.

'I'll give Patricia another call. She hasn't been answering this morning — she has the launch of her new line tonight, at the Foundling Museum...'

Jay interrupted, 'The Foundling Museum? Weird... that was on the news at breakfast; I wasn't listening properly so missed what happened there. But you can ring her on the way. We'll take my car.'

Dread settled in Andrew's stomach. With no choice other than to go with Jay, he prayed *The Old Curiosity Shop* was shut, Nicole off doing a house clearance, or at least helping Trish with her show set-up. He buckled himself into Jay's BMW, the leathery scent clinging to the seats, and the radio flared into life as Jay turned the key, with the tail end of the ten o'clock news bulletin.

'*... the police are calling for any sightings of an armed man seen running from the Foundling Museum last night...*'

Without thinking, Jay changed the station to one with Hindi music, filling the car with the sounds of the harmonium and a plethora of ancient stringed instruments. In a uniquely British way, Andrew started his next sentence by apologising, 'So sorry, Jay, but do you think we could just go back to that news report?'

Jay switched it back to Radio 4, where the presenter had moved on to the weather. 'Sorry, thanks, we missed it. Switch it back, if you like?'

Andrew banged out another text message to Patricia. He understood she might not pick up, surrounded by technicians, make-up artists and models, but she could take the time to reply to one of his messages he'd sent over the past twelve hours. Then his phone rang.

'Patricia!'

'Who is this?' replied an authoritative voice on the other end.

Andrew's tone changed, 'Who is *this*?'

Jay turned his head towards him at the change, nearly colliding with a lorry sneaking past them on the inside, and jerking the steering wheel back just in time.

'This is Inspector Fujimoto of the City of London Police. Who am I talking with?'

Not good. Not good at all. Covering the microphone, he whispered to Jay, 'It's the police.' Jay responded by turning the radio off, pulling into a side street and parking in an empty loading zone. Killing the engine, he motioned to Andrew to continue.

'This is Andrew Harvard.'

'Mr Harvard, we understand that you know a Miss Patricia Bolton?'

'Er, yes... I'm Patricia's... um... her boyfriend.' He felt a blush travelling up his cheeks, aware of Jay's intent gaze on him. This mixing of his private life with work was getting to be a habit.

'Mr Harvard, when was the last time to spoke with Miss Bolton?'

'I tried to call her yesterday, and this morning, so not since the day before... um, in the evening. Is she okay? Where is she? Can I talk to her?'

'That isn't possible. We haven't seen Miss Bolton since we found a dead security guard here at the museum. We're reviewing the surveillance tapes, and Miss Bolton was here with another woman...'

Andrew's heart stopped, and he interrupted, 'Nicole — Nicole Pilcher — she was helping Trish get ready for her show...'

Inspector Fujimoto barely paused for breath, 'Thank you for that. We located Miss Bolton's phone among the boxes she had been unpacking. There's a small issue with the CCTV footage, with a period of time missing. We've sent the video to our technical team but I'll need you to come in to view the footage, to identify Miss Bolton and her companion.'

'You don't think Trish had anything to do with the security guard's death do you?' Andrew's voice cracked. The thought of Trish being hurt filled him with fear. He'd been such an idiot, letting their relationship drift, not wanting to disrupt things by attempting to make it more permanent, or to even put a name to it — and now she was in trouble.

'I wouldn't like to speculate at this stage. If you could meet me at the Wood Street police station at three o'clock.'

'Thank you, yes I will.'

'One last question, Mr Harvard, what vehicle does Miss Bolton drive? We couldn't find any vehicles registered in her name.'

'She doesn't.'

'Doesn't what?'

'She doesn't drive. Well, she *can* drive, but doesn't, not unless she has to. She would have been in the van from *The Old Curiosity Shop*. So Nicole would have been driving, I guess. They had a lot of stuff to move over there for the show, props and things.'

'Right, thank you. I'll see you this afternoon.' Inspector Fujimoto rang off.

'My girlfriend is missing,' Andrew said.

Jay had already composed a long text to Don Claire, detailing verbatim the conversation Andrew was having with the policeman. He pressed 'Send'. Putting his phone down he turned his attention to Andrew. 'There's nothing we can do now, Andrew. Shall we pop along and look around there, till you have to go to the station. I'll drive and wait with you, as moral support?'

Andrew fiddled with his phone, turning it over and over, weighing up his options. If they went to the shop, it would be closed because, in theory, Nicole was wherever Trish was — or she might be there, oblivious to any issue at the museum; meaning someone else was with Trish. If he turned Jay down, he might lose his job. Should he go straight to Trish's flat? But the police would've already checked there. But then again, how would they know where her flat was? The phone company, of course. He nodded at Jay.

Jay couldn't conceal his pleasure. His childlike excitement trumped any concern regarding Andrew's missing girlfriend.

THE INVESTIGATION

*I*nspector Fujimoto pressed the rewind button on the digital player and watched the footage again, 'So you're telling me no one has tampered with this video — that this is exactly what happened? They just disappeared?'

The IT technician replied enthusiastically, 'That's right. There's no evidence of anyone tampering with these files. The guard's notation in the security log about losing sight of them is out by two minutes, but it still gives us a good frame of reference for his time of death, and their disappearance.'

Fujimoto looked on. 'You can't be serious? When we go to court, or to a judge to ask for a search warrant, or whatever, am I to say, under oath, "Your Honour, the women disappeared"? I can tell you now, that's the last thing I'll say. Take these files and run them again. I'm not an idiot, so don't play me for one. Those women didn't just vanish, any more than the guard shot himself in the back of the head.' Tapping the screen where the shadow of a person appeared at the edge of the frame by the body. 'And this image, work on that. Get me something I can use.'

The technicians hurried off, back to their computers and their coffees, to deliver the impossible once again.

Inspector Victor Fujimoto raked his slender fingers through his thinning hair. This case would be the end of him. Two missing women, one murdered night guard, and no suspects. What made it even more perplexing was that nothing was missing; nothing the Foundling Museum had identified, anyway. There was nothing of value in the museum — the tokens left by distraught mothers were worthless trinkets, not worth any burglar's time, and not worth murdering over. No, it must have had something to do with the women. His cellphone interrupted his thoughts, 'Fujimoto here... yes, that's my case... how can I help?... yes, we think we've identified one... yes, Patricia Bolton... it's possible the other woman is a worker from... hang on while I just check... ah, *The Old Curiosity Shop*... no, no I didn't know that, thank you... yes, yes I'll let you know. I have the boyfriend coming in to ID her from the video footage... yes, I'll let you know, thanks.' Ringing off, he sat looking at his phone, as if all the answers were within its intricate operating system.

'Victor? What's up?'

'Can you pull up all we have on *The Old Curiosity Shop*, an antiques place in London.'

'In the market for an invalid's cup for your advanced age, Fuji?' joked one of the uniformed staff. The office erupted in laughter.

Fujimoto stroked his thinning hair, 'That's enough of that, just pull the files. I want a photo of the woman who owns it, a Sarah Lester. The Met have a Missing Persons file open for her, and for both her parents. It's all connected.'

Silence filled the office as Victor scribbled in his notebook. Regardless of all the technological advances in the world; all the smart phones and tablets, Apple watches and 'the Cloud'; nothing beat a good old-fashioned notebook. This development could be the lead he was looking for, the reason the guard lost his life. Homicide rates in London had been plummeting, with only eighty-three recorded for the previous year which meant any new ones would guarantee maximum media coverage. If any reporter linked that murder to a 'missing persons' case, he wouldn't be able to leave headquarters without being mobbed.

'Here's a picture of Sarah Lester. Pretty for a tinker,' Corporal Sean Jones proffered a printout of Sarah's licence.

Victor gazed at the image of the woman in the printout. Lifting his eyes to his computer screen, to the frozen image of two women unrolling what looked like an animal skin. One of them was *definitely* Sarah Lester, proprietor of *The Old Curiosity Shop*; reported as missing; and wanted for questioning about a knife used in a murder for which they had arrested a man, who was currently awaiting trial. 'This is a pile of shit we've waded into,' Victor announced.

THE V&A

$\mathcal{E}$liza gazed at both samplers, laid side by side on her workroom table. The stitching was identical, as were the colours, and the style. Undoubtedly stitched by the same girl, and now they were both hers. *I won. And that bloodsucker Harvard didn't.* That was the best part.

In her mind she pictured how she might display them. In her world they needed their own exhibit, something befitting their coming together after their separation through in time.

The arrival of two police officers interrupted her musings, and she thrust her dreams away, for later.

'Mrs Broadhead?'

Flustered, Eliza fluttered her hands as she tried covering up her tapestries, as if they had caught her manufacturing methamphetamine. 'Just a moment... one minute, I'll just...' she trailed off. The officers' faces were impassive in the stark fluorescent lighting. 'Right, well, how can I help?' Wheezing, she sunk into her chair, the sheepskin rug on it enveloping her in a woollen hug.

'Mrs Broadhead, we are investigating the whereabouts of a woman who the V & A recently purchased goods from via auction—'

Eliza interrupted, 'I'm hardly able to help there, am I?' Her voice full of haughty dismissiveness.

The sergeant stepped forward, trying to make her face appear relaxed. This woman's attitude was becoming more and more common, regardless of the enquiry. *What turned the general populace against us?* A perennial question.

'Mrs Broadhead, we're just interested in the sampler you purchased from Christie's, the one by R. J. Williams. We'd like to see any paperwork that may have come with it, and to know if you've uncovered anything else about the sampler since buying it. As you may appreciate, despite being only loosely related to Miss Lester's disappearance, we have to follow all lines of enquiry.'

Mollified, Eliza heaved herself up out of her seat, and over to a historic filing cabinet, where she retrieved a folder from the drawer marked "Acquisitions", before taking a chair once more, perspiration beading on her forehead.

Clutching her jet necklace for emotional support, she opened the folder. She knew the contents by heart, but made a show of leafing through — a complete farce, when there was no benefit from such amateur theatrics. Clearing her throat, she replied, 'There's not much I can tell you. The V & A put up the funds to buy this sampler, given its superior condition. We don't have the seller's details — that just isn't the *done* thing in the auction world — although I asked one of their staff if the seller had any similar items, which they hadn't. It did not come with a provenance, annoying, but not unusual. There's nothing more I can add. I was just this minute trying to decide how the museum would display it in an upcoming exhibition, and... that's all I can offer.'

An officer peered at the sampler on the workbench, tugging at the plain calico covering the second sampler. 'This one has the same name embroidered on it — that's unusual, isn't it?' Both officers examined the samplers, the constable taking a quick photo with his phone.

'Now, that is unnecessary, and please don't touch it. I've told you everything I know about the sampler from Christie's. We had to pay a fortune for it. Daylight robbery. If *only* the country recognised the treasures they sold into private ownership. It's a travesty, and *that's* the crime you should be investigating.' Eliza slammed her folder shut.

'We can't comment on Britain's antiquities laws, but we would like to know about this second sampler. They are both by the same person, yes?' Sergeant Foster smiling as she asked, her finger resting on the second sampler, almost sending Eliza into cardiac arrest.

'Don't touch the fabric, you don't understand what damage you could do,' Eliza squealed.

Tania Foster's smile broadened, but she removed her finger, 'The other sampler, Mrs Broadhead?'

Huffing, Eliza responded, 'Fine. I had to fight for that one. *Physically* fight. Against one of those cretins from Christie's, Andrew Harvard. He's one of the worst. All gussied up in his expensive suits, swanning about the Embroidery Guild meetings and exhibitions, like a leech. Well, he didn't get his hands on this one. It was a donation to the V & A. Donated, *not purchased*. Makes such a difference. You should speak with him... about the assault.'

'Right, we'll do that, thank you. Ah, the identity of the person who donated the sampler please? I presume that's in the folder?'

Eliza disliked Sergeant Foster's false smile. Women should be on the same side, against the misogynistic men who thought they ruled the planet, and yet here was one of her 'sisters' giving her the third degree about the sampler she'd fought tooth and nail for. *Was there* no *justice?*

She reopened the file with a huff and violently leafed through the pages. Sergeant Foster smiled at the constable who was himself making a show of taking notes, adding to Eliza's discomfort.

'Here,' Eliza shoved a page of self-carbonating paper at Foster, the details of the donation almost illegible.

Sergeant Foster turned the sheet over in her hands, 'Where is the top form, with the original information on it? This one says "Copy For Donor".'

That was it, the final straw for Eliza. Throwing her hands in the air in defeat, she shrieked, 'What am I? A miracle worker? I'm not in charge of the filing. I don't keep track of the donors. Why aren't you on my side? I'm not the criminal here. Just leave. Please leave now.' Thrusting herself from her chair, she attempted to usher them from her office, her sanctuary.

Sergeant Foster planted her regulation uniform black boots firmly on the floor, 'Mrs Broadhead, you are making this much more difficult than it needs to be. If you could just give us the *legible* name of the person who gave this sampler to the museum, we'll be on our way. Or Inspector Fujimoto, the head of this investigation, will have to make enquiries with the museum director.'

Unfazed, Eliza puffed out her chest, firing her own volley. 'May I suggest you get your slant-eyed *inspector* to contact the Director. He'd be most interested to know you were in here without a warrant.'

Tania Foster's face lost her smile, replaced instead with steel, 'Mrs Broadhead, do I need to remind you that England has very strict anti-discrimination laws in place, which cover racial slurs? We will be back.' The officers left, leaving Eliza pale-faced in her office doorway, mortified at the inquisitive looks from nearby workstations.

'What are *you* all looking at?' Eliza screamed at them, before subsiding into a hacking cough, and slamming the door in their faces.

THE EVIDENCE

'Fiona, write it up on the board. Would've been nice if we'd got the file earlier from the Art Loss Register. Not that they've made any progress either.'

'Are the IT guys right, Fuji? No one tampered with it? They really *disappeared*?' Fiona Duodu couldn't keep the incredulity out of her voice.

'Of course they didn't disappear. But at the moment, the tech guys can't figure how someone manipulated the footage — they will, they just need time. Let's work out again the players in this game. Write them up, Fiona, as I call them out. We've got *Ravi Naranyan*, he's the dead night guard from the museum. Put a column next to him. *Patricia Bolton*, our fashion designer, setting up for her show; and next to her *Andrew Harvard*, boyfriend of Patricia, works at Christie's. After this it gets complicated, and links two, if not three or four other cases. My head hurts just thinking about it.' Running his fingers through his thinning hair, he thought hard about the next name. 'Put up *Albert Lester* next. Write him in a different colour, to indicate he's a missing person — a different file, but still interconnected. Right underneath him, write *Annabel Lester*. His wife. Same colour. A missing person too.' He stood frowning at the board. Pointing to the empty left-hand side, he spoke again. 'Draw a line down there, and write the name *Sarah Lester*, and next to that write *The Old Curiosity Shop*, and put lines between the shop and all three Lesters. Somehow Sarah Lester is the key. I don't know why, but it's something to do with the murder at Christie's.' Pointing to Ravi's name, he instructed Fiona to write the murdered Christie's clerk's up too, *Leo Hayward*.

Fiona paused, pen still in her hand, 'But we *know* who killed him — there was a room full of people with phones who recorded the whole thing, for posterity, to share on their Facebook pages.'

'Yes, and that's why the next one I want up is *Richard Grey*. There's a link to all of this. We just need to work it through. Let's take a break and come back to it after lunch. I want to read through these files again. Did you get the acquisition files from the V & A?'

'Still waiting. I'll chase them up.'

'Good, you do that first, then join us here when you're done. Go on everyone, get some food.'

The room emptied, leaving Victor Fujimoto staring at the whiteboard. It may as well have been in Arabic for all he could decipher what he was looking at. *What is the key? Who is the key?* 'Damn it!' The shop was the key. He circled the name in red. *Why the hell haven't we been there yet?* He threw the pen at the board, before shrugging on his coat, and stomping out, incredulous at his own blindness.

THE MEETING

*R*yan Francis sat in the austere police meeting room, surrounded by people he didn't know, and files he did. His bespoke suit was an anomaly in a room filled with cheap suits and chain store ties, loosened in response to the ineffectual air-conditioning — common to public service buildings the world over, the City of London Police room at the Guildhall no different.

'Let's begin then, shall we?' announced Inspector Victor Fujimoto, running his hands through his hair as he took the empty seat at the head of the table.

An unusual crowd sat arrayed round the table. Ryan Francis and Gemma Dance were both there representing the Art Loss Register and, by extension, Richard Grey. Detective Sergeant Owen Gibson was there, for his involvement in investigating the killing at Christie's, the one they had charged Grey with committing. The police prosecutor was there, a man dressed head to toe in various shades of grey, with a personality to match. The solicitor for Christie's was also in attendance, although clearly under the sufferance of Fujimoto, who didn't acknowledged his presence. Ryan surmised that the Inspector's superiors must have jacked this one up. Two other hangers-on filled the remaining seats. Who they were, Ryan never found out, no one introduced them, and they may as well have been mute for what they added to the discussion.

'I need everyone's cards on the table. Now isn't the time to hold anything back because it happened on someone else's patch.' Back at the board, he gestured with the red marker. 'You can see here that something links these cases.' A chorus of conflicting arguments met his sweeping statement. 'Yes, I realise it's as farfetched as you can get, but it's the only conclusion we can make. I'm not saying that Grey murdered both men, absolutely not,' he shot a warning look at one attendee who'd interrupted his presentation. *Public Relations-type*, Ryan realised, *here to minimise any potential damage to the Force's reputation.*

Fujimoto carried on, his disdain for the political game clear on his face. Running his fingers through his hair again, he waved at the folders in front of Ryan, 'Why don't you start?'

Ryan frowned, stumbling over his words. It wasn't unusual for the Art Loss Register to work with enforcement authorities, but this was the first time he'd worked with the police on an investigation involving a murder and a missing person. 'Um, well, as you're aware, Mr Grey asked us to trace the whereabouts of several items which once belonged to his family. He is a long-term client, and we have successfully located articles for him before, which Mr Grey has then acquired...'

'Is that a euphemism for "stolen"?' Fujimoto interrupted.

'Um, no I don't think so,' Ryan began, a blush gracing his cheeks. He and Gemma had theorised that Grey's luck in getting the pieces they'd identified was nothing short of miraculous and was more likely nefarious in nature.

'Go on,' Fujimoto instructed, the smile on his face nowhere near his eyes.

'The Register traced back the pair of *katar* to a minor Indian noble. What happened next is murky, but the next time they appear, and we think they're the same ones, is when they're listed on the manifest of household effects shipped from India back to London by Lord Henry Grey. And, er... from there, there's nothing more till one went up for auction during the forties, to aid the war effort. Consigned to Christie's by Mrs Elizabeth Williams and purchased…'

Here, Ryan paused, shuffling through his meticulous notes.

'Purchased by a Mrs Audrey Grey, the mother of Richard Grey. And, well I think we can all recall what happened next…'

'If you could indulge us, and for the benefit of those not as familiar with the knives as you are…' Fujimoto prodded.

Ryan glanced at his notes, 'The only other time the second *katar* comes to note is when it's offered for auction at Christie's by Miss Sarah Lester, who owns *The Old Curiosity Shop*, an antique store here in London.'

Fujimoto held up his hand, stopping him mid-sentence. 'We know from our interviews that Richard Grey attempted to purchase the *katar* pre-auction direct from Miss Lester. How he found out she had consigned it to Christie's is an aspect we're working on but, and with their help, we hope to track that through.' He nodded to the auction house's solicitor, a silent observer at the far end of the table who'd spent the entire meeting scratching on his legal pad with a pen worth more than Fujimoto earned in a month. 'What we don't know is where Miss Lester acquired the *katar*, because no one has seen her since an alleged armed robbery at the shop just before Mr Hayward's murder.' He turned toward Detective Sergeant Owen Gibson, 'Owen, any progress on at your end?'

Owen Gibson, the youngest man in the room, shook his blonde head — a head of hair more at home on an Australian beach than inside a police headquarters. 'We have a roomful of people who saw Richard Grey gut Leo Hayward. He died instantly. Grey is out on bail, despite us appealing that decision. Seems money does wonders for some…'

'Just the facts thanks, Owen. Most of us in this room agree with you on the bail thing, but we don't have time to rehash that. Go on.'

'Seems that the only person I haven't been able to interview about the knife and the period before the auction is Sarah Lester. I had some push back from her friend Patricia Bolton, whose boyfriend works for Christie's but, to be fair to her, she's doing her best to run things while Miss Lester is missing. We thought we had a lead that she may have gone to India, but there's no record of her having left the country. There's also no record of Sarah Lester's parents having left the country either. They are both listed as missing persons and have been for several years. I've got no idea what's going on. All I know is Grey killed Leo Hayward, in a room full of witnesses. And if he gets found not guilty, I may as well give up.'

'You're too young to be so cynical about our legal process, Owen,' joked Tania, her perpetual smile filling her face.

'Thanks, Owen, now's not the time to worry about Grey's eventual conviction, we'll get there. We need to focus on the death of Ravi Naranyan now. Tania, can you talk us through that, with no side commentary. Just the facts, thanks.'

'You know me too well, Fuji.'

Fujimoto smiled at his sergeant, 'The facts, Tania, go.'

'Patricia Bolton booked the Foundling Museum four months ago for the launch of her clothing collection titled, get this, *Victorian Gilt*. The assistant at *The Old Curiosity Shop*, Miss Nicole Pilcher, told us she'd helped Miss Bolton load up the shop van with articles from the antique shop they were using as props in the show. A normal arrangement, nothing unusual, but this is where things get spooky-'

Fujimoto interrupted, 'Spooky, Tania? This isn't an episode of *Doctor Who*.'

'Right, yup, sorry, moving on. This is where it gets complicated. Miss Pilcher said in her interview that Sarah Lester, whom she'd never met before, turned up out of the blue, covered in grazes, which she helped clean and dress, before Sarah disappeared next door to speak with Patricia Bolton for maybe ten minutes, before returning to the shop. Miss Pilcher and Miss Lester argued, and after Miss Pilcher left the shop that night, she didn't return to work again till the Monday morning. On the Sunday she was at the Alexandra Palace Antiques Fair. She had agreed to help Patricia Bolton set up for the fashion show, but didn't after arguing with Lester.'

Fujimoto took over, 'We have CCTV footage of Bolton and Lester arriving at the Foundling Hospital in a white van. They chatted with the security guard Ravi Naranyan for a while, before he helped them carry several cartons into the museum. We see the guard making his way back to his booth and we can see Lester and Bolton via the CCTV unpacking cartons. Lester briefly visits an adjoining room, where it seems like she was looking at the exhibits, before rejoining Bolton. Then they disappear from view. The CCTV timings differ from the note made by Naranyan about the time they vanished by a few minutes. He leaves to investigate. There's an area of the driveway where there's no camera coverage, and that's where the murder occurred.

We compared the timings with those from other cameras and this is where the techies have some concerns; there's either a problem with the camera in the exhibition room, or someone tampered with it, but Miss Bolton and Lester are in shot one minute, and vanish the next. And afterwards, someone shoots Naranyan. So where does that leave us?'

Silence overwhelmed the group; the same uncomfortable quietness a teacher faces when asking for volunteers to answer to a complicated algebra problem. There was embarrassed shuffling and clearing of throats, but no one offered any theories.

'Do you have a motive for the security guard?' Owen asked, underlining notes on his pad as he spoke.

Victor slid into his seat, running his hands across his head, as if he expected to see clumps of hair in his hands. 'We thought theft, but the museum has assured us there's nothing missing. Checks into the guard's background don't show anything of concern, so, what now?'

THE DEAL

heir handshake was short, decisive. The two men separated and walked away, no further words required, the handshake sufficient for their business. Face-to-face, whispers, handshakes. Better than email or phone. Going old school was safer now that everyone's digital communications were as secret as if someone projected them onto the side of London Bridge for everyone to read, given how much 'big brother' monitored those channels in these uncertain times.

The second man slipped into the back of the black sedan idling on the street. Of the first man, there was no sign. 'What have you got for me then?' Richard Grey asked, his hands firmly in his lap lest he sully himself by touching the other.

The shadowy man cleared his throat, raspy from a two-pack-a-day habit which fouled the air in the car, 'She's gone missing, her and her friend. The police think someone altered the CCTV footage, but can't figure out how. No suspects for the guard's murder, and the boyfriend of the other girl knows nothing. That's it.'

Steel in his voice, Grey replied, 'That's it? What do you mean *that's it*? People don't just disappear. Your source is holding out on us — or you're holding out on me?'

The other man spluttered, 'No, no, no. I'm telling you straight. Lester's gone missing. No sign of her, nothing. No credit cards, no cash withdrawals, no passport movements. She just disappeared, *poof*, like magic. Exactly like the CCTV shows.'

'You've been watching that shop for weeks now, yet you didn't see her return until she was leaving it with her friend — so how can we trust your assertion that she has vanished without a trace? Hmm?' Grey wound down his window a fraction, the smell of stale cigarette smoke too much in the confines of the car.

'She disappeared. You asked me to find out more, and I did. That's all the police know, the City lot, *and* the Met. She's disappeared. The detective working on it is thorough, he'll find her, and we'll know as soon he does.'

Grey dismissed the other man, who slunk back out to the darkness, the only sign of him the red glow of his lit cigarette.

Richard Grey pondered the developments. Seeing Sarah's face peering out at him from the front page of *The Sun* had been a jolt. He'd had other men watching *The Old Curiosity Shop* since his arrest and they'd all missed her return. *Unforgivable.* He couldn't go himself — he was under Draconian bail conditions, strict in the sense that he couldn't go near the shop, nor Christie's. His conditions didn't allow him out after dark either, but he drew the line at that. He wouldn't allow any public servant to curtail his private life, or his business dealings, many of which took place at night.

In his twisted mind, he held Sarah Lester responsible for his plight. She only needed to have sold him the *katar*. Where she'd got it was another matter. *Yes, this whole mess is her fault.* The murder of the guard at the museum was an unfortunate by-product of using subhuman intermediaries, and he washed his hands of any involvement there. That had been the other man's decision, done without his knowledge. Grey brushed off any remorse and instructed his driver to take him home. He'd started to formulate a theory but would not give voice to it until he was certain. He gazed out of the tinted windows at the neon world beyond — its garish commonness normally an affront to his refined tastes, but tonight it hinted at the impossible.

THE CHURCH

*B*ishop Daniel Shalfoon dismissed his assistant, who scurried from the room, quietly closing the door after him. It was in his best interests to do so, as the Bishop was prickly about noise. Shalfoon slid behind his desk, checked his watch, and picked up his phone. Quarter to six. He may be a powerful man but this was one call only he could make.

'Hello, Mother, how are you feeling tonight?... have you turned your heater on?... what are you having for tea?... good, good... yes, I'll pop by Thursday... I've been working on a tricky acquisition this week but it's worked out well... some loose ends remain, some pieces are still in the hands of the seller that we'll work towards getting, but very exciting... I'll tell you all about it when I bring your groceries... yes, Mother, I'll take care. Goodnight.'

With his nightly call done, he allowed himself a rare smile. Other than his mother, there was nothing he loved more than collecting treasures for the church, the only lover in his life. The Paul de Lamerie candelabra would be a feather in his cap, and finally the Archbishop would notice him. His mind wandered; when one treasure surfaced, there were usually more. And, with the right inducement, he could trace everything back to the church, and therefore claim ownership.

What he needed now was something else to chase. He opened his red leather notebook monogrammed with his initials. There he ran his eyes down the list of pieces missing from various churches and cathedrals around the world. This wasn't an exhaustive list, nor an official one, but one he'd spent years researching and listed some of the more valuable pieces; pieces whose return would garner much media attention and acclaim from his superiors. Shalfoon knew God destined him for great things — his mother had been telling him so since he was born, and he'd yet to disappoint. One of the youngest bishops ever appointed, his master plan for moving up the ecclesiastical food chain rested on his network of art dealers and auction houses delivering the right information in a timely fashion. He had a budget to draw from but a cost-effective return to the bosom of the church was more desirable.

His eyes marched down the pages, pausing over an entry with a thick black line through it (highlighting an article already recovered), but there were still far too many not crossed out. There wasn't a single completed page, yet. His finger came to rest halfway down the page, sparse in detail, it merely said *"Collection of Roman statues, missing from St Thomas's, following a German bomb strike on 10th May 1941"*.

St Thomas's hadn't kept photographic records of the articles, only typed descriptions, which could have described half a hundred Roman statues with no degree of individuality. However, within the churches archives, Shalfoon had located references to a former minister, long dead, who'd fancied himself an artist. He'd sketched various items from the church's collection; his works presented as part of the local Women's Institute show, and the proceeds donated to the orphanage.

Weeks ago now, Shalfoon had visited the premises of the old orphanage which, over time, had been a school, a war hospital, and was now the tatty headquarters of a humanitarian charity, whose asset register was as loose as their finances. He'd accessed their attic storage under the pretence of trying to locate church records for orphan reconciliation. Eighty years of accumulated detritus looked very much like a hoarder's basement; moth-eaten tapestries, worm-riddled chairs, frames void of their contents, small leather suitcases still filled with the worldly belongings of their former diminutive owners, left to decay, forgotten in the attic. And, just as he'd suspected, there was a tea chest full of things which had once graced the walls of the orphanage, including half a dozen sketches by an artistic reverend of middling talent. Slipping the pictures into a suitcase, and looking for anything else of interest, he'd thanked the hemp-wearing activists for their assistance, and took his leave.

The pen and ink drawings were competent renderings of an assortment of Roman antiquities, in varying states of repair. But to Shalfoon they were as valuable as a Rembrandt. Now he had something to work with. Hooligans looted the church in the aftermath of a German bombing raid but time was a great revealer of stolen property. The next generation was usually unaware of the original origin of family treasure, and history was littered with legal claims for restitution once something appeared on the open market, being sold off by grandsons and nephews for a quick return.

He'd removed the sketches from their cheap frames, scanned them, and had fired them out to the Art Loss Register, high end auction houses, and the like. And he'd waited. He'd found, as age advanced, sleep was harder to come by. To fill in time, he ran Google image searches for the items still in his notebook. Tonight was no different. The Google search for a *small Roman statue*, within the timeframe of the last week, took less than a second to return one hundred and fourteen new results. He scrolled through the images: *Julius Caesar — images from an exhibition at the Vatican; marble rendering of a small boy in a toga — publicity photo from the British Museum; a Roman copy of a Greek statue of Hercules — destroyed in a fire at a provincial Italian museum.* And then the fourth image, a *carved head of a Roman boy*, a young curly haired Adonis-like child, listed on the website of a London-based antique shop. Shalfoon was about to scroll down further when his finger froze above the mouse. *Adonis-like curly-haired child.* Flipping open the only folder on the immaculate desk, it fell open at the page he needed, the Roman sketches by Reverend Brian Moss. A match.

THE EMPLOYEE

*N*icole had tossed around in bed as if fighting an army of ninjas. The police had rung the night before advising of Patricia and Sarah's disappearance, and the murder of the night guard. All night she'd shivered as she lay there thinking 'What if?' *What if I'd helped Patricia set up? Why didn't I ring the police straight away to tell them that Sarah was back? Am I considered an accomplice now?* To what, she didn't know, but it terrified her, regardless.

Dawn arrived, heralded by her alarm clock, and the increased hum of traffic outside her window. She missed the call of birds at home. She'd seen no sign of bird life in London, bar the pigeons which infected every public building in the busy city. *Will this investigation send me back to Tamworth? God, I hope not.* Time would reveal everything when the police arrived for a ten o'clock appointment. Stumbling out of bed, eyes puffy from lack of sleep, her hair a tangled mess, she forwent breakfast in exchange for a long bath to prepare herself mentally for the day ahead.

A coffee in hand, she unlocked the shop. She normally stayed away from newspapers and online news sites; they only made you miserable, but as soon as the police rang, she'd gone online, pulling up anything she could find on the murder at the Foundling

Hospital. Once she'd unlocked the door, she crept upstairs, calling out Sarah's name in the hope of an answer. She'd done a quick circuit of the rooms — not much to look at apart from a pile of filthy clothes on the floor, and the usual detritus any woman accumulates on her own. She should know, she was now single herself — not that she'd dwell on the fact that she'd uprooted her entire life for the pathetic loser who couldn't comprehend what commitment meant, even after he'd had it tattooed on his arm. After that, she'd trawled through the various news pages till she found she was rereading the same cut-and-paste paragraphs. Journalists were as useful as her ex.

While she waited, she toyed with tidying another shelf, but didn't want to get dirty. She hoped no one bothered coming in today — she didn't want them to see her talking to the police in case they got the wrong end of the stick. This new development would catapult *The Old Curiosity Shop* straight back into the headlines, once they released Sarah's name, and Patricia's, she supposed. So, instead, she wiggled closer to the fan heater, trying to soak up what little heat it put out waiting for the police to arrive.

One of the first things Nicole had done once she'd accepted the role at the shop, was to set up a basic website. Using free software on her laptop, luckily the domain name "The Old Curiosity Shop" was still available. Snapping it up quick smart, she threw together a home page, and read up on how to add a shopping cart to the site. Nothing was ever easy, but a dash of online help, and trial and error had seen her finally create a shopping cart that worked, and then the world was her online oyster.

She'd started out by loading a dozen odd things a week — the more eclectic pieces she'd found in the shop, and there were plenty of those. Each auction started at the ticket price, leaving no opportunity for haggling — a nice respite from her normal customers. Some asked for discounts of up to fifty percent. It may have been their culture, but she still considered it the height of rudeness for people to try it on. Usually if a customer asked for her best price, she'd knock ten percent off, making them both happy. For her regulars — the collectors and the other dealers, something between fifteen to twenty percent was standard — but only if they asked. Most of the time she kept people happy by rounding the price down to the nearest pound — one way of keeping regular customers happy and ensuring the likely return of new patrons.

This week she'd uncovered a trove of what looked like replica Roman statues in one of the unlabelled cartons downstairs. This wasn't her area of expertise, but she doubted that any antique dealer would have left a carton of genuine Roman antiquities in storage. They would've sold like hotcakes if they were legitimate. As it was, the ones she'd listed had already had over a thousand views. She'd watched with utter amazement as the clicks kept coming through, and the bids kept climbing.

Nicole closed her laptop, knowing that watching the auction wouldn't make them climb higher any faster, nor would it make the police arrive any sooner.

THE POLICE

'Here's the warrant. Search this place from top to bottom. The insides of books, the basement and any cavity you find. I want all stock records brought back here, and I want you to go through every one of them. *Where* did that knife came from? The Lester's are the key to this, and whoever sold them the knife. Grey is giving an Oscar-winning performance of being a mute, and I can't touch him till the trial, bastard.' He carried on, a sneer on his face, 'The judge *graciously* signed a second warrant prepared for the shop next door, Bolton's clothing shop. Search that too. Let's go.' Victor Fujimoto shooed his team out, the way you would a gaggle of geese. He was about to rake his hair with his fingers, before vanity reminded him this habit was contributing to his premature hair loss, and reached instead for his cold coffee, its temperature not even registering in his crowded mind.

Turning back to the whiteboard, his eyes traced the lines connecting the players together. It galled him that they hadn't searched *The Old Curiosity Shop* before. They'd had probable cause: three missing people; a murder using an object owned by the proprietor. He'd uncovered a file note from months ago where Patricia Bolton had reported gunshots at the shop, but with nothing stolen, and no one found on the premises, they had taken no further action. A giant disaster they would rectify today.

Fiona Duodu nosed the car into the empty loading zone behind the shops — an unmarked car which screamed 'police' to those who needed to know. A uniformed policeman, barely old enough for the job, opened the back door. 'They're waiting for you, Sir,' he mumbled, every word carefully chosen in case he messed things up on his first ever search warrant.

Fuji smiled at him, remembering his first days on the job where he was even more cowed by the experienced officers around him. 'Thanks. Shut it and lock it now; don't want to let anyone slip in while we're all busy somewhere else.' He moved through like a tidal wave, with Fiona trailing in his wake. The sheer scale of the task ahead daunted her, and *she* wasn't even going to be doing the searching, just the exhibits register, and that scared her.

Nicole stood defiantly behind the desk, the warrant clutched in her hands, eyes wide at the number of police who filled every inch of aisle space in the cluttered shop.

'Miss Pilcher?' Fujimoto offered his hand to the apprehensive woman. 'Inspector Victor Fujimoto. I presume you've had the search warrant explained? You need not stay and you're welcome to leave any time. You're not being detained. Was that made clear?'

Nicole made a show of reading the warrant before looking at the inspector. 'Can I wait here, or should I go upstairs? It's just that, well, upstairs is Sarah's flat, and I'd feel uncomfortable waiting there. Should I ring anyone?'

Fuji shook his head, 'We're looking for anything to help find Miss Lester and Miss Bolton. I know they've interviewed you already, and I've read over the transcripts, but have you thought of any additional information which might be useful?'

Nicole shook her head. *This dream job is turning into a nightmare.* Maybe she should return to her uncle's hotel, to serve wealthy Germans and new-money Russians. What a thought. 'I could find all the stock books since your warrant mentions them. Would that help?'

Fuji looked to Fiona, who replied for him, 'That would be fabulous.

I'll come with you till anyone finds anything. They'll give me a yell when they need me.'

Nicole smiled at the warmth in Fiona's voice. 'The most recent ones are here.'

Fuji left them to it, Nicole grateful to do something to calm her anxiety, and Fiona in her element surrounded by tangible files, figures and words — her area of expertise. He wandered around the shop, pick up random Shelley vases, and tapping the unmoving hands of a barometer stuck on "Change". This was a whole different world, and he wondered how many of these treasures were languishing on a list of stolen articles. A small Roman statue caught his eye. The weight of it surprised him. Surely this piece belonged in a museum instead of in a shop, destined for a private collection, where people like him, public servants, would never get to see it again. He turned to ask Nicole, but she'd disappeared with Fiona, leaving a stack of stock books on the counter, waiting for someone to log them as evidence.

Fuji left the statue there, content to ask about it later, and turned his attention to another officer with a query.

A small knot of bystanders had gathered outside, drawn by the police cars and the flurry of simultaneous activity between the two shops. Standing amongst them, a priest, listening to the excited mumblings of those around him. They gave no consideration to the priest's nimble fingers dancing over the screen of his phone. Message sent, he left them to their voyeurism.

Fuji wandered through Sarah's flat, taking in the plethora of reference books bending the shelves of the wall-length bookcase in the lounge. *Derby Porcelain, Staffordshire Portrait Figures, Coalport, Shaker Furniture, Antique Golf Collectibles*. The list was endless, and they all looked well-used, held together with tape, or elastic bands. The flat was noticeably devoid of antiques, as if the owner wanted nothing to do with them in her private life. It wasn't luxurious; spartan would be a better word to describe it. He poked his head into her bedroom. Once you'd searched one millennial's flat, you could almost predict what would be in all the others. Piles of dirty laundry, half-read novels by the bed, an overabundance of scented toiletries of dubious age.

What you *didn't* normally find were nuggets of gold, and one-hundred-and-fifty-year-old letters.

With the letter bagged up and sealed for safety, the nugget lay in its own sequentially numbered bag.

'The boys thought it best we didn't leave this lying around for someone to nick,' Fiona informed him, writing it up in the exhibits register.

Fuji turned the bag over. This was worth more than his annual salary. It was crazy, but he'd attended more than his fair share of armed robberies where gold was all the criminals had been after, given the sky rocketing gold price. 'Why'd she have this next to her bed?' he said.

'You think *that's* weird, look at this stuff. She must be into reenactments or something. One time up at Vindolanda, this busload of Italians turned up, dressed to the nines in Roman centurion costumes. Amazing, but bizarre at the same time.'

'What were you doing there?' Fuji asked, sensing a side of his colleague he'd never seen before.

'I did a year of archaeology before quitting to do this, but quitting was the biggest mistake of my life,' Fiona laughed.

'Come look at this statue downstairs then. Looks like the real deal,' Fuji offered, slipping the nugget into the evidence box.

'Just need a minute,' Fiona called out. 'I've left Nicole downstairs pulling out the rest of the stock books, so I'll examine those, then come see your little statue.'

Fujimoto nodded, already moving on.

Nicole Pilcher locked the door behind the last apologetic police officer. Exhaling for what felt like the first time that day, she sunk onto the tatty stool, and waited for her hands to stop shaking. Her gaze travelled around the shop. It didn't look too disturbed from the inspection by the police. They'd done a half decent job of tidying as they searched, although they'd still broken a couple of large cake plates, but that was no worse than what she normally broke. There'd been assurances they'd pay for the damage, but she didn't hold out much hope of that. What was worse was they hadn't allowed a single customer in all day, so her sales total was zero.

It was bizarre how guilty she'd felt as the police searched the shop and Sarah's apartment, as if she herself had been complicit in Sarah and Patricia's disappearance and the murder of the museum guard. She'd helped the policewoman pack up dozens of stock book, written in a variety of hands. Some were overly verbose in their descriptions, but most were just one line saying "Chinaware", or "Wooden Articles", which could have covered anything from a Māori feather box, to the Ark of the Covenant. *Good luck to the lucky sod who gets tasked with reading those.*

Her mouth parched, and with the shop's meagre coffee supply depleted by the police, she slipped upstairs, thinking she might find something in Sarah's kitchen. Up here was a different story. The place looked like a tornado had hit. Books pulled from shelves, the couch, devoid of its cushions, squatted in the middle of the lounge. Jaw clenched, she walked into the kitchen which only made the situation worse. She grimaced at the mess which confronted her. *Jesus.* Every cupboard emptied, leaving tins of baked beans tangled with half-empty packets of pasta and store brand rice crackers. A roll of paper towels had unravelled from its cardboard and lay stranded on the floor. Someone had tipped the cutlery drawer into the sink — the miasma of mismatched bone-handled knives and odd forks, coffee spoons and ancient bottle openers given no more consideration than a beggar on the street.

Pushing up her sleeves, she started tidying up, huffing as she went. This was the last thing she wanted to do, but she couldn't have Sarah coming back and thinking she had made the mess. She wouldn't have liked to have come home to a flat which looked like someone had robbed it and doubted Sarah would either.

After the kitchen, she returned to the lounge and started re-homing the books. For a woman who owned an antique shop, there was little of value in Sarah's flat — a classic railway clock on the wall, a brass stand in the shape of an umbrella which used to contain an assortment of old walking sticks. The sticks now strewn in a corner. One looked like a sterling silver top once adorned it, now missing, crudely wrenched off. She hoped it wasn't the police who'd stooped to nicking it. But, apart from those few pieces, it was similar to her own place — lifeless. It wasn't a home without someone to share it with — a cat, a partner, a friend. But Sarah had nothing, and no one to share her life, and her flat reflected that.

Without prying too much into the detritus of Sarah's life, Nicole poured herself a glass of water, and perused the titles she'd replaced on the bookshelves. Life never worked out the way you wanted. There was no large diamond ring on her finger she'd expected to have by now. Not even a small diamond. All she had was an empty flat since the love her former boyfriend had promised her disappeared, like Sarah and Patricia. *Maybe it's me?* At this rate, she could continue running the shop and keep the profits. *Tempting.* She tumbled the idea over in her mind, then remembered Patricia's boyfriend Andrew. He knew she was here. Suddenly, being in Sarah's personal space made her uncomfortable. She may not have had any customers, but her Internet sales wouldn't let her down, they'd all be closing soon, including the auction for the Roman statue.

Back downstairs, she fired up her computer, checking on the bids, oblivious to the man outside her window, peering in through the newly cleaned shelves.

THE BUYER

*S*halfoon checked his watch. The online auction for the little Roman statue was due to end in fifteen minutes, well after the closing hours printed on the shop window. *Is it acceptable to knock on the door as soon as the auction finishes? The girl in the shop might be keen enough to complete at least one sale.* He'd watched all day, albeit from a distance, and knew no one had been inside, which meant there'd been no sales. He wasn't familiar with why the police were today – his only concern was that it didn't involve his statue.

And there, as the minute hand swept past the twelve, the auction finished. The price was of no consequence. He'd placed the highest bid to ensure no one else could spirit it away, again. Once he had the authorities involved, the statue would return to the church, at no cost, and with much media interest.

He checked through the window again. The girl was immersed in her laptop. Given the appalling state inside, she should tidy up, but that was none of his business. If he'd known the shop was usually that cluttered, he'd have been even more distressed.

He was about to knock, but hesitated as another car rolled to a stop outside, its windows covered with that dark film favoured by unsavoury types the world over. He felt self-conscious loitering on the street in his work clothes, his clerical collar a white beacon in the fading light. Shaking himself free of his dreams of plaudits, he hurried off, throwing a glance back towards the idling car, before being swallowed up by the crowd of workers eager to return home for mediocre dinners in front of their flat-screen televisions.

THE SAMPLER

'*I*'ve finally got that old biddy to give us the details of the donor of the other sampler. The one which matched the sampler Sarah Lester put up for auction.' Tania Foster bounced on her feet, a smile filling her face.

'Not sure how you think it will help...' Fuji said, before Tania interrupted, spluttering out her words in her haste to reveal her thoughts. Fuji held up a hand. 'But, as I was about to say, you've followed this through, so tell me what you've got.'

'The original sampler, the one from Lester, we don't have a *provenance* for that. But this second one, the one the experts say the same person did, does finally have a *provenance*...'

'You enjoy saying that word, don't you?' Fuji interrupted, his eyes crinkling at his own joke.

'Stop it, Fuji, this is serious. The second one came from a woman who took it from her own wall at home. She's a spinster...'

'God, do woman even call themselves that any more?' Fiona said, nursing a coffee at the other desk.

'This one does. Now, can you two stop interrupting me?' Tania's smile faltered a little as she rechecked her notes. After a quick scan her smile returned, 'So, she took it off the wall where it's been hanging all her life. She was born in the house, and *her* mother, who's dead now, of course, told her that one of her ancestor's, some great-great-something grandmother had embroidered it when she was small.' She slapped her notebook shut, with a finality Fuji was about to question.

'Right, so we have a piece of fabric embroidered by an unknown grandmother which matches another piece of fabric an antique dealer sent off to auction, prior to disappearing, then reappearing, before she disappeared again, after somehow being connected with, not just one, but two, murders. And that helps us how?' Fuji's hair stood on end, as his hands raked through it. This case would leave him with no hair by the end, he was sure.

'No, I've got all the names. The donor, her mother, and all the grandmothers' names. Maiden and *married* names. Fortunately, the donor is a genealogy freak...'

'A spinster *and* a freak. There's not enough coffee here to process this.' Fiona threw over her shoulder as she loafed off to the canteen.

'I give up.' Tania sat down, stroking her notebook, as if reassuring it that she believed it.

'Keep talking us through it, I'll draw up the links. I think we're all frustrated here. Start with the donor.' Fuji walked over to the cluttered board. They had added nothing new in the past few days, and his whole stance explained his feelings about the case.

'The donor is Miss Barbara Woodly. That's her maiden name. She's never married, and she's in her late eighties now, and she donated the sampler because she'd got no family to leave it to, and wanted it to go to a good home instead of the tip when she finally dies. She worried that whoever came in to tidy up her estate wouldn't realise its age...'

'Uh huh,' Fuji jotted it up, his back to her, wincing at the extraneous information coming his way. Tania was a talker, but she had a way with witnesses, so it was something he put up with. It just took her such a long time to impart the critical pieces of intelligence.

'Right then, her mother, who's dead, died in nineteen seventy-five. Well, her married name was Kathleen Woodly, maiden name York. *Her* mother's married name was Betsy York, maiden name Williams,

Rebecca Jane Williams. But everyone called her Betsy. She showed me her family photos, and they're all labelled Betsy, but the birth certificates are all for Rebecca Williams. Initially I thought that's *our* R. J. Williams, but the dates don't work. But she had this whole chart tracking back the paternal side of the family, and, if you go back about five or six great-grandfathers, there was another R. J. Williams — also Rebecca Jane Williams — *that's* the R. J. Williams who embroidered the sampler. Anyway, the census records her occupation as "Companion". It's amazing the information she had in her files. She'd make a great investigator!' Triumphantly she closed her notebook again, her smile the brightest thing in the room.

Fujimoto had stopped writing the names up on the board as soon as he realised there wasn't enough wall space, let alone whiteboard, for the sampler's family tree. Massaging his temples, leaving black marker smears, he finally asked, 'Tania, it's great that you followed this through, but I just can't see how this helps us? I'm looking at the names and can't see any link?'

'Oh... oh, hang on,' she flipped open her notebook, eyes scanning at supersonic speed. 'The census says Rebecca Jane Williams was a "companion". I didn't know who she was a companion for, but then Barbara showed me a super old bible, with an inscription in it — wait for it, you'll love this...'

Fuji sat down, resigned to Tania stringing it out — it was just her way.

'The inscription said, *"Dear Betsy, in appreciation of your companionship. Kindest regards, Edith Grey, Grey Manor, Grosvenor Square."* See! Grey — Edith Grey. Related to *Richard* Grey by some great-great-great-grandmother, I don't know how many greats, but a ton of them.'

'This is weirder and weirder. I don't even know *how* this fits with everything that's happened. Has anyone told Grey about his ancestor's samplers?'

Tania smiled, 'Why would we tell him when he's about to go to jail for murder.'

Fujimoto circled the names Edith and Richard Grey with a red marker, linking them with a snaking red line.

'I'd be interested to see what happens *after* we tell him. Let's play with this.'

Fiona put her hand up, waving it around like a schoolgirl, 'Let me, I'll notify him,' she winked at Tania.

'You can inform his solicitor, but monitor his phone calls from the moment you do. I realise Grey's on a curfew, or whatever bail conditions he's on, but I want actual eyes on him. What will he do with this information? He's already killed one man over a knife, and not for financial reasons, which is what worries me.'

Instructions given, the room hummed with activity, phone calls, computers, the whirr of printers, and excited conversations all competed for precedence. Fuji could feel his pressure headache receding for the first time in weeks as he recognised that this insignificant scrap of old information was the key. Yes, it all linked back to that damn shop, but the link to Grey was the breakthrough he'd hoped for.

THE SOLICITOR

*G*rey's solicitor wasted no time in ringing his client to arrange a meeting to discuss the latest information in what was turning out to be the weirdest case he'd ever had.

'Richard, we need to meet... this afternoon... the police have been in touch regarding a new piece of evidence... no, I won't go into it over the phone... no, it's not an attempt to bill you for extra hours. I can guarantee you that the bill for your defence will be enough to make me comfortable for quite some time — one more billable hour is neither here nor there for me... yes, three o'clock works, I'll see you then.'

Grimacing, he ended the call. Thank goodness his client couldn't see his face now. Richard Grey was a difficult creature to work for, and, as his solicitor, he should believe his client innocent, but he doubted any legal team on the planet could exonerate a man recorded by three dozen smartphones disembowelling another man on the stage of the most venerable auction house in the world. He regretted not retiring to Jamaica the previous year. A doctor friend of his was selling his private general practice on the island, and was looking for a business partner to help run a low-key tourism adventure, more a tax write-off than an actual business, but he'd been keen. Like a fool, he's asked for another year before he committed to the venture. One more year of billing his clients an obscene amount of money for the privilege of being represented by one of the most successful solicitors in the country.

He prepared himself for the afternoon's pain which was his meeting with Grey. The time passed too fast.

In Grey's apartment, the Thames was the dominant feature where every room had an uninterrupted view of the river full of life: boats; canoes; birds; and even marine life, much to the surprise of Londoners. The never-ending stream of locals and visitors alike, pouring over bridges, and along the refurbished waterfront parades reminded him of ant colonies left to run unchecked in a confined space.

Grey intruded on his reverie, 'You've interrupted my afternoon, and you are no doubt billing me for this time, regardless of what you say, so perhaps we could get onto it. I won't be able to afford the view you're enjoying much longer, given what you charge.'

Chastised, the solicitor took an uncomfortable seat at the dining table, turning his back on the window, he withdrew his meticulously prepared notes from his briefcase, and laid out coloured printouts of the two samplers.

'I received a call from the police this morning...'

'Yes, we've already established that. Move on.'

The solicitor cleared his throat, shuffling his papers into straight piles before he continued. Grey liked to think he was menacing, instilling the fear of God into everyone he met, but he wasn't any different from every other descendant of the upper class — he suffered from an overdeveloped sense of self-importance in a world which had moved on from revering someone because of their family name. There were much scarier people in England than Richard Grey. He should know, he'd helped defend many of them.

'While investigating your antique dealer's disappearance...'

'*Not* mine, but please don't let the facts get in the way of a good story.'

'While investigating Sarah Lester's disappearance, the proprietor of *The Old Curiosity Shop*, the police followed the trail of the articles she sent to Christie's…'

'Wait. There were *other* items? Other than the *katar*?'

'Yes.'

Grey swore, slamming his fist against the polished chrome of the table.

The solicitor didn't flinch. Unnecessary shows of strength were commonplace amongst his clients and the posturing didn't faze him. 'It seems she sent a pair of silver candelabra off to auction, and a piece of embroidery. And it's the embroidery which has proved to be most interesting.' He paused waiting for the inevitable sarcastic interruption from Grey. When it was not forthcoming, he carried on. 'The V & A purchased that embroidery at great cost. But then a donor gave a second piece to the museum, and their experts believe the same person made the two pieces…'

At this, Grey threw his hands up in the air, 'Am I in the middle of an episode of *Antiques Roadshow*? Get on with it. I fail to see how any of this is of any interest to me, or my case.'

'I think you'll be very interested to know that the police have tracked both pieces of embroidery to the companion of your great-grandmother, several times removed.' The solicitor leaned back in his chair, satisfied at the look of utter shock on Grey's face, the only time he'd ever seen a true emotion on the man's face.

'And this is the paperwork from the police?'

The solicitor nodded.

'And these are my copies?'

'Yes.'

'Good, you may leave now. I'll be in touch after I've read through the paperwork.' Almost as an afterthought, he added, 'Thank you,' which was the first time the solicitor had heard him utter *those* particular words. *A miracle.*

~

'The brief is leaving, standby.'

The radio call made, the small cohort of undercover officers readied themselves for action.

After much negotiation, a judge had approved a phone tap, in addition to the surveillance on Grey. As much as the general populace thought the police could tap phones on a whim, without the slightest bit of 'just cause', in reality it was a time-consuming and rigorous judicial effort to obtain permission.

The console in the indistinct tradesmen's van lit up, as Grey made a call.

'Who's he calling?' Fujimoto asked, stuffed in the van's corner. The experts ran this phase of the investigation. Fuji's only role was to question the data they collected, make the connections and then steer the next phase of the operation.

'It's a number at Christie's.'

Fuji leaned forward, 'A direct line or the switchboard?'

'Direct line.'

'Do we know who it belongs to?'

The technician rolled his eyes. It didn't matter which boss was in charge, they'd all forgotten what it was like to sit in a surveillance van for days on end, or behind a wall of Post Office boxes, waiting for someone to pick up a letter. Patience was a virtue when everything took time. The technicians weren't miracle workers.

Then a tinny voice, 'Good afternoon, Hannah Gardner speaking.'

A slight delay, then the deep autocratic boom of Grey filled their headphones, 'Miss Gardner, you have been less than honest with me. How is it that today I find out Miss Lester had consigned other items to auction?'

Silence filled the van and Fuji nudged the technicians, 'Did we lose our link?'

'Nope, she just isn't answering.'

The crew in the van leaned forward, as if leaning forwards would improve reception, when Gardner spoke again.

'Why are you calling me here? Wouldn't it be better to meet at the club?'

'What club?' Fuji hissed at Fiona. She shrugged, waiting to write Gardner's words verbatim in her notebook, despite that they'd be paying someone to transcribe the tape in the coming days.

'Shush,' she said, her pen poised.

'No, I want to understand this now, I don't have time to swan around the tennis club you can only afford to belong to because of me. What else did Sarah Lester auction through you?'

An uncomfortable silence stretched through every person in the van, before Gardner spoke again.

'An embroidered sampler from 1726 and signed by an R. J. Williams. And a pair of silver candelabra by Paul de Lamerie, lacking any provenance. That's all. Nothing I considered of interest to you.'

'Nothing *you* considered of *interest*? And since when have you become an expert in what interests me?'

The police raised their eyebrows at the venom in Grey's voice.

'Do you think Gardner's in trouble with Grey now? Should we keep an eye on her?' Fiona whispered.

Fuji shook his head, fascinated at the insight they were being given. Gaps in their investigation were being filled every minute. Gardner must have told Grey about the *katar*, but what else had she shared with him?

Grey continued, without giving Gardner the luxury of answering, 'The police, Miss Gardner, the police have just told me they tracked the sampler back to my family. *The police*. Isn't that your company's job, to research the items before you auction them? Those bumbling idiots who couldn't get jobs in the real world, unearthed the provenance of a scrap of fabric, and traced it to my family.'

Silence greeted him at the other end, before Gardner answered, 'I'm sorry, I didn't know there was a connection. Andrew Harvard was dealing with this. It's not my area of expertise. The computer shows it went to the V & A. A hefty donation ought to secure it for you. I don't know what else to say, or do?'

'I want you to do what I'm paying you for.'

'And I've told you, I want no part of this any more.'

'You'll carry on informing me of *anything* that comes in of interest to me, or your employer will find out about your dealings with me. Now, I want all the details of that transaction. And, for good measure, send me all the information on the silverware too.'

When the call disconnected, the officers turned to look at each other.

'Wow,' said Fiona.

'You could say that,' Fuji replied, running his hands through his hair, his brain firing off in every direction.

'Shall we let Tania have the pleasure of telling Christie's what Gardner's been doing?' Fiona asked.

'We'll all pay a visit to Christie's. Fitting, don't you think?' Fuji said with a slow smile.

THE MOLE

*W*hen Fujimoto, Tania and Fiona arrived at Christie's they had to dodge an army of workmen in pristine white overalls carting furniture and artworks through the enormous marbled lobby. The concierge hurried forward, ready to ask them to leave, before they set him in his place.

Fujimoto flashed his warrant card, 'We'd like to speak with Don Claire please.'

'Have you scheduled an appointment, sir?'

'I wasn't aware we needed an appointment whilst investigating a murder which occurred here.'

The concierge tried explaining that Mr Claire was a very busy man, but Fujimoto had little time for people who considered themselves above members of the public service and made it quite clear he should escort them to Mr Claire's offices quick smart.

Sniffing his displeasure, the doorman swiped his card for the elevator, stabbing at the button for the fourth floor.

'Mr Claire, may we please have a moment of your time?' Fujimoto announced as he walked straight into the opulent office.

Don Claire looked up from his computer, and was about to stand, when he lowered himself back into his chair, gesturing for his guests to take a seat.

'Coffee?' he asked.

'No, but perhaps you'd like us to close the door? We have some rather sensitive information to share with you?'

Fiona leapt up to shut out the questioning glances of the secretary, and the concierge who was loitering in the outer office. Fiona smiled at him, refraining from winking at the unpleasant lackey.

'Sensitive information? Should I get my solicitor in?'

'No need for that yet, but I recommend getting legal advice after you've heard what we're about to tell you,' Fujimoto motioned towards Tania, the youngest person on his team. It was only through her diligence they'd linked Grey with Gardner.

Tania beamed, she couldn't help it. What a triumph to be sitting here, and all because of her. She opened her notebook and tried to arrange her face into a more serious demeanour. As she talked, explaining her findings, she felt herself becoming more confident, more grown-up. She needn't have worried, her methodologies were sound and her evidence solid. And by the time she described the phone call between Gardner and Grey, Don Claire had stopped viewing her as a child dressed up as a policewoman. She was now the Angel of Death, delivering the worst news to a man whose whole life revolved around the people and objects in this building. Every word Tania uttered was another brick falling from the walls, its mortar flaking away until soon there'd be nothing holding up their venerable house.

THE JACKET

*N*icole laboured over her handwritten sign, balancing her cellphone between her shoulder and cheek. 'Hi, Andrew, it's Nicole... no nothing's wrong, just confirming I'll have the shop closed this weekend... It's the worst timing after what's happened, but they only hold the *La Grande Braderie de Lille* fair a few times a year. One of the best ones in France... and I'd already booked my accommodation, and the Eurostar... you'd love it. I'll see if I can find you some old embroidered pieces,' she laughed. 'No, I'm not planning on disappearing while I'm there. Sorry I laughed. What would the police say if I never returned from my buying trip? Can you imagine the newspapers?... I'll be careful, I'll have my phone, and you let me know if you hear anything from Trish. Cheers.'

The call ended, Nicole added the final full stop. She would never be an artist, that was clear, but the sign was legible, and explained why the shop would be closed. A trip to the annual *Braderie de Lille* flea market. Ten thousand exhibitors over sixty-two miles. *What an adventure.* And she'd thought the antique fair at Alexandra Palace was large. She'd already packed her most comfortable shoes in her largest suitcase, which was empty, except for the smaller suitcase she'd packed inside. And she planned to fill them both.

She needed to replenish her stock of militaria; trench art and compasses, medals and maps. It was amazing how many people still collected that stuff, and not just the old guys. She couldn't keep up with demand. There was a whole area of the market dedicated to books and paperwork, ephemera, so she'd hit there first, then the little dealers who traded in medals from around the world: Norwegian War medals; Queen's Visit medals; sterling silver sporting medallions awarded by running clubs and tennis clubs. All those she'd be buying. Right at the end of her trip, she was planning on looking at the vintage clothes — not because she had any great interest or knowledge in that area, but she thought she might find some old leather flying helmets, or gloves. Small things, easy to identify, but leaving the old Dior gowns and Reboux cloche hats to dealers who knew more about that specialist segment of the market, which was a different kettle of fish.

The sign taped to the window, she locked up and climbed into her waiting taxi, 'St Pancras station please.'

The time she spent in London traffic was about the same as it took the Eurostar to travel to Paris, then it was another hour to Lille. Her excitement levels rising, she was like a small child on Christmas Day by the time the train pulled into the station.

She'd booked into *L'Art de Livre*, a quiet bed-and-breakfast in Saint Michel, a short walk from the *Braderie*. She checked in to the nineteenth century home, decorated Indian style, with pictures of long-dead Maharajas adorning the walls. Fortified by a strong coffee, she set off to stalk the traders as they set up. Buying couldn't start till two o'clock, that was the rule, although every guidebook she'd read said most merchants would happily sell if you asked.

The crowds were reminiscent of Hogmanay in Edinburgh, with the same festive air. She wasn't the only one pulling a large trolley bag. If you weren't sporting a large back pack, or pulling a wheeled bag, you looked out of place. The number of bags at the market would have rivalled a plane load of antipodeans on a Contiki tour.

Overwhelmed by choice, Nicole tried to stick to her plan, but everything distracted her. Toast racks. One trader was selling their personal collection of toast racks. They had everything from Georgian silver, to novelty toast racks with the seven dwarves as dividers, and the tiny ceramic Royal Winton ones from the breakfast sets, with just enough slots for two slices of toast. She couldn't help herself, she asked how much the seven dwarves rack was, and if she could buy it now. She didn't even haggle once she heard the price. As cheap as chips.

She carried on. She'd only been there seven minutes, and was already the proud owner of one toast rack, and a small pair of brass-tipped bellows. Given London had banned open fireplaces, it amazed her that people rang constantly looking for fire screens and bellows in good working order. Perhaps there was a dark underbelly of London where residents lit illicit fires at night? Regardless, she'd snapped up this pair. *So much for the fair not starting till two.* There were deals going on everywhere she looked.

She stumbled across a militaria stand by accident. A large group of American tourists had barged past her, their girth multiplied by their bags and cameras slung round their necks, made passing them impossible, pushing her into a stall selling various small whatnots, music and folio stands, and a fine collection of canterburies — open-topped racks, designed for holding music, but more commonly used to hold magazines. She'd examined a walnut example with handles inlaid with mother-of-pearl, before she realised that this stall backed onto another one in a different street.

Nicole left the canterbury behind, because how on earth was she going to get it back to London, and focused her attention on the next stall. Large old bakers' trays crammed full of helmets, from every theatre of war in modern memory. British, French, German, Prussian. Bayonets grouped together in an old brass shell casing. And tray upon tray of Perspex-covered medals. Tarnished dog tags hung around a shop mannequin's neck, with a Swiss Army helmet balanced on the bald head.

'May I leave my bag here?' Nicole asked in passable French. Her holidays at her uncle's hotel in Germany had prepared her well in the basics of most of the main European languages; French, Spanish,

Italian, and German, *natürlich*. She'd have trouble conducting a full conversation about politics in any of those languages, except German, but if it involved directions, refreshments or luggage, she could hold her own.

The grizzled trader muttered a gruff *'Oui'*, reading his newspaper, which looked to be as old as he was.

Nicole browsed the uniform hats on display, selecting some old RAF caps. Placing them on the trestle table, she caught the eye of the stall holder, and his blink gave his word he'd hold them for her as she continued browsing. Other punters came and went; the stall never empty. A pair of Chinese ladies looked like they'd wandered in by accident, but still left with a military field compass in its original leather case, and a handful of Chinese-Russian friendship pins. Mass-produced in the nineteen fifties, they were more kitsch than collectible.

Nicole ran her hand over a flying jacket. British-made, lined with sheepskin, it looked like it had suffered a hard life. It was bulkier than she would have liked, but there was something about the supple leather, and its sheer Englishness which appealed.

'Combien?' Nicole asked. *How much?*

'Deux cents cinquante,' came the gruff reply. Two hundred and fifty euros.

Cheapish, Nicole thought, *for a genuine World War Two flying jacket.* Once she added her mark-up, there'd be a good bit of profit in it, but no harm in trying to negotiate a better price.

She paid three hundred euros for the jacket, the two hats, and half a dozen unnamed service medals from the Second World War, the sort given to every serviceman. Nicole turned to thank the seller, but he'd hidden himself behind his newspaper.

By the end of the day, her feet were aching; her bag felt as heavy as the Shackleton ice shelf in the Antarctic, and the crowds had become overwhelming. The smell of dust and decay intermingled with that of the famous *moules* — mussels — served at every bistro she passed. She pondered what Lille did with the mountain of black mussel shells during their biggest weekend.

Collapsing in her room, she considered having a shower before going out for dinner, but that required too much energy and, besides, she wanted to spread out all her treasures, to assure herself she'd been a canny buyer, and hadn't fallen prey to any impulse buys or counterfeits. Replicas were slowly infiltrating the famous fair. As much as the organisers tried to stamp them out, they were like cockroaches, and appeared everywhere, in every sector of the industry.

With her treasure spread all over her room, the floor resembled the shop. Nicole carried the jacket to the full-length mirror and put it on. Miles too big, it enveloped her. Warm and snug, it felt special, as if its previous owner was smiling at her trying on his coat.

She thrust her hands into the deep pockets, wondering who it was who'd first put his hands in them. What had become of him? She heard the faint crackle of paper. Confused, she couldn't feel any paper inside. She opened the jacket and spied an internal pocket and withdrew the paper from inside. A letter, undated, it began *"Darling Elizabeth..."*

Engrossed, Nicole settled into the armchair, curling her legs underneath her, and read the letter, fascinated by the glimpse into the past, until she came to the end, when reading became impossible because of the tears in her eyes.

THE EMAIL

With Bishop Shalfoon's auction bid for the small Roman statue the highest, he confidence was high that the piece wasn't at risk of going anywhere in the immediate present. He'd recovered from his almost rash decision of trying to uplift the statue the night the auction ended, which would have caused administrative complications. Instead, he'd returned to the apartment he kept in London and had made his nightly call to his mother, sharing with her his frustrations at the business acumen of some sectors of society, with which she naturally agreed. *Her clever son*, she was fond of telling people.

After his conversation with his mother, he'd fired off an email to Gemma at the Art Loss Register, explaining his findings, and requesting she attends *The Old Curiosity Shop* with him on Monday morning.

Unbeknownst to Shalfoon, his email sent ripples around the Art Loss Register office.

'Ryan? Can you come here, please?' Gemma called across the room, causing a few meerkat-like heads to pop up from their computers.

'What? You've never heard me say *"please"* before?' she shot back, her morning already way out of balance from the moment she'd read Shalfoon's message. Admittedly he'd sent it last week, but she'd been on leave, a mini-break to Scotland for a wedding, so hadn't checked her email until today.

Ryan walked over to her desk, coffee in hand, 'Morning, Gem, you're in a good mood,' and he winked at her.

'Not helping, Ryan. Read this,' and she pointed at her screen.

'*The Old Curiosity Shop*? That's Sarah Lester's place, right? Jesus,' he laughed, 'Literally, Jesus now. This is far too complicated for me. What are you going to do?'

'The only thing we can do, is hand it over to the police. And you know why? The way things are going around here, Grey's fingerprints are all over this, I can feel it in here,' she said, pointing to her head. Gemma closed her eyes, 'It's giving me a headache just trying to unravel the links. He makes a convincing case, so we have to get the police involved. And also because he doesn't know what we do about the place.' Looking at Ryan's mug of coffee, she held out her hand.

Ryan laughed and handed it to her, 'I'll get myself another one. What time do you want to meet him?'

'I'll just ring the inspector, make sure he can meet us. So, you'll come with me then?'

'I'm not missing this show. Most exciting thing that's happened since my last murder,' he joked.

'Not funny, Ryan, not funny. Well, kind of funny, but not really. At this rate everything in that store needs investigating. The sole thing not in it, is her.'

THE LETTER

"What happened to that toast rack your mother had? Can you have a look for it in the box in the bottom of the cupboard in the back room. I put some stuff there, but I don't remember checking through it. I know I promised to sort stuff after we moved those cartons.

Don't know why I'm thinking about toast racks! Too much time on my hands I guess. You can't fly in bad weather, and there's plenty of that. But at least there's a heathy supply of toast, cold mostly, but they never run out.

How's the house holding up with all the rain? Did you get someone to look at that leak? Don't you go up there. Don't think I've forgotten about the chisel marks from when you tried fixing the door handle. I love that you tried though.

Some of injured lads are being schooled up on the engine stuff, means we can put more able bodied boys in the cockpit. I'm doing my bit too. You'd never know I broke my arm. It's only on the really cold nights that it bothers me.

Sorry I haven't sent this yet. It really will be the longest letter ever by the time I sent it. Hopefully the censors enjoy reading it as much as I know you will.

At least the weather is playing as much havoc with them as it is with us. Although we have managed to get a decent amount of training in this week. The boffins have modified the wings of the latest Spit's. So trying to get to grips with that. Controls are still touchy, so got to get used to the new lines.

I wish you could come fly with me. I dream about it every night. Up there is like rolling through silk. Don't get scared, but sometimes during training flights, I turn my engine off. The silence is overwhelming. Every sense strains to make sense of it. And when you can see the green below and the blue above, you are free. So free.

Anyway, I know I go on. You'll be pleased to hear our new jackets are warm! Fleece lined, leather, even better than hot toast with fresh butter, at this time of year anyway.

Sorry, have to dash. Will write more tomorrow.

THE REVENGE

_T_he Jowl brothers kept to themselves in the weeks after the altercation in the street. Jimmy ventured no further than church and, even then, he wore his hat down low there, slipping into one of the rear pews with Joe at the last minute. It was time to concentrate on business, with no female interludes, no harassing the natives, no fighting. Just distilling and bottling.

Joe Jowl spent an inordinate amount of time in the public bar he and his brother owned, the _Shakespeare Tavern_. The habitual drinkers neither knew nor cared about a minor kerfuffle on the road between their publican, a girl and a native — standard fare in a settlement such as this. The churchgoers and English matrons judged him. He could feel their condemnation oozing from every frigid cavity — but they weren't his customers, so damn them all to hell.

While, behind his wooden counter, polishing cloth in hand, Joe exercised his mouth, questioning all and sundry about the girl and, by extension, the native. Everyone loves talking, and those in their cups more so than others. The girl was proving an enigma. Some fancied they'd heard she'd disappeared. Others claimed she'd run off with the native. They called him Tau, or Sammy, Winston or Pita. But they suggested the name Wiremu more often than the others, leaving Joe certain it was a Wiremu he was hunting down. The girl's whereabouts he shelved until she surfaced. She would. It was a small country.

He carried on serving his regulars, who travelled miles for his gin; a reminder that the girl still owed him for those bottles. Meantime he'd experimented with brewing beer. Hard liquor may be a good seller, but as more British settled in Auckland, demand for a palatable beer had grown. Jimmy was growing the raw ingredients he required — that was about all he could trust his brother to do, so it was up to him to brew an ale worth selling. The bottles he'd ordered were expensive, although he needed them to advertise his wares to other taverns, which were sprouting like mushrooms in the township. Only in the April, *The New Zealander* listed fifty applications for a publican's licence. *Fifty* in a population of only twelve thousand persons. Or lives that counted. English, Scots, the Irish. A smattering of Germans and Dutch made up the balance. Of the natives, they mattered not one bit. They had no coin to buy his grog. If he had his way, he'd sell them off as slaves.

Two customers were having a heated discussion at the bar. Joe moved closer, ready to defuse any violence before it erupted. Glass was hard to replace, and he wasn't having any man wreck his place. Those that tried always regretted it.

'I tell you, the flour writhed with weevils. The Māori said it wasn't his flour, that I'd mistaken it for someone else's. Can you believe it? He questioned whether I knew where my flour came from?'

'How're you meant to make bread with flour filled with vermin? No one will buy that filth.'

'Filth. To think I was trying to give a local boy a go. Last time I raise a finger to help one.'

'The boys should just shoot the lot, especially the ones who assume they can do an Englishman's job. *Trying* to be a miller. As if he knows anything about it. They didn't even have wheels before we got here.'

'I heard they eat their captives. Perhaps that's what your miller's been adding to his flour.'

The man turned apoplectic, 'What are you saying? That my bread tastes like it's made from dead darkies? You better shut your mouth, or I'll shut it for you.'

'Now, now, gentlemen, I could pour you another drink, but Steven, your wife will want you home for tea, or *you'll* be feeding those weevils.' The men laughed, the sting taken out of the situation. Steven swilled the dregs of his ale, and shrugged on his jacket, its threadbare elbows evidence of where he didn't spend his money; his florid complexion evidence of where it was.

'Steven, before you return to that fine woman of yours, who's the miller you were *discussing*? Need to ensure my flour isn't coming from his mill.'

'You wanna steer clear of Wiremu Kepa then. He doesn't supply that many bakers — won't be supplying many more after I spread the word.'

'Wiremu, eh? I know who you mean. Good, he's not my supplier. You head off now, or you'll be in the dog box with those hounds of yours.'

Joe carried on cleaning glasses, pouring drinks, and eavesdropping on the conversations that flowed around the bar. The truths he overheard constantly surprised him; stories of adultery, theft, abuse, and worse. This was why his life mantra was *family business is for behind family doors*. And now he knew which door Wiremu Kepa was behind.

THE ADZE

*W*iremu Kepa struggled with his fifth sack of grain that morning, the hessian hard to grip in the humidity. Two of his boys hadn't turned up today, leaving him to get on with things on his own. Dropping the sack to rub his still swollen jaw, he thought back to when he'd stepped in to protect the English woman. Aroha was furious — reminding him that they had a family, and *they* were the ones who needed protecting. And he'd heard Joe Jowl was asking about him. Word travelled and people loved talking. It had always been that way, and it would always be. It was only a matter of time before they sought retribution, and it wouldn't be long. Orders had dried up to a mere trickle of what they were before the fight. Wiremu ran his hands across the stacks of milled flour, *certain* weevils contaminated none.

Coughing with the disturbed flour dust, he wiped his mouth with the back of his hand, and considered the very real possibility that, if Jowl didn't get him, his own mill would. Breathing the dust was slowly killing him. He didn't how long he had left, but he still needed the money it brought in for the future of his family.

Overtaken by another coughing fit, he abandoned the sacks where they lay. He thought he'd quit this part of the job behind him when he'd taken on the apprentices, two other Māori boys. But with them not there, it was all on his shoulders. Given the way his lungs were reacting, he'd be better off calling it a day and heading home early. His baby needed him more than the mill today.

Matariki was coming up — the Māori celebration of the new year — and he needed to get home to help his wife build the kite they'd fly together on the dawn of *Matariki*, to remember their dead, and to give thanks for the blessings the land, the sea and the sky had given them. He hoped he'd be able to celebrate with his baby in the coming years. After locking the mill door behind him, he laid his palm against it. This was his livelihood, but a man needs his family, for they were the true food for the soul. It was time to move back to his roots, to his tribe. He just didn't know which was safer. Here, where a stranger to him was hell-bent on ruining him; or down country where he'd never lived; where tribe fought against tribe, some with the British, others against — all of them using British weapons.

Outside the mill, his coughing doubled him over. Maybe this was the decision made for him. His health couldn't continue like this. He was a giant tree being felled by the minute scratchings of the fantail resting on its branches. He'd place an advert in the *Daily Southern Cross* to find a buyer, for what it was worth. Perhaps someone else could make it profitable, a man with a more English-sounding name. Spitting phlegm into flax nearby, he startled a white heron. In silent awe he watched it take flight, its ungainly run met with the effortless majesty of its flight over the living harbour. A bird hunted almost to extinction, its snowy plumage prized by natives and settlers alike, it was a rare sight in the settlement — an omen. As the heron flew alone in the vast sky, Wiremu took it as a sign that he too must take flight. To be closer to his ancestral home, to his family.

With his back to the mill, he made his way homewards, his shoulders unburdened from the expectations of society. Now to tell his wife of the journey they needed to make. The journey home.

Wiremu's wife took the news of the imminent departure stoically. Their belongings few, it hadn't taken longer than a day to pack away the necessities for a new life down country.

'What will we do with these?' Aroha Kepa asked her husband, gesturing towards a wooden crate. She flicked her jet-black hair out of her eyes, and it fell like a veil down her back. For forays outside, she tamed it in a long braid; when it was just them, she left it loose. Wiremu liked nothing more than to run his fingers through her hair as they lay tangled in each other's arms at night. The babe was an expert at grabbing tiny handfuls of her mother's hair at every opportunity.

Wiremu considered the crate. Years had passed since he'd looked inside the box. He hadn't needed to, he knew what it contained. His head exploded with memories, as if from yesterday, when he'd sat at his father's knee, watching him slowly grinding and smoothing pieces of stone into beautifully formed adzes. He'd kept the adzes; a solid link to the past. Do possessions serve as the only tangible link with those who came before, or do the memories held within the heart nourish the soul, linking it to the past? Possessions couldn't give nourishment. Possessions tied you to the past, their weight pulled you backwards, stunting growth and denying the future.

Decision made, he passed his hand across the rough slats of the wooden box, 'No, we will sell those. Father's knowledge is within me to make them all over again, with as much love and care. There's a man in town who's put adverts in all the papers seeking our *taonga* — our treasures.'

'You'd sell your heritage to the British?'

Wiremu placed his hand on her heart, 'It's not abandoning our heritage, it's being practical. They pay good money, there are people over the ocean who desire these pieces of our world. And that cash will take us home, with the baby, in more comfort than we could have ever hoped.

Aroha stroked Wiremu's face, the bristles on his chin rough against her hand, 'If it's of no concern to you, then it will be okay. I was worried you'd regret the decision. Walking isn't so bad, I've been walking since I was a baby. What's one more long walk?' Aroha smiled, they kissed, and the baby cried, breaking them apart. This was the way now, time was no longer their own.

'I'll go and be back tonight, and I'll eat in town so don't bother preparing me anything.' With that, Wiremu placed a chaste kiss on her forehead, scooped up the crate, and left the cottage.

Wiremu sat in the public bar. The *Shakespeare Tavern* publican had served him, but he could feel the filthy looks from the other punters as he waited to meet the man from the newspaper ad at two o'clock, but he was late. Wiremu was trying to gauge how long he should wait, when a stranger dressed in a dark three-piece suit with a starched white shirt, arrived. A gold fob chain marched its way across his waistcoat, following the line of a white moustache groomed into a smooth plane on his face.

'Mister Kepa?' His enunciation marked him as a member of the upper class.

'Mister Robley?'

Moses Robley took a seat next to Wiremu, shaking his head when Wiremu offered to buy him a drink. 'I understand there are some Māori artefacts you're looking to sell?'

Wiremu sipped his ale, his decision a stone in his stomach. His eyes flicked towards the crate on the floor. The adzes in the box reached back two generations. His father, and grandfather had made them, but in the end, they were just stone. They weren't flesh and blood, so why did he feel like he was selling his soul?

'Mister Kepa, I don't have all day. Since placing the advert, the offers of native memorabilia have overwhelmed me. I have almost reached the point where I can now only accept items of exceptional quality,' he said, flicking open his gold pocket watch to check the time.

Wiremu swallowed another mouthful of ale. It tasted bitter, and he pushed his unfinished glass away, 'It's not a wasted journey, Mister Robley. Sorry, my emotions... my ancestors made these, but my family needs the money more.'

'It's a reality of the times, Mister Kepa, hard to wrap your head around I know. There are many collectors who would put your treasures on display for future generations to enjoy.'

Wiremu answered, 'That makes it easier to accept. I must sell them, but it doesn't make it any better.' He lifted the crate onto the table, loosening the nails with a ragged-looking pocket knife.

Robley's eyes shone in anticipation. This trip to New Zealand had netted a mountain of artefacts he'd have no trouble moving on back in England for a tidy sum. Waiting at the wharf, already crated up, were several *poupou* — Māori wall panels, clubs, chisels made from greenstone, four carved feather boxes filled with *huia* feathers. His pride and joy were the three *mokomokai*, the tattooed and preserved Māori heads. They would join his personal collection. As Wiremu lifted the lid of the crate, Robley sighed with relief. The adzes were superb.

'There are about thirty or so, I haven't counted them in a long time.'

Robley smiled as he ran his fingers over the smooth stones. Yes these would be perfect. Sir Augustus Franks at the Department of Antiquities of the British Museum had been hankering after some examples as fine as these. *Perfect.*

'If we can agree a price, we will have ourselves a deal.' Steepling his slender fingers he smiled at Wiremu again. *Make friends with the natives, and they'll give you more.* 'Perhaps I will have that drink now. Shall I buy you a refill?'

Over their glasses, the two men worked out a deal. Robley pulled a wad of notes from his waistcoat pocket, peeling off half a dozen pound notes, and laying them on the table.

Wiremu replaced the lid, hammering the tacks back in with the base of his knife. Every tack shooting through his heart.

Robley sipped his fortified wine, savouring the richness in his mouth. It rolled around on his tongue like velvet but his companion made no move to pick up his money. Still, they'd agreed on a deal and time was of the essence. 'Thank you for your time, Mister Kepa. Here is my card. Should you come across any other artefacts, please contact me at the address on there. I visit New Zealand often, but should I be out of the country, my associates will act on my behalf. It's been a pleasure.'

With his goodbyes said, Robley, struggling under the weight of the box, stumbled from the pub. To the casual observer, it looked much heavier than when Wiremu had carried it in with the ease of someone who hauled bags of flour for a living.

Wiremu scooped up the crisp notes, their fancy script made blurry through unshed tears. He went to stand up, but a pair of hands on his shoulders pinned him to his chair.

THE CONFRONTATION

𝒫inned to the seat by a pair of meaty hands, Wiremu couldn't move. As he strained against the person holding him, the cold eyes of Joe Jowl met his.

'Hello, old friend. What a coincidence you're drinking in this bar — it's mine. I've wanted to catch you for a while, so this is very convenient.'

Wiremu squirmed, the crisp notes in his hand heavier than lead. *Not good. Not good at all.*

'I didn't realise it was your bar. I was just leaving.'

'Leaving, were you? I hope you were planning on settling your bill before you left?'

'We've paid for the drinks.'

'Oh, you paid for *those* drinks, that's true, but that's not the bill that I was referring to,' Joe said, sitting next to Wiremu, his bulk filling the space.

Wiremu tried shoving the handful of notes into his trouser pocket. The movement did not go unnoticed.

'I have no other debt with you and, as I said, I was just leaving,' Wiremu said, getting up to leave.

Jowl reached out, clasping the smaller man on his arm, digging his fingers in, dragging Wiremu back into his seat.

'The thing is, *Mister* Kepa — oh yes, I know who you are. I've heard all about you. I know more about you than your mother does. See, you interfered with my family business, and the Jowl brothers don't take kindly to others interfering in our business. We're good churchgoing folk who abide by the word of Lord Jesus our Saviour, but we also need money to live, to follow the word of God. And when you owe the Jowl brothers, you pay the debt. You, sir, are well overdue on paying what you owe.'

Wiremu looked around the bar, trying to catch the eye of anyone watching, hoping they'd intervene, but no one would meet his eye. Since Jowl had sat at his table, most of the other patrons had decided they had things to do elsewhere. The room was almost empty.

No one would help him; he was on his own. Resigned to his fate, Wiremu replied, 'Fine. How much do I owe you?'

'You owe me for the bottles of liquor which smashed, two shillings ought to deal with that.'

Wiremu exhaled in relief. Two shillings was fine, it left him enough for the trip down country. He thrust his hand into his pocket and pulled out the cash.

Joe changed his grip to Wiremu's wrist, 'I said two shillings would cover the bottles which were broke, but that won't cover the loss of the girl.'

Wiremu frowned, 'What girl?'

'Don't play the smart-arse with me. The one you helped escape. Are you shacked up with her? You boys are all the same, can't keep your hands off the white women. But if you want her, you pay for her. And given how much money I saw you pocket, it's best you pay off her debt too. She owes me for a bottle of gin, and her lodgings. So make it easy for yourself, and just put your hand back into your pocket and pull out the dosh that fancy man gave you. Maybe then you'll be able to move on, but not with that mill of yours...'

Jowl winked; the accompanying smile never making it to his eyes.

'No.'

'I beg your pardon? Did you just say "no"?'

Wiremu stood up, wrenching his arm from Joe's. The sudden movement took Joe by surprise. Years of lugging bags of flour had given Wiremu a surprising strength, hidden by his English clothes.

'Good day, sir,' and he flung two shillings on the table before walking out, chin up, looking braver than he felt.

Joe let him leave, well aware of the path Wiremu would take home to his woman and child. A path which wound its way through some thick areas of scrub, rarely used. Joe knew the man's routines — that he avoided the roads where the work gangs were, keeping to the quiet paths. Which suited the Jowl brothers perfectly.

THE WIFE

*A*roha Kepa shifted the babe from one hip to the other, and checked outside, again. With dusk falling, her field of vision inched inwards. Shadows were brushing the bay. *He should be home by now.* Aroha's mind was a muddle of thoughts and worries. One option was to ask a neighbour to walk into town; to make enquiries. Or she could do it herself. A final glance towards the darkening hills, and she returned inside. *Not tonight.* She wouldn't go tonight. *Tomorrow.* She'd look for him tomorrow. Unless he came home soon. *He must have got delayed,* she negotiated with herself.

She placed her daughter in the middle of their bed. Their meagre belongings sat waiting for Wiremu to load them into the cart. They had to leave soon, before winter struck. She wouldn't travel with the babe in winter. Her heart would break again if she lost another one.

Leaving the babe to sleep, she sat down at their little table, and picked at the now-cold meal she'd prepared for tea. Worry gnawed away at her. Any ills could have befallen Wiremu, but mostly she worried because there'd been a rash of Māori being beaten for no reason other than they were Māori. As if the settlers were trying to erase them from the land.

Clearing Wiremu's uneaten dinner only intensified her disquiet. In bed, she curled into her daughter, protecting her with her body, her warmth. She wanted her to grow up strong, and confident, surrounded by family, with unbreakable bonds. And siblings. Aroha wanted so many things, but right now all she needed was her husband there beside her.

The night took over where every whisper threatened to be Wiremu, and every creak falsely heralded his return. Even the tiny noises made by her daughter were reminiscent of his whispers to her.

Aroha woke with the sun. Wiremu's empty side of the bed cast shadows of her fitful sleep under her eyes. The baby cried. Named Sophia after her aunt, the babe's cries were as strident as Aroha remembered her aunt to be. Soon she'd be with her again, and her cousins; her *whanau*, her family. But today she needed Wiremu.

Aroha fed Sophia, stroking her tufts of strong black hair. It was growing curly, just like Wiremu's, although he kept his short, smoothed back, as per the English way. Wiremu tried so hard to be British, to fit in. It would be a relief to go down country. To be free of the restraints of pretending to be someone you were not.

Throwing Sophia into an improvised sling, she set off to find her husband.

The day was clear. Around the Onehunga settlement, other early risers were heading off to their jobs. Some were even tending their flourishing vegetable gardens. Everything flourished. The climate was perfect for almost every fruit and vegetable. The settlers had brought with them seeds from plants discovered elsewhere in the world. Exotic plants flourished next to the native species — an ecological experiment no one expected would get out of hand in the decades and centuries to come. Watermelons still scared her. So big, and such a vivid shade. Only flowers should be that colour.

Like Wiremu, she kept off the road, preferring the well-worn path through the remaining scrub, confident the only other people she'd meet on the track would be her own.

Fantails danced up ahead of her, revelling in the insects disturbed by Aroha's progress through the bush. Spiders paused in their elaborate webs, ready to ensnare the unfortunate few who escaped the fantails insatiable hunger. She hummed an old song to Sophia, who gazed around at the foliage, reaching a chubby hand for low hanging leaves, giggling in her pouch at the birdsong accompanying her mother's sweet voice.

Nothing sounded sweeter than her child's laughter, and Aroha sang even louder.

The haze of Auckland appeared on her horizon. *Where do I look for him in the city?*

She rounded a corner, her eyes on the smoke from the city, her mind elsewhere, calculating distances, times, and the need to stop and feed Sophia soon, when she tripped on the path.

Aroha cried out, as she fell on her side, trying to protect her daughter. Bruised but not hurt, she rolled onto her back, loosening the sling and removing Sophia before she tried standing up. She dusted herself off, berating herself for her carelessness, when Sophia spoke, her first word, her only word, 'Papa.'

And there was Wiremu. His curly black hair matted with blood, not pomade. His suit ripped and muddied. Sticky burrs clung to the fabric, decorating the muted brown weave.

'Wiremu!' Aroha bent down, brushing the grass away from his face. Almost unrecognisable. Both eyes swollen shut. His upper lip torn almost to his nose. A nose kinked to the left, whereas before it had been straight, aquiline.

'Wiremu, can you hear me? Wake up.' Aroha shook him harder. 'Wiremu?'

A moan.

'Wiremu, please... please, wake up,' she whispered before tucking Sophia, who'd been threatening to crawl away, back into her sling. Aroha stood up, screaming for help. It was early, yet surely other people used this track? 'Help me! Help, please!' She bent down again, shaking Wiremu. She held her hand under his nose and felt a tiny gust of breath as he exhaled.

Sobbing, she lay her head against his chest, cradling Sophia with one arm, who was squirming, and trying to escape the confines of the sling. She wanted to be with her Papa.

'Aroha? Aroha, go now. Before they come back.'

Aroha shot up, smiles wreathing her face 'Wiremu? What? Thank goodness. Are you OK? Can you get up?'

Wiremu coughed, a spittle of blood passing his lips. His voice little more than a whisper, 'Listen, my love. Take the babe and go. Don't go back to the house. But go...' A cough took hold, stronger this time. A great heaving cough leaving bubbles frothing from his mouth, tainted pink.

'I am not leaving you, Wiremu Kepa. Someone will be along, and they can help me get you to a doctor. Don't you dare try to tell me what to do. I am not some white woman, tied to her man by the church. I'm the daughter of a great chief...'

Wiremu pushed himself up, wincing. 'And you will go to your people, and they'll protect you. Go now. They know who you are and where we live.'

'You're speaking in riddles. Who's *they*? The people who did this to you? What did *they* want?' Comprehension washed over her face. 'The money? They took the money from you selling the adzes?' Her face paled. Their plans, meticulously made, now ruined. *How will we travel all the way down country, with a babe and no money?* 'What will we do?'

'Go...' Another spasm wracked his body, the cut on his lip reopened. Aroha tried staunching the flow with her hands, her tears mingling with the blood. 'Go, go now, Aroha.'

'No! You tell me who did this. Tell me now. Damn you, Wiremu Kepa, I'll drag you to hospital myself.' With the deftness only managed through practice, she spun the sling round to the back, and manoeuvred herself behind her husband, grabbing him under his arms. 'This will hurt, but you're not dying in the dirt like some old tinker.'

Wiremu cried out, agony crystal clear in his voice.

Aroha ignored his cries, focussed on getting help for him. He was so heavy, and with the babe on her back, she... no, she wouldn't think about it. She *had* to get him to a doctor. She could rest after that.

Sophia wailed. Hungry and squashed, she wanted out.

'Stop, stop, Aroha, put me down, please. I'll tell you who did it, it was the Jowl brother, the...'

The pain was weakening his voice, till it was little more than a whisper, his words lost to the breeze.

'You shut up. Be quiet, I have to do this. I will not leave you here. Someone will be along soon, I know it. But I *have* to do this.'

Wiremu coughed. At least in this position his beautiful wife couldn't see the blood he was spitting out. Every step she took sent daggers of pain through his lungs. The other Jowl brother, the quiet one, had set upon him on his way home. His work boots were a fine weapon which he used unceasingly against Wiremu, who hadn't expected an attack on this little-known track.

The beating had been relentless and, as a final indignity, Jimmy had urinated on Wiremu's body, just as Wiremu lost consciousness. For all that Wiremu thought the beating was the precursor to robbing him, he didn't realise Jimmy hadn't checked his pockets. Joe hadn't told his brother to search the native's pockets for any money. Joe had instructed Jimmy to butcher the man. No more, no less. And he followed his instructions. He'd learnt his lesson with the girl.

Aroha dragged her husband backwards along the common shortcut, praying for help around every bend. Sweat dripped from her forehead. Sophia wailed. The bird calls filled the air, competing with Sophia's objections and Aroha's grunts. Wiremu had fallen silent. She swore as she saw he'd lost one of his boots as she'd heaved him along the dirt track. She'd have to go back later to find it. There'd be no spare money now.

Just one more corner, then someone would come. *Just one more.* She stopped to catch her breath. Despite her fitness, she wasn't fit enough to carry her husband on her own into town. She wouldn't cry. The daughter of a chief wouldn't allow herself the luxury.

Then, a pair of suited gentlemen materialised. Not the sort whose decisions affected the Dominion, but more those who carried out the orders other men gave. At once they both rushed forward to relieve Aroha of her burden.

Aroha couldn't thank them enough. Over and over she thanked

them until her words were so commingled with her tears she was incomprehensible.

The gentlemen laid Wiremu down on the ground, their faces worthy of a championship game of poker.

'Madam, what has befallen him?' the elder of the two asked, his whiskers brushing well past his collar and down towards his rotund stomach.

Between sobs, Aroha told a partial story, 'They attacked him, and stole our money. I found him on the path. He was there all night.'

The men exchanged glances. The younger man, clean-shaven, his suit of a more modern cut, his ear pressed against Wiremu's chest, looked at his companion, and subtly shook his head.

Sophia filled the silence with her cries.

'Madam, we will convey him to the surgeon. You must go on ahead with the babe and warn them of our coming. We will be much faster without you both, and you will be much faster without us. You may trust us; the Governor General employs us as his surveyors.' The elder man helped Aroha to her feet, and steered her away from Wiremu, towards the path to town.

'Do you know the Provincial Hospital, madam? It's the best place to take him.'

'Yes,' Aroha responded, glancing at her husband until the hungry cries of her daughter galvanised her into action.

'I will see you there. Please hurry.' And, with that, she took off, alternating between walking and jogging, holding Sophia tightly in front of her, shushing her, reassuring her that Wiremu would be well now that there were men to help her.

After she left, the younger man stood up, announcing clinically, 'His body isn't cold, but he has gone. I know not how long ago. She must not have noticed.'

The bearded surveyor bent down himself to check. Not that he didn't trust his young colleague, but youth was always too quick to pronounce something. Every aspect of life, and death, needed the utmost care. Double checking his colleague's work was his way.

Careful to secure his whiskers, he leaned his face in towards that of Wiremu. There was a lack of breath from the man's face, and no movement of his chest.

'And you checked for any sound of his heart beating?'

The other man couldn't conceal his impatience at the second guessing of his companion, 'Yes. I checked for a heartbeat. I heard nothing.'

'Perhaps the baby's cries disguised it?'

At that, the younger man could control his impatience no longer, 'No, Clarence, the baby made no difference to the fact that this man's heart has stopped beating and, even as we sit here, his body grows colder. Can we please stop this ridiculous conversation and transfer him to the hospital, or am I the only one concerned about the time this is taking away from the task they mean us to complete?'

Clarence Whittaker sniffed, his mouth set like a ruled line. *It is very hard to find suitable staff, but I must make do with the dross I am saddled with.*

'Fine, but we will write this up in our report before we leave the hospital. We should record events such as this. Someone has beaten him, and our evidence may be of use, or our records required at some stage. As I have told you time and time again, Roger, the smallest things sometimes become the biggest. No one knows what the future may have in store for our records.'

THE MONEY

*A*roha stumbled from the hospital, baby Sophia in one arm, and a brown paper bundle in the other. Her face was emotionless, heartbroken. She'd consigned Wiremu's broken body to the Municipal Burial Ground, to the north of Symonds Street. By rights, she should take him to his ancestral home, but she had neither the funds nor the support to transport him. With great reluctance, she'd left him in the care of the nurses, and with him she'd left her heart. There was nothing in her now except a foul anger.

Looking down the line of shops, she finally spied what she needed, a pawnbroker. Wiremu's clothes, his good suit, wrapped in paper and pressed into her hands by the nurses, would give her enough to travel home. She'd wanted Wiremu buried in his best suit, but one nurse, an elderly sort, more practical than emotional, suggested his suit was more valuable to her than it was to him.

Swallowing her pride, she entered the premises of *Henry Neumegen, Pawnbroker*.

The proprietor stood behind the polished counter in person, his bald head framed by impressive bushy sideburns and a full moustache. His face remained impassive — he saw all sorts here, and it was not his place to judge his customers. Native women were, however, rare visitors to these premises.

With the package on the counter, Aroha forced herself to meet the eyes of the man in front of her.

'I have a gentleman's suit I should like to pawn,' she said, shifting the sleeping form of her daughter to a more comfortable position now both arms were free.

'Of course,' Neumegen replied. A recent immigrant, he'd built up a reputation as an honest dealer, one in which even the police had faith. Unwrapping the parcel, he ignored the dark stains on the black material, fingering instead the weave of the fabric, examining the workmanship. Made by Archibald Clark and Sons, it was a suit of fine quality.

'It is a fine suit, madam, but what of the fellow to whom it belonged? May I enquire as to his well-being?'

Aroha replied, without emotion, 'He has passed on, suddenly, and I am to return to my family, but I don't have the funds.'

Neumegen ran his hands through the pockets of the suit. You never knew what gentlemen left there. He pulled out a handful of pounds.

Aroha lit up, her eyes darting from the notes to the pawnbroker's face, and back again.

'These must belong to you,' Neumegen said.

Aroha reached for the notes.

'They killed him for nothing,' she whispered.

'Excuse me?'

'The Jowls, they killed him for nothing.'

Neumegen looked to his door, shifting behind his counter.

'Madam, I know nothing of what you speak, but may I be frank in my advice to you? Take this money and leave. Tell no one of your good fortune and never again mention that name. It will do you no good, and will not bring him back. Come now, hide your money...' he implored her to put away the cash as he repackaged the suit, trying to pass it back to her, wanting nothing further to do with the transaction.

Almost every businessman in Auckland knew to steer clear of the Jowls. It did you no good to be on their wrong side.

Almost pushing her from his shop, he directed her to the Redan Hotel, where the horse bus would return her to Onehunga on the half hour. Neumegen checked the road, before shutting the door, closing away the trouble which could befall him. The last thing he needed was anyone asking questions about him and his business. Or worst of all, asking questions about his past...

THE BISHOP

'Where on God's earth is my water? I can't be drink this. If I wanted to be a heathen, I'd rip off my clothes, tattoo my face, and join the local savages. This tastes as if you sourced it from the night soil collector.'

Annabel recoiled from his vitriol. For a religious man, he hadn't bought into the *Love Thy Neighbour* rhetoric at all. Bishop Dasent was one of the most vile men she'd ever encountered. If she'd been in her own life, she'd have told him to *bugger off* a hundred times now. She'd have walked out, relying on family and friends for a place to stay. But here it was a different story. Here she choked down her anger, swallowed her disbelief at his misogynistic attitude, and she carried on, for a roof over her head and food on her table.

'I can go to Sutton's General Store, to replenish your bottled water?' Annabel offered, through gritted teeth.

The Bishop waved her away, saying 'Be quick, Mrs Lester, be quick.'

Annabel muttered to herself as she gathered her things from the kitchen. It wasn't as easy to 'pop out to the shops' as it had been back in England, where there'd been a store on every corner, as prevalent as pubs and curry houses. No, to go shopping, she needed to find enough coins from the housekeeping money, a hat, the right footwear for the appalling roads, and a basket to carry everything. And nothing was light... it all weighed a ton. She had biceps like an Olympic wrestler from the regular shopping she'd had to do.

After replacing her indoor shoes for more sturdy lace-up boots, she left the Manse, lifting her face to enjoy the sunshine. Catching herself, she hurried off, well aware that Norman Bailey was watching her, waiting for her to mess up so he could tattle to the Bishop. Well, she wouldn't give him that luxury; she'd enjoy the sun around the next corner. As she hastened down Manse Street, her mind wandered — although, today, it wasn't her former life she thought about, it was more about the strange man she'd bumped into, last time she'd come this way. *A stranger.* She'd seen him at church, his head constantly scanning the congregation. *Tall, dark and handsome. He'd make a fine cover of a Mills and Boon romance, with long black lashes the envy of every woman in the congregation. Younger than me, but not by much,* she thought, as she allowed herself the luxury of imagining his hands running over her hips, her back, her breasts. A dog of uncertain parentage raced in front of her as she passed yet another building site, and she stumbled. As she fell, an arm shot out, catching her before she fell into the muddy roadside. Her momentum carried them both into the morass of mud piled by the edge of the building site. Far from rescuing her, his bulk pinned her to the rubble.

'Jesus Christ, get off me,' Annabel screamed, her hands scrambling at the dirt.

A deliveryman outside Sutton's General Store abandoned his drayhorse and cart and rushed to her aid. Edwin Sutton himself deigned to emerge from his shop to see what the fracas was. The builders, always eager for a scrap, bounded over, hauling the woman's attacker off her. A burly Scotsman threw a couple of punches, until a well-timed uppercut to his jaw sent him backwards into the building materials, eyes dancing in their sockets. Dazed, he could only watch as his colleagues converged on the fellow who'd put him in the woodpile.

Annabel Lester, covered in filth, hat crushed beyond recognition, fled to the safety of Sutton's doorway. A street brawl was the last thing she expected to experience on her way to the store. The man who'd assaulted her was giving the remaining builders, and the deliveryman, a good drubbing. She wasn't sure anyone knew who they were fighting, nor why. *Men.*

'I've had enough of this,' Sutton said, before using a galvanised bucket to scoop water from the horse trough, and threw it over the men.

As they came up for air, Annabel gasped. The stranger from church was on the ground — one eye already closing from a thwack to the face, knuckles bloodied, coat torn, but still recognisable. The builders ordered back to the site by the foreman who'd appeared at the end to the fight, and the concussed builder staggered off with the support of his friends. Sutton chastised the deliveryman for shirking his duties — time was money, and the bloody cart wouldn't unload itself, being the gist of the conversation, leaving Annabel alone to watch the man dusting himself off.

'Are you okay?' Annabel called out from the doorway.

William Price looked over, struck again by the woman's similarities to Sarah. The slope of her eyes, the way she held her shoulders, further back than most women, as if there was an air of confidence built into her bones. He examined the sleeves of his coat — torn and covered with blood — his own from the cut by his eye. 'I'll live,' he replied.

'Can I help?' Annabel ventured a few hesitant steps towards him. 'You're bleeding?' A question, not a statement.

'Am I? I'm surprised you care, madam.' He couldn't help snapping at her. She'd tripped, he'd tried to catch her, they'd fallen, then someone had attacked him. He wasn't feeling generous.

'I'm sure Mister Sutton wouldn't mind if we used his kitchen to clean your injury...'

'After what just happened, Mrs Lester, I don't think my health could hold up to being alone in your company.'

Annabel thought she saw a smile crease the corner of his one good eye, but it was as fleeting as a fantail through the bush, and she dismissed it. She'd had enough of men being tossers in her life, and this man she didn't have to be polite to. 'Well then, bleed to death, I don't care.' She bent to pick up her wicker basket, just as Price also went to retrieve it for her. Their heads collided. And their dual laughs split the air.

'Seems the loss of vision has affected my perception, so sorry. Did I hurt you?' Price asked.

'Only a little,' she laughed. 'Come on, I'll clean it up for you. They'll lock you up for causing a disturbance if I let you loose on the streets like that. This town is so straight-laced, I'm surprised any of them can breathe.'

Price gazed at her face. Up close, she *was* beautiful. So similar to Sarah, yet older, and there was something else indefinable. *An acceptance of life?* She was a woman not searching for anything. Comfortable in herself. And that was a powerful force, and rare in a woman. She led him through Sutton's shop, where the dusty smell of flour mingled with that of strong carbolic soaps and sweet Jamaican rum.

Sutton showed them through to his kitchen and left them to it. Customers and their coin were of far greater interest than an injured man consorting unchaperoned with the widow from the Manse. Annabel rummaged through cupboards searching for the things she needed, a bowl for water, clean cloths. The kettle was soon boiling over the black range.

Price removed his coat, mournfully perusing the damage to one sleeve.

'I can fix that too, if you want? My sewing isn't fantastic, but I can do it...' She blushed. *What am I, twelve? Tongue-tied, at my age.*

'Yes I'm a man, but I've been on my own long enough to learn how to sew.'

'Is your wife not here with you then?' Pouring the tea, she couldn't believe the words coming from her own mouth, the flush on her cheeks not from the heat of the boiling water.

Not talkative in normal circumstances, he replied, 'I've not had that good fortune.' Like a true gentleman he didn't comment on her blush as she passed him a mug, the porcelain the same colour as her skin, an English rose.

Pulling up a three-legged milking stool, Annabel set to cleaning his wound, dabbing around the cut, revealing a decent gash. 'This should have stitches.'

Price didn't comment, his good eye following her every move.

Annabel hadn't been this close to a man since she'd arrived in Dunedin years ago. And nothing could have prepared her for the impact his proximity made on her. Like a flower opening under the summer's sun, she bloomed, the cares of her life swept away by his lashes. The possibilities of life suddenly seemed endless.

'I was coming to see you,' he interrupted her ministrations.

'Why?' Her heart skipping a beat.

'I was hoping we could speak about Sarah? Sarah Bell? They led me to believe she was a relative?'

Annabel froze, her illusions shattering with those words. 'I have no relations here.'

Price frowned, 'But she looks just like you, as if you were sisters, or you her mother.'

Annabel's eyes widened, the mirror image of Sarah's. 'I had a daughter, in England, not here. Here I have no one. Sorry, I have to go, I was buying water for the Bishop.' She fled the kitchen, pausing only to fill her basket with bottles of Thomson's aerated water for Dasent. Struggling, she manhandled the basket down the road, tears streaming down her face and regardless of how much she wiped them away they still fell. Oblivious to the curious stares at her racking sobs, she stumbled, bottles clanking in the basket which grew heavier with every step, just like her heart.

An arm reached out, relieving her of the burden, her physical burden. Annabel stopped. Without even looking, she knew who it would be. Price lowered the basket and turned her with his hands. Tall for a woman, like Sarah, she towered over the Bishop, and his minion. But to Price, she was the perfect height.

'Perhaps she tried to find you, but didn't know where you were? We all fall out with our families, but running away from them isn't the answer. I will be honest and say I was trying to find her for my own reasons.' Price ran his hands down her arms, stopping at her hands, holding them in his. 'It felt personal, but we didn't have an understanding. It's possible I was under an illusion cast by time.'

THE MOTHER

$\mathcal{A}$nnabel Lester smoothed her hair as best she could in the primitive living conditions. Not primitive like living in a cave, or a tent in an overcrowded refugee camp, but in the sense that she had no electricity. Dunedin wouldn't see electricity until 1885. Of all the things she missed, electricity was the main one. That and hair conditioner. And hair straighteners. Still, she'd tidied herself as far as possible, and checked her reflection in the small hand mirror. The Bishop allowed no mirrors in the Manse, considering them 'a sign of vanity,' he'd said. So she kept this one in her chest of drawers, under her underwear — the most utilitarian creations ever designed, and ones she was certain even the cretin Bailey wouldn't dream of disturbing. She'd found the mirror in a pawnshop. It wasn't of any great value, being plain ebony. It had once been part of a larger ladies' dressing table set, but the pawnbroker had divided the collection, selling each item individually. The mirror was usually the most desirable piece, but because of a small nick in the handle, it had remained unsold. This was why complete sets commanded such high prices at auction in the modern world. She'd broken up suites of jewellery, dinner services and sets of silver cutlery herself, anything to get a sale. She regretted those decisions now. But, you achieved nothing in life by hanging on to the past.

A final glance in the mirror and she was ready for her walk. They were meeting at Hubert's Café and Club on Princes Street for lunch. It was her afternoon off, but still she slipped silently out of the house, afraid her employer would see her, and question her intentions. The Bishop assumed she'd come to Dunedin under the Assisted Female Immigration Scheme. It was no secret that many women coming to New Zealand on the scheme had turned to prostitution, for a variety of reasons, but primarily because of the lack of work in the province. As a result, she never felt at ease with him, and constantly worrying about being thrown out contributed to her insomnia.

Walking to the café, she reflected on the changing society in which she lived. Dunedin had been a smug Presbyterian community when she'd first landed, but since the flood of miners, the settlement's moral and religious tone was teetering on the brink of collapse. If the Bishop and his lackey knew where she was going, they'd accuse her of contributing to that downfall.

At least Price hadn't suggested they meet at night. Walking about town in the evening was not for the fainthearted. The swathes of tents, combined with the criminal element who'd fled New South Wales in search of glory on the Otago goldfields, increased the chances of being set upon by a ruffian *en route* to one of the newly formed musical societies. No, going out for lunch was respectable, and she shouldn't worry about the Bishop. There was no chance he'd have any idea what she was up to this afternoon.

THE SON

*A*nnwr Lloyd wrapped the shawl tighter around her shoulders. Standing outside the pub, she kept watch for her son, missing these last two nights. She stood in the shadows, to avoid attracting attention from a man who might mistake her as a 'lower' sort of woman.

Their home in Wales was so distant from the ports of London and Glasgow, but that hadn't stopped the sinking feeling in her stomach when she considered her second son may have gone off on a grand adventure to join his brother in the colonies.

She cursed herself again for keeping the letters from her eldest boy. Isaac had learnt his writing from the minister who'd made sure all the boys under his care could pen their names, and those of their families. Not in Welsh though, in English. It seemed young Colin had learnt his too.

When she'd first come home from the factory to discover Colin gone, and her pile of correspondence from Isaac's time in New Zealand scattered across the kitchen table, she'd known instantly that Colin had run off to find his eldest brother. There was no bond as strong as the hero-worship a younger brother has for an elder one.

Now she waited, in the slender hope Colin would get a cuff round the ear from the nearest sailor, and sent home to his mam. Her two smallest children inside, grumbling about getting supper ready. Seven, and nine, not so little any more, almost old enough to earn their keep, which would barely put them back where they had been when Colin was home and working at the mines. If he didn't come back soon, they'd lose their room at *The Sailors Return,* and be out on the street before they knew it. Annwr shivered. Hope was a powerfully warming drug, but it could only warm you for so long.

C olin Lloyd shivered on the ship. He'd been cold before — that was par for the course when you lived in Wales — scrimping and saving every penny he and his mother could earn to keep them alive. Alive but not warm. But he'd never been this wet and cold for so long, salt-water spray making his trousers and shirt stiff, rubbing his neck raw, and chafing his skinny thighs. The peculiar balmy weather they'd had earlier on in the voyage was now a distant memory, but standing there on deck, shivering in the wind, watching a poor soul thrown overboard, was far preferable to being below in steerage, where the stench of vomit was all pervasive. His stomach had stood up to the rigours of an ocean crossing better than most; he'd at least been able to keep down his meals. Regular food was a luxury he was unfamiliar with, and he wouldn't let an upset tummy stop him from eating everything put before him.

He hugged himself harder. Standing on his own, he let down his guard, becoming the boy he truly was, instead of the man he was trying to be. He'd marvelled at the flying fish they'd seen, and for the past week dolphins had escorted their ship, weird shiny things, smiling and gibbering at him every time they caught his eye with their silly antics.

He'd barely spoken to the poor soul they'd just wrapped in an old sailcloth and tossed over the side, albeit with a Christian service. The man hadn't distinguished himself onboard; he travelled alone — headed for the glittering goldfields of New Zealand, before a tragic accident robbed him of his dreams. God gave no warning before calling your name.

Colin's brother was in New Zealand, finding his fortune, according to the letters he'd found from Isaac to their mam. In the beginning, they'd described the abundance New Zealand offered, the opportunities, begging her to bring the rest of the family out. But his more recent correspondence hadn't been as glowing. The letters spoke of hardship and unrest and urged their mother to stay put; promising he'd be home as soon as he'd made some money. And then they'd stopped.

Colin was here for two reasons: to find his brother; and to strike his fortune. His family deserved better than living in one room above an inn, their tenancy constantly a struggle. And he deserved more than working in the dark coal mines of Wales.

The captain had said New Zealand was only a few days voyage, weather dependent, although this wind would help. Tearing his eyes away from the dead man's disappearing body, he strained to catch sight of land, but the vast expanse of empty ocean teased him with its dancing waves, and its choir of porpoises.

Munching on his ration of raisins, he savoured their sweet taste, wondering if they'd provisioned Isaac's ship with such things. He wanted to send some back to his little brothers, but they were too good. He'd write once they got there and describe them. Colin smiled as he swallowed; the sweetness clinging to his tongue and teeth. He had no desire to go below deck, to play chess or another interminable game of cards with the other lads. Being up here, taking in the world outside was enough entertainment for him.

Colin's mind wandered to the problems he would face once he arrived at Port Chalmers. The task of getting from there to Bruce Bay was the biggest one. The lack of food and shelter never once presented themselves as a problem — a typical teenage boy frame of mind.

THE LUNCH

*H*ubert's Café was filling up. Not the most illustrious in Dunedin, despite its claims of grandeur, but it was affordable for the average person — hence the numbers who filled it every weekend.

Price waited outside, nodding at the enquiring glances thrown his way. Most diners too focussed on their own relaxation to worry about the handful of shiny men waiting for their lady friends. Price, however, cast his eye over every man and woman who walked past, still looking for Sinclair and Sarah. He didn't think he'd ever stop searching for them. His life needed to go on, but could it without *her*? Then he caught sight of Annabel.

She smiled at Price, subconsciously touching her hat. It still felt like she was playing dress-ups every time she went out. Initially, she thought she'd never tire of it, but a couple of Otago summers had cured her of that romanticism. But, on chilly days like today — and there were many of them, she welcomed the voluminous skirts, quilted jackets, hats and gloves society dictated she wear.

'Good afternoon, Mrs Lester,' Price said, offering his arm to his guest.

Together they entered Hubert's, and sat at a table for two, set

English-style with white linen tablecloths, and polished cutlery. A cold luncheon was on offer — there was no picking courses off a menu, so the plates arrived with no great fanfare. The noise was bearable, quiet murmurings between couples; the largest group of guests numbered only four — merchants making their way north, selling their wares to the various towns en route.

Price held Annabel's eyes. *So very green.* He had to stop comparing them to Sarah's. A small piece of him desperately wanted her to walk through the door. There'd been a time on the road, that he would have traded his life for another moment with Sarah. But this woman, Annabel, she was casting a spell over him, washing away all but his deepest memories of Sarah, and he was powerless to do anything about it.

'So, do you come here often?' Annabel asked, lowering her lashes to hide her fear that this was a regular habit of his, taking strange ladies out for lunch.

'No, this is my first visit. Someone from work recommended it. He is more the type to frequent establishments like this.'

Annabel took a small sip of sherry which Price had ordered for them both. It'd been ages since she'd last had a glass of sherry. Years earlier, when Sarah was little, and even before that, she and Albert drank a glass before dinner every night. It was 'their thing', and cheaper than wine. They drank out of tiny crystal glasses, the sort that weren't in vogue any more, but here she was, drinking out of identical glasses, but with another man.

Small talk dominated their conversation. It was easy enough to get caught up in the minutiae of life in a new town, and they talked about the roads, the immigrants, the influx of merchants from New South Wales, and the convicts who'd fled the hard slog in Australia, swapping it for an even harder time on the gold fields of Otago. With the weather turning, they theorised about the numbers who'd leave again once they realised how cold it could be.

'Why anyone settles here is beyond me,' Annabel offered, taking another sip of the sherry, savouring the sweet taste on her tongue.

'But you did, Mrs Lester. You settled here?'

Caught out, Annabel blushed. *How am I meant to answer this?* 'I had no choice,' she said, picking at the crocheted tablecloth.

'But you can leave. There's nothing holding you here, is there?'

Looking him in the eye, she answered sharply, 'Only a roof over my head, and food in my stomach. In case you haven't noticed, it isn't Noddy's Toyland here. No one's handing out free houses, and the jobs available aren't that salubrious.' Waving a hand around the room, she carried on, 'Look at all these women. Either they're already married, or they're desperate to get married — preferably to a man with some money — so they aren't working on the streets.'

'I don't know who Noddy is, but there are opportunities out there. I was only asking if something tied you to this town.' He looked away, his eyes not seeing anything other than an empty future stretching ahead of him, surrounded by thugs and vagabonds, lonely nights in boarding houses or his ramshackle hut in Bruce Bay. 'I'm curious if you can leave, or whether you were under some obligation to stay?' he asked, sinking back into Sarah's, *no, not Sarah's,* sinking into Annabel's green eyes.

'I shouldn't think the Bishop cares if I'm there. Another ten women are waiting to take my place. Women with better credentials than I; whose linens revert to their original white colour, and whose hems stay up. Ten women with references and the right breeding. A hundred Christian women who don't swear and aren't gigantic behemoths stomping around the Manse in size eight shoes...'

Price held his finger up to his lips, 'There aren't ten women in this city who can hold a candle to you. It's true that I haven't heard other women swear like I have heard from you occasionally,' he beamed at his dig, and once Annabel had returned the smile, he carried on. 'There isn't a single woman here as good as you.'

Annabel laughed. 'You haven't seen my laundry skills. The number of pillow slips I've had to rewash, the tablecloths I've hidden in the bottoms of drawers so the Bishop and his smarmy aide can't see the iron marks.'

Price shushed her. 'Those are of no consequence. They matter not to God, nor to man...'

'Have you met Bishop Dasent?' she exclaimed, too loudly for the diners nearest them, who looked aghast at her words. 'But no, I'm not tied to him. I could walk out today and not be beholden to him. Although there are some things I'd like to take with me if I ever left. Why, were you inviting me to run away?'

Price squirmed in his wooden chair. *Do I want her to run away with me? She's nothing like any other woman I know.* 'I don't think I have enough to offer you...' he started, before being interrupted by Graeme Greene.

Greene rushed up to the table, tripping over chair legs in his haste to get to Warden Price, landing on the table, sloshing sherry all over the pristine white of the tablecloth.

'What on earth are you doing here, Greene?' Price was barely controlling his frustration at the interruption.

'Sorry, sir, but there's been an accident. The *Watermark* has run aground at the entrance to Port Chalmers, there are bodies everywhere,' He stopped short as he noticed Annabel. 'Sorry, ma'am, but it's all hands on deck, so to speak. I knew you'd be here, and we need all the help we can get.'

The moment lost, Annabel and Price exchanged glances filled with things unsaid. 'You should go, Mister Price,' Annabel said, gathering up her own belongings, 'And I should tell the Bishop — he'll want to be there.' Under her breath, she muttered, 'He always goes to the important stuff.'

Price hesitated, before laying three shillings on the table, to cover their uneaten meal. He clasped her hand and then left the café. Two other constables, off duty themselves, followed him out of Hubert's, and the four men commandeered the nearest taxi cab, racing off to the port.

Annabel paid no attention to the other diners and, in her haste to leave, didn't notice the weasel-faced Norman Bailey, lurking in the corner, a cup of tea cooling in front of him.

THE BOAT

*T*he scene at the entrance to Port Chalmers was chaos. Men in shirtsleeves waded out as deep as they dared to drag in the survivors, and those not so lucky. Further out in the channel, the wooden sides of the *Watermark* had split like a ripe tomato, spilling its guts into the icy water.

Customs Officers set to in their small boats, dragging survivors over the sides. Weighed down by lashings of petticoats, and heavy woollen trousers, most of the passengers were being pulled under.

'Can you swim, Greene?' Price yelled, stripping off his outer garments.

'Yes, sir?'

'Get your boots off, your jacket and your trousers too, and get in there.'

Before Greene could argue, Price had waded out past the other rescuers, ignoring the men they were dragging up to the shoreline. He kept his eye on the patch of water where he'd spied a young lad trying to hold up a girl. Both had disappeared underwater as he'd yanked off his boots.

Powerfully, he swam out to the spot, surrounded by empty barrels and the detritus common to sailing ships around the world. Taking a deep breath, he dived past bolts of cloth lurking beneath the frigid waves, past the carcass of a piglet, originally destined for the captain's table. *There.* Two figures tangled together, turning like feathers on a spring breeze. He struck out for the top and, filled his lungs once more before diving again, the water dulling the sounds above him. Kicking towards the bodies, he grabbed handfuls of their waterlogged clothes, tugging them towards the surface, willing himself to have the strength to bring them both up. They were so heavy, and with his lungs screaming, he prepared to make the irreversible decision to abandon one before he too drowned, when Greene appeared.

All skinny legs and wide, scared eyes, Greene grabbed the girl around her waist and wrenched her free from Price's weakening grip.

They broke the surface, and Price gasped for air like a beached whale. 'There's no time to waste, Greene, got to get them to land,' he screamed, coughing up water, hacking his way through the choppy sea, the unresponsive boy towed behind him.

His feet found the soft silt in the shallows, and rough hands reached out to grab the boy's body, to add it to the growing number of lifeless immigrants, lined up like silent school children. Price refused to relinquish him, 'No, no, lay him down here, on his back, the girl too,' he rasped, spitting out the salty water which threatened to suffocate even him.

Kneeling, dripping salt water over the limp body, he thumped the boy's chest, again and again, over and over. Greene copied him, fearful he was doing more harm than good to her.

'Harder, Greene, harder, you've got to get the water out of her lungs,' Price ordered, before he lent to kiss the boy.

Greene's eyes widened in shock, 'Are you kissing him?'

Price ignored the question, intent on blowing air into the boy's lungs. *How long was he under? Only a couple of minutes?* The boy had a chance. Coming up, he turned to Greene, pushing the young man's face down to the girl's unresponsive face laying before them, 'Give her your air, breathe into her mouth.' With the instruction given, he turned back to the boy. Two more breaths, and another wallop to the chest with the side of his fist, and the boy convulsed, water erupting from his mouth like a geyser. Price turned him to his side, lest he choke. Behind him he could hear the satisfying sounds of the girl doing the same, and the gasps of wonder from the audience.

'You have a hospital here, right?'

Greene nodded, looking bewildered at the girl now huddled in his lap, hiccuping and gulping in noisy lungfuls of air.

'We need to get them there. Give her your coat, man, she's freezing.' Price himself was draping his own jacket over the pale boy shivering in the tussock.

Luckier passengers were being rowed to shore in a montage of dinghies, sail boats, even a Māori canoe — a *waka*. Each vessel disgorged sodden passengers, and bodies, onto the increasingly crowded shoreline.

Together, the Customs staff and the police sorted themselves, and the chaos calmed. Shouted commands settled into orderly instructions, and a mountain of willing hands assisted survivors, and covered the dead.

Price scooped up the young lad, nodding at Greene to do the same. 'Come on, we must get these two to hospital. They'll know what's best to do with them there. Leaving them here's no good.' After summoning a carriage, they hurtled into town. The girl refused to let go of Greene, resulting in a damp trip to the Dunedin General Hospital.

THE PATIENT

Colin Lloyd lay in a pristine white bed, in a long room filled with identical beds. The General Hospital was still new enough that fresh wooden floorboards offset the scents of decaying butchered limbs and the dirt poor.

It felt like a thousand stinging bees had swarmed in his throat, before nesting in his chest. Every breath hurt like buggery. He cast a glance down the line of beds trying to find anyone he recognised. He'd no idea if he was the only survivor or not. Every bed was full of men in various states of disrepair. A nurse clad in white swished down the centre of the room, crisp efficiency exuding from each pore, as she assessed her patients. She stopped once to tuck a wayward sheet around an elderly gentleman, his head bandaged with snow white wraps. With the other patients also swathed in crisp white sheets, the overall effect was as if fresh snow drifts surrounded him. Or what he imagined fresh snow would look like, untainted by coal dust. The only snow he'd ever seen looked more like coal slurry.

He pushed himself up, 'Nurse?'

The woman paused, looking for the owner of the voice, rewarding him with a flicker of emotion before reaching his bed. Gently pushing him back down she said, 'So, you're back with us then, lad?'

'Do you think I could have a drink please, miss?'

Her skirts swished again as she filled an invalid's cup for him, then returned to hold the beaker to his mouth. He sipped, grimacing as his throat protested at even the most benign of liquids.

'Is your throat in pain?' she asked, staring at him.

'Yes,' Colin said, his watery blue eyes filling.

'The surgeon will be back from the barracks. There are more patients there for him to see, we must share him between us. The water will soothe your throat, drink up.' She put the beaker against Colin's lips. He opened them obediently, trusting her face, her greying hair. The nurse reminded him of his mam. 'The surgeon needs some details about you, we don't even know your name or your age. No one's come forward to claim you as their own. I'll be right back with my folder.' She swished off down the ward, once again casting her eyes over the rest of her patients.

Colin lost sight of her as she vanished through the doors at the end of the ward. He coughed uncomfortably. This was not how he'd imagined his adventure would start. At least he wasn't cold any more, and they weren't skeletons in the surrounding beds. The men looked well fed enough, so he presumed they'd feed him at some stage — hopefully only a broth; he didn't think he'd be able to manage anything more solid.

When the nurse returned, she wasn't alone. Warden Price strode up to Colin's bed, a slight smile on his face as he saw the young lad was awake. 'Back with the living, then?' Price pulled up a chair, settling down. 'So what's your name, son? The passenger manifest disappeared with everything else, so we're waiting on the telegraph service to send through a complete list. Meanwhile, I said I'd help put together a list of the survivors. The police here have enough on their plates without worrying about this.'

'That's a big job, sir,' Colin rasped. Price offered him some water from the invalid's cup. Colin took a few sips, before continuing, 'As near as I know, there were about ten score on board, including the crew, sir.'

'And what's your name, boy? The nurse here needs it for her records.'

'Colin Lloyd, sir. I'm here to see my brother, Isaac. Maybe you know him, sir?'

Price laughed, 'It's a big country, boy. Dozens of immigrants arrive almost every day. There's a flood of Welsh boys just like you slogging their guts out on every new goldfield the papers hint at. The odds aren't high I know him. Sorry...'

'And how old are you, Mister Lloyd?' the nurse interjected.

Colin closed his eyes. They couldn't send him back now, so it'd do no harm to tell them the truth, 'Sixteen, ma'am.'

The nurse stifled her dismay, her pencil scratching on the form. 'And your address?'

Colin coughed, and reached for the water, managing it on his own now. 'Here, or at home?'

'Do you have an address here?' She didn't sound hopeful.

'My brother is in Bruce Bay, so I'm on my way there to see him. I'm not that sure where it is. But can I put that down as my address? Or I can give you my mam's address in Wales...'

'No address,' she muttered under her breath. 'The surgeon will be along and I'll be back later. You help the Warden with his questions, but keep sipping that water.' She then went about her business, already putting the young man out of her mind as she concentrated on the other men in need of her nursing.

Price had been looking at the boy silently since he'd uttered the words 'Bruce Bay'. The coincidence was too much. 'What did you say your brother's name was, boy?'

'My name's Colin, sir.'

'No, not your name, your brother's name?'

'His name's Isaac, sir. He's been out here a good couple of years now. He was writing regularly to our mam, but nothing for a long time now. So... well, I thought I'd come find him, and help him on the goldfields... for the family. It's the coal mines or the slate mines at home, and... well, this seemed more exciting...'

Price slumped forward. *The poor boy. Should I tell him?* The general surgeon arrived, saving him from answering. The surgeon's giant mutton chop sideburns, a swathe of silvery white on his chin, completed the snowy landscape of the ward.

'You had a lucky escape, Mister Lloyd. It's not many drowning survivors I see in here. You and your lady friend were very lucky the Warden was on hand to pluck you from the hands of Death. Now, I have this instrument here with which I wish to listen to your lungs,' and he pulled out his flexible stethoscope, applying one end to Colin's bony chest. Deep concentration filled the surgeon's face, 'Pulmonary oedema, or what the normal man calls water in the lungs. Rest should cure it. No running off to the goldfields. Is that where you were heading?'

Colin's eyes widened at the surgeon's uncanny ability to read his mind.

'I'm not reading your mind, Mister Lloyd, but of the men in these beds around you, there would only be a couple who aren't in here for gold-related ailments. One piece of advice, get a proper job. Forget the goldfields. You've only a couple of months before the temperatures plummet, and the minders will flood back into town, looking for work. Find yourself a job now,' he said, winding up his stethoscope, and smoothing down his whiskers. 'Perhaps the Warden here can help you find work. He's the one who saved your life. God has bigger plans for you than dying penniless in the provinces looking for alluvial gold.' And he took his leave.

'He didn't say how the water would get out of my lungs?' Colin whispered.

'Time, Colin, time. I'll come back tomorrow, and we'll talk more then. Why don't you write your mam a letter, tell her you're okay?'

Colin nodded, relieved someone was looking out for him, relieved he didn't have to be a grown-up, just yet.

W arden Price returned to the hospital to find Colin looking perkier and, whilst still propped up against cushions, he was playing cards with another patient.

'Hope there's no money riding on that game,' Price joked with the boys.

'Oh, Mister Price, you came back,' Colin enthused.

'I did. I've saved very few lives in my time, and, given you're one, I thought it best to look in on you. Make sure the Surgeon hasn't knocked you off in his haste to repair you.'

Colin's eyes widened, 'Oh no, sir, he's been brilliant. But busy, he has to see to the men over at the barracks, and the ladies.'

Price had a little gem of an idea percolating away. He needed to keep this lad safe, otherwise he'd end up the same as his brother — buried with no ceremony, in a nondescript cemetery they would lose to time as nature reclaimed the wooden plot markers, once the settlers moved on, following the gold, leaving the land breathing in relief.

'Did you write home? Like we discussed? To let your mam know you weren't dead in an alley back home?' Price raised one eyebrow.

'Oh, yes, but the nurse wouldn't send it. Said she needed money for the postage. But everything I own is at the bottom of the sea, so what should I do?' Colin's voice faltered, revealing again how young and alone he was.

'I think we can post it for you. Happens that I know the lady up at the Manse and, since you tell me the Church taught you your letters, I'm sure the Church can stump up a penny to send your letter to your mam. You give it to me and I'll sort it out for you. I'll be back tomorrow to check on you again. So don't you go anywhere until I've been in,' Price instructed.

As obedient as ever, Colin nodded again, before a short coughing fit took over from his bobbing head.

'You rest, I'll see you later. And while I'm gone, perhaps consider what you might like to do with your life now you're not going to the gold fields.'

Price left, leaving Colin protesting that gold mining was *exactly* what he wanted to do.

Exhausted, Colin lay against his mountain of pillows. He couldn't lie flat, had to sleep sitting up. Every time he tried to sleeping horizontal, the nurse had to come and help him because it felt like he was drowning all over again. He couldn't breathe and ended up gasping for air, pain tearing at his throat. So he'd given up trying. Sitting wasn't so bad, it meant he could talk to the other men, although listening to their stories of life on the goldfields filled him with a sense of trepidation. Maybe he'd go, just to visit Isaac, to see if he was okay, and then he'd find a proper job. Finally the distance to Bruce Bay scared him. *How am I ever going to get there without money, and without being able to breathe properly?*

THE ORDERS

*P*rice reported in at the station, asking, as always, if there'd been any sightings of Sinclair, although, today his heart wasn't in it. There were other more pressing matters to consider.

Sergeant Jock Crave was manning the front desk, his ever-present pipe barely a hindrance to his daily tasks. Legend had it that Crave had subdued and arrested someone once, with his pipe still clamped between his lips. It didn't even go out.

'No sightings, Price — ain't likely to be any now,' he prophesied, before adding, 'There's a letter here for you, though.'

Price took the letter from Jock, before walking through to the briefing room. As he read it, he noticed Greene sitting on the far side. The lad's shoulders were square, and his chin held high. A peculiar light shone in his eyes.

'Morning, Greene,' Price said, 'Something's different today. Can't pin it down.'

Greene's face lit up, 'It's Una, sir.'

'Una?'

'Una Neville, the girl from the boat. You know — the one we saved?'

'Oh yes, Miss Neville. How is she doing?' Price had forgotten the young woman they'd dragged from the chilly waters of the harbour. That was a lifetime ago.

'Miss Neville wanted to thank me for saving her…'

'That's good,' Price interrupted.

'But that's not all. She's asked if we could meet for a cup of tea, so she can thank me in person. This weekend. She was coming out here to join her aunt and uncle, so her aunt will chaperone her. I can't believe it.'

Price smiled at the younger man, 'See what happens when you save someone's life?'

'What's in the letter?' Greene changed topics as fast as the seasons did in this new country.

Price looked at the paper in his hand, folded over and over, until it was as small as a calling card. 'Oh, orders. I'm no longer required in Bruce Bay. As I told young Colin, there's no gold left in those hills. Most of the miners are making their way north, wreaking havoc as they go, like locusts. I'm being reassigned to the Bay of Plenty. There is *plenty* of trouble there, which needs quelling. Heaven knows what's happening. Living with the Māori need not end in bloodshed, but it sounds like that's what I'm in for.'

Greene's mood was evaporating with the knowledge his unofficial mentor was leaving him.

'But what about Sinclair, and your friend Sarah?'

'We have to face the truth that Sinclair has gone. Where? I know not. Whether Sarah is still alive is unclear, although now believe she's not. Sinclair wouldn't drag a woman around with him this long. She'd just be a hindrance.' Sadness flashed across Price's face. He felt a certainty as to the fear he'd just voiced and realised that the thought had been at the back of his mind the whole time he was chasing Sinclair down country. Sarah would have been a liability to Sinclair. She wouldn't go quietly; or *remain* quiet. She was strong and strident, so like Annabel that, despite Annabel's protestations, they were mirror images.

Assuming Sarah *was* dead, her body was most likely hidden deep in the impenetrable bush covering this land, decaying, returning her to nature. He only hoped Sinclair was quick about it. *He* would resurface, with the candelabra, unless he'd melted them down — which *was* a possibility — then they would be little more than misshapen lumps of silver, minus their assay marks.

'When will you leave?' Greene asked, his shoulders slumped forward.

'In a couple of days. There are things I need to sort out here first.'

'Mrs Lester?'

'I beg your pardon?'

'Everyone knows you took her out. How do you think I found you at the restaurant? There are no secrets in this town. She needs to be careful though — the Bishop's man doesn't like her...'

'She's a grown woman. A widowed woman taking tea with an employee of the Crown. That isn't a cause for any gossip. I thought we'd escaped this judgemental behaviour by leaving England?'

'You don't know the Bishop. Any smear of impropriety, and he's all over it. He's still new to town, but there's nothing he doesn't have his finger on. He's trying to shut down anything that's...' The Sub-inspector interrupted Greene by entering the room and the general hubbub of a dozen constables ebbed away.

'Right, lads, be on the lookout for a Samuel Beeby. He assaulted a constable last night who was questioning him about a break in at Simpson's store. He took off, with two or three accomplices. We've not been able to track him down. Constable Swan is recovering at home, and will be back on board tomorrow but, all things considered, it's your priority today to locate Beeby and bring him in. Last night, a cart took out Mr Solomon's shop window, damaging its framework. You'll remember someone robbed his shop earlier this year, being that he is a gold assayer and jeweller. That robbery remains unsolved, but it's possible this latest break in was by the same persons,' the Sub-inspector allocated various officers to the crime, and other ongoing cases.

Price listened to it all. Crime was the same regardless of where you lived. Criminals followed the money, and gold was an easy portable target. Alcohol was nearly always the culprit for petty misdemeanours and public nuisance complaints. If you outlawed alcohol, and eliminated greed, life would be utopian.

The Sub-inspector dismissed the officers, and like a wave, ranks of blue serge-wearing colonial men flowed out of the room, their ruggedness an echo of the land they inhabited.

'I'm off too. I've got a letter I need to get to the Manse,' Price said to Greene.

'Don't forget what I said about the Bishop, and his man,' Greene replied. 'Better to use a boy to deliver it for you,' he suggested.

'It's a letter from the lad in hospital, to his mother. I was rather hoping to utilise the goodwill of the Church to post it for him, given the Church has taken the time to teach him his letters.'

'Uh-huh,' Greene said, eyebrows raised.

Price laughed, 'Fine, you don't believe me. Off you go, you've a robbery to solve. I'll catch up with you at midday. Remember what I said the other day, follow the money. After the robbery of a jewellery shop, they want to get rid of the jewels as swiftly as possible. Most criminals don't have the wherewithal to hold on to their ill-gotten goods till the heat dies down. Back when I was in New South Wales, two weeks after a robbery, another member of the gang tried selling some of the stolen stuff back to the jeweller.'

'How'd that happen?' Greene asked, perplexed.

'Simple case of the left hand not knowing what the right is doing. Ended up arresting the lot. Jeweller got back some of his things, and a fist-sized lump of gold — they'd already melted most of it down. That's another thing to look for, someone who has the right gear to melt gold; a crucible, and extreme heat. And you don't find those on every street corner. Be smart, Greene, and you'll find the stuff before I'm back from my errand.' Price shoved his hat back on his head, and left, leaving Greene scribbling in his notebook.

Price made his way to the Manse, marvelling again at the rate of progress in what had been, only a few years ago, a tiny Presbyterian settlement. In his paper this morning, there'd been adverts for an operatic performance of *The Barber of Seville*, and billiard games, and a ball for the Benevolent Society — all activities considered unseemly by the strict religious founders of Dunedin, and the Otago province. There had also been an advert for the auction of a four-roomed verandah cottage, complete with a vegetable garden and fruit trees, well adapted for a respectable family. And he wondered, will *I* ever have a family?

Price walked up the path to the Manse. Its garden was a mere shadow of what it had once been under the green thumbs of Reverend Cummings. The autumnal chill was now attacking the flowers left in once-glorious beds either side of the pavers. *Would a family cottage have a path lined with flower beds*, Price mused before his hand reached for the gleaming brass door knocker.

Annabel answered the door before his heartbeat had even reached a count of ten.

'Warden Price,' her eyes darted back behind her, checking the gloomy hall for any sign of Bailey.

'Mrs Lester, sorry to call upon you so early in the day, but I had hoped to ask you for a favour?'

Annabel's eyes widened. The longer the door was open, the greater the chances Bailey would discover her talking to Price. While parishioners often called, they were usually middle-aged women with pressing concerns about the state of the settlement. The Bishop lapped up their gossip and vitriol like a cat with cream in its saucer.

'Sorry, William, but you being here isn't great timing...'

Price's heart thumped at her using his first name, a touch of familiarity he was entirely unprepared for.

'I assure you, it's with the best intentions. There's a young lad in the hospital, he's no family here. I don't have the nerve to tell him his brother died in Bruce Bay...'

'The poor boy. But I don't see how I can help. You should go. You've no idea what they'll do if they see me fraternising with you at the door-'

'We're not *fraternising*, Mrs Lester. Please, I just have this letter for you to add to your outgoing post. It is but a small favour I ask,' he pushed Colin's letter towards Annabel. She reached for it.

'Mrs Lester, why not invite our guest inside,' came a voice from beyond the gloom.

Annabel jumped.

'It's nothing, just a delivery.' She stuffed the envelope into her pocket, her eyes apologetic as she closed the door on Price, the brass knocker clanking, ending the conversation. *And the relationship?*

Annabel turned to face the disembodied voice.

'A delivery? But I see nothing in your hands?' Norman Bailey spat. The whore had been entertaining the man from the café, *and* at the door of the Bishop's house. *The nerve of her*. Wait till the Bishop heard.

'Perhaps I wasn't clear — it was a query about a delivery. He wasn't sure where to deliver it, here or the church. It's sorted now.'

'Lies, Mrs Lester — filthy lies, straight from the mouth of Satan. The Bishop will hear of this as soon as he returns. Mark my words, you'll be on the streets, with naught but the clothes on your back. And not a second too soon for my liking.' Smirking, he watched her stride down the hall. *No, Not natural. Too tall. Too bold. Sent by the Devil.*

THE STATION

*A*nnabel Lester trudged up to the police station, a small leather suitcase gripped in one hand, her face pale.

The whole situation was ludicrous. She had *never* asked for this life. At home she barely ever went to church for Easter or Christmas. The one time she'd tried to go to a Christmas Day service, in Edinburgh, she'd slept in and when she'd arrived at the cathedral, she'd found it locked up tighter than the Crown Jewels. So much for Christian charity, she'd thought at the time. The same thoughts were going through her head now.

Thrown out of the Manse. No notice. Without her final pay and with no reference. She wouldn't dwell on it. They couldn't bring her any lower than she was when the Reverend Cummings had rescued her, before the Bishop had turfed him out on his ear.

At least she'd had time to rescue her treasures — *worthless things now*, she thought, grimacing as she calculated how very little she had to get by. Which was why she was about to throw herself on the mercy of the Warden, only she didn't know where he was.

Approaching the desk, she swallowed her pride, donned her colonial persona, and asked for Price.

The pipe in Sergeant Jock Crave's mouth stilled as he eyed the

fh
x
m

woman in front of him. They had a fair few women come through the station, mainly for the one reason, and few, if any, had sauntered up to his desk, as calm as you please, asking for one of the Queen's men.

He took his rich-brown *puriri* wood pipe from his mouth, knocked out the dottle before tightly repacking the bowl with fresh tobacco, while he considered her question, 'Warden Price isn't here, they've reassigned him...'

Annabel's face fell. If she hadn't been leaning on the counter she would have crumpled to the floor. *No.* She was stronger than that. She tried again, 'Do you know where they've reassigned him?' she asked, her voice betraying her rising panic.

'Mmm... mmm,' Jock replied, a delightful Scottish answer which is neither a 'yes' nor a 'no'.

'He's only gone to his lodgings to pack and settle his bill.' Greene said, appearing behind Annabel and answering for Sergeant Crave. 'Come with me, and we can catch him before he heads off. He was eager to speak with you before he left.'

Annabel averted her eyes from the sergeant who'd allowed his pipe to extinguish — unheard of inattention to his favourite pipe — and followed Greene from the station, allowing him to take her bag. The chivalrous manners of Victorian gentlemen continued to surprise her, and she'd quickly become accustomed to accepting their offers of help.

'Will he mind me turning up?' Annabel asked as they walked.

'I've not known him long, but this has been the happiest I've seen him. I'm certain you've helped put his demons to bed.'

'The weather is biting, winter is knocking,' Annabel added, completely changing the topic.

'Aye, and this town will be full of unemployed men looking for a warm place to sleep, a bite to eat, a job. The goldfields are hell in winter. Soil as solid as ice. Weather that'll turn your fingers and toes black, if you've got any left from the last winter...'

'You sound like you've lived that life,' Annabel observed.

'Not me... my father. Made our lives miserable. Would have been better if he'd stuck to farming, but no, when the fever strikes, it hits hard. My brothers never followed him, though. They saw how it broke our mother. There's not much you can do when you're only left with four fingers between your two hands.'

The sounds of progress filled the streets, carriages ferrying passengers home or away, to business, or for pleasure. Annabel loved playing the guessing game; who was behind the door? Where were they going?

Greene interrupted her daydreams, 'Here we are.'

Annabel hadn't registered their location, but they'd just walked back the way she'd come, and were outside *Wains Hotel.*

'Best wait here, until I've told him you're here,' Greene offered, aghast at the disregard for propriety, regardless of the circumstances leading to the Manse's housekeeper turning up at the station with a suitcase.

'No, Mr Greene. Thank you for bringing me, but I'll take it from here.'

'But, you can't go up there,' Greene protested, 'They'll assume you're a...'

'Should I care what people think of me? I know who I am. The best piece of advice I can give you is, stop worrying about what other people's opinions. Their thoughts about you do not matter.' Then she laughed. 'But you'll only realise the truth of what I say when you're older. Now, which room is his?'

Annabel made her way up the carpeted stairs to the first floor. The hotel still had a newness about it, where the skirting boards were pristine; and the expensive wallpaper — stylised oak leaves on a maroon background — unmarked or marred by water stains.

She found herself outside Price's door and brought her hand up to knock.

'Mrs Lester!'

'Mr Price, could I come in?'

Price hesitated — the landlady had been explicit when she'd said "No Female Companions". Given he was leaving today, this minor breach of the rules was acceptable, and he welcomed Annabel to his room.

'I never expected to see you here, at the hotel.'

'And I didn't expect to be here either, but things turned pear-shaped after you left.'

Price rubbed his chin, 'With the Bishop?'

'Yes, but his lackey fired the first shot. Bishop Dasent didn't need much persuading.' Annabel's shoulders sagged with the weight of her predicament.

Price directed her to the chair by the window, 'Sit down. Where will you go?'

'I have nothing here to hold me any more. My *friends* are fair-weather friends from church and they'll shun me like week-old milk.'

'Do you have somewhere to go? Back to England perhaps? To your family there?'

Annabel covered her face, as silent sobs shook her body.

'I have no family here. As for my family there, I have no one any more. No one but you.' She looked up at Price, her eyes red with tears.

Price knelt down, 'No one, Mrs Lester?'

Annabel looked into at his quiet eyes, and replied, 'Only you.'

Price nodded, heart racing. What he was about to do went against everything, all he knew.

'Come with me north, to the Bay of Plenty. I can't predict what awaits us there. It could be war, or it could be peace. Life will be hard, and I cannot promise you anything, apart from my love.'

THE LETTER

"The NZ lads are doing a fine job of keeping our spirits up. They did a stirring dance for some of the lads who died after a training accident here (I expect the censors to cross this bit out!). It's called a haha, but it made my blood run cold, whilst at the same time it brought tears to my eyes. Bugger the old 'stiff upper lip', they know who to celebrate the life of someone.

I can hear the foxes called at night now. They have a burrow somewhere near the airfield. The Adj. talks about hunting them every night. Don't think he likes them much. Don't tell him, but I think they're cute little things and hunting them seems so wrong.

I know you've got a fox coat, and I never really thought about it too much until I saw the cubs with their mum the other night when I was out for a stroll after supper — it's hard to get a moment to yourself around here. Children give you a different perspective on life, don't they? Don't take this the wrong way, but maybe sell the fur? If you want to, of course. These are the musings of a man who loves you, and misses you, and wishes you were closer.

I'll write more tomorrow. I can imagine you rolling your eyes as you read some of the silly things I've written here. And I love you even more for it."

THE MAJOR

The hail lashed everything in its path, both natural and man-made. It stripped blossoms from fruit trees and sent the mercury plummeting. With visibility reduced to zero, the soldiers hunkered down, miserable on the edge of the road. Only fools would venture out in this. Brutal winds accompanied the dangerous ice, damaging more than a dozen villages, and the equivalent number of British troops caught unawares outside.

Major Warren Brooke huddled against the trunk of a baobab tree, having decided that being hit by lightning was less of a risk than death by hail.

His men were miserable, and gloom settled over him as the weather focused his mind on everything wrong with his life. Not only was he wet and cold, but he was homesick too. He'd been in India for years, but now the sudden the pull of England had made itself quite clear. And the catalyst was obvious — a woman.

It was not as if there weren't any females to keep him company — far from it — but most of them had one goal in mind whenever he spoke to them, marriage. Every time he breathed near a single lady, Simla ran rife with the news they were engaged. Which was why he preferred being with his men. The likelihood of being shot was preferable to marrying any of the lacklustre social climbers surrounding him. That was why he was sheltering under a tree amidst the worst hailstorm in India's history, imagining he could see the only woman who'd ever fascinated him — Sarah Williams, the girl bundled out of Simla faster than the hail was falling.

The chatter round the troops was about the body they'd stumbled across the day before. It had once been a man, a local. His torso sliced open, resembling an overripe peach, burst after dropping from its branch to the ground. India's eclectic, and abundant scavengers and insects had done their best to clean up the corpse, rendering it unidentifiable. Captain Doulton and Brooke had discussed the comparison with Simeon Williams' body. The wound, though well cleaned by tooth and mandible, appeared identical in length and positioning. Similar enough that they felt discomfited by the similarities, as if the same person had killed both men. The identity of the killer still unknown.

An indistinct shape materialised in the gloom, arms held ineffectually above their head, providing no protection from the brutal chunks of ice whipped against them by the howling winds.

Catching sight of the person, the men broke off their quiet discussion, the dead body a topic for another day. 'Look at that idiot,' muttered Doulton.

Brooke shielded his eyes, peering out, 'Hell, James, that looks like a woman.' Brooke charged out into the weather, drenched within seconds. He felt a thousand ice daggers try to pierce his skin. It was only his uniform which saved him from real damage. A uniform so unsuited to the Indian climate that it was a continual source of complaint by the troops.

He shepherded the woman under the meagre protection of the tree. Doulton abandoned his dry position under the leafy canopy to make room.

There in the half light, the unmistakable face of Sarah Williams emerged, forcing them into a stunned silence.

'Miss Williams?'

Sarah looked up into the incredulous face of Major Brooke, noting at once the pain in his eyes — pain not caused by the hail.

Shaking the fuzziness from her head, and a residual headache, she nodded, before leaning against the tree for support.

'What in heaven's name are you doing here, out in this weather? They told us you'd returned to England.'

Sarah struggled to work out the timelines of her varied lives. The logistics of travel in the mid-nineteenth century wasn't something she'd grasped yet. If she had gone back to England from Simla, how long would that take? And then to come back again? Major Brooke was an intelligent man, would he believe her if she fudged the truth? Patricia's arrival saved her from answering.

With the men focused on Sarah, they'd failed to notice a second woman walking the same path as Sarah, a dozen paces behind, hidden by the squall, although this one was half stumbling, crying out in the wind, her voice lost to the surrounding mountains. Another soldier had ducked out and, scooping her up like a groom on his wedding night, carried her back under the tree.

Out of the apocalyptic weather, it took Patricia mere moments to grasp the situation. Her parents had always referred to her as a 'smart penny'. Her good humour remained alight, and her first comment took them all by surprise. 'You promised me the weather was better here, Sarah,' which lifted the mood all round. The biggest problem was not finding enough soldiers to go to India — it was getting them to return to England, and to the universally acknowledged dire weather.

'I can't imagine what you're doing this far out of Simla, Miss Williams, but, given how wet you both are...' He raised his eyebrows as he took in the fabric clinging to each woman's body, before averting his eyes to somewhere over Sarah's shoulder.

'Thank you, Major, out of this rain and some dry clothes would be great.'

'We weren't expecting this freakish weather either, Miss Williams, and, as far as I'm aware, there's no shelter close by. So there's little hospitality I can offer other than this tree, and a share in our rations once young Lawrence over there has started a fire.'

With the bedraggled appearance of the women causing much excitement among the patrol, the officers directed the men to start a fire for tea, and to erect whatever shelter they could muster from their packs to give them something to occupy their time. Unequipped for more than a couple of nights away from headquarters, rations and comforts were few. However, like most young soldiers of the time, they took it upon themselves to rally to the comfort of the gentler sex.

'Are you going to introduce us, Sarah?' Patricia asked, the reality of the situation sinking in.

'Yes, sorry. This is Major Warren Brooke and Captain James Doulton. And these are, what would you call them, your men? Your platoon?' she asked.

'My men will suffice,' Brooke answered, returning to his reticent self, his shock at finding Miss Williams pushed away for later, the only sign of his unease, a subconscious turning of a copper bangle around his wrist.

Captain Doulton interrupted the uneasy silence, 'The lads have made you some tea. Best you get that into you. Once Mrs Abbott finds out that you're back, she'll have me court-marshalled if she believes we didn't do our best for you.'

Breaking the tension between Sarah and Brooke, the officers ushered the women from the shelter of the tree, to a canopy rigged up by the men, where a billy was boiling away on a small fire. They filled white enamel mugs with fragrant tea, which sloshed over the side as Doulton lobbed two sugar cubes into each mug, and then his own, before handing the mugs to the women.

'No milk?' Trish asked, a smile dancing on her face.

If the men had noticed the streaks of mascara running down her face from the rain, they didn't say. A smile renders even the plainest person into a beauty, and hers lit up the makeshift camp. Before long, Patricia was being quizzed about her accent, making them all guess her origins. Brooke sat back on his hunting stool, sipping his tea, his eyes never once leaving Sarah. If she knew of his gaze, she gave no sign, bar catching his eye once or twice. Sarah put his staring down to the memory of what had happened to Simeon the last time she'd been in Simla. That image made her shiver, and although he'd been no true relative, no man deserved to what happened to Simeon. *Almost* no man, she corrected herself.

With Patricia burbling on about having never visited India before and asking everyone to regale her with the best places to visit, Sarah avoided the anxiety of further questioning about why she was there, when she was supposedly travelling back to England — which was news to her. The last thing *she* remembered was picking up the photo frame lying at the feet of her dead 'brother'. From there, time had whisked her back to the present day, and she knew nothing of the real Sarah Williams' descent into a deep depression brought on by complete and absolute memory loss.

Sitting under a canopy sipping tea might suit the army, but to know her father was so close, and to not be running down the road to be with him, made it difficult to swallow her drink. Chancing it as a question of no importance, she asked Brooke about her father, 'Major Brooke, a small question... is Albert Lester still at the Viceroy's lodge?'

Brooke's protracted silence scared her. What if her father had moved on? She'd found him by luck once, and she'd never imagined a second chance. To her relief, Brooke answered, 'Yes, he's still advising the Viceroy. I didn't know you knew each other?'

'It was the night of the troubles...'

The memory of Christopher Dickens' death stopped her from continuing.

Brooke noted the catch in her voice and probed no further. And leaving her to her thoughts, he conferred with Doulton, 'Can you send two of the quickest men back to town? At least they could get a carriage dispatched tonight. By the time they return, it will be the early hours of tomorrow.'

'I'd counsel against it, in this weather? Foolhardy. What if there's another hailstorm? With this drop in the temperature, we're better setting up a proper camp till the morning. I can escort them back with two others, and we can return for the rest of you before night falls again, depending on the conditions.'

'I'd rather they didn't walk back. Are there at least two competent men who can double back to Simla?'

'In this, Brooke? That's madness. You can't even see your own hand in front of your face, and none of us have winter kit. With all due respect, let's dig in here, and we can set off at daybreak. These storms never last long, but the sun is setting, the little of it you can see behind the storm clouds.'

The two men reached an impasse. Stepping into the weather, Brooke ducked back under the canopy, shaking the rain from his hair, the moisture making it curl up at the ends. His decision made, he only had to nod at Captain Doulton to make his instructions clear to the other officer. Doulton wasted no time in directing the men to make a temporary camp for the night. Years of training kicked in, each man knowing their role as if by some telepathic communication.

Soldiers draped jackets around the women's shoulders, instantly providing an additional level of warmth, and their shivering diminished. Huddling into each other, they found themselves alone for the first time since they were in the Foundling Museum, unwrapping the stiff tiger-skin rug. It finally clicked into place for Sarah — the skin was from the tiger which had attacked the Raja of Nahan, the very same one she'd shot with Christopher's rifle.

'Do you believe me now?' she asked Patricia.

'More than you can imagine,' Patricia replied, her teeth chattering.

'I didn't know this would happen. It's as much of a shock to me as it is to you,' Sarah offered.

'It is a shock, I'll give you that. I've always wanted hailstones the size of golf balls fired at my head,' Patricia quipped, smiling, despite being wet, cold and hungry. 'Do you think these boys have any food we can eat?'

'Undoubtedly. They say an army marches on its stomach, don't they?' Both women laughed aloud at the absurdity of their conversation, and their situation.

'What do we do now?'

377

'We try to find Dad as soon as we get to Simla,' Sarah said.

'Can't we go to your house first, clean ourselves up?' Patricia asked, her mind already wandering to the luxurious taffetas and silks she imagined were hanging in the wardrobe of Sarah's *doppelgänger*.

Sarah pondered the question, her forehead furrowing as she thought through the ramifications of her leaving Simla after Simeon's death. 'I don't think my things will still be there. I have some vague memory that most of the officer's houses were rentals. Rented from the local nobility — like the Raja of Nahan for instance, he owned some, and rented them to the East India Company. But I'm not sure, to be honest.'

'Shall we just ask then?'

'No, then I'd look like an idiot! Surely *I'd* know whether my belongings were still in India or if they were in England. It's best if we try to find my father as quickly as possible, and hopefully he'll have some idea of how to get us home. For all I know, he may have even found my mother.'

THE LODGE

*A*fter delivering Sarah and Patricia into the surprised arms of the Viceregal Lodge's household staff, Major Brooke nodded to Sarah before pulling the door closed behind him, and he and Captain Doulton disappeared into the recesses of the lodge.

'That soldier likes you,' Patricia announced, with no thought to the ears of the servants still in the room.

'Shh!' Sarah said, motioning to the Indian servants pottering around, ostensibly ignoring Sarah and Trish, but listening to every word, which they would broadcast throughout Simla before nightfall.

'Don't be silly, they can tell he likes you too. The only people who can't see it are you and him. Is he the one you were telling me about — that night with the wine, and the curry? Or was that the one in New Zealand?'

Sarah cast her mind back to that long ago night. It *hadn't* been Brooke she'd been referring to. And as for Bruce Bay, it didn't matter because she'd never see Price again. Now, reviewing her recollections of Major Warren Brooke was like a series of black and white photos developing into a prismatic feature film. Every glance, every word a declaration.

'Sarah? Hello? Earth to Sarah?'

'Yes, I'm just… in shock to be honest.'

'Typical. Tell him. Don't let this drag on any longer. Chop, chop. What better place to have a love affair than in India.' Trish got up and opened the door, ready to usher Sarah out into the arms of Major Brooke, and came face to face with a different man. A man white with shock as he glimpsed Sarah inside. 'Oh sorry, hello,' Patricia enthused, not for one second recognising the man.

'Sarah?'

Sarah stood on autopilot and walked over, 'Hi.'

'Oh. Oh my.' Trish clapped her hands, 'Come on, ladies, let's leave these two alone, and you can show me to a bathroom, and I'll need some new clothes. Let's sort those out first — oh yes, *lead* me to the wardrobe.' Trish gathered up the serving girls and shepherded them out of the room, nattering about fashion. All of them casting curious glances at Sarah and at the man, Albert Lester.

At last, the two were alone.

Albert stared. 'It can't be you. You left, and then the person you left behind returned to England. Christ almighty, you shouldn't be here. You can't be here. Why *are* you here?'

Sarah burst into tears. She needed her dad, yet he was dismissing her out of hand, without emotion. No hint of love. Every girl deserves the unconditional love of her father.

His resolve faltered, and he gathered her into his arms. Slipping into parental mode was as easy as that. 'I'm sorry. I can't believe that you are truly here. Your mother? Have you found her? I never in all my dreams expected to see you back here. Sarah, look at me.' Tilting her chin up till she was looking into his eyes, he carried on, 'Sarah, you know what's coming, to stay here is madness. The whole country is about to turn to custard. Britain is losing its grip here only doesn't know it yet.'

'Then come back with me, Daddy. We found a way last time, so we can do it again. Take me back to Simeon's house and I'll find something from home. Something to take us both back, and I won't screw it up this time. Then we can figure out how to find Mum, together.'

'I'm sorry, Sarah love, but I can't now. My life is here.'

She pushed him away, and screamed back, 'No! Your life is with me, at home. With Mum. You can't stay. You can't.'

'Sarah, keep your voice down. For God's sake, shut up.'

'You don't get to tell me to shut up. Not any more. If you won't be my father, then you've lost the right to order me around.'

'I'll always be your father, Sarah. Now calm down.'

'No. My real father would never have left. Never. You're not my father. Just go. I'll figure it out alone.' Sarah's face fell into a sullen scowl, worthy of any teenage girl.

Albert Lester, recognising the futility of carrying on the conversation, took a seat, waiting for sense to prevail.

Sarah pulled at his shirt, 'I said, just go. Go on, bugger off. Go play soldiers, or whatever is more important than your daughter and wife.'

'There is nothing more important than you and your mother-'

'Well, you've got a poor way of showing it,' Sarah interrupted.

'If you could listen for a moment?' Untamed white eyebrows raised in exasperation at his daughter's petulance. 'I've lost your mother. I spent years trying to get back to you both. Perhaps it's as the police said, and she *ran* off with someone. By some twist of time, we have both ended up here. If your mother was anywhere other than home, she would be here. With us, now.'

'Dad. Do you not remember when I told you...' Sarah broke off. She couldn't recall if she'd told him about her adventures in New Zealand, and as Betsy in London.

'Go on.'

'I haven't just been here, I've been other places too.'

Albert frowned. 'What do you mean *other* places?' Comprehension struggled across his face.

'I've been to Simla, but I've also been in New Zealand, during the gold rush. I've been a servant in a lord's house in London, and I've been back to the same house as a potential bride to Lord Grey. And now I'm back. The trips are all linked. They all involved something from an estate I bought. One lady owned everything, Elizabeth

Williams. You must have bought something off her? Something that sent you here.'

Albert sat thinking. He'd all but persuaded himself that his wife had left him, and he'd put her out of his mind, embracing this life with his extensive historical knowledge, the only subject he'd shown any aptitude for at school other than maths. Turning his thoughts to his business, he trawled through his almost photographic memory of sales and purchases, but couldn't recall any goods from an Elizabeth Williams. 'Whereabouts in London?'

'No, not London, Salisbury. Surely you'd remember something from that far away?

'I used to go to Salisbury occasionally because my godmother lived there. Our families were very close when I was younger, and I tried to do some buying when I visited. Your mother never came — she had to look after you. Let me think? Was it a house, or flat?'

'Her house. Well, her estate. The most glorious Georgian mansion. Made of flint. History says King James the First once stayed there.' Her father looked at her. 'I Googled it. Anyway, seems it was just her and her husband, who'd died before her. No children. I dealt with the solicitors, and someone had packed most of it up by the time I arrived.'

"Ah, I loved those sorts of deals. Never knowing what sort of treasures were there until you got back to the shop.'

The combined passion for the trade bridged their earlier difference of opinion. Like father, like daughter. His face lit up like a firework. 'Yes, I remember now! In Cathedral Close, enough windows to make you think the house was looking into your soul. Elizabeth Williams was old, but a lady who embodied the word "class". Someone put me in touch with her because she was a friend of my godmother. I bought some chinaware, nothing exciting — good stuff, though, a Royal Albert dinner service, and a shell collection. Made some money out of that. They'd boxed the shells up when I got there, with some large conch shells on the top, a teaser for what was in the cartons. At the bottom of a carton was a silver trinket box studded with jewels and decorated with engraved seashells. I never clicked that it was the trinket box which led me here. After all these years it's just becoming as clear as day. But how does that explain your mother's disappearance?'

His question stumped Sarah, and she chewed her lip. 'Maybe Mum met her somewhere? Bought something off her at a fair? Or she came the shop when you weren't there?'

'You're grasping at straws. No, she's not part of this. I've tortured myself thinking about it. I didn't realise she was unhappy, but, my love, it's the only explanation. Which is why I won't return. There's no life for me there now. Here, it's an adventure every day; like living inside a Clive Cussler book — every time you turn a page, something exciting happens.'

Sarah took a deep breath, her next questions flooding out like water running over rapids, 'I don't really want to know, but can you tell me, if... if you have a new family here... it's not my business but... well, I'd like to know that you were happy?' She paused and looked her father in the eye. He had the most annoying habit where he would tap the side of his nose with his index finger, as if to say *don't be so nosy*. 'Dad! Stop it. I asked you a completely reasonable question.'

Albert laughed, 'No, I don't have another family. I live here in the Lodge in what I can only describe as "bachelor" quarters. To be fair, I have escorted a few ladies to the theatre, but I don't have to tell you that my favourite pastime at the theatre is usually catching up on my sleep.'

Sarah recalled several occasions with him nodding off when he'd taken her to a stage show. Only her father could fall asleep during *'Allo, 'Allo* or *Cats*.

'What I have is the most perfect collection of antiques. And, before I die of some tropical disease here, I need to work out how to ship them to England and to keep them in storage for you. That way, when you go back-'

'When *we* go back.'

'No, when *you* go back, you'll be able to-'

'Again, Dad, just when I thought I'd finally seen some sign you do actually love me, it all comes crashing back down. You love antiques more than your own daughter. Fine. Whatever. Stay. You can gift me some leaky warehouse full of antiques. But until you help me get back into Simeon's house to find a way home, you're stuck with me — and Patricia. And she tells me that an officer quite likes me. I think that's worthy of investigating further, don't you?'

Sarah stomped from the room; petulant and hurt at the same time. Once she'd slammed the door satisfyingly loud behind her, she stood in the hall. She didn't know what to do now.

Nirmala appeared by her side. 'Memsahib?'

THE DINNER

*D*ressed by silent servants — servants on whose backs Great
Britain built their Empire — Sarah and Patricia prepared
for dinner. The girls looked at each other, both nervous in their own
right. Patricia's fears tempered by dressing in the most divine outfit of
blue and cream panelled silk, with a cunning floral motive spun into
it. Lace at the sleeves, and applied in a 'V' shape on the bodice, made
it a surreal costume, one she'd remember for the rest of her life.

In contrast, Sarah was wearing a blood-red silk, cinched at the
waist with a simple sash from the same fabric. A thin line of ribbon at
her demure neckline, and at the short puffed sleeves, completed the
outfit.

'You ready to leave the trenches? Once more unto the breach, dear
friend?' Sarah jested, the fear in her eyes at odds with the forced
joviality in her voice.

'What on earth could go wrong? Imagine it as an episode of
Downton Abbey. Tell you what, you pretend to be the Dowager
Countess, and be dire and morbid the whole night, and I'll play the
part of Lady Sybil — all sweetness and light. We've got our story
straight, your father's unlikely to come out and say, "Oh, by the way,
these two girls are from the future, and that one's my daughter," now

is he? For God's sake, cheer up. It's not the end of the world, Sarah. Stop being so miserable.'

Having lost patience with her friend, Patricia walked out of Sarah's bedroom, eager to get on with her own grand adventure.

Sarah followed behind, stung by her friend's words. *Am I dour and miserable? Is that how everyone sees me?* Thoughts tumbled over themselves as she rationalised her behaviour. She was acting like a bubblehead. Any other person in her predicament would grab it with both hands and run, singing the *Mary Poppins* soundtrack while doing so. *What do I want?* That was the first question she needed to answer. The *only* question she needed answered. From there, she could plan for everything else. Still questioning herself, she followed Patricia, almost unaware of her surroundings.

They walked into a room dominated by the longest dining table either of them had seen outside of Windsor Castle. Surrounded by forty-two chairs and covered with a white linen tablecloth. Patricia whispered how difficult it would be to fit it into a washing machine, before pristine servants separated them and escorted the women to their respective seats.

A floral carpet on the floor mirrored the foliage just visible through the windows in the fierce yellows and blush pinks of the setting sun. Arabian fretwork and heraldic shields in the European style jostled for space on the walls, the mixture of heritage working well. One wall of decorative shelving displayed the most glorious pieces of silver tableware and giant porcelain chargers. The staff, as numerous as the guests, stood behind the chairs as everyone waited for the Viceroy to arrive. Here was all the pomp and circumstance expected when dining with the Queen's representative, His Excellency, the Viceroy of India.

The formalities of the Viceroy's arrival completed, the dinner service began. The bill of fare announced eight courses. All along the table were ladies, young and old, preparing themselves for a feast of which they could partake only sparingly; for their dresses did not allow them to eat to the point of fullness. Sparrow-like, they must peck and scrape at the fine offerings. The staff served hors d'oeuvres first; a platter of *Devils on horseback* made its way down the table, pink pork strips wrapped around dark sweet prunes, a delicacy devised and adored by the Victorians — and revived in the seventies. Trays of pork tartlets made with saffron and currants further affirmed the table as one of wealth, already self-evident from the silver serving dishes, the cutlery and the sheer majesty of the room.

Sarah tried reading the menu, her schoolgirl French stumbling over the third course — *Cailles aux pommes de terre à l'Indienne.* She'd have to wait until it appeared before figuring out what they were.

A creamy tomato soup came next, served in delicate Royal Crown Derby footed Imari bowls, the luscious reds and blues made even richer in the flickering candlelight, reflected by hundreds of crystals hanging from the lustre vases adorning the table.

During the soup course, Sarah's companion on her right finally acknowledged her. 'Miss Williams, I trust you have recovered from the unfortunate death of your brother. No mourning dress for you?' Major Brooke looked *almost* concerned as he enquired after her grief.

Sarah laid her spoon on the Imari saucer, 'Thank you for your concern, Major Brooke, but, to be honest, I didn't feel the need to mourn my brother. His behaviour towards me was horrific. I applaud whoever did away with him.'

Stunned into silence at Sarah's frank opinion, Major Brooke attacked his soup. Her honesty stole the power of speech from him. It had been no secret in Simla that Simeon Williams had hit his sister, and his wife before that. Curious, he chanced another look at the woman sitting next to him. *Could she have killed her brother?* Leaning back in his chair he pondered the question. He'd seen Simeon's body; it was a violent death he'd suffered. No woman of Sarah's stature could have managed that. A knife was a man's weapon. Women, in his experience, preferred poison or something more subtle. Several husbands had 'accidentally' fallen from one of the many lookouts in the Indian hill country. *No,* he decided, *she isn't a murderer.* She wasn't transparent in her dealings with him, nor with those around her, he was certain of that, but why she was back in India he knew not. He'd noted the inquisitive glances Mrs Abbott had been casting Sarah's way all evening.

The two women had only just missed each other, given how late Sarah had left coming downstairs. Mrs Abbott was rabid with impatience that she hadn't had the chance to quiz Sarah about her return to Simla. She was still 'miffed' about the unanswered letters she'd sent while Sarah was 'recovering' in Delhi. Unusually for Naomi Abbott, she'd not shared her suspicions about Sarah's pregnancy with anyone. Frustration threatened to boil over that she had no clear view of Sarah's post-birth waistline — if she *had* been pregnant when she'd left Simla.

'I know what you're thinking, Major Brooke,' Sarah interposed.

Brooke choked on his mouthful. 'I beg your pardon, madam? I think not.'

Sarah lowered her voice, 'You're wondering if I killed Simeon. I can see it in your eyes. You'd make a useless poker player, Major.' She leant back into her seat to allow the waiter to remove her soup bowl to make room for the unfathomable *Cailles aux pommes de terre à l'Indienne*.

The other conversations around them included the self-righteous talk of preserving peace in India; the difficulties with servants — said within earshot of those selfsame servants — and how to better deliver the proper British way of life to the people of India, whether or not they wanted it. Sarah part-listened to their conversations, acknowledging comments made by her companion on her other side, a district administrator invited to dine as a favour for his work enticing English coffee growers to his region, while she chased the quail around with her fork.

'You perturb me, Miss Williams,' Major Brooke broke his silence, her social simpering galling him. To him, she was playing a part to which she was ill-suited. How different she was from the other ladies at the table, their conversations as flippant as their dresses — all lace and froth, but no substance.

Sarah gave up on her quail and potatoes, and aligning her cutlery, she turned to face Brooke, 'I'm not perturbing, Major. As we discussed, I am a woman and of no consequence.' She challenged him with her eyes to query her further. The service of the next course delayed his answer. Salmon with a short crust pastry; herb sauce oozing out between layers of fish, pooling on the plate, flavouring the peas served with it.

Brooke stabbed his pie. No other woman had vexed him as much. He didn't understand her, yet he couldn't thrust her from his mind. He devoured mouthfuls of pie, the currants tart on his tongue — each mouthful bringing him closer to uttering some other inanity towards Miss Williams.

Naomi Abbott wasn't the only one confused, looking at Sarah. Albert Lester, despite being seated next to the Viceroy, shot glances down the mile-long table with great regularity, causing his neighbours on both sides to look in the same direction, trying to guess who was captivating their dining companion. He could almost predict the conversations of those ladies after dinner. This was *not* the future he wanted for his daughter. He didn't want her stymied by the Victorian way of life: the gossip; the social constraints; and the Christian judgement. *Why can't she understand that?*

Chicken with watercress, artichokes stuffed with sage and onion followed, along with asparagus in sauce. Sarah had waved that away, turning up her nose with a small murmur of disgust. At the far end, Albert Lester laughed, a sound completely out of synch to a story about the state of the road out of Simla. Sarah had never liked the green spears; it was a long-running family joke. An overwhelming sense of loss hit Albert. He'd decided this was his life, and he'd come to terms with it, resigned to the grief of losing his family. But... but during moments like these, all he wanted to do was hold her hand, and tell her stories like when she was six years old, with her whole life ahead of her.

'Asparagus not to your liking then?' Brooke observed, kicking himself for such a frivolous observation. *What must this woman think of me?* For, now, he *was* viewing her as a woman. The silks and laces disguised the certainty that she was a diamond; her elusive nature as much of an attraction as her blunt answers. So he took a gamble. 'Could call upon you and we could take a walk together?'

Sarah coughed, covering her shock. 'Are you asking me out on a date, Major?'

'The date? Sorry, tomorrow, Friday the tenth.'

Sarah laughed, the context of her question lost on this man. She'd had more advances in India than she'd had her entire life, and that amused her. Where were all these dashing men in the modern world? Or had a diet of reality TV and *sub par* American sitcoms bred out the charm and charisma from the contemporary man? She took a bite of *Le pudding ā la diplomate*; candied fruit cloyingly sweet with custard; something her mother would have served at Christmas in her best Webb Corbett crystal bowl.

Thoughts of her mother cleared her head. If this life was enough for her father, then let him live it. Although every girl needed her father, she *knew* where he was, and he seemed happy. As much as she needed him, she also needed her mother. *What is life without a mother in it?* After wiping her mouth with the napkin and returning it to her lap, she met the dark eyes of Major Brooke, 'Absolutely, but may I suggest we walk past my old house — there are some items that never returned to England, and I'd like to find out where they might be. Perhaps after dinner tonight?'

Brooke nodded, his world erupting into one of opportunity.

Warren Brooke and Sarah walked companionably down the wide driveway of the Viceregal Lodge, shunning offers of a carriage or a palanquin. The evening's meal successfully navigated, Sarah left Patricia engrossed in discussions about the latest fashions with the other ladies, confident her friend could bluff her way through any conversation involving textiles and fashion. She'd avoided Mrs Abbott by slinking out a side door, like a nervous teenager slipping out after curfew.

The light had changed to the deep pinks of late dusk, with shadows filling the edges of the night.

'You have poor luck with the carriages you choose,' Major Brooke began, looking out over the vista of the Simla township, and not at the young woman by his side.

'Mmm,' Sarah replied, choosing instead to take in the

magnificent Himalayas. He was right but this last time, she'd invented the problem with the carriage. Brooke was an intelligent man, and she expected him to see through the subterfuge.

'Your friend Miss Bolton is an effervescent character. A fashion designer, I overheard her saying. An unusual vocation for a woman?'

Sarah stopped walking, resting her hand against the guard rail protecting unwary walkers from the precipitous drop down the steep hill. 'An unusual vocation for a woman? What century do you think you're living in?'

'The nineteenth century, the same one as you, madam. There's no need for the indignation, it was merely an observation. You seem to gather the most peculiar friends around you.'

'Seriously? You're passing judgement on my friends now?'

'I wouldn't presume to judge your friends, Miss Williams, it was an observation. Your choice of companions make you that much more interesting. You've more depth to you than most of the women I've known in Simla. You're an intriguing woman.'

That shut her up. She moved off, walking down the cobbled road, stars twinkling as dusk turned to night. Gaslights winked on one by one, illuminating the roadside. The balmy evening was a far cry from the hail the evening Sarah returned.

Too quickly they arrived at the house Sarah had called home for such a short time. Shrouded in darkness, it had yet to be re-let, its traumatic past common knowledge in the community, and enough of a mystery to bring shudders to the memsahib's considering a move to larger premises.

'We should have brought a torch with us,' Sarah said without thinking.

Brooke looked at her in confusion, 'There'll be a lantern on the porch. I have matches. The light will be sufficient for our needs I should think — regardless of what they are,' he added as a quiet afterthought.

Whether Sarah heard him, or ignored his throwaway comment, she didn't make clear. Even walking up the front steps sent her heart rate climbing, shortening her breath.

'Is it safe?' she asked. That question transformed her from a modern woman back to one of the times — one dependent on a man for all things.

Brooke struck a match against the silver vesta box squirrelled away in his inside pocket. The sulphur flared, illuminating the Major, his features soft in the unnatural light. For a moment, Sarah's heart caught in her throat. This man, so hard and suspicious, suddenly became something more than that. *Desirable?* She hesitated to give flight to that thought. After losing Price, there seemed no point in giving any time to a relationship which had no future other than in the past.

The wick in the kerosene lantern caught and Brooke opened the front door, lighting up the terracotta tiles. Sarah followed him into a house that was at once almost as familiar as her own growing up. Someone had cleared the devastation away, leaving the few remaining pieces of furniture shrouded in drop cloths, the light sending grotesque shadows ducking and darting about the walls.

'Tell me once again, what is it that we are searching for?' Brooke asked, tilting the lantern towards Sarah's face.

Sarah noted the condition of the lantern; its original glass chimney secure in its mount, the brass untarnished by time. *It would be a fast mover back at The Old Curiosity Shop*, she mused to herself, almost hypnotised by the dancing light.

'Miss Williams, what are we looking for again? Could it be under one of these cloths?'

Broken from her reverie, Sarah looked up at Brooke. 'Oh, some picture frames,' she improvised, 'Family photos. I'm sure half my things never made it back to England, but I guess that's because no one was here to supervise the packing.' From here, Sarah had to be careful what she said. She had little knowledge of what had happened to the real Sarah Williams after Simeon's murder, piecing together the snippets overhead at dinner, weaving them into something tangible to understand the real Miss Williams had suffered a breakdown after viewing her brother's body, and had returned to England via Delhi quick smart. Sarah should have quizzed Naomi Abbott, but Major

Brooke wanted to go before night fell, so there'd been no time for fond reminiscing with her old friend.

Brooke cocked his head, 'Picture frames, of course.' He busied himself lifting every drop cloth in the sitting room, then the dining room.

Sarah trailed behind him, taking care not to touch anything herself. The prospect of returning to the future, without Patricia, a frightening reality. 'Perhaps we should come back tomorrow, in the daylight,' she ventured. 'And with a tea chest, you know, to pack things up in. I thought I could waltz in and find what I needed, but...' She waved her arm around at the house, smothered in fine dust and insect carcasses. 'Well, tomorrow would be better.'

Brooke settled the kerosene lamp on the barren mantelpiece, disturbing a lizard clinging to the brick of the chimney breast. 'Tomorrow is fine. Tonight has not been without its enjoyment though.' The distance between them covered with two of his long strides before Sarah knew what was happening, and Brooke cupped her face in his hands. Time slowed.

Sarah tipped her head back; his touch as welcome as the sun slipping out from behind a summer storm. Her lips parted as he brought his face down to hers. Their kiss swept away the snide remarks, their exasperation with each other born from their unconscious attraction. The kiss wiped Warden William Price from her mind.

THE KISS

*P*ulling away from Brooke, Sarah touched her lips. Still tingling from the kiss, she didn't know what to do next.

'Should we come back tomorrow, when there's more light, then?' Sarah asked, her hand brushing against Brooke's, fingers entwining.

'That doesn't suit you,' Brooke answered.

'I beg your pardon?' Sarah said, shocked at the sudden change of atmosphere.

'You don't get to turn into an insipid female, all fluttering eyelashes and coy glances. You are so much more than that. So don't pretend to be something you're not, it's unbecoming.'

'It's unbecoming? What the hell gives you the right to comment on my behaviour? You walk me to a deserted building, in the dark, one lantern between us, and you kiss me. What am I meant to think? That you're in it for the thrill of the chase? Unbecoming, my arse.' Sarah stomped off down the hall, moving away from the lamplight, further into the shadows cast by the violent act which had gone before.

'Sarah... Miss Williams, wait... you don't know what's down there.' Brooke hurried after her with the lantern.

Sarah stood in the doorway of her old room — the furniture still in place, draped in the same white cloth as the other rooms. A tiny piece of red silk remained caught in the doorway's corner, a remnant from a garment Simeon had slashed into a rainbow of ribbons before he died. She bent down, picking it up. Running it through her fingers, she sensed Brooke behind her.

'There can always be more dresses.' Brooke reached out and slid the silky fabric from her hand. He looked past her into the room. 'I would have thought they would have shipped everything back to England, unless it came with the house. Some of them come furnished, but not many. They like to make you buy the stuff to fill the houses with. Makes it more awkward for everyone except them.'

'You know that's racist, right?' Sarah was still smarting from his last stab.

'Not racist, Miss Williams, it's just the way it is in India. Surely you've been here long enough to know that?'

'You've got no idea what's coming. After trampling an entire culture under your English boots, and they're about to slap you in the face.'

Brooke laughed, 'You've spent too long listening to Albert; all doom and gloom too. For what it's worth, I think you're right. But I'm just a soldier, following orders.'

'You know how to show a girl a good time, that's for sure.' Sarah wheeled away, retracing her steps to Simeon's room. She paused at the closed door, her hand on the knob. *Do I want to go in?* She doubted that his body was there, and expected no sign of the blood remained, the furniture shrouded. But would his essence remain?

Brooke put his hand over hers. 'You don't have to do this. Tell me what it is you're looking for, and I'll find it. Let me do this for you. There's no need to be strong. Let someone else shoulder it for you.'

Sarah slid her hand out from underneath Brooke's and stepped to one side. She smiled at him, her first smile since the kiss. He turned the handle. Swinging he lantern ahead of him, the room looked as barren as the salt plains of Utah. Even the bed had gone, the floors stripped of their coverings displayed perfect round circles — the only evidence that rugs and furniture had once filled the room.

They stepped inside, the lantern casting their separate shadows into one.

'There's nothing here!' Sarah exclaimed, the shock on her face exaggerated by the lamplight.

'That *is* odd,' Brooke agreed. He strode over to the windows, nudging open the shutters with the lantern. 'There's nothing outside either. The untouchables cleaned it, and they took their role a dash too far. It is strange though, compared to the rest of the house. Whatever you were hoping to find is long gone. I'm sorry.'

The wallpaper in the room remained magnificent. Sarah trailed her finger along the ivy tendrils painted on the paper, its convoluted loops and whorls impossible to follow with the eye. *What was it I hoped to find?* The necklace from the Viceroy was uppermost in her mind. She knew where the *katar* had come from, but didn't understand how they'd landed in Lord Grey's house. She wasn't aware of Simeon gambling them away. If she'd been a party to that information, she might have guessed where the Viceroy's necklace had ended up.

'Why empty this room and none of the others? It doesn't make sense,' Sarah said. Turning to look at Brooke, she swallowed her pride, 'I'm sorry,' she said.

'There's nothing to be sorry for, Miss Williams. Sorry that your brother was a delinquent? That's the way his cards fell. It's nothing to do with you.'

'No, that's not what I meant. Jesus, men are all the bloody same.'

If her unnatural profanity startled him, he gave no sign bar the slight lift of an eyebrow. 'Are all men the same, Miss Williams? Do none of us excel in your eyes?'

'Now *you're* playing the flirtatious fool. Nothing has changed in the last hundred years.'

The comment confused him, but he shrugged it off, as men do when a woman speaks and they don't understand.

'Shall we go back? There's not much we can achieve here tonight. We can arrange carters for tomorrow, if the remaining pieces belong to your family. I can even make enquiries into who cleaned up, if it's imperative?'

Sarah nodded. What a complete debacle the night had been. There was nothing here from the shop. She'd ruined an intimate moment with a man interested in her. *I'm an utter idiot.* If she could save anything from the situation, perhaps she'd be able to ship a few of the pieces back, pay a very, very long storage fee, in a warehouse which wouldn't get bombed during the Blitz. *Who am I kidding?* She was a bubblehead for even thinking she could salvage anything out of this. Unbidden, a solitary tear snaked down her cheek.

'You are a peculiar woman, Sarah Williams,' Brooke announced, placing the lantern on the floor, wiping away the one tear with his fingertip. 'Enough of this dancing, now.' Taking her in his arms he crushed his mouth against hers; cigars, and whisky, and man enveloping all her senses.

As shocked as she was by his sudden change, like a summer squall moving through a sheltered valley, she threw herself into the kiss. Entwined, their two bodies cast a single shadow against the papered walls.

⁓

N aomi Abbott stood like a sentry at the grand entrance of the Viceregal Lodge. Stout legs apart, hands on ample hips, her critical eye took in every detail of the returning duo as they approached her. The bruised lips, the mussed hair, the concerted effort they were making to appear disinterested in each other patently obvious, even to the casual observer, and she was hardly that. She smiled. The Major was a far better suitor than the Raja, and she approved, although she was aghast at the subterfuge by the pair, sneaking off after dinner to God knows where, and she was going to say so, when Albert Lester loomed up behind her. He pushed her out of the way and hissed at Sarah, 'Where have you been?'

'Come now, Lester, that's no way to speak to Miss Williams.' Brooke stepped forward.

'Stay out of it,' Albert Lester grabbed Sarah by the hand, 'You can't go running off round the countryside; you've no idea what you're doing.' He tried pulling her inside, when Sarah wrenched her hand from his.

'What the hell is wrong with you? One minute you want nothing to do with me, and now you want to know what I've been doing? You're trying to control me. Well I've got news for you, buddy, I'm a grown woman, and I've managed fine without you, and you know what else? I don't need you. Bet that hurts, right? So let go of me and let me live the life I want to lead. One without you.'

'Sarah, you don't understand the damage you can cause, that you *are* causing, even now, with this childish display.'

Brooke interrupted, 'Lester, the lady told you to take your hands off. I don't have a clue what this is about, but when a lady tells you to remove yourself, you do. Or I can do it for you.'

Lester backed away, holding up his hands in supplication. 'Seriously, Sarah, you cannot have a relationship with a man here. *No* man. Go home,' he implored.

'I've tried that — there was nothing left in Simeon's room.' A light dawned in her eyes. 'But you'd know all about that now, wouldn't you?'

Naomi was lapping it up like a cat with the cream. What a *delicious* scene. *Has Albert Lester been dallying with Sarah this whole time, right under my nose?* As much as she loved the girl, she was turning out to be a hussy. This always happens when a young girl had no parents or responsible adults to chaperone them; they took up with an entire retinue of improper men — not that Major Brooke was unsuitable, no, not by a country mile — but the other two... Albert Lester was old enough to be her *father*.

Albert reached again for Sarah's hand. This time Brooke wasn't about to stand by to watch the woman he'd chosen being harassed by a man with no discernible background, or breeding. He was a competent advisor to the Viceroy, but it was undeniable that no one knew anything about the man. He was an enigma who'd just dared lay a hand on the woman he loved. *The woman I love?* As that fact crashed into him, he wrenched Albert's arm off Sarah, and up behind his back. Yelling in pain, Albert tried to throw off the younger man.

'Stop it! Stop it!' Sarah screamed, her loyalties torn. *What an absolute nightmare.* She tried stepping between the struggling men.

'Get away, Sarah!' her father yelled at her.

Naomi stood by, alternately clasping her hands and fluttering them like a hummingbird.

Captain Doulton appeared and pulled them apart. 'Jesus, Brooke, what are you doing?'

Major Brooke shook himself free of his friend. 'It's nothing. Lester here was harassing Miss Williams. I'm sure that's finished with now, though. Am I right, Lester?'

The older man gazed at his daughter through hurt eyes, rubbing his shoulder. 'Sarah?'

Sarah skirted past him, and into Naomi's waiting arms, as if touching him was tantamount to approving his actions. 'Can we go inside, please?' she begged Naomi, who was more than happy to spirit the younger woman away, where she'd be able to draw out the juicy details.

Doulton gave Brooke a shove, and with a tight grip on his major's arm, he yanked him down the driveway.

Albert watched the men leave, imagining their conversation. Rubbing his arm, he walked in the opposite direction, onto the sweeping lawn and through to the manicured gardens. The visual display of Victorian excess always impressed him. He'd embraced this new life, surrounding himself with the elegance of the craftsmanship of future antiques, while they were still in their prime, before becoming worm-riddled and dented, altered and defiled. *Like life — everyone starts out pure and unadulterated, and over time they get kicked, and scratched, misused or ignored, changed irrevocable by someone else's idea of beauty.*

He felt no guilt over his role in packing Sarah's belongings. He'd ordered her servants to empty the rooms and pack everything away for safe keeping as soon as his Sarah had disappeared the first time. After the breakdown of the *real* Sarah Williams, everyone agreed it prudent that they close the house and ship everything to England with her. But the troubles in India had delayed shipment, and the goods sat in a

399

warehouse, slowly decaying. As if shutting them away closed the lid on his past, on his family. How easy it was to forget someone when you believe them lost to you. *Now she's back, what should I do? Stay? Encourage her to stay?* The country was teetering on the edge of an eruption. He cared not one whit about himself, but Sarah was his daughter. There was a time when he would do anything for her, but he wasn't sure now whether that 'anything' extended to giving up this life for her, not now that she was an adult. If he went back, he would only cause heartache for everyone. His only memory of buying anything of Indian origin, from anyone in Salisbury, was a small gold snuffbox. When he'd bought it, he hadn't realised it was gold, thinking it instead to be brass. On polishing it up for sale, reality hit. And, like several other valuable pieces, he'd put it away, for a rainy day, when bank funds were low, or unexpected expenses cropped up. He'd often referred to those items as his 'retirement fund', and it would have destroyed him if he'd known how little his collection of Doulton Lambethware was worth now, and that Sarah had slowly been sending them off to auction, one at a time, including his favourite jardinière, the one by Hannah Barlow, the first female artist to work for Doulton in 1871. It was the embossed snuffbox he was thinking about now. He hadn't recognised it when it was in Simeon Williams' possession, but he *had* recognised it after Sarah's return, and he hoped like hell Nirmala had packed it away as per his instructions. If Simeon still owned it and hadn't gambled it away like almost everything else of worth that came into his possession. And now... now if Sarah demanded access to the stuff from the house... well, he would have to put a stop to it. She had to return home, but he would orchestrate the when and where. His daughter couldn't stay because it wasn't safe.

THE WAREHOUSE

*B*reakfast in the Viceregal Lodge was a quiet affair. Guests came and went, eating an odd mixture of standard English fare and an assortment of adopted Indian dishes.

Patricia regaled Sarah with the intricate details of her outfit, gushing over the stitching and the quality of the lace. A conversation the other ladies at the table were more than happy to take part.

If Patricia noticed any quietness from Sarah, she gave no sign, already entrenched in the world into which she'd landed.

'Yes, a game of croquet sounds divine! I've never played, but I'll give it a go. What do you reckon, Sarah, some croquet this morning?' Patricia looked at Sarah.

'What? Oh, here?'

'Well, we're not playing in London today are we!'

The table tittered. Almost every lady there would have given anything to be back in England, away from the giant bugs which even invaded the Viceregal Lodge. The bugs were incessant, the heat relentless, the servants terrible, and the melancholy incurable. Little did they realise, the first-timers at least, that life in India was a pantomime. Its reality a moment in time — a time they, and the world, would never have again. The Victorian era was like no other for the British as a race, especially for the ladies in the English upper classes.

'Sorry, Trish, but today I need to find my things, and sort through them. I must arrange transport, and shipping and stuff. Mr Lester has offered to take me. You should come with me.' Sarah gave Patricia a look.

Patricia frowned. 'You don't need me for that,' she said.

Simultaneously, Albert Lester bellowed a 'no,' from the end of the table.

Ignoring him, Sarah responded, 'Yes, Trish, I need you with me. To help me get things organised to get everything home. *You know*, the whole reason you came back to Simla with me?' Her eyebrows raised, and her eyes narrowed. She understood Trish was in her own little *fashionista* heaven, surrounded by fabrics and designs she'd never get to experience again, but she needed her friend to come home too. That was her plan. She would go home today. Her father would be on his own. *Why can't Trish understand what I'm getting at?*

A deep voice interrupted the glowering down the table, 'I'll come with you, and Miss Bolton can learn the rules of croquet. There's no need to deny her that enjoyment when she's only just arrived. If you're here for the season, it won't take long to get your things moved here, or we can move it back into Firgrove House. It's still for lease, so you could stay there, if you're comfortable. I understand if you're not?' Brooke said, spreading a slice of toast with English marmalade, as if his offer hadn't put the cat among the proverbial pigeons. Albert Lester needed taking down a couple of pegs, to a level more befitting his position. Brooke wasn't having him dictate what Sarah could or couldn't do. The man was far too interested in Miss Williams for his liking.

Sarah's heart thumped. *No. I mustn't think of him.* She was going home. Once there she'd find her mother. She wasn't in India. She must be in New Zealand; that was the only possibility left. She must return to the shop and prayed that the girl hadn't sold what she needed to find her mother. *Blast it.* Torn between her girlfriend's happiness, her feelings for Brooke, and the imminent loss of her father, she muttered, 'Thank you, Major Brooke. You don't mind, do you, Mr Lester?' She challenged her father.

Lester shook his head.

Patricia clapped her hands. Never had a woman revelled in layers of petticoats, restrictive jackets and headache-inducing hats than Patricia at that very moment. Oblivious to Sarah's discomfort, she had but one thing on her mind, and that was fashion. She was spiralling out of control with ideas and had already begged a sketch pad from the Viceroy's wife.

Sarah swallowed a spoonful of porridge, which turned to stone in her stomach, as she contemplated her next move. Like a game of chess, she needed to be three moves ahead of herself. Everything she touched had consequences. Every future she altered now, could affect the past, and she didn't even notice Trish wave a cheery goodbye when she left for her game of croquet, a game which called for another wardrobe change.

'Are you not hungry, Miss Williams,' Brooke enquired, his own plate a barren wasteland. A smear of yellow egg yolk was the only evidence there'd been anything there.

Sarah shook her head, trying to force down some tea. *What to do? What to do?*

Brooke leaned forward, his voice a whisper, 'Why is it that Lester assumes he has any say over your life? It intrigues me, his obsession with your activities.'

Glancing at her father, Sarah replied, 'I've no idea. He has no hold over me. Maybe he feels responsible for what happened to Simeon?' As soon as the words left her mouth, her mind protested. Was her father capable of murder, to protect her? She gazed again at Albert, engrossed in a conversation, his grey head bowed to listen to the woes of an ancient Englishman seated next to him.

The same thought had taken root in Brooke's mind as well. 'I'll come with you, just to be on the safe side. Shall I meet you outside in an hour?'

Sarah was deep in contemplation. Everything seemed more

believable. That her father had potentially murdered someone to protect her felt comforting, if not a tad macabre.

The three of them made an odd trio, with Lester refusing to meet Sarah's eyes, and ignoring Brooke. They conducted the ride down the Mall, past the butter-yellow Christ Church, entirely in silence. Sarah gazed out across the valley, every colour squeezed fresh from tubes of an artist's oil paints onto the palette.

Past the fashionable shops, past the browsing *memsahibs*, parasols sheltering them from the Indian sun, filling in time before another party, a ladies luncheon or an afternoon tennis match.

They left the fancy shopping precinct, bouncing their way to the lower mall, where throngs of people shopped. Here the noise of the crowd would have drowned out any conversation. Hawkers selling stacks of multicoloured shawls; potters squatting on the ground next to their pregnant terracotta gourds. Traders surrounded by woven bowls filled with mountains of spices, their peaks echoing those of the Himalayas. Pots and pans jostled for space among woodturners, and racks of dead poultry and small mammals hanging in the open air. The flower pedlars tempered the stench of the market. Dahlias and marigolds intermingled with chamomile and golden *champa* — frangipani. A cascade of colour through the street.

And, all too soon, they were outside a set of warehouses, two of them occupied by smaller traders, who watched with interest as the silent trio waited for the doors to be unlocked.

'Sarah, stop and think...' Albert started.

'Don't,' was her response as she marched into the warehouse, the mixture of dust and decay as familiar to her as it was to any antique dealer. Things in storage exude their own scent, the slow smell of neglect.

Silverfish scuttled from the light, and faint rustles under the furniture sounded like rodents gorging themselves on leather and lace.

Brooke wandered around as if he were shopping for some trinket for himself. Peering beneath drop cloths, or feeling the heft of an ornament laying atop hastily packed crates.

Brooke broke his reverie, 'I'm trying to imagine how you've been living these past few months. Miss Williams.'

'What?' Confused, Sarah turned towards Brooke, her arms crossed across her chest.

'How you've been living? In hotels I presume?'

'You're not making any sense. I've been home and have come back to find out what happened to my belongings.' And here she turned to Lester before continuing. 'You wouldn't think it'd be that hard to ship someone's things back to England, not when you have the greatest navy in the world at your beck and call. When you're the world's superpower.'

'Now I've no idea what you're talking about. But I think you haven't been exactly honest with me.'

Spinning back, her anger bubbling over from the night before, 'For God's sake, I never asked to be here. I'd give anything to go home. To see my mother again. To have my father hug me, for him to call me *love* just once more. I'd give up all of this in a heartbeat to see my parents again, together. Alive. And yet here you are, all puffed up in your stupid uniform, your whole life is about to go up in flames and you have no idea. And you want to accuse me of not being honest with you?'

Brooke flinched. There was heartbreak in her words. He reached out, but Albert got to her first.

'Sarah, love,' he pulled her into a hug, her sobs stifled in his shoulder. 'I'm so sorry. I wish I could say you don't have to go home. If only I could say "stay and make a life here", but I can't. Sorry I pushed you away, that I didn't try harder to find you, and that I gave up trying to come home.' His voice lowered to a whisper, 'You have to go home. You can't change history. Everything you do now will change something. We just don't know what the ramifications might be. You can't make a life with Brooke, you know that, right?'

Brooke cleared his throat, the scene as unsettling as Sarah's words. A stack of lace edged handkerchiefs, starched within an inch of their lives, lay on top of an unsealed packing crate. Brooke selected one, and coughed politely, trying to ignore the incomprehensible happening in front of him. 'Ahem, Miss Williams, perhaps I may be of some assistance. I'm sorry I questioned the veracity of your statements. I am intrigued by them, but perhaps we could do this task another day. You seem very upset. This can wait,' he said, offering her the handkerchief.

Sarah pushed herself away from her father, and reached for the lace hanky, her fingers brushing Brooke's. And then disappeared.

THE FATHER

*A*lbert Lester blinked. Unease settled on his shoulders, much like the dust they'd disturbed when they'd entered the warehouse. He spun around, distress gripping his heart. *This was bad, the worst outcome.*

Albert did a quick circuit of the warehouse — nothing. He thought back, trying to recall what she'd touched. That idiot Brooke passed her a handkerchief. *Of all the bloody stupid things, a scrap of fabric. Stupid.*

Lester found the open carton, his hand hesitating above the stack of starched white squares. *Should I?* He knew the ramifications. What good would come of his return? His fingers wavered in midair like a desert mirage. What would his life be? Full of questions about his absence, his wife and child, his business?

Lester closed his eyes, trying to bring up his wife's face. It had been so long that her memory had become unfocussed, like an old movie shuddering on its reels, the film decaying from age. Wherever Annabel was, she wasn't his.

Lester snatched his hand away. *No.* Going back wasn't the answer. Spinning on his heel, he strode from the warehouse. He'd have to deal with the consequences of their disappearance, but he could do it. India lent itself to disappearances. It was still a dangerous country. Wild animals abounded. Deserters hid in the shadows. And elopements were *de rigueur*.

He pulled the door behind him, slamming the padlock shut. The locals paid no attention, focused as they were on sharing a bowl of dates in the sun, whilst ignoring anyone who looked like they might want them to work.

Taking a deep breath, he smoothed his jacket down now he'd decided. He need never open that warehouse again. Sarah's friend was an unlucky consequence. *I can tell the truth to her, later. Much later.* She seemed happy enough living out the fantasy that was Victorian India. He was pragmatic, but not heartless, despite what his daughter must think of him. Sarah would always *be* his daughter, but this life was his adventure now that his parenting duties were over. She was a grown woman who didn't need him.

Summoning a passing rickshaw, still a new phenomenon in Simla but a welcome one, he climbed up, giving the puller his destination. Straight back to the Viceregal Lodge. The natives wouldn't comment on whether they'd seen Brooke and Sarah leave the warehouse, and he wouldn't raise the alarm until someone else mentioned them. He had his own neck to protect. God knows, they'd all need protection. The rebellion was coming.

THE SHOP

The sound of two bodies colliding against a stack of plastic crates echoed through the basement. An old tin Disneyland tray slipped from its perch, clanging on the wooden floor, followed by silence.

Warren Brooke stirred first, 'Christ, was that an earthquake?' He tested his arms and legs, stretching one booted leg out at a time, before turning his attention to Sarah, 'Are you hurt?'

Sarah groaned, everything aching, her mind foggy with the pain.

'Miss Williams? Are you OK?' Brooke reached for Sarah, groping in the dark before his hands found her on the ground. They brushed over her legs, her waist, skimming her sides, inadvertently brushing one breast, until satisfied she was unhurt. He pulled her into a sitting position. 'It must have been an earthquake. They're fairly common, but damn it if I don't remember a thing.'

Sarah coughed, holding her hands to her head, realisation dawning.

'Where the bloody hell is Lester? Lester? Albert, where are you?' Brooke called out. Silence the only response.

'It wasn't an earthquake, Warren, it's worse than that. I'm sorry,' Sarah muttered.

'Roof must have come down,' Brooke observed, 'Come on, I'll help you up, best we get out of here before there are any more tremors,' Brooke tugged on Sarah's hands until she stood up.

Sarah walked past him, her familiarity with the space the reason she could walk with such confidence. She flicked the ancient Bakelite switch, and yellow light flooded the basement of *The Old Curiosity Shop*. Shelves lined the walls, bowing under the weight of old crates, filled to the brim with unpriced stock, spare convex glass for oval frames, crystals for lustre vases and coils of chain for chandeliers.

She steeled herself for Brooke's reaction, gazing at the floor rather than the bewildered major in the middle of the room.

'Bloody hell,' Brooke spun round, his hand reaching for his rifle, which he'd laid to one side once they'd entered the warehouse, never for a moment thinking he'd need it.

'Ah, not an earthquake. Before you completely freak out, which I'm doing enough for both of us, can I suggest you take a deep breath and come upstairs. We'll have a cup of tea, and I'll explain.'

For a man so in control of his emotions, Brooke's looked dumbfounded. 'What is this magic?'

'Please, just come up while I explain everything. It's not witchcraft or magic, it's… to be honest, I'm not quite sure what it is, but can you come up? Please?' Giving him no time to answer, she turned and walked up the stairs, hoping he'd follow.

Brooke made his way slowly behind, skirting the naked electric bulb before stepping into the shop. He froze. The scant light from the fluorescent tube in the window disguised everything inside with draped shadows, hinting at unfamiliar forms, reinforcing the nightmare he'd just entered.

Another wash of light fell down the stairs as Sarah tugged on the pull cord at the top. Brooke looked up, shielding his eyes from the unnatural sunlight above. Still protecting his eyesight, he followed Sarah upstairs.

Emerging into the shabby lounge, he walked straight into Sarah's frozen form.

Oomph

Reaching out, Brooke stopped her from falling.

'Oh,' her only response, her voice breaking with that one word.

Forgetting himself, ignoring the implausible position he found himself in, his first instinct was to worry about Sarah and the state she was in.

'What's wrong,' he asked.

'Someone's been here,' Sarah cast her arm around the room.

Brooke looked around, taking in the tiny pieces of Sarah's life. It was untidy, but not messy. An old clock adorned the papered wall, books filled the bookcase. Books the colours of parrots, every cover a rainbow. The furniture was neither here nor there, more fabric and filling than he was used to, but still identifiable. Apart from everything being so colourful, he could have been in any time.

'How can you tell?' he asked.

'It's not how I left it,' and she pointed to the bottom of the bookcase, 'There, see the atlas? It's the wrong way round, spine facing in instead of out.'

She walked through to the tiny kitchen, moving rolls of cling film and foil back into their respective places in an open drawer, before backing out, and walking into her bedroom. Sarah saw signs everywhere that someone had had a good rummage through her things. Her eyes flicked to her bedside table; the pile of half read books remained, but something was missing. Sarah racked her brain, before her heart sank — Isaac's gold nugget and his letter. She placed her hand on the void where the letter had lain. 'Oh Isaac, I'm so sorry.'

'Who is Isaac?'

Brooke had followed her, his discomfort growing — loitering in a young lady's bedroom was not something he was entirely comfortable with.

Turning to reply, she remembered the situation they were now in.

'Isaac was a friend from long ago. I had a letter for his mother I should have sent, but it's gone. Someone has taken it,' Sarah said.

Brooke was none the wiser, but the whole day wasn't panning out as he'd imagined, so he thought it best to take one thing at a time.

'You promised me a cup of tea,' he replied.

'Oh, yes,' Sarah replied, but didn't move. 'Do you think I could just get changed before I do that?'

Confusion filled Brooke's face, but ever the gentleman he left the room, pulling the door behind him. He considered making tea for them both, but after surveying the kitchen for any sign of tea-making facilities, he'd given up, and had taken refuge on the couch. Finding a newspaper, the most recognisable thing in the place, he settled in to read the September 2015 issue of the *Antique Trades Gazette*. He tried hard to ignore the date, to focus instead on the feature article detailing the new offices Sotheby's was opening in Mumbai, India. His mind drifted back to India trying to recall a place called Mumbai, but its name escaped him. His breath also escaped when Sarah emerged from her bedroom, jeans clinging to her legs, an olive hued T-shirt tight across her chest, and her hair in a ponytail. Her clothing was as surprising as the ease with which she wore it.

She glanced at Brooke, fully aware that an English woman wearing trousers was as far away from the norm as her cellphone was from the Morse code machines used by the postal services in his time.

Ever the poker face, he asked again for a tea, and retreated to the comparative safety of his newspaper. As Sarah disappeared into the kitchen, he hazarded a glance at her buttocks, hugged by the denim of her jeans. *Just as I imagined.*

'There's no milk, but I've plenty of sugar if you need some,' Sarah called out.

'Sugar's fine,' Brooke replied, flushing at the possibility she caught him admiring her shape.

With comforting mugs of tea in her hands, she'd become a different person. Gone was the hesitant Miss Williams, her cautious approach to the world her overriding persona. In its place, a woman who carried herself well, who strode with confidence. Even her voice had grown in stature.

Sarah sipped her tea, grimacing at the lack of milk, but it at least gave her something to occupy her hands as she contemplated what to do next.

Brooke made it easy for her, by starting their necessary conversation, 'Miss Williams, this is a peculiar method of arranging a moment alone with me. We could have gone to a play, or the opera, or a walk. Yet here I find myself, what, I can't even bring myself to say it, but this newspaper says it is true. That this is the future?'

Sarah wondered how on earth to explain she'd skipped them forward a hundred and fifty-odd years?

'You've some explaining to do, Miss Williams.'

'It's Lester, Sarah Lester. Sorry. There *was* a Sarah Williams, Simeon's sister, just to make things confusing, but I'm not her.'

'Lester? As in *Albert* Lester? You're his wife?'

Sarah spat out her tea, convulsing in laughter, 'Sorry, no. He's my father. Jesus, married to him! That'd make him laugh,' she continued laughing into her mug, shaking her head at the absurdity of his question.

Brooke pondered her answer, 'That explains his peculiar obsession with you, and those around you. But... does that mean he's from the future too? But he's been advising the Viceroy for several years.' Then the penny dropped, and fear washed over him, 'What of the future, what happens? Both of you alluded to trouble in India, what do you know? What's in your history books I'm yet to live through?'

'I'm not entirely sure I should tell you. We should try to figure out a way for you to get home, before I do any further damage,' she said.

'And what of Miss Bolton? Are you telling me she's from this time too? That explains her odd manner and exuberance...'

'Trish! Oh my God, I completely forgot about her,' Sarah's eyes widened as she considered the fate of her friend. This was turning into a complete fiasco.

'This place, it is yours?'

'Yes.'

'And downstairs, a shop? Also yours?'

'Yes, a shop, *The Old Curiosity Shop*, an antique shop. It was my father's — Albert's — but when he disappeared, I took over. Jesus, everything's a disaster, the shop, Trish, you being here...'

'Come now, me being here isn't a complete disaster is it?' Brooke placed his mug on the table, stood up and stretched. Standing there, looking at Sarah, he felt an overwhelming sense of calmness descend. He'd been in worse places than this, none as odd, but certainly worse. His life wasn't at risk, no one was firing at him, nor was he being pressed to send his men into battle. For the first time since he was a child, he could just *be*.

'May I suggest something a dash stronger than tea, and then you can fill in the gaps for me?' Brooke said.

'We should try getting you back,' Sarah's face crinkled with worry.

'Miss Lester, it could be I'm here for good. Wouldn't it be best if you prepared me? You had the luxury of knowing the environment you entered. Shouldn't I receive the same benefit? But in the meantime, a whisky would help...'

THE NIGHT

*W*ith Brooke in such close proximity, Sarah admired his *sangfroid*. There were no hints of panic or wary looks, no surreptitious prayers to God. He'd observed his surroundings, drunk a dire mug of tea, and had taken her at her word.

Every time she'd needed him, he'd been there. On the ship, on the road, after Simeon. Aloof to the point where she'd imagined he hadn't cared. But Brooke had proven otherwise. He was in a world he couldn't possibly fathom. She should march him downstairs, tossing the place, till they found something to send him back. That was the only fair thing to do. But then again, she could stay in India, with him. Live a quiet life, and maybe move back to England, away from the uprisings. She'd adjust to the lack of electricity, and wouldn't miss mobile phones, or neon billboards, Pizza Hut or McDonalds. Easier for her to adapt than him.

All these thoughts, and a thousand others flashed across her mind, like meteors.

'You're thinking about how I don't belong here. How to get me home — is that not true, Miss Williams?'

She flushed, 'It's Miss Lester, Sarah Lester...'

'Yes, my mistake. You can forgive one mistake, yes?'

'Of course.'

'Could you forgive two?'

'What's the second mistake?'

'This one,' and he leaned towards her, kissing her, his unshaven face rasping against hers.

Sarah relaxed, her body answering his question.

Pulling away from her, he grasped her by the hands, and pulled her to standing.

'Am I to assume that society has loosened its standards somewhat?' Brooke asked.

'A little,' Sarah replied, as he pulled her into his body, nestling against him like a Russian doll.

Brooke nuzzled at her, the softness of her cotton T-shirt intoxicating. His hands traced the shape of her waist, and down over her thighs.

Sarah sighed, exposing more of her neck. She'd imagined this, so a sense of *déjà vu* washed over her when he kissed her again.

Sarah broke away and confusion crossed his face, until Sarah took him by the hand and led him to the bedroom.

'Miss Lester?'

'You're in the twenty-first century now, Major Brooke,' Sarah said, pulling off her T-shirt, revealing one of the greatest inventions of the twentieth century, the Wonderbra.

Brooke's hand moved to cup one breast, his other arm circling her waist.

'No corset?'

Sarah laughed and unhooked the bra with the practised hand of a professional.

Brooke's eyes never once left hers, save a small flicker downwards towards her naked breasts.

'I think I will enjoy this century,' he murmured, nuzzling back into her neck.

Sarah pulled away, again. 'You can't stay here,' she said, shocked at the thought of Brooke running rampant on the streets of London with his Victorian morals and concepts of justice and racial tolerance.

Brooke shook his head, clearing away the lust. 'You are a perplexing creature, Miss Lester. Am I not here now? Am I not flesh? Do I not have a say in this future? A future together?'

'A future?'

'Us, together. Is that not what you want?'

Sarah's mind went blank. She wanted her mother, and her father; to rewind life back to normality. But she also wanted this man.

'Yes, that's what I want,' Sarah whispered, 'But how?'

'Let's start with this,' he suggested, ignoring her breasts, instead taking her face in his hands and kissing her, lowering her to the tangle of the unmade bed.

His uniform lay in a crumpled heap next to the bra on the floor, their bodies joining the way two lovers do after a long time of dancing around their desires.

And then they slept, entwined together, like natural lovers, comfortable with each other, and themselves. Their worries forgotten until the next day.

THE UNPACKING

*N*icole unlocked the shop's door, pulling behind her the two wheeled suitcases she'd lugged on and off trains, the same way the world's strongest man practised for his competitions. She could have sworn *she'd* developed similar muscles in the few days she'd been in Lille.

She paused — the atmosphere inside felt different from when she left. *That was just stupid. But when you're surrounded with things from the past, they absorbed the feelings and emotions from their previous owners, and then shed them in their new environment.* A silly thought, but it was a vibe she'd had, even when she'd worked at Tamworth Castle.

Nicole flicked the switch on the kettle and unzipped the first bag. Such a moment of excitement. She may have bought all these treasures thinking they'd be great sellers in the shop, but the *real* moment of truth, when her purchase decisions made sense — or didn't — was when they were sitting on the counter, mingling with everything else in the cluttered space.

How do they fit with the overall vibe of the shop? Did their flea market eclectic coolness translate to a little brick shop in London? Will our customers love them?

First she unpacked a box of old keys — long iron keys, the sort a *chatelaine* would have carried about her person, as she managed her chateau. Popular, and not cheap, even at the flea market. At a minimum, she'd be selling these for ten pounds each. Still, some good profit in it.

Her system was methodical, and simple — unpack, enter in the purchases register, price, moved to one side. That way there'd be no chance of getting into a muddle. Nicole tried not to think of the stock downstairs, waiting for a home, or space on a shelf. And blanked from her mind the potential outcome of Sarah and Patricia's disappearance. She'd keep working till someone with authority told her not to. Her pay was automatic, so, as long as she kept filling the bank account by selling stuff, she'd keep getting paid. It was a terrifying thought that at any moment a solicitor could walk in here and shut it down.

Next came a set of apothecary jars, their gilt labels pristine, and their cork stoppers intact. The cork stoppers *weren't* original — they would have been glass originally — but the cork looked the part, and most people bought the bottles for display only.

Find after find filled the counter. Nicole hummed away to herself, a German pop song she'd overheard on the train, its beat catchy and repetitive.

The last thing she pulled from the suitcase was the flying jacket. She'd carefully placed the letter in her folder of receipts back in France, its poignancy tugging at her heart. After pricing it, she hung the jacket off the handle of the silver cabinet, its leather still supple after all these years. She fancied she could smell the cologne of the pilot, and wondered what had become of him, and of the Elizabeth he had written to — the Elizabeth who had never received his final words.

Zipping shut the larger bag, she moved onto its smaller cousin, removing first the shoebox of militaria she'd bought from the same seller at the market. She tipped it out, and disentangled the jumble of dog tag cords, the red and green discs a brotherhood of servicemen, in death as they were in life.

Still humming away, she shot out of her skin when a customer hammered on the door.

Damn it. The whole reason she hadn't opened up yet was that she wanted to get this stuff priced up before any of her regular customers came in. Her pushier regulars would see something unpriced, offering to buy it before she'd researched it, escaping with an absolute bargain. Especially the 'Toy Guy' as she called him. He bought all her lead toys, old Meccano, and lately he'd been branching out to actual car memorabilia, and military badges. Nicole didn't mind a customer getting a good deal on an obscure Stanley sharpening stone #4, but for things like war medals or military insignia, they needed researching *before* being put out for sale.

Switching back the black evening dress hung on the front door to cover the grille-covered window, she found a small man, his neck cinched in by a clerical collar. Conditioned to trust a man of the cloth, she fumbled with the lock and opened the door to the agitated priest.

Fastidiously presented, the reverend looked like a ruffled rooster, up in arms over her tardiness in opening the shop.

'Good morning. I have been waiting for you to open, after finding you closed all weekend. I have urgent business to attend to, so may we come in?'

'We?' Nicole asked, seeing no one with the man.

'I have colleagues on their way, who will be with us soon.'

Nicole interrupted, 'I'm sorry, but I'm not open yet. Is there something specific I can help you with? I'll be open at lunchtime otherwise.'

'The auction for the Roman statue. I had the highest bid, so I'm here to pick it up, to take it to its true home.'

If his peculiar statement puzzled her, she gave no sign, 'Oh, sorry, yes, I hadn't looked online this weekend. Please come in.'

Nicole allowed Shalfoon into the shop, closing the door after him, 'Can you text your colleagues to tell them to knock when they get here, otherwise every Tom, Dick and Harry will want to come in. That's always the way when the door's shut. But when it's open, no one comes in,' she laughed.

Avoiding the suitcases on the floor, she slipped in behind the counter. A few keystrokes on her laptop and she had the auction up in front of her.

'Are you paying with cash or credit card?' Nicole asked, looking at Shalfoon, her eyes bright, the sale a substantial one.

Shalfoon cleared his throat, this was the part he found most distasteful. He would have preferred the help of the inept Art Loss Register people and the police. Pulling himself taller, he spoke, 'The statue is...' before another knocking at the door. 'That'll be my colleagues,' he said.

Nicole sighed, squeezed back past the bags and down to the door where she found Inspector Fujimoto, Fiona Duodu, and two people she'd never met.

'Oh, hello. Now's not a great time, can you give me a few minutes? I've an actual customer in the shop buying a statue, and as you know, I didn't have that many sales last week, so I kind of need this one.'

'Morning, Miss Pilcher. Sorry, but as improbable as this sounds, we're here because of the statue...'

Time stopped for Nicole. This was the real risk of selling stuff whose provenance was unknown. A customer could waltz in and claim someone had stolen the article. There were processes in place to protect dealers from unscrupulous claims, but more often than not, the police sided with the customer, tarring all second-hand dealers with the same criminal brush. She'd heard of one dealer, who'd been buying odd bits of Doulton, silver, and assorted bric-à-brac for years from a middle-aged matron, but it later transpired she worked in a rest home, and had been stealing from the elderly residents for years before being caught.

'Right, best you come inside then. This is awkward, because the guy buying the statue is a reverend.'

With this many people in the little shop, space shrank, and Nicole had to squeeze past the four of them and the minister before reaching the relative safety of the counter.

'OK, hit me with it. This is the biggest sale of the year, or at least since I started here,' the dismay in her voice matching the look on her face.

'This is not your business?' Shalfoon interjected. *A potential wrinkle in the plan.*

'Sorry, no, I'm just an employee, the...'

'Well then, I need to speak with the proprietor about returning the Church's property.'

'That will be difficult because she's not here. Surely the police told you that?' Nicole said, trying to keep the smugness from her voice. Her mother had always warned her to watch her tone; it was a downfall of hers when dealing with idiots. One former employer had even tried to discipline her for narrowing her eyes at him. *Nutter.*

'Then where did you find my... the Church's statue?' Shalfoon spluttered his face reddening, his dreams of ecclesiastical adoration slipping from his grasp.

'I think I'll step in here now,' Fujimoto interrupted, his hands in his pockets. This shop made him nervous. The pancaked china bowls looked like they were waiting for him to breathe near them before they careened off the stack of old enamelware. 'Sarah Lester, the owner of this shop, is missing, and we'd like to question her about several things, but your statue is at the bottom of that list. We are only here at the request of Miss Dance from the Register, but...' and here the Bishop tried to interject. 'Let me finish... for the sake of completeness, we'll take the statue for safekeeping while you lot thrash it out amongst yourselves.'

'I found it downstairs, in the basement. There's no way I could tell you where it came from.' Looking beseechingly at Fiona, she added, 'You've seen the stock books — that statue, however remarkable, could be in the register as "Statues (10)", with no other defining feature. You're dreaming if you think it's yours. It's probably just a replica, anyway.'

'Ah-ha, so you knew you were selling a fake, a counterfeit statue, pawning it off as the genuine article.'

'No I wasn't, if you'd read the auction listing, you'd have seen that I made no claims as to its actual age, in fact I even said I wasn't sure. Buyer beware and all that stuff.'

'See, officer, see what criminals these people are. You should just arrest her now.'

'Thank you, but that's not quite how we run our investigations. Once we locate Miss Lester, I'm sure she'll answer most of our questions.'

At that moment, Sarah appeared at the bottom of the staircase. Barefoot in jeans and a rumpled T-shirt. She made her way forward.

'You're looking for me?'

THE LETTER

"This will be the last page of this letter, I promise! We've got another flight tonight, and I'll post this tomorrow.

Got your postcard today, thank you. Keep them coming. The lads are damn jealous that you're such a top correspondent. If there was an award for who got the most post, I'd win hands down because of you, my love.

Weather is playing ball now. So it's up, up and away. Not quite the trip to France I would normally choose — no wine or cheese, but we'll go drink all the wine after this damn war is over, which won't be long, I'm sure.

Going there by boat is the only downside... Maybe we could look at buying ourselves a little aeroplane? What do you think, good idea?"

THE MISSION

*P*hil sat at the back of the room. Despite the frigid temperature outside, sweat beaded on his forehead. He extended his arm, and while it protested, he had full movement, and was almost pain free.

The briefing room was full to overflowing, the doors locked before the night's briefing. He wouldn't be flying tonight, but soon. *Just required the base doctor's sign-off.* In the six weeks he'd been out of action, they'd lost thirteen of their crews. Lads were being sent up with less than one hour's flying experience. The doctor would sign him off, they needed every last man.

After he'd crashed his Spitfire, they'd transferred him to another unit, where he had the luxury of time to get to know his replacement aircraft. The new lads, the ones who arrived with shining eyes, and shinier uniform buttons, all joked the war would end before they'd get to have a go at the Germans. The old hands like him — and there weren't many around now — knew better. But But even so, he was itching to get back behind the controls and give it another go.

The Adjutant was burbling on about some visit from some high-ranking government official, so he let his mind wander to Elizabeth. She'd taken the little Roman statue off his hands, writing how a bloke

426

at the local foundry ground down the base so the statue now sat flush in her display cabinet. Phil had cringed when he'd read that, mindful that there could be more of the statue still in Barry Wentworth's field. He'd tried begging leave to go back to Wentworth's farm, to thank the man for saving his life, but the war had moved on from there. No time for that sort of thing. It was as if the war had stopped good manners, and they were all expected to carry on regardless of societal expectations. In reality, Phil wanted to have a good look in the hole. After the war, he promised himself. After the war.

Phil Williams jiggled his knee, his foot tapping out its own tempo. Cigarette smoke threatened to envelope them all. The smoke was better than the fog outside, which was winding its way around the propellers and the engineers scurried around, prepping the planes for the night's run.

'Come on, Williams, you're not nervous about going up tonight, are you?' A meaty hand slapped Phil's leg, putting a sudden stop to his involuntary jiggling.

'I'm as jumpy as you will be when you finally get a girl to agree to hop into bed with you,' he rejoined, with mock bravado.

Gales of laughter greeted his comment. Their banter an integral part of relieving the palpable tension in the room. One of the Polish pilots had to have it interpreted for him, before he too chuckled with the rest. 'Hopping' into bed hadn't translated well.

The men in the group were as close as brothers, yet there was a level of detachment between them too. An invisible barrier between the old hands and the new recruits; the British and the foreigners. True, they were on the same side, fighting the same fight, but it just 'didn't do' to get too attached to the new lads.

'Five minutes, men,' the Adjutant announced, fiddling with his watch strap. The energy in the room lifted, electric anticipation flashed across the faces of a generation. A decimated generation leaving behind widows, spinsters, and heartbroken mothers.

Cigarettes extinguished, maps folded and shoved deep into pockets. Friends acknowledged each other, their young eyes flicking away before fear engulfed them, before they froze to their seats.

With the briefing room door opened, the pilots strode to their aircraft, running their hands over wings, checking props, and one by one the engines roared into life. Ground crew pulled wooden chocks out from under the wheels, and each plane rocked slightly, eager to escape. Adrenaline trumped fear, and each pilot focused on the task at hand. Germany.

As he taxied along the runway, concentrating on staying between the lines, Phil gave no thought to Elizabeth. No thought that tonight might be the night they prepare a telegram advising her of his demise. To think of that would be madness.

With the planes in a tight formation in the air, he recalled his childhood and the memories of his gang hurtling as a group to the river, racing their bikes, jostling to be the first to get to the rope swing, to soar over the raging water. The difference was that tonight, only the mad among them wanted to be first.

Fog embraced them, rendering them ghost-like over the cliffs of England, wraiths in the night, come to spirit you to your death. The low drone of the aircraft, the moaning of a hundred souls in purgatory.

As the tightness in his neck intensified, he tried shaking it off, but the unease settled, much like the fog. He checked his instruments again: altimeter; air speed indicator; artificial horizon; Each check was as natural as breathing. The instruments presenting as they should. His left companion, a dark smudge, the regulation distance away. Straight and level. His right-hand side companion a dash too close but, as he checked, the pilot made the tiniest correction, and settled where he should. Like an astronomer's star chart, each plane a dot in the sky, equidistant from each other, in their right places, ready for action when the call came.

Static-toned voices filled his headset. Calm and measured. Nothing amiss. *Why do I feel dread seeping in through the canopy, wrapping itself round me, constricting my lungs? My heart?*

A warning call over the radio, 'Half a minute, lads.'

Phil shifted in his seat, ready.

Another command, 'Reduce altitude.'

Phil pushed forward on the throttle, the nose of the aircraft dipping down, the purr of the engine subtly changing. Measuring off against those on his wingtips, he levelled out. He could no longer see the plane in front of him, but at this stage of the flight, it was possible he'd pulled ahead — especially as it was old 'Kiwi' Parker, the New Zealand chap, who'd waltz straight into Hitler's house at supper if he ever got the chance.

They were over France now, an inky black land filled with legions of Germans. But they were not alone.

The blackness below hit lit up like Chinese New Year. Arcs of light raced towards him. He peeled off to his left, praying the Pole on his left was doing the same thing. Like a waltz, the two of them danced in the sky away from the shots ringing through their formation. He had no time to look for Kiwi, or Mitchell Brady, his wingman on his right-hand side. Craning his tight neck, he swivelled his head trying to pinpoint the source. They were only here as an escort, had to get the bombers through.

Crazed radio calls assaulted his ears. *Bloody hell.* 'Where they are?' he yelled, slipping in behind Kiwi, the two of them forming a shield on the tail of the bomber they were escorting.

'They've gone right, gone right,' came back the frenzied cry.

'Let's go under and right,' radioed Kiwi to Phil. Phil clicked his mic in response, his head still craning to see any enemy aircraft.

More light lit the sky to his right, and he dipped down, executing a perfect wingover as they banked to their right.

Phil's whole plane shuddered in shock, as strafing bullets decorated his metal tail. He tried his rudder, *easy movement, but for how long?*

'Can anyone see my tail?' he transmitted. His voice calm, matter-of-fact.

No answer. All he could do was to continue. He'd know soon enough if the shots had done enough damage to take him down.

'On your right, Phil, three o'clock,' Kiwi's long vowels distinguishing him from the rest of the men in his unit, the rolling 'R's symbolising the placid country life Kiwi hailed from.

Every fibre screamed at him to get out of there, to look after number one, but no, the mission was to protect the bomber and its payload.

The plane shuddered again, as he took another hit. Whoever was behind him must have been off his aim, given his plane was still functioning, albeit sluggishly.

Tracking the enemy at his three o'clock, he manoeuvred his craft behind the German *Focke-Wulf Fw 190*.

Rat-a-tat-tat. Rat-a-tat-tat.

His finger hesitated on the controls, before pressing the fire button one more time, for luck.

The *Focke-Wulf* paused mid-air, then gave up, plummeting towards the scarred earth.

Phil looked for Kiwi, swivelling his head, when, from the edge of his peripheral vision, he saw another *Focke-Wulf*.

Hell, I'm hit!

He banked away, his tail gone. His geographical knowledge of this area was sketchy. He was near Wittes, so nowhere near anywhere. He couldn't see Kiwi, or anyone else from his squadron. His height dropped two thousand feet, then even further. He tried to level out, and heaved the nose up, slowing his descent. With the engine signalling its last gasp of life, it went silent.

As a teenager, long family summers in Yorkshire were a highlight after he'd joined the Yorkshire Gliding Club. And it was those long-ago skills he now called upon.

Forgetting those above him, he concentrated on landing, his rudder almost non-existent, the pedals heavy. The elevators needed surgical precision, they were overly sensitive, a constant complaint of the Spit pilots. It was all he could do to hold it steady.

The rambling countryside flew up towards him; fields stained by war.

And he ploughed into the ground.

THE GIRL

*W*ith a countryside torn to shreds, one more plane coming down was of no great consequence to anyone other than the pilot.

As his mangled legs lay entwined with the metal wreck of his Spitfire, Phil prayed to all the gods who'd ever lived, to end his life quickly.

His short life was but a blip on the timeline of the world. His lasting imprint nothing more than words on paper, and the tattered dreams of his widow.

Phil shut his eyes against the pain and imagined the children he'd never have; the love he'd never feel again; Elizabeth's touch. He let the tears fall, their saltiness diluting the deep red of the blood staining his uniform.

Slipping away to a safe place, where suffering couldn't find him, where heartbreak had no entry. A place filled with life's treasured moments, a kiss, a kind word, good deeds, sunsets. Phil was oblivious to the furtive figures running towards him, materialising out of the night, as if the darkness itself had made them.

Wooden handled tools in their rough hands attacked the plane. Wrenching, pulling, gouging the canopy. Prising it off. The Spitfire

431

under siege by these apparitions. Muffled curses, quiet orders. As one, this group operated like surgeons on a patient, till they freed Phil's useless legs, his body plucked from the wreckage, spirited away. To safety. Then they stripped the place of anything useful. Done in silence, a production line of destruction. Then, like mist, they disappeared. Back to their beds, their farms, their families.

Tonight one French family would have a new member, although he lingered outside the gates of heaven. Waiting for the moment they would allow him enter, free of pain, of fear. Released.

Clara Bisset bathed the blood from the Englishman, the light of the stubby candle showed he wouldn't be with them for long, just like the others who'd passed through their door in the middle of many nights during this war. *A senseless war run by foolish men, for stupid reasons.* But she was just a girl, what did she know?

She'd stripped him of his jacket and overalls. The overalls, unsalvageable, cut into ribbons, rolled up and squirrelled away. They'd be of use at some stage. His jacket, she'd slipped on — the sheepskin lining making her the warmest she'd been all winter — and she snuggled deeper into it as she watched her patient in the wavering candlelight, deaf to the crinkling of a half-written letter in the pocket.

Phil struggled through the night. His mind a flickering film of his life. Childhood memories wrapped up in sunlight, with warm dinners, and laughter and joy. The lightness of freedom as he took his first flight; his first kiss, and his last kiss.

That kiss a reminder of what he was about to leave behind. He battled through the blanket of death settling upon him, forcing his eyes open where they focussed on Clara at his side, her face telling him what he already felt.

'A letter, will you write a letter for me?'

Clara scrabbled for a pen and paper in the candlelight.

Sentence by sentence, Phil dictated his last letter, which began with "*Darling Elizabeth, this was not meant to be the last page of my letter to you; not the end of our story...*"

The letter finished, Clara stretched her cramping hand. She tried to give solace to the man with so much love in his heart for another.

He closed his eyes, his letter done. And took his last breath.

Clara and her family dug a new grave, a private grave. Unmarked to anyone's eyes except theirs. Dog tags removed and secreted in a tin under a floorboard. His location concealed.

Clara slipped the dead pilot's letter into his jacket pocket and packed it away from prying eyes. After the war, she'd send it home, but until then, it needed to remain hidden.

Girls grow up. Some marry, some don't. Clara never left the farm. Her memory grew hazy, till she couldn't think to tell her nephews about the young men they'd rescued a lifetime ago. Men whose families would never know the truth that their sons and husbands, their brothers and lovers, had the touch of a caring heart right at the end. And she forgot about the warmth of the jacket; a jacket from too many years ago.

And like all good things, Clara's time ended. Funny old Aunt Clara, who told foolish stories about planes falling out of the sky, and handsome pilots holding her hands, when everyone *knew* she'd never left her family farm. Their simple spinster aunt, as bland as boiled cabbage. It's a curious thing dismantling someone's life after they're gone. Their life reveals itself through old love letters, faded photographs of relatives long gone. But Clara's nephew could never have guessed the secrets concealed within Clara's old farmhouse. If he'd given more thought as to the origin of the dusty box of dog tags, or the preserved flying jacket, he might not have flogged them off so readily to the tinker who came knocking on his door one summer.

THE LETTER

My dearest Elizabeth,

I love you.

I'm not going to make it home this time. I'm so very sorry.

You are the love of my life. Beautiful, and funny, you are my soul.

It's unbearable to think of the pain I leave you in. You must be strong.

I will always love you.

Phil x

THE ROUGH

'You ou want me to go into that crappy little shop?' Melissa asked Sinclair, her face as incredulous as the Botox allowed, when she took in the peeling paint around the window frame — what remained of the paint.

The dated window display would be more at home in Russia's Cold War era department stores than a modern London street. 'It's not the same calibre as the shops I've taken you to,' she added.

'Won't take more than a minute. Try it, you might pick up a bargain in a slum like this.'

Rearranging her face into a delicate pout, well practised over the years, she watched as Sinclair opened the door, and beckoned her to follow.

Used to getting her own way, Melissa stood firm on the footpath, hands on her bony hips. This turn of events was entirely dissatisfactory. *This is what happens when you try a rough diamond, they don't play by the rules* she thought to herself. She didn't want to be seen going into this secondhand shop, or charity shop, or whatever it was. And had no problem telling her companion. No qualms at all…

Thank you for reading *The Last Letter*.
The story concludes with *Telegram Home -*
book #3 of *The Old Curiosity Shop* trilogy.

REVIEW

Dear Reader,

If you enjoyed *The Last Letter*, could you please leave a review on your favourite digital platform?

Reviews are invaluable to authors, and only need to be a couple of lines, or more if you like.

Thank you.

Kirsten McKenzie

CAST OF PLAYERS

THE OLD CURIOSITY SHOP SERIES

Sarah Lester/Grace Williams/Sarah Bell/Betsy

Art Loss Register
> Gemma Dance
>
> Ryan Francis

Auckland, New Zealand
> Aroha Kepa, wife of Wiremu Kepa
>
> Henry Neumegen, a pawnbroker
>
> Jimmy Jowl, a publican
>
> Joe Jowl, a publican
>
> Moses Robley, collector of artefacts
>
> Sophia Kepa, daughter of Wiremu
>
> Wiremu Kepa, a miller
>
> Clarence Whittaker, a surveyor

Bruce Bay, New Zealand
> Bryce Sinclair, ferryman
>
> Christine Young, wife of Reverend Young
>
> Felicity Toomer, daughter of John Toomer

Frederick Sweeney, publican
Grant Toomer, shopkeeper
Isaac Lloyd, a gold miner
Margaret Sweeney, wife of Frederick Sweeney
Samuel Sinclair, son of Bryce Sinclair
Saul Hunt, ex convict
Seth Brown, a gold miner
Shrives, a bullock driver
William Price, Warden
Reverend Gregory Young

Christies Auction House
Andrew Harvard, Senior Specialist Costumes and Textiles
Don Claire, Senior Partner
Hamish Brooke
Hannah Gardner
Jay Khosla, Senior Manager of the Indian Art Group
Leo Hayward, a clerk

Dunedin, New Zealand
Amos Wood, army deserter
Annabel Lester, mother of Sarah Lester
Colin Lloyd, younger brother of Isaac Lloyd
Edwin Sutton, Sutton's General Store
Graeme Greene, police constable
Howard Cummings, a clergyman
Jack Antony, army deserter
Jock Crave, police sergeant
Mervyn Kendall, Collector of Customs
Norman Bailey, assistant to Bishop Dasent
Thomas Dasent, Bishop of Dunedin
Una Neville, on the boat with Colin Lloyd

England
Adelaide, maid to Lady Laura Grey

Arthur, a silversmith
Arthur Sullivan*, composer
Audrey Grey, mother of Richard Grey
Barry Wentworth, a farmer
Benjamin Grey, brother of Edward Grey
Daniel Shalfoon, a clergyman
Edith Grey, ancestor of Richard Grey
Elizabeth Williams (née Grey), daughter of Edward Grey
Grace Williams, daughter of Robert Williams
Jessica Williams, sister of Robert Williams
Jonas Williams, foster father of Robert Williams
Josephine, a prostitute
Lady Laura Grey, mother of Edward and Benjamin
Lord Edward Grey, brother of Benjamin Grey
Lord Henry Grey, husband of Laura Grey
Mary Grey, wife of Edward Grey
Melissa Crester, an American
Mr Sutcliffe, manservant to Lady Grey
Mrs Phillips, housekeeper to Lady Grey
Nicole Pilcher, the manager of *The Old Curiosity Shop*
Patricia Bolton, a fashion designer, friend of Sarah Lester
Paul de Lamerie*, a master silversmith
Philip Williams, husband of Elizabeth Williams
Ravi Naranyan, security guard
Rebecca 'Betsy' Jane Williams,
Richard Grey
Robert Williams, illegitimate child of Sarah Williams
Samer Kurdi, a trader
Sally Glynn, a converted Muslim in Liverpool
Stokes, goon employed by Richard Grey
Tracey Humphrey, Royal School of Needlework
Wick Farris, a knocker
W.S. Gilbert*, dramatist

Customs and Excise

Alan Bullard, Surveyor of Customs, London
Clifford Meredith, a customs officer
Mervyn Bulford, Collector of Customs, Liverpool
Paul Shaskey, a customs clerk

France
Clara Bisset, resistance fighter

London Police
Fiona Duodu, Constable
Owen Gibson, Detective Sergeant
Sean Jones, Corporal
Tania Foster, Sergeant
Victor Fujimoto, Inspector

India
Abe Garland, army officer
Ajay Turilay, assistant to Patricia Bolton
Albert Lester, husband of Annabel Lester, father of Sarah Lester
Alice Montgomery, Anglican Missionary School
Amit, servant to Simeon Williams
Christopher Dickens, army officer
Elaine Barker, Anglican Missionary School
Jai Singh*, the Maharaja of Jaipur
James Doulton, army officer
Kalakanya, servant to Sarah Williams
Karen Cuthbert, Fishing Fleet Girl
Layak, servant to the Raja of Nahan
Madame Ye, an opium dealer
Maria, Fishing Fleet Girl
Naomi Abbott, wealthy wife
Navin Pandya, a stonemason
Nirmala, servant to Sarah Williams
Raja of Nahan
Ram Singh II*, the Maharaja of Jaipur

Reverend Montgomery
Sally Brass, Fishing Fleet Girl
Sanjay, a street urchin from Jaipur
Saptanshu, driver for the Raja of Nahan
Simeon Williams, brother of Sarah Williams
Warren Brooke, army officer

Victoria and Albert Museum
    Brenda Swift, curator
    Eliza Broadhead, Department of Furniture, Textiles and Fashion
    Jasmine Gupta, manager
    Steph Chinneck, intern

Wales
    Annwr Lloyd, mother of Isaac and Colin

* Real historical figures. Their names have been used in a fictional sense, although their achievements mentioned in this novel are real.

ACKNOWLEDGMENTS

Thank you for reading *The Last Letter*. It would be wonderful if you could post a review on Amazon or BookBub or Goodreads, or any other digital platform you use to record the books you've read. Reviews really help authors.

This edition of *The Last Letter* is quite different to the first edition. Changing the order of the chapters was like doing a puzzle where you don't have a picture on the box as a guide. I hope the new layout makes it easier to follow Sarah and her journey.

I want to acknowledge the feedback from earlier readers. They have shaped this edition. Thank you.

ABOUT THE AUTHOR

For years Kirsten McKenzie worked in the family antiques store, where she went from being allowed to sell postcards in the corner, to selling Worcester vases and seventeenth century silverware, providing a unique insight into the world of antiques which touches every aspect of her writing.

Her historical time slip novels have been described as *Time Travellers Wife meets Far Pavilions*, and *Antiques Roadshow gone viral*.

She is also the author of the bestselling gothic horror novel *Painted*, and the medical thriller, *Doctor Perry*.

Kirsten lives in New Zealand with her husband, her daughters, and two rescue cats. She can usually be found procrastinating on Twitter.

You can sign up for her sporadic newsletter at:
www.kirstenmckenzie.com/newsletter/

CPSIA information can be obtained
at www.ICGtesting.com
Printed in the USA
FSHW011011261219
65466FS